THE ACRID SKY

Book One of
The Malice of Light

BRADY J. SADLER

THE MALICE OF LIGHT

BY BRADY J. SADLER

The Acrid Sky (2023)
The Withered Roots (2024)
The Smoldering Vein (2026)

ALSO BY BRADY J. SADLER

WITH ADAM SADLER

Ransom Creek Remains (2025)

RELIC MEYERS

BY BRADY J. SADLER

Relic Meyers & The Rhythms of Ruin (2024)
Relic Meyers & The Harmony of Hexes (2025)

LORENGUARD

BY BRADY J. SADLER

Eve of Corruption (2012)

OTHER WORKS

BY BRADY J. SADLER

In Short Order (2025)
Emerald Decay (2025)

THE ACRID SKY

Book One of
The Malice of Light

This is a work of fiction. Names, characters, business, events and incidents are the products of the author's imagination. Any resemblance to actual persons, living or dead, or actual events is purely coincidental.

THE ACRID SKY

Copyright © 2023 by Brady J. Sadler & Twin Tale Studios LLC

www.twintalestudios.com | www.bradyjsadler.com

Cover Art & Graphic Design by Evan Simonet

Maps by Mya N. Osburn

Interior Art by Ellie TenBrink & The Creation Studio

ISBN: 978-0-9853679-4-7 (Paperback)
ISBN: 978-0-9853679-3-0 (Hardcover)
ISBN: 978-0-9853679-3-0 (Hardcover, IngramSpark)
ISBN: 979-8-3494-5645-9 (Paperback, IngramSpark)
ISBN 978-0-9853679-2-3 (eBook)
ISBN: 979-8-9993640-2-9 (Deluxe Pocket Hardcover Edition)

For my daughter, Rylie.

Be heroic.

The Unthroning † 348 Years Ago

"Of all the places I have been in this world," Kartha said through crooked, rotting teeth, "I never thought I would be descending these unholy depths."

The torch she held in her withered hand lit just a small portion of Myretha's swollen belly. The stone goddess' towering likeness marked their progress down the twisting stairs. It was said that dwarven miners had dug their capital city of Myrethold out of solid stone, in the heart of Farhelm Mountains. Dwarven artisans had sculpted Myretha to serve as the pillar of their kingdom.

And to bless their home, Kartha thought, smiling bitterly at the irony. Stepping carefully, she hugged a black leather-bound tome against her breast as if it were a newborn child. The book looked more ancient than its carrier, but possessed an indestructible quality which Kartha lacked. Burnished gold from an ancient time adorned its edges, dully reflecting the torchlight.

Behind her, Luishen spat into the dark void between the stairs and Myretha's eternal unborn children. "Why would you want to? These stupid dwarves dug too deep and pierced the Abyss. Fools! Ah!"

Kartha heard the elf's feet slip and turned to see him frantically brush a bit of dirt from his soft blue sable cloak as if it were poison. His Key of Transience—the sapphire called Skythe that hung from his neck, set in a white gold pendant of clouds—shone brightly, casting their pocket of the underworld in vivid blue light.

"Do you feel him still?" Kartha asked, nodding to the key.

Luishen looked up with a scowl on his pale face, looking offended as always. "Yes. It would seem he is quite angry about being imprisoned. I sure hope your theories about Stane's prophecies are right. If Eyen breaks free—if *any* of them break free…" He paused just as his voice began to sound panicked, straightening himself back into the spoiled high elf that Kartha had grown to despise. "Well, we may be the very cause of the end of the world that Stane wrote about, not the saviors."

"The signs do not lie," she said, staring deep into Luishen's stone. "The fact that the bindings even worked should be proof enough that his words are true. Do you believe it was mere coincidence that you found Skythe exactly where the book said it would be?"

Luishen looked down at his necklace and then back up to her, his arrogant scowl unchanged.

"Or any of the Keys?" Kartha pressed, now looking up into his eyes. "The steps were all laid for us—thousands of years ago—awaiting discovery in a time of need."

"Your love of reflection is quite a wearisome trait, witch. The deed is done. The storm god is bound." Instinctively, Luishen reached a pale hand up to grasp Skythe, casting a dismissive glance at Myretha's statue. "One last god awaits her usurpation. Let us be done with it and hope all of your assurances are sound."

Kartha turned back to their descent, carefully guiding her steps. Despite the warmth that ran through the runic stonework along the stairs, a shiver went down her crooked spine. Where she once felt an eager thrill, there was now dread settling within her for the apocalypse they had worked to divert. She was so focused on her steps that she let out a sudden gasp when she almost stumbled over a fresh goblin corpse on the stairs.

Luishen peered over her shoulder, letting out a scoff. "Looks like Irvik's work, foul brute. Never one to clean up after himself."

After Kartha carefully stepped over the dead thing, Luishen casually kicked the cadaver into the vast nothingness.

"Ware, Purveyors!" Luishen's voice echoed. "Clean up after yourselves, for Light's sake!"

Kartha caught a glimpse of the goblin's body as it flailed limply into the darkness below, a pale green light illuminating the end of the winding stairs where the body inevitably landed with a sickening splat.

"Filthy Shadowfiends," Luishen spat. Kartha could hear him adjusting his fine cape as they continued their trek.

Watching the Shadow-taken creature become swallowed by the darkness made Kartha wonder about Luishen's sudden doubts about their purpose. "Do you fear the Shadow?"

Luishen's cleaning stopped for a breath, but his quiet steps continued behind her. "Are you weary of witchery? Trying your hand at philosophy now, are you? We all fear the Shadow, that is why we share this glorious burden."

"I do not fear the Shadow," Kartha said, her eyes growing distant as she continued her descent. "Stane says that Shadow takes root in fear and doubt, and I have no fear or doubt in regard to our task. Perhaps you fear the Light?"

"Why should I fear the Light?"

Kartha shrugged as much as her weary bones would allow. "I wonder if your doubts are seeded in a fear that the Light might expose the darkness in people."

"You speak of darkness in others?" Luishen scoffed. "How long have you walked in Shadow, you ambling affliction? We all know that you've outlived any natural life you could have hoped for, but it's not the feysleep that keeps you breathing. Do not tell me you have not toiled in Shadow."

"I have not," Kartha said plainly. "Believe what you will, but my additional years come at a heavy cost you would not understand. The path of Shadow would have been an easier one for me to tread, but the gods forbid us from reaching it—just like Light."

Luishen had no clever retort, and they continued in silence.

A shriek sounded from below, echoing through the high passage. Kartha's body tensed, nearly causing her to tumble down the stairs. "Myretha," she breathed through her few teeth that remained.

"Lead on, woman," hissed Luishen from behind. "For all your talk of doubtless conviction, you stop now? Play your part and say the damned words," he scowled at the book, a hint of fear betrayed in his sapphire, almond-shaped eyes, "and we'll have saved the world from certain doom, right?" He offered her a mocking, wicked smile as he took another step, his fine sable boots collecting more dirt. "The Purveyors of Light will be worshiped in place of these heaven-sent tyrants for ages to come."

"Not that," Kartha hissed between those rotting teeth. "Let the world know an age of mortal toils, without bearing the weight of worship or supplication…"

Luishen rolled his eyes and scoffed. "For certain, witch. Now on with you."

They continued their descent in silence, aside from Luishen's occasional curse—"Do you have any idea how many merchants sell cloaks this fine? Damned this dirty hole and the dirty dwarves who carved it!" Kartha withdrew into herself, reflecting on her own toils that brought her here, aligned with this motley band of god-slayers. The task at hand continued to fill her with dread, even though she was certain it was her destiny.

We are saving the world, she told herself. *We are saving all the Joined Realms from certain doom.* Repeating the mantra did little to calm her nerves, but it was a welcome distraction from the continued shrieks from below.

We are saving the world.
The gods have abandoned us.
We had no other choice.
Light, forgive us.

"Hope we aren't too late," Luishen said in a low voice, his hand nervously fumbling with his Key. "I can feel Eyen's power—he stirs already, calling a storm most likely. Quicken your gait, you rotund bag of withered flesh! It's bad enough I'm being held accountable for a human's punctuality, but a fat and old one such as yourself is simply preposterous!"

Kartha smiled inwardly as she ignored the elf's rising venom, and continued stepping carefully. It would not do to break a hip or otherwise incapacitate herself so close to the final rites. There was no one else walking the realms in this age who could read the *Book of Stane*, otherwise she never would have been able to acquire the thing. And she would be damned if she did not enjoy the power she held over squirming beings such as Luishen.

Elf and witch finally reached the bottom of the stairs, stepping into a pool of pale green light emanating from a diminutive figure—their ally, Ruke. The painful shrieks had subsided, but echoing voices could be heard coming from the great hallway that stretched before them.

"Any goblins give you trouble?" The halfling priestess of Oakus fixed them with a discerning stare, the glowing emerald held within her gnarled staff pulsating in rhythm with her twitching left eye. While she stood no higher than Kartha's chest, her presence was no less commanding. She wore her graying hair tightly bound up in her yellow hood. As was common with halflings from the Acreage, she had a round nose and pudgy cheeks, and Kartha knew under the woman's hood there were two large ears as well.

The elf strode past both women, scoffing and brushing the settled dust off his fine quilted doublet. "You mean the goblin corpses we had to wade through to get down here, Ruke? Absolutely ruining my wardrobe? No, they gave us no trouble whatsoever." He spat against the wall, defiling the runic praise to Myretha. "Let us be done with this. As the witch said, the bindings will not hold unless a balance is met and each one is restrained, and Eyen grows restless."

The women shared a brief look of mutual dread and determination before turning to join Luishen's swift walk to the dungeon.

"You were right about the signs, my friend," Ruke said softly, her round eyes watching Luishen warily—elf ears were notoriously astute, but their companion would most likely be too caught up in his own self-important thoughts to catch any exchange between the priestess and witch. "Oakus has sent me visions of the orcs and goblins— among other creatures—turning into…monsters. Slaughtering and reveling in cruelty. It is the coming of Shadow."

The stone in Ruke's staff glowed stronger at the mention of the harvest god's name. The halfling looked up at it, then back to Kartha. "He still speaks to me, pleading for reason, placing the blame on Wick for letting his flames grow weak while the Shadow encroaches. The gods seem so…confused."

Kartha slowed her step to place her torch in a nearby sconce, no longer needing it with Ruke's light guiding their way. "It is to be expected, friend," the witch assured her. "Desperate pleas, nothing more. They have kept the Light to themselves since the dawn of time, and would have snuffed us out entirely had we not deciphered their cruel purpose." She hefted the book, finding solace in its weight. "We cannot sit idly by while our very world is held in the destructive hands of celestial tyrants." She gave the halfling a curt nod. "This must be done. The Shadow is coming, the signs have all come to pass."

Ruke looked into Kartha's eyes as if seeing her every thought. "Do you assure me, old friend, or yourself?"

Kartha had no answer.

And the elf accompanying them had no more patience.

"Stop your mewling," Luishen shouted back at them, sighing with an overwrought sense of drama. "I won't have it be said that I died saving the world while stuck in a dwarf hole being bored to death by you two. Onward!"

Three distinct figures entered the antechamber to join the gathered four. A fifth was bound to the floor by manacles, black iron bindings that seemed to drink the flickering light coming from the circle of candelabras that framed the ritual site.

"We may begin," said a gruff voice. A robed dwarf stepped forward on stocky legs, his gray garments hanging loosely from the broad plated armor on his shoulders. An axe was hooked to his belt, with smeared goblin blood on its blade. He motioned to Kartha with a hand adorned with nearly a dozen rings, each one socketed with a different colored stone that glittered unnaturally. "Lady Kartha, if you would lead us," Irvik said through a thick beard also studded with jewelry. Ironically, the crown he wore that denoted him as a Border Thane was hammered from old metals without a single gem adorning it.

Kartha stepped forward as Ruke and Luishen found their own places among the gathered. Ruke fell in between a big-bellied sailor with a curled mustache and a brutish woman that towered over the halfling priestess. Luishen took his position between Irvik and a crooked old human man bent under the weight of bits of plate mail with a knight's sword strapped to his thin waist.

As Kartha made her way to Myretha's altar within the circle of her companions, she tried to keep her eyes from the bound goddess. Failing miserably, she gasped in unexpected horror as she observed the prisoner.

Myretha's gray eyes stared skyward into the high darkness that hung above the gathered. She looked altogether lifeless, save for the slow rise and fall of her breasts. The stone goddess had been stripped of her heavenly raiment, and the shackles forged by Irvik and his dwarven priests clasped firmly around her wrists and ankles, leaving her limbs no slack for struggling. Her earthly brown flesh was flawless, except for the burns where it had touched the unholy metal bindings.

So young, Kartha thought, knowing the foolishness of it—of course the goddess was anything but young; this was just an earthly vessel born of necessity. Myretha was as ancient as the stones she created at the foundations of Aetha, but the body laid before her looked like a lass who had barely bloomed. Even Kartha's cold heart broke a little as she stepped around the body.

Placing the heavy tome on an altar, she made a show of carefully opening it to the final rites, written in the forgotten scrawl of the Ghultans. The language was still a wonder to behold—elegant glyphs flowed into cascading patterns, a work of art more than a language. The price Kartha had paid to learn the words locked within those mystical pages was steep, but she would pay it happily again, as the knowledge had made her indispensable to the Purveyors of Light—the convened saviors of the world itself.

They waited with bated breath—except Luishen, who released his own freely with an elaborate yawn—watching the old witch, anticipating the words she would soon read from the *Book of Stane*. Each member of the Purveyors, with the exception of Kartha, held one of the Keys of Transience—the unholy relics that the First Man, Stane, had hidden across the world as a means to protect Aetha from its gods.

The high elf lord, Luishen of Fehir'whin, with his sapphire, Skythe, binding the sky god Eyen.

The dwarf thane, Irvik Urknst, and his Ironband, meant to seal the stone goddess Myretha.

The halfling priestess, Ruke Ebbers, with her short ashen staff named Elysun, which now barred the harvest god Oakus from returning to his heavenly fields.

The tired old knight, Sir Branton Pembrook, of the declining human empire Eastlund, proudly—if not a little pathetically—wore what armor his old frame could still support, and now drew the jewel-hilted sword, Kindler, from its decorative scabbard.

Wick chose a short candle to burn there, Kartha thought to herself as Sir Pembrook made the three-pointed sign to the flame god with the sword that served as Wick's seal.

Plump Archcaptain Hugh Heyer from the rich merchant coasts of Velcarthe on Xe'dann twirled a finger through his oiled mustache as he flipped the coin, Deepfare, into the air to catch it with the same sausage-fingered hand. No one alive had sailed Corsa's watery domain more than Captain Heyer.

And finally, the warrior queen from the Jagged Swales, Ethenna Praal, scowled in her hunting leathers. A worn longbow in one hand, the enchanted horn, Siren, in the other. Tattoos crept across Ethenna's dark flesh, each one a devotion to the Bestial Maid, Syrina.

"Light of Creation," Kartha began, turning her attention from the

Purveyors to the book. She took a deep breath, considering all the events that brought her here: the deceit, deaths, and blasphemy. "By the words of Stane, your chosen prophet and heavenly messenger, we call upon your infinite power and wisdom to stay the coming injustice—"

Sudden laughter burst from Myretha, still fixing her eyes to the darkness above. "Injustice," she repeated, her voice a whimsical lilt. "What is injustice without the existence of justice?" Now she turned her head, celestial eyes piercing Kartha's. "And what is justice without a mortal to decide?" She laughed again. "I can see now…"

"Continue," Luishen said casually. "Before she goes on about betrayal and shifting blames. Let us be done with this."

Myretha let out another laugh, much weaker than before. "Betrayal." She tasted the word, returning her eyes to the darkness above as Kartha's wavering voice continued to beseech the Light. "What is it without trust? Can you trust the weather? Trust a plains cat to not maul your child?" Her laughter was still weak, confused.

Kartha pressed on. "In the name of Light, we—"

"Light!" The goddess sat up violently, her arms held back by her bindings. "What is Light without Shadow?" Myretha's eyes widened, turning to the old witch. "It is Shadow you call! The Light craves the Shadow as the sword craves blood! Do not—"

"Finish it," Irvik commanded, his voice seeming to shake the antechamber.

Kartha swallowed before reading on, trying desperately to ignore the goddess' ranting. *They all claim to be deceived*, Kartha reminded herself as she finished another passage of Stane's rites. She could feel the power rising, a cold grip around her heart that gave her the absolution she needed to press on. But she could not look at Myretha, not if she wished to get through the words without stumbling.

"In the name of Stane," Kartha continued, raising her voice, "the First and Only of his name, we renounce the dominion of the gods. We bind the ones who would destroy our world rather than give it the means to protect itself. As the Shadow descends, we beseech the powers of Creation, bless us with the Light!"

"—believe the Light," Myretha begged. "Good needs evil, as peace needs war." Her maddening laughter turned to sobbing, but she calmly lay back, turning her teary eyes back to the blackness above. Her body resigned while her eyes darted worriedly, as if unable to express to these mortals the direness she felt. "We have been betrayed," she said softly, her voice fading, "by those who made us." She turned her head to look at each of the Purveyors. "...by those who made us..."

Kartha finished the last rite as the energy from Myretha seemed to drain. "Dethrone from their heavenly reign those who would destroy their makings. Bind them to the world they created and could so easily cast aside..."

The light from Ruke's stone pulsated weakly from atop her staff, dimming and drawing shadows closer to the gathering. Each of the Purveyors reached for their Keys. Even Luishen's arrogant expression washed away, replaced by uncertain fear.

The world began to shake, slightly at first, but soon a steady rumble. "It comes," Myretha mouthed. "The seeds will take root. The seeds will take root. The seeds will take root. The seeds..."

"Bind them," Kartha repeated, her voice beginning to thunder deep in Myrethold. "Their work is done, and so begins their rest. Bind them in reverence, and bind them in worship, but allow them not to return to the Nethering. Let the fate of Aetha be born this day." Kartha held her breath after releasing the final word—time stopped, and the gathered froze in expectation.

Then the world shook more violently, debris falling from the unseen ceiling above. A stone fell with a mighty thud in the halls above.

"By the Flames," old Sir Pembrook cursed, falling to a knee as he braced himself on Kindler. His eyes were fixed on the chained goddess. Kartha turned back to Myretha to see her arching her back in silent pain, her belly beginning to swell.

"What is this?!" Irvik demanded, rubbing his hands together as if he were trying to rid himself of his rings. Kartha saw Luishen tugging at his Key as well, Skythe pulsating with a pale blue glow that seemed to grow brighter as Myretha's stomach bulged.

"Betrayed," the goddess repeated through clenched teeth. "It comes..."

Ruke stepped toward Kartha, her staff now giving off a blinding glow. "Something is wrong! Are you sure your readings were correct? Did you—"

Silence fell with sudden darkness as the light from the Keys flickered out abruptly. Kartha's breath still held in her throat. She was afraid to breathe, afraid to speak. Afraid for the light to return.

She no longer heard Myretha's heavy breathing or the crumbling stone above. Utter silence.

After what felt like nearly a whole evening passed, the sound of Myretha's breath returned—painful breathing through clenched teeth. The breathing quickly turned to grunting, and then guttural screams. Kartha dared not move in the darkness. She listened and slowly began to release her breath, reaching blindly for the book but not knowing why. As Myretha's screams reached a crescendo, Kartha clutched the *Book of Stane* to her breast and prepared for a hasty exit.

But then the Light came.

It was not a subtle glow that pulsated like a heartbeat; it was an immediate brilliance unleashed upon the world, blinding Kartha. Even before her eyes adjusted or the newborn's cry split the silence, she knew a child had been born. *The Child of Light*, Kartha thought with a certainty that she did not know, but rather felt.

The blinding Light slowly became a soft glow, the fading embers of a dying fire became flesh in the form of a pale, wriggling newborn on the stone floor. There was no sign of the Purveyors; only their keys remained, abandoned. Kartha was alone with mother and child. Instinct took over, despite the circumstances, and Kartha hurried over to take Myretha's child in her trembling arms—the *Book of Stane* fell to the ground, forgotten.

As Kartha cradled the child carefully, Myretha began to convulse again, her back arching upward and breath hissing through her clenched teeth. Unnatural warmth came from the child in her arms, and Kartha stared in amazement—the glow coming from the child's flesh had become faint but lit the antechamber like a torch.

The second child—another girl—drank the light that her sister gave off and didn't make a sound as she entered the world. *The Child of Shadow*. She looked up at Kartha as if she saw perfectly already and waited patiently to be picked up. Kartha obliged and held Myretha's daughters as if they were her own, rising unsteadily to her feet.

"I am sorry," Myretha's voice came from the grave, weak and miserable. "You are alone now... The war is coming... Keep them safe...but far from each other." A tear rolled down Myretha's cheek. "They are...of your making. The war...the war..."

"What war?" Kartha managed, not expecting an answer as she watched Myretha's final breath leave her borrowed body. The ground shook violently as if the stone goddess' essence found a new home, and more debris began to fall, crashing into the antechamber. Kartha held the children close as she turned and hurried toward the stairs, hoping she had the energy to climb back to the surface. "Brace us, children! Forgive us…"

In the abandoned antechamber, a fissure split the tiled stone floor, swallowing Myretha's body into the dark abyss below. The *Book of Stane* wobbled on the edge of that crevice, tottering toward the gaping stone maw. From below, a massive arm of broken red rock reached up, slamming a clawed hand on the book, as a huge winged form was birthed from the goddess' grave.

The Perfect Gift

The town of Blakehurst was a frequent stopping point for merchant wagons making their way through the sprawling Lohkrest Woods, which served as a relatively peaceful border between the rival kingdoms of Eastlund and Vale. Unfortunately, the poor farmers, carpenters, and hunters of Blakehurst were not the best customers when it came to mystical wood elf trinkets and tonics that were the primary export from the treefolks' realm. So Anika was surprised to see Elza's wagon open for business. A lavish purple awning supported by two sturdy oaken poles led up to a unique selection of silver and gemstones.

"Maybe it's just for show?" old Lana said as she strode past Anika, making her way across town square to The Early Mule. Anika shifted the bag slung over her shoulder as she waited under the shade of a great elm and watched Lana's head nod toward Elza busily arranging her wares.

Anika's dark eyes watched Elza as the gnome continued preparing her display. While she had seen dozens of halflings come through Blakehurst, Anika had seen no gnomes other than Elza, and that fascinated her. While gnomes were said to be fey-touched halflings, they looked similar enough in appearance, aside from gnomes looking more like human children than halflings tended to.

From Elza's clothes—loose-fitting silks in exotic shades of purple and silver—to the way her slightly tanned skin seemed to glow like an elf's, she was a taste of the mystical in Anika's otherwise routine life.

No other wagon was setting up this morning. Anika could only ever recall merchants setting up their mobile shops to sell on festivals. Sure, there was the occasional harvest market when wagons would pack the small square, but those were reserved for selling crops and local wares, not far-off oddities that Eastlunder merchants—especially Elza—specialized in.

"I don't reckon I care much," Lana's wrinkled husband, Geddy, said under his breath. Anika always had good hearing, much to her brother's chagrin. *Where is he already?* she thought to herself under the weight of the bag. "Gnomes," Geddy spat, giving Elza a narrowed eye over his shoulder, "ain't welcome here, I say. Always digging around in places they don't belong. Ain't proper, says I. Eastlund can have 'em all. I trust a halfling just fine, but not one of these that take up in elf business…"

Lana patted her husband on the back as they continued toward their morning tea. Anika could see the halfling Ransil Osbury through the windows of the inn, hurrying to finish the morning bake, his stunted legs gracefully carrying him about his kitchen as if it were a dance. She couldn't help but smile watching him. Ransil was almost like an uncle to her, always watching out for her and Gage when he wasn't keeping an eye on his troublesome apprentice, Robin.

The aroma from Ransil's bread filled the town square and made Anika's mouth water. Maybe she would pick up a loaf with the money from her deliveries—Father wouldn't mind; he loved the halfling's baking as much as everyone else in Blakehurst.

A flash caught Anika's eye and she turned back to Elza's wares. Something shimmered from the gnome's display, reflecting the rising sun like a star in the night sky. Without fully realizing it, Anika took a step toward the wagon, and then another. Even from across the square, she could see the source of the shine—a blue gem encased in intricate silver, polished smooth like a crystallized raindrop. A sense of weightlessness drew Anika closer, the world around her darkening as the stone's glow pulled her forward.

"Ah, Lady Lawson," Elza said, jolting Anika's attention from the stone. The gnome offered a quick smile as she ran her fingers up a colorful plumage of feathers attached to an elven headdress. "Glad tidings from the east!"

Anika smiled awkwardly, resisting the urge to look back at the blue stone. "It's good to see you again, Elza." And it was, despite the discomfort that Anika felt. Not all merchants that passed through Blakehurst were as pleasant as Elza, and Anika had vivid memories of the elder woman offering her and the other village youths sweets during Moon's Bounty when most other merchants were charging coppers. "How fares the Eastway?"

Elza scoffed and waved a dismissive hand. "Plagued with bandits as always. I'm almost losing more queens paying for guides than if those outlaws plucked my wagon clean."

It was in that moment that Anika first felt the eyes on her—the feeling of being watched overcame her in a surge and her eyes darted around. A hooded figure leaning casually against the wagon had somehow blended into its surroundings like a ghost and now gave Anika such a start that she almost lost her balance. She managed to shift the weight of the bag over her shoulder and offer the mysterious watcher a slight nod of recognition.

The figure did not move. Their arms were crossed over intricate armor of dark green and brown, with leaf-shaped silver rivets worked across the dyed leather. A cloak and hood hid their face in shadow, but Anika could see watchful eyes glinting at her. The watcher had a fine whitewood longbow leaning nearby as well as the decorative pummels of two long knives on either side of their slender waist.

"Don't mind Farrah," Elza said as she wiped her hands on her baggy pants. "She's not very sociable, even by wood elf standards."

"You pay me to keep you and your wares intact, not to be sociable," the hooded watcher replied, still unmoving.

Elza gave a little laugh. "That I do, my speaking statue! And you've been worth every coin."

Ignoring the banter, Anika leaned closer to the gem hanging from silver. The depths of the blue stone went on forever, an encased abyss that Anika felt herself falling into. Time stood still and the world around blurred once more—all but the stone.

In Anika's mind, a mountain rose surrounded by unnatural clouds of gray, brown, and sickly green. Deep in the stone's depths, she saw a figure take shape above those shrouded mountaintops, a winged creature that was part human and part bird, altogether god-like in presence. The figure spread its wings and a ray of sun burst through the poisonous clouds behind it. Anika couldn't breathe; the image clutched her heart and she felt as if she were suffocating.

The light burned her; she felt it warm her skin, slowly at first, and then painfully.

The winged figure opened its beak-like mouth to shriek, but instead said, "Can you afford that?"

Anika blinked the vision away and saw her dirty fingers reaching to clasp around the blue stone. She pulled her hand back as if it were about to touch a burning coal. She jerked her gaze to Farrah, whose black almond eyes narrowed on Anika from beneath her hood.

Elza gave a quick laugh. "Oh, the Lady Lawson is no thief, my dear." She stepped over to Anika, standing just up to the young girl's stomach. "It's beautiful, isn't it? Came across it when the Green Lake thawed—was just sitting on a sandbar near the mouth of the Bracing River. Took some cleaning, but should fetch a pretty price in the south, if I can make it that far."

Transfixed by the gleaming gem, Anika could only offer a small nod. "It looks...magical."

Farrah offered what must have passed for an elven snort. "Magical? Certainly not."

Anika shifted her eyes to the elf, catching something in her voice. *Was she hiding something?*

Elza's laugh was less guarded, but still strained. "Yes, let's not talk about magic items, lest we bring an Oather down on us." The gnome's normally boisterous voice grew quieter when she spoke of the sworn disciples of the Arcania that traveled throughout Vale to ensure no wizards broke their oaths to the Hall of Sorcery. "What brings you to town today, young Anika? And with such a burdensome load!"

Anika smiled as she let the bag over her shoulder drop to the cobbled ground. The relief in her shoulder was exquisite. "Gage and I are helping with deliveries. I'm still apprenticing under Father, who is training me in tanning and Gage in hunting." Anika motioned to her pack. "These are the first leathers I cleaned and dried myself. I'm supposed to deliver them to Neff, but Gage is to meet me here first so we can deliver his hunt to the butcher." Anika cast an annoyed glance toward the forest's edge, hoping her brother was on his way.

Farrah gave another delicate snort.

"I've been waiting on you."

Anika spun around to see her younger brother, with his fair skin and easy smile. Born of Eastlund stock, Gage was a spitting image of their father; thick hair grew wildly from the top of his head and his long face had a noble quality to it, despite their family's common standing.

Gage made a show of casually leaning on his longbow as if he had been there all morning. Elza gave a chuckle, but Anika was less amused. She looked to his belt where a single hare was dangling lifelessly by its hind legs and her mood soured all the more.

"Is that it?" Anika asked, motioning to the sorry excuse for game that had apparently taken Gage all morning to acquire. "Father set over a dozen snares."

Gage shrugged. "They were all sprung. Must have been something big. I had to cut new rope for each of them. Looked like they had been chewed through."

Anika found that odd. The lightly wooded outskirts of Blakehurst where their father hunted were home to mostly small critters, and even the deep forests of Buckley Woods beyond Banbrook Ferry rarely saw anything more threatening than the occasional fox sniffing after livestock. Additionally, their father was an expert trapper, and his snares rarely failed.

"What makes you think the ropes were chewed?" Farrah asked.

Gage started slightly as he turned toward the questioner, obviously as surprised by the elf's presence as Anika had been. He gave a shrug and scratched the back of his neck in a show of casualness, despite the red creeping up his face—a face much paler than Anika's own, which was dark chestnut.

"Well, the ropes were split," Gage offered. He didn't look her in the eye. Elves weren't necessarily rare in Blakehurst, but they certainly weren't common, and enough tales were spread of their mysterious reclusiveness that it was rare for anyone living in town to be completely comfortable around the fey folk, gnomes included.

"Perhaps cut?" the elf asked.

Gage scowled, reaching into a pouch at his waist and producing the ropes. "I suppose they could have been." He offered them to the elf.

Farrah reached out a gloved hand—the gray-green material looked completely foreign and mystical to Anika, like silk but more durable. She handed the ruined snares back to Gage. "Goblins," Farrah said, shifting her watchful eyes to Elza.

The gnome turned her head knowingly and waved the elf on with her small hand. "Well, off you go then. I'll be fine here—the reeve's guards are on their patrols. I'm more concerned with goblins on the roads than Blakehurst bandits in broad daylight."

Farrah spun on her silent feet and departed for the woods. Her cloak billowed in her wake and Anika felt hypnotized by its shifting nature.

"And off you both go to your duties." Elza winked, turning back to her wares.

Anika nodded to Gage and motioned him to come along.

As they left, she tried to catch one last glimpse of the necklace, but it was nowhere to be seen.

"That can't be, Neff. Father said you would buy the whole bag."

The swarthy trader pulled the mint stem from his mouth—a common practice of the northerners from Copera who took special pride in their breath—and offered Anika a shrug. "Wagons are near to bursting already," he said. His eyes fell down to the open bag of carefully folded leather that Anika and her father had tanned. "Since that storm showed over Rathen, there's been a growing food shortage all over Vale. Crops aren't taking near the mountains—those strange clouds are more than unsettling. Making people panic and stock up for the winter, just in case. It's not likely there'll be buyers for anything they can't eat or store."

Anika wasn't sure what storm Neff was referring to, but a rising demand for food certainly explained why the local farmers were celebrating these past several days. Just last night she had been in The Early Mule when Matty Cullen announced he was buying rounds for the entire place. Anika's heart began to race a bit just thinking about handsome Matty in his rugged farming clothes hardly containing his muscled form, but she quickly averted her thoughts back to the current transaction.

"What about this?" Gage asked, presenting the hare. "There's probably enough for a stew here."

Neff considered the offering, his big dark eyes flittering between it and the half-full bag of quality leather. There was sympathy in the way his shoulders sagged. His gaze fell on Anika, giving her a small smile. "I can throw in an additional queen for the game. And tell your father I will try to take twice his normal load next month, given this storm passes."

Anika had no other choice than to nod her approval of the offer, collecting the meager stack of queens that she'd have to take back to her father along with half their wares. She began to shoulder the lighter bag, but Gage caught her arm and took it.

"Let me," he said, avoiding her gaze as if he were ashamed. "It's your birthday. You shouldn't have to lug this around."

Anika smiled—she had thought he might have forgotten. Birthday celebrations had become scarce since their mother had disappeared over ten years ago—*She's not dead*, Anika reminded herself, *no matter what Father believes, I know she's not*—so it was easy to forget the passing of a year for any of the Lawsons.

"You remembered."

Gage shouldered the bag, shrugging. His cunning eyes shifted down the road, watching for someone or something. "Of course I did, you told me this morning—I'm not *that* forgetful."

Anika followed his gaze, but all she saw was typical morning activity down the road: Bruck Undrel the dwarf smith returning from the creek lugging two pails of water to his shop, the pale-skinned beauty Polly Cenclaire confidently striding past them on her daily trip to— *Wait, this morning?*

She turned back to her brother. "What do you mean, this morning? You were gone when I woke up…"

Gage didn't respond, his eyes still seeking some hidden danger.

"Gage!"

He looked at her, startled.

"What are you looking for? And what did you mean about this morning?"

"Nothing."

Anika saw the tell—Gage bit his lower lip whenever he lied. "It's Robin, isn't it? That's who you're looking for."

"I got you something," Gage said with a sly smile, a master of bait-and-switch. "The perfect gift." He flourished his gloved hand, unfolding his exposed fingers to reveal the captivating necklace from Elza's wagon. "I saw you staring at it back there."

Anika was frozen in place, all thoughts of this morning and Robin gone. She fell into the blue stone's depths again, twisting forever in the span of a breath. She blinked and snapped out of the trance, taking a furious step toward Gage to close his hand on the stone before anyone could see it.

"You stole it?!"

Gage offered a quiet laugh. "Of course I did, we'd never be able to afford something like this."

"Well, you're taking it back!"

He forced the stone into her hand. "Do what you want with it—it's yours now. Just remember what they do to thieves." He leaned in close, looking over his shoulder as he said, "The reeve sent those two travelers that tried to pinch from the Brook & Stable up to Oakworth and the baron strung them up as Guild agents."

Overcome with rage, Anika could have choked him. He was right—she couldn't take it back to Elza without questions being asked, especially with Gage now spending so much time with Robin, who was rumored to have Guild associations. The Baron of Oakworth had been making a grand show of hanging thieves in an effort to send a message to the Guild in Andelor.

And dammit if I don't want to keep it, Anika thought frustratingly.

Every curse Anika had learned in her entire life was welling up within her to unleash on Gage, but when her brother's eyes shifted to something over her shoulder, she turned to see their father approaching.

Bennik Lawson was a broad man with a slight belly, his long unkempt hair at odds with his trimmed graying beard—and yet Anika couldn't help but always see her brother when she looked at their father, bringing that painful feeling of displacement. He gave his children a slight nod before his questioning eyes fell on Anika's bag.

"Was Neff gambling in The Early Mule again?"

While Anika's mind raced with thoughts of thievery, ancient relics, and goblins in the woods, Gage informed their father of Neff's situation.

While he listened, Bennik ran a thick hand through his wild hair. He looked tired—which was notable, since despite his busy schedule, he was a man that stayed relatively light on his feet and quick-witted, especially in the morning.

"I heard murmurs of the storm," Bennik replied as his eyes went to the clear sky. "Old Ackerly says she heard tales of an evil witch from the mountains, stealing all the rain to quench the thirst of the monsters in Myrethold." He offered his children a weak grin, as if he were trying to convince himself that Ackerly's nonsense was indeed nonsense.

Visions raced through Anika's mind again of the winged creature in the mountains, but she shook them away and gave her father a grin. She slipped the blue stone into a pouch on her belt, clueless on how to handle that situation currently.

"I'm going to check the snares again," Gage said, his voice faltering from its normal nonchalance. "Make sure the elf didn't disturb them." He hefted his bow, dropped the bag of leathers, and trotted off toward the woods before his father could inquire further.

It was then that Anika caught sight of Robin as he slipped out of The Early Mule. He was a handsome boy—*A man now*, she reminded herself, remembering that he was only a year behind her—with long blond hair pulled back in a tight knot, his rich crimson leathers making him seem a noble lord and not an orphan working in Ransil's kitchen.

Anika lost sight of Robin and Gage when her father's firm hand took hold of her shoulder, bracing himself to retrieve the bag of leathers from the ground. "I'll take these," he told her. "I have something else for you."

Curious what job awaited her now, Anika followed her father toward the smith's shop. Bruck was stoking the fires of his forge when the Lawsons ducked their heads into the dwarf's meager smithy. The ceiling was a little lower than most buildings in Blakehurst, and the Lawsons were taller than most of the inhabitants. Bruck smiled warmly through his gray beard.

"Morn' to you, Ben, and to you, lovely Ani!"

"Morning to you as well, Bruck." Bennik hoisted the bag of leathers onto the dwarf's workbench. "That item I requested—I know we spoke of coin, but I was curious if a trade might interest you?"

Bruck scratched his bald head with one gloved hand as he shook his other glove off to feel the leathers. "Aye, you know I love your work, Ben. I'm not sure I have need of so much currently though. Maybe if I had more swords to make, but round here it's mostly tools and horseshoes." He regarded the man and raised a bushy eyebrow. "If coin is tight—"

Bennik waved away the thought. "It's not that. Neff just couldn't take the rest of these—his wagon is full of crops with Rathen still dried up."

Bruck shook his head. "Aye, it's a shame. I heard from him over drinks last night." He pondered over the leathers another moment, running his thick fingers through his beard. Finally, he smiled up at Anika. "For your birthday, Ann? Of course! A trade it is!"

Anika blushed but gave her father a questioning look.

He just smiled at her and turned to empty the bag of leathers while Bruck turned and disappeared into the back. The dwarf was only gone a moment before he returned with something small wrapped in a fine red satin cloth. Bruck beamed with pride as he handed the item to Bennik.

Anika's father knelt down so their eyes were level. He held out the item in both of his hands. "You have taken to our family trade better than I could have imagined, Anika." She could see tears welling up in her father's eyes, and the feeling of pride he must have felt sank its hooks into her as well. "This may not be the gift every lady dreams of getting on their seventeenth birthday, but it's the only way I know how to tell you how important you are to me."

Overcome with emotion, Anika slowly reached out and pulled the red satin away to reveal a brilliant silver blade and a deep green leather handle. A skinning knife.

"It was my father's," Bennik said, taking hold of the artifact and turning it over to show Anika how well it had been restored. "It was the rusted one that sat on the mantel."

"A fine blade," Bruck offered. "Just needed a little time in me ol' forge."

Bennik spun the blade around and offered the handle to Anika, his face betraying a smile that Anika had not seen since her mother's disappearance.

Anika could not find the words. She stared at the knife, knowing everything it represented. Her father's legacy—her entire family's legacy—was being handed to her. She had no choice but to reach a hand out and grasp the fine green leather.

All thoughts of the stone left her as she hugged her father.

"Happy birthday, Anika."

CHAPTER TWO

Dry Season

The city of Rathen was a shadow of its former self. The ruins of the battlements that marked its borders were grown over with moss and lichen, never repaired from the days of the Nether War. In the distance, the slanted array of mismatched roofs were patched and mottled like some timeworn quilt, sewn over and over again instead of being remade.

This was not the Rathen that once stood as the only free city against the tyrannical rule of Eastlund's Grulain dynasty. This was now a collection of buildings under limp ivory banners that no longer flew the city's once-proud three eagles crest.

Even the numerous and quaint farmsteads that Deina Brasson remembered seeing during her journey south only two years ago now looked abandoned and dried up. Spitting a foul taste from her mouth while turning her eyes skyward, the dwarf wasn't altogether surprised.

"This be a curse," Deina said, as much to herself as to the priest. She instinctively ran her broad fingers across the blade of the axe slung at her hip. The pale green clouds above made her stomach turn and her nerves uneasy, and her keen dwarven eyes held to the sky as if she expected a foe to descend at any moment. Behind them to the south, the gray clouds receded and there was still a hint of serene blue on the horizon. But to the north, a disease-like rot came from the mountains and kept the lands below in a hazy dry spell.

"It has been over two months," Avrim said, one hand on the holy star hanging from his neck and the other leading their weary mule. The priest's blue eyes regarded the unnatural green and silent storm hanging over Rathen. "The duke's letter said they haven't had any rain yet this spring—I admit, it sounded like an exaggeration."

"This be a curse," Deina repeated.

Avrim nodded, giving the dwarf a grim look. "Very well could be. I've never seen anything like it—never read anything about it either, or heard the vicar mention it in any of his darker sermons."

The dwarf scoffed. "This don't seem like no heavenly gift, that's for damned sure. A gift from the Abyss, says I."

Avrim shook his head. "You know as well as I that the Final Thane sealed the Dark Ways. Unless you have heard of his recent awakening, I don't see how this could be the work of a demon."

Deina relaxed slightly, reaching for her pipe as she turned and gave the priest a raised eyebrow. "What's your theory? Does the Luminaura have experience with this kind of…occurrence?"

Avrim tried to avert his eyes from the scornful green sky—it made him feel small in the opposite way the Light did. "If I had to guess, I'd say this is arcane in nature, not demonic. The vicar had received word that the Arcania sent an Oather to investigate this…storm several weeks ago. I imagine they will get to the bottom of it. Besides, we have our own concerns."

Nodding, Deina lit her pipe with a small flint and tinder device of dwarven ingenuity. "Aye, the duke's wife. Forgive me if I wait at the tavern nearest the duke's estate. I have no desire to come down with whatever ails her. I'm already indebted enough to your temple, I don't need ya healing me again."

Avrim grinned, welcoming the levity. "I don't imagine I'll need your protection once we reach the gates, Deina, as welcome as it has been on this journey."

"Betchya wishin' you didn't stable our horses back at that priory." She reached down to rub a cramp out of her thick, short leg as she walked.

"They will be cared for better there than in the city," Avrim said. "Besides, as the Enlightened wrote: To walk in the Light, one must walk through Shadow."

As if in response, up in the green shadows above, Avrim could have sworn he saw an angel's form—a winged feminine shape. But it was such a brief flash that he had to have imagined it.

The Fourth Eagle was a little more rundown than Deina had expected, being so close to the duke's estate and in the wealthier part of the city. Hoping the drink prices would match the tavern's aesthetics, she took a chance and pushed open the door. She was immediately welcomed by thick pipe smoke, calm conversations, and the gentle plucking of a lute by a lavishly dressed gnome bard bathed in candlelight.

Deina sighed deep and closed her eyes to relish the ecstasy surrounding her.

This was home.

"What'll it be?" asked a sober, high-pitched voice in the distance.

Without opening her eyes, Deina said, "Ale. Dark as you got."

"Came to the right place," the voice replied. "Grab a chair, got some nice accommodating seats over where my two favorite halflings are. Say hello, Suzy and Chera. Welcome our new guest."

Deina opened her eyes to see two seated halfling maids waving at her, smiles so sweet that the dwarf felt a bit queasy, but nodded in greeting nonetheless. She walked to the bar to grab her drink. The rest of the patrons looked rather subdued, which didn't surprise Deina, given the circumstances. Several human farmers, a spattering of halflings, the gnome bard, and a hulking half-orc woman sitting in a dark corner looked to be Deina's company for the evening.

"They aren't doxies, just friendly," the barkeep said, nodding to the halfling women that still watched Deina with eager smiles, sipping their ales daintily. The barkeep was a plump halfling with an eyepatch, standing on a raised plank behind the bar to adequately tend to his patrons. He regarded Deina with one eye. "But if you are seeking company in that regard, you know where to come. With so many of our farms dried up, many have taken to new occupations, and the Eagle here is where coin is most plenty."

Deina grabbed her ale and dropped a few queens on the bar. "Just the ale for tonight. Keep it coming, Mr...?"

The halfling scooped up the coins and gave her a smile that only displayed a few remaining teeth. "Boggs, Tremly Boggs. Master brewer and not-so-bad pickler."

"Deina Brasson. Bodyguard."

Tremly raised his eyebrows. "Sounds important. Who's your patron? Most of our wealthier lords have been cutting their staff, not hiring more guards."

Deina wiped her mouth with the back of her hand, shaking her head. "Not a local. I travel with a priest of the Luminaura, from the Temple of Dawn outside of Sathford to the south."

Tremly nodded knowingly. "Ah, for our fair duke's poor lady wife." He flipped one of the queens Deina had paid him back onto the bar.

"I won't have anyone in Rathen saying that Tremly doesn't support a righteous cause. The Light shine on both your paths."

"Another!" A patron at the end of the bar slammed an empty tankard down.

Deina scooped up the coin and raised a small toast to the halfling as he returned to his duties. She turned and noticed Suzy and Chera still regarding her with eager smiles. Seeing nowhere else to comfortably sit, Deina nodded and lumbered over to the shorter table.

"Traveling through, are ya?" Suzy asked. She looked a little older than Deina, with wrinkles on the edges of her eyes and sun-beaten skin.

This one was certainly a farmer, Deina noted.

"We mostly see regulars in here lately," Chera said, "what with the sky as it is and all, and…well, it's good to see a new face." The two could be twin sisters, except for Suzy's blonde hair and Chera's darker curls. Both halflings raised their drinks in greeting.

Deina clanked her mug to theirs, taking a quick liking to the women. "I can imagine. It was not the most welcoming sight as we came into town. I can't imagine living under this. You lasses be braver than me."

Suzy shrugged, her smile seeming a little more forced now. "It's not bravery that keeps us here, it's the duke's grace."

"There's not many other lords in all of Noveth that would share their own wealth with his people," Chera said soberly. "When the storm came, most of our farms were ruined. Many moved south to try their luck with less fertile lands, while others took up whatever other crafts they could to get by. But for us," Chera motioned to Suzy.

Suzy leaned in and lowered her voice slightly. "Since you're a traveler, it seems, I'm sure you're aware how most halflings in Vale stick to the big folks' kitchens. Round here though, most of us have our own farms and shops, just like our kin back in the Acreage, and this storm won't be chasing us out that easy. And those of us who stayed were rewarded."

"Rewarded?" Deina couldn't hide her shock at the positive spin on their current predicament. "How so?"

Chera pointed a small thumb over her shoulder. "Duke Ambrose. He saw how dire things got for us—no rain, no crops, no queens. He's a wealthy man, the duke. And the Shadow take me if he did not reach into his own coffers to give us an advance on next year's crop!"

Deina slugged the last dregs of her ale and slammed it down on their table as Chera rocked back with a giddy smile. "A high lord sharing his coin! Now that's more unnatural than your storm!"

The women shared a merry laugh together as Tremly brought them each another round. Deina drained another dark ale, bitter and muddy and glorious, delighting Suzy and Chera with her tales of adventure in the south. She didn't share the details of the grievous wound she suffered, or the debt she owed Avrim for finding her and healing her. Partially because the evening was too pleasant to revisit her near-death experience, but also because she had to share many more drinks with someone before she revealed to them any manner of past mistakes.

The drinks continued, as did the laughter. And while the halflings were clearly drunk after the third round, Deina was just loosening up, and she could clearly see the half-orc staring at her from the darkness—watching and waiting.

Avrim spent some time collecting his thoughts in the duke's estate gardens. He knelt below the gruesome sky, his eyes closed. During his brief time in Rathen, he realized that the feeling of absolute dread that the storm inspired on the way into the city was thrice as strong within the city walls.

It's this city, Avrim thought, closing his eyes tighter as he tried to focus on his evening prayers. *This is the heart of it.*

"Father?"

Startled, Avrim dropped his luminary—the holy book of the Light. He opened his eyes to see a knight in brilliantly white armor, etched in onyx arcane patterns. She rested a mailed hand on the pommel of a broadsword at her waist and regarded him with an accusatory stare. Against the dying flowers in the duke's gardens, the Oather looked almost as ominous as her order's reputation.

Avrim got to his feet, offering her a polite smile. "Oh, I'm not a Father yet—just a Brother of the Light." He stepped cautiously toward her, inclining his head. "My name is Avrim Kaust, from the Temple of the Dawn near Sathford."

The Oather's face remained unchanged. Her hair was short and neat. She motioned to her narrow chin. "I'm sorry, I saw the beard and…"

Avrim's own hand went to his close-cropped beard, dark but with specks of gray. He laughed. "Yes, I guess I would be quite reprimanded if I were to visit the Lighthold in Andelor looking like a Father with no stole to show for it. Fortunately, the Dawn's vicar does not hold too deeply to such superficial traditions."

The knight held her gaze on him for a long moment before nodding. She clearly did not approve. "I am Dame Kasia Strallow, Oather of the Arcania. You may call me Kasia, Brother Kaust."

"Please. Avrim. It is a pleasure to meet you, despite our," he motioned to the sky that had darkened to the color of swamp water, "ominous predicament."

Kasia nodded, frowning. She couldn't have been much older than Avrim—who had just seen his thirty-first birthday—but the Oather's eyes were those of a tired old woman who had nothing but cynicism left for the world. "I will admit, it is quite perplexing. But I have theories."

"So your investigation bears fruit?"

Kasia regarded him with cold eyes and a condescending smile. "In my thirteen years with the Arcania, I have yet to fail in rooting out unsanctioned arcane activity." Her smile faded slightly. "Witchcraft, I prefer to call it. I assume you are here to tend to the duchess?"

Avrim turned to retrieve his forgotten luminary, dusting the dirt off the bent pages. "Yes, I understand she is afflicted. Duke Ambrose has requested the Light's healing and it seems his own priests had been called away on Lighthold business."

"How many priests does it take to heal an affliction?" came a mocking voice from beyond one of the hedges. A young elf with angular features and long black hair stepped into view along the paved path near Kasia. "I don't believe I remember the answer to that riddle." The elf didn't even look at Avrim. "I still think we should have a look at Lady Ambrose ourselves."

Kasia motioned to the elf. "Avrim, meet my companion, Blane Hassok. He is a high mage from the Arcania. He is here to assist in my investigations, and is second-in-command of the city watch until the situation in Rathen is resolved." She turned to Blane. "And I'll remind my companion that the duke has requested we not risk exposing ourselves to whatever ails his wife until an experienced healer is able to confirm that her affliction is not catching."

"Has no one been in to see her then?" Avrim asked.

Blane finally regarded Avrim, as if annoyed he was still there. "It seems that your church had sent all of the good duke's healers out to Wickham and its surrounding holds where the harpies have resorted to raiding." He flourished his hand, and lightning subtly danced between his fingers. "I personally drove most of those bitches off when we arrived—the archers with the city watch couldn't hit a dead cow with their aim. The harpies haven't attacked since, but have pestered those foolish enough not to come stay under our protection within the city."

"A word of warning, Avrim," Kasia said, motioning for Blane that it was time for them to be off. "The duke seems to be beside himself with grief for his wife, and might not be of sound mind. I just spoke with him and he refused to let us speak with his son, Percy, who I hear has a fascinating collection of talismans found in the northern ruins that I'd like to speak with him about. Report to us if you suspect anything…suspicious. We will be continuing our investigations at the city's keep should you need our assistance."

As Blane followed Kasia out of the garden, Avrim noticed the wizard carrying a bag of oddities. A few scrolls and a jeweled statue of Rathen's three eagles could be seen protruding from the sack, along with a couple colorful jagged stones. The elf was inspecting a gray stone that looked almost like a gem as he walked away, quickly returning it to his bulging bag as they left the duke's garden.

Curious, Avrim thought.

The duke's manor was beyond the garden on a hill that overlooked the market district of Rathen. Avrim made his way up the winding path, exchanging quick pleasantries with the duke's personal guards. Through several short exchanges, Avrim learned that the city watch was entirely under the Arcania's control during Dame Strallow's investigation, with the duke's personal guard being the only military force within the city that was not under Andelor's control.

The more Avrim learned of the situation in the city, the more palpable the tension became, to the point that he felt like he was suffocating when he reached the duke's large doors. Surprisingly, no guards flanked the entrance, and with the exception of the guards pacing the gates surrounding the manor, Avrim didn't see any guards near the manor.

Taking a deep breath, Avrim pounded on the massive oak doors with his fist.

BOOM BOOM BOOM.

After the echo that followed, there was silence.

Avrim raised his fist to pound again, but paused as he heard the faintest whisper that sounded like the sigh of the wind—even though there had been no wind since he came under the storm.

"...the stone..."

The whisper sounded like it came from beyond the door, so Avrim leaned closer. Silence. He pressed his ear to the door, focusing. But only silence.

BOOM BOOM BOOM.

Avrim stumbled back, his heart racing. He instinctively reached for the holy star around his neck and raised his luminary in defense.

There was a soft click on the other side of the door and a high-pitched squeal as it opened inward to reveal an older but sturdy halfling man dressed in a perfectly clean ivory tunic that displayed the three deep green eagles of Rathen on it. His broad-booted feet clicked together as he motioned to the lavish foyer. He smiled at Avrim.

"Welcome, do you have Ruke's stone?"

"Ruke's stone?" Avrim asked.

The halfling's smile widened. "Welcome to the duke's home, Brother Kaust. May I offer you some refreshments?"

Before Avrim could answer, or even collect his wits, he heard the thumping sound of boots on the carpeted floor above getting louder and louder until a figure appeared behind the ornate banister overlooking the two staircases winding down to the foyer's first floor.

Duke Petrik Ambrose was a disheveled man with weary eyes. He had a bald head with wild hair remaining above his ears.

"Come in, shut the doors! Hurry, Kasper!"

The halfling motioned for Avrim to hurry inside.

The duke was scrambling down the stairs. "Is she gone?"

"Yes, my lord. Dame Strallow has left the grounds," Kasper replied in a calm voice.

Avrim gathered himself as he stepped into the foyer, ready to meet the duke. "I came as quickly as I could, Duke Ambrose. If you'll show me to your wife—"

The duke waved the thought away as he stepped onto the landing, his clothes looking two sizes too big for his emaciated frame. "Oh, she's quite dead. Come, you must tend to my son immediately."

"Dear," came an ethereal voice from above, "is that any way to welcome our guest?" Gentle laughter followed, sounding as if it came from some other plane.

Following the voice, Avrim looked up to the balcony where the duke first appeared. The barely visible form of a bloody woman stood there in a tattered dress. She reached out a crimson hand to motion for Avrim to come toward her.

Avrim held his holy star up as far as the chain around his neck would allow. His mouth went dry staring at the ghostly form of the duchess, and he struggled for the disciples' words on banishing lost spirits.

"Begone, bitch! You are no longer my wife!" The duke waved a dismissive hand toward the spirit as he reached for Avrim's elbow with his other hand. "Lock the doors, Kasper, and have the guards keep anyone from entering the estate grounds. We shall be in Percy's quarters."

Avrim allowed himself to be led by the duke, his eyes fixed on the spirit of Duchess Ambrose. Her form faded slightly, and her smile twisted into a mockery of a human face before she released a horrid peal of laughter.

"Brother, you have seen ghosts before, yes?" The duke led Avrim under the stairs into a great hall that ran under the balcony. The duchess' laugh echoed throughout the foyer.

"Y-yes," Avrim managed, licking his cracking lips. "But not quite as…malevolent as that." The lie had a hint of truth in it. He had seen a ghost when he was an acolyte, but it was bound to a Lightshard and not remotely dangerous.

The duke clicked his tongue. "Then brace yourself, Brother. This house is unclean, and my son is the source of this scourge plaguing our city."

CHAPTER THREE

The Eaves of Oakworth

The sun began to set behind the second tallest building in Oakworth, the massive three-story inn that Renay liked to admire from her high window in the baron's keep. The Harvest Breeze Inn was often a bustle of activity, and this evening was no exception.

Renay stood naked near the wide window of her sizable quarters, letting the fading sunlight warm her skin as she brushed the day's tangles from her long red hair. Her eyes were fixed on the town's thoroughfare below, where people of all shapes, sizes, and colors milled about. Oakworth's location so near the Valeway meant travelers coming to and from Andelor were bound to rest their weary feet at The Harvest Breeze—its reputation as Vale's busiest inn was probably the main reason that Renay decided to make a new life in the otherwise dull town.

The baron's keep overlooked the entire town and most of the baron's holdings outside the walls of Oakworth, including Buckley Woods to the east as well as the banks of the Bracing River and the Horin Hills to the north and south, respectively. To the west were the farmlands that flanked the winding road leading to the Valeway. Renay's lofty quarters in one of the keep's corner towers afforded her varied scenic views, but she only ever watched The Harvest Breeze.

Each traveler had a story—whether exciting, dull, or pure fabrication—and Renay liked to imagine what those stories were as she watched them shuffle about. As she ran the brush through her hair again, she saw a weary one-armed dwarf shouldering a heavy bag stomp up the inn's front stairs. *Did he just come from the hills?* she wondered, recognizing the figure from somewhere. *Must be a miner, coming to find buried treasure.* Baron Alburn Caffery was known for his lucrative mining operations, drawing prospectors from every corner of Vale to his lands.

Following the dwarf came a pair of lovers—a dark-skinned

Karranese man and his pale elven maid—in a hurry to find a private room on the third floor. Holding the door for the two was a halfling woman leaving the inn; it was Dolly the cook, and her adorable tiny twin daughters. Dolly scolded the girls to watch where they were going as the twins scurried down the steps into the thoroughfare.

Renay smiled tightly, letting a sad sense of nostalgia wash over her, sending an unexpected chill down her spine. The scene below darkened as the heavy fog of memory shrouded the window. She saw a baby's contorted face beneath rippling water as her own trembling hands gripped its little shoulders and held it under. The sounds of distant choking and gurgling echoed in her ears.

The vision blurred and vanished and the sound became her own cry of pain as her head jerked back—her brush was on the ground and her fist gripped a chunk of her own hair, pulling it violently. She gasped and released her grip, biting her lip before taking a deep breath.

A knock at the door startled her and she instinctively covered her nakedness as best as she could with just her hands, giving up when she realized she was safe in her quarters.

"Yes?"

"Are you decent?" came a hushed familiar voice beyond the door. "I've sent your guard on a small errand."

Renay relaxed, her face softening from fear to resignation.

"You may come."

The door creaked about halfway open to reveal Vivian Caffery, who tried her best to look discreet as she slid her considerable form through the opening, closing the door behind her. The baroness was about five years Renay's senior and dressed as if she had just stepped out of a painting from Caim, where the vampires ruled. She was nearly spilling out the top of a corset that did its best to slim her ample waist, and her graying hair was bound up tightly in a lavish web of pearls and jewels. Her gown was less elaborate than the rest of her attire, but she rarely walked the grounds without looking like a queen.

She was a large and beautiful force, and Renay still had trouble not lowering her eyes in the woman's presence. As Vivian enjoyed her silent view, Renay stepped toward her wardrobe and retrieved an open shift to slip into, tying its small belt around her waist—though it did little to conceal what the baroness could see whenever she desired.

"Did I disturb you?" Vivian asked teasingly, taking a step away from the door.

Renay shook her head. "Of course not, my lady, you are always welcome. I was giving the children time to finish their studies before dinner."

"That's very well," the baroness replied, shifting her gaze from Renay to the window overlooking the inn. "Their father just finished an audience with the queen's newest envoy—an upstart elf lord from the Wane Coast." As Vivian stepped near, Renay caught the scent of Coperan mint on her breath and her stomach fluttered slightly. "Last year he was nothing but a wharfmaster, and now he's apparently docked his skiff so well in the queen's harbor that she's granted him dominion over the entire coastal trade." The baroness lightly ran a finger down Renay's back—the younger woman held her breath. "Now, our dear baron is meeting with the Guild, which should keep him busy for a spell."

The baroness stalked around Renay. It was a familiar game, one that reinforced the woman's power over the household and reminded those in the Cafferys' employ that Vivian Caffery shared equal footing with her husband in all matters.

From behind, Vivian's hand slipped under Renay's arm and firmly took hold of a heavy breast.

Renay exhaled carefully, closing her eyes. The sound of the baroness' voice complaining of diplomatic matters faded away, and a ghostly humming from her past brought another vision to Renay—she looked down, and instead of the matriarch's hand, there was a beautiful baby boy feeding from her while a phantom mother from the past hummed a calming melody that melted Renay. The ecstasy was deep, and fear was as distant as Vivian's voice.

For a moment.

The vision of the baby faded slowly until it became a shadow, and then blood burst from the shadow child's mouth as pain exploded through Renay's body.

The present came back forcefully as Vivian pinched a nipple and Renay gasped, nearly doubling over. Relief and pleasure drove out the memory of pain. She grasped Vivian's hand with her own, welcoming the baroness' rough touch, more so today than ever before. She wanted more than anything to stay the Shadow from her waking dreams.

It had been worse than ever today, but the Shadow seemed to always chase her—ever since she ran away.

Vivian spun Renay around, tearing the shift away as she got to her knees. Renay looked toward the setting sun while the Light still remained.

"You have some nerve," Alburn Caffery said through gritted teeth. He leaned forward in his chair, its back rising up to shape the ornate oak tree that served as his sigil. "You come into my keep under the guise of diplomacy and seek to rob me in broad daylight?"

The halfling named Brood reached up to scratch the thick patch of hair that separated his plump cheek and round ear—an ear that had a sizable chunk cut off it. The top of the bushy hair on his head barely reached his companion's waist.

Grip was short for an elf, but smiled like she stood taller than any other person in the hall. She regarded the baron dispassionately, her one good eye unblinking and her black glass eye as unsettling as ever. She was a dark-skinned elf—born from the Shadow, some said—but her black leathers made her flesh look more like a fresh bruise in the hall's bright torchlight. "Rob you? Dear Baron, the Guild forbids us to mark a fellow thief." Her voice was as musical as a funeral dirge.

The baron shot to his feet, his long, brown and gold embroidered cloak swirling behind him as he stepped down the dais toward his guests. He pointed a broad finger at Grip, assuming as threatening a posture as he could while unarmed and flanked by two of his armored house guards. "You will not name me thief in my domain, you Netherspawn! I rid these lands of your filth—worthless vagabonds! Vagrants! If the queen was not bound by whatever blackmail your master holds over her, I'd hang you both up with the rest of your lackeys!"

"Is that your answer then?" Brood asked in a voice much deeper than the shrill baron's. He was the burliest halfling Alburn had ever seen, as well as the rudest. Dressed in black leathers like his companion, Brood rested a hand on the hilt of a short, broad blade at his hip while he picked something out of his teeth with the other hand. "We can go back and tell Knife you declined our offer—that you ain't looking to stock your coffers for the coming winter in exchange for that paltry trinket. I reckon you're plenty aware that Knife's good for the coin."

The baron looked down at the impudent creature, not hiding his disdain for having to even acknowledge a halfling in his hall. In his mind, the small folk belonged in the kitchen or the fields, not treating in his hall as if they were dignitaries!

"You tell Knife whatever you damn well please, halfling. My patience is at an end. Next time you intend to treat with me on the Guild's behalf, you will remember that I won't be threatened, and Oakworth won't negotiate with brigands." He turned his furious gaze to Grip. "You will not have the stone."

"Well, that went well."

Grip waved a dismissive hand. "We knew how that would go, Brood. That's not why we're here." She kept her voice low as they crossed the baron's courtyard. She focused on the bridge ahead leading over the moat into the market, not the lifeless thieves that hung like banners in the baron's grisly garden.

He is not subtle, she thought, knowing this grisly display was specifically for them. Grip could barely fight back the blinding fury that threatened to overtake her as she thought about all the young pickpockets that had been murdered in the baron's vain and futile attempt to frighten the Guild.

"Enlighten me," Brood replied. "I got a good memory, Grip, and I seems to recall Knife telling us to get that stone and we ain't supposed to ask questions."

"Well, subtlety has not always been your strength, friend." She patted Brood's head, pulling her hand back before his swipe could get it. "We know how proud the baron is. He would never agree to an amicable trade with our organization, no matter how lucrative. Knife knows this too, which is why she sent us empty-handed. Also, the queen cannot risk openly opposing Caffery, not with a possible war—she needs Oakworth."

"And?"

"And they both know that we solve problems. We're here to figure out a solution." Their soft boots barely made a sound over the drawbridge as they made their way to the baron's gates. Night was falling, and the bustle on the market street was dying down. They continued under the gates in silence, passing the last of the keep's guards on their way to The Harvest Breeze.

"So we can't steal it," Brood began again, "unless we want to end up on display in that pompous goon's gardens. And we ain't expected to get anywhere with negotiations…"

Grip stopped, turning to look back at the baron's keep. Its high walls always had archers pacing the perimeter, and both gates were under constant guard. Even if the underway that carried the high lords' filth from their privies was large enough for Brood to squeeze through, there was too much risk for them to try to sneak into the bowels of the keep to blindly search for that damn stone.

"We need to find someone that's been inside," Grip thought aloud. She turned back to Brood. "Let's reconvene with Scratch."

The two changed course away from The Harvest Breeze and left the market's cobbled thoroughfare, turning around the southern tower of the baron's keep. The gentle waters of the moat ran into a stream that divided a quiet row of several two-story apartments where many artisans from the market made their home. Outside one of the quaint residences, two halfling girls chased each other, giggling breathlessly. As the thieves from Andelor approached, Brood rushed toward them.

"Uncle Rosh, Uncle Rosh!" they both shouted as the burly halfling lifted them off the ground and spun them around.

"You two are giants!" Brood said. "I won't be able to do this next time I visit." He hugged them fiercely.

"Why can't you stay?" one of the children asked as Brood set them down. "Mother said the spare room is for you whenever your knife doesn't need you."

The other girl pointed at the knife at Brood's hip. "I don't think it needs you anymore, Uncle. It looks fine to me!"

Brood chuckled. "I wish I could stay, Sadie. And my knife needs me for a little bit longer, Kadie." He rubbed their heads. "We have to speak to your mother for a bit; keep playing and stay out of trouble."

Grip knelt and rustled their hair as she followed Brood into the apartment.

The pair found Dolly making a racket in the kitchen, cursing as she shoved a giant lazy cat out her way with a large bare foot. "You two here for dinner? I left you some grub at the Breeze. Not much here, but I can put a loaf in and cut up some cheese if ya like."

Brood waved a hand. "We'll eat at the Breeze. We're just here to speak with Scratch."

Dolly let out a guffaw. "You know Scratch's dead—has been since she squeezed out those little scamps. Cute as buttons, they are, but damn near useless in the kitchen." She appeared in the kitchen's tall doorway with a pitcher of wine and a handful of glasses. "I almost curse that sly sailor that put them in me, but I guess it could be worse—I could be trying to treat with our slimy baron." She set the refreshments down on the short table. Grip sat on the ground and crossed her legs.

Brood took a glass of wine and saluted. "Well said, sis."

"We let him name his price," Grip explained. She told Dolly the details of their meeting as they drained the glasses. "I'm sure Knife knew that he would not sell the thing."

"And the queen is absolutely certain that he has Ruke's stone?" Dolly raised an eyebrow. "I hear these things are linked, so I can only assume she has another piece of Elysun?" She turned to Brood. "Or did you not think to ask, sweet brother?"

Brood shrugged. "I don't get paid to ask questions."

"I trust Knife and she trusts the queen," Grip said. "I believe it's here, and the baron more or less confirmed it with his rejection. We just can't retrieve it ourselves."

Dolly leaned back and kicked her broad feet up onto the table, calloused and furry. "Well, don't look at me. Like I said, Scratch's dead. I'm just Dolly Osbury, head cook at The Harvest Breeze and diligent mother." She drained her glass. "Speaking of which, brother, make sure the girls aren't dead out there."

They shared a laugh while refilling their glasses.

"We wouldn't ask any senior members of the Guild to risk exposing themselves in this kind of operation," Grip said, returning to the topic. "Especially with these hangings."

"He's trying to lure the queen," Dolly said with a nod. "Our brilliant strategist of a baron expects that if he hangs enough thieves, he might get an important Guild member and force the queen's hand. He already suspects the Guild are her personal spies, but he's too dense to see the greater picture...the greater threat the queen is trying to prevent."

Grip nodded, confirming her own suspicions. "We need someone that's no longer tied to the Guild—someone we can trust, preferably that knows the baron's keep."

Dolly froze, turning her eyes from the open window where she watched Kadie and Sadie back to Grip. She smiled.

"What?" Brood asked, leaning forward.

"There was a certain half-elf that Knife raised from a babe. I always suspected it was her own kin, but who knows without ever having seen her face. She turned half the ladies of the Guild into mothers watching over that boy, myself included—it's why I'm such a damn fine mum! Anyway, that boy grew up after Scratch passed on and Knife sent him away, had him escorted to Sathford—don't ask me why."

"Robin?" Grip asked.

Dolly nodded. "He must have gotten into trouble, because not just two years past, our fine baron had him in chains in his keep. This was before all the hangings, mind you, but still—Robin knew a lot about the Guild. When I found out, I was going to take myself on up to Andelor to report to Knife directly, but damned if I didn't see our cousin from Blakehurst march right on up to the baron's gates and come back out with a freed Robin in hand." She laughed heartily, slapping her knee.

Brood smiled. "Ransil?!"

Dolly nodded again. "The very one that swore off Guild business and opened The Early Mule all the way on the other side of Vale." She chuckled again and took another drink. "He stopped to say hello—I don't think the girls were even old enough to remember him then. I can only assume Knife sent word to him to keep an eye out on Robin—again, don't ask me why she worries so much over the boy."

Grip smiled wickedly, casting a quick glance to Brood before turning back to Dolly.

"She's going to be glad she does."

"Can you tell me the story of Queen Sopheena?" little Lenora Caffery asked as Renay tucked the child into her massive four-post bed.

"You know that story better than I do now," Renay said with a smile, patting the girl's head. "Haven't you read more books than Viktor on the history of Vale?"

"Yes, but you tell it differently than the books," Lenora said, her childish voice enunciating the words like an articulate scholar. "Why do all of Father's books speak of the elves as if they don't belong here? Didn't we come to Vale from Eastlund, just like the elves came from

Luastreal? Didn't we fight the Shadow together?"

Renay shrugged. "Many people do not understand the elves, and people fear what they do not understand. Fear causes us to push things away."

"Like you pushed me away?"

Shaken, Renay frowned and saw a shadowed face where Lenora's once was. She blinked the vision away until she saw the baron's child again, closing her eyes and nestling sweetly into her pillow.

Taking a deep breath, Renay gently stroked the girl's head. "You are so thoughtful for one so young, my Lady Lenora. I do hope you stay so curious."

Lenora did not offer a response, already drifting off to sleep.

Taking the candle from the nightstand, Renay left the child's quarters and peeked in on Viktor across the hall. The boy was snoring loudly on his side, his arm hanging off his bed. *The quartermaster must have pushed him hard today*, Renay thought, shutting his door.

She walked swiftly down the hall, hoping Mother Agathene was still at the temple this late. As she rounded the corner to the stairs, she nearly collided with Baron Caffery. He stood erect, although he was only of a height with Renay. She smiled after she collected herself, offering, "Excuse me, my lord baron. I was just putting your children to bed."

"Yes," Alburn said, his eyes fixed on hers, his expression soft. He betrayed the hint of a smile beneath his thick mustache. "It seems my wife and I both require a bath, if you are not otherwise indisposed."

Renay tried to drive the Shadow out of her mind enough to offer him a genuine smile, but she feared he would see it as placating him. "Of course, my lord. Perhaps I could tend to you both when I return from the temple?"

Alburn's face darkened, but only slightly. "After the day I have had, I am in no mood to wait. We will expect you shortly." The baron raised his eyebrows, looking more like a beggar than a lord.

Renay ran a teasing finger across his moustache before continuing toward the stairs. On her way to the temple, she had to pass through the courtyard, which she always dreaded. The shadows of dead thieves swaying in the breeze brought more disturbing visions. Despite his grisly trophies, Renay couldn't help but feel eternally grateful toward the baron for taking her in. She made a mental note to pray for him after tending to her own troubled soul.

The Temple of the Lightborn stood just to the north of the keep. Two great braziers burned at the gates that surrounded it and the adjacent cemetery, ensuring that the Shadow was kept at bay. She felt relief flood her as she crossed the fiery gateway. She was greeted inside the temple by two Brothers kneeling in silent prayer to the decorative oversized lantern.

"It has been almost a month," an old voice said to her from a dark alcove beyond the temple's altar. Mother Agathene stepped into the pool of light coming from the great lantern. "Has the Light started to fade in your high tower?" She gave Renay a sly smile as she approached.

Mother Agathene was an elderly woman, but it only really showed on her wrinkled face. She stood tall and had no trouble getting around, and her wits hadn't even slightly declined. When she was close enough to make out Renay's face, her smiling expression slipped into worry.

The elder woman reached out a hand. "Come, child."

Together they left the silent nave, navigating the rows of pews to a side hallway that led to a vacant glowery, where worshipers could sit and contemplate in the Light. The small room was adorned with dozens of candles that seemed to burn brighter than any candle should, and almost immediately the shadow-visions that plagued Renay all that day faded into memory.

"What troubles you, child?" Mother Agathene had no trouble getting to her knees on the padded pillow.

Renay knelt down on the pillow as well, considering her words. "I have told you before of the visions that plague me. But I haven't told you about my past."

"The Light does not care about your past," Mother Agathene said, quoting the luminary, "The past is where the Shadow lies. The Light is always ahead, showing the way forward."

Thinking of her Shadowchild, Renay breathed deep before asking, "The luminary says the Shadow consumes. The monsters that now plague our world that have fallen into Shadow, completely lost to the Light… Is there hope for them?"

Agathene shook her head. "Those lost to the Light are hopeless. The Shadow is absolute when it consumes, leaving death to be the only absolution. We must always fight the Shadow and never believe its lies. Once it takes hold, the Light is extinguished."

Even in the bright light of the glowery, visions of the night she fled still darkened her mind—

The child slept peacefully as the man grabbed her arm, begging her to stay, promising that he would find a way. Renay pulled her arm free from the Shadows and wiped away the tears from her past, throwing open the door and running into the night.

—Agathene's hand clasped over hers. "Do you feel the Shadow, my child?"

Renay smiled, shaking her head. "I escaped it long ago, I think. And I won't go back." A tear ran down her cheek. "I'll never go back."

They turned to bask in the Light.

CHAPTER FOUR

The Shadow's Reach

Anika worked into the night, spending the late morning massaging the family dog's urine and dung into freshly cut cattle skins. She then folded the treated skins tightly before arranging them in stacks in their tanning shed, where they would putrefy to an extent that their hair could be more easily removed. As she inspected the hanging skins that had been cured with salt and stale beer from The Early Mule, she could remember when the smell of the structure was enough to make her sick. But this would be nearly her seventh year working in the shed, and though it wasn't a pleasant place to spend her time, she found the wretched aromas almost reassuring.

It was the smell of purpose and intention—belonging.

Their family provided an important service to the community, opening up valuable trade opportunities that both kept them living comfortably and contributed to Blakehurst's good standing. Their leathers were used for shoes, clothing, armor, tool grips, and bags that carried livelihoods from place to place. She took great pride in the stink, and she knew she had her father to thank for teaching her how to appreciate how much such a simple life could mean to someone.

The rest of Anika's afternoon was spent learning, watching intently as Bennik carefully displayed the proper way to skin the two wolves that Matty's father, Hugh, brought from their farm. The beasts had torn apart three of the family chickens and Matty had taken vengeance with his bow.

"Take 'em," Hugh said when he dropped the beast corpses off at the Lawsons' home. "Rug 'em or trade 'em, however you see fit, Ben. Just give me their heads—I want Cassy to stuff 'em to hang outside our coop. That Syrinic priest that came through last year says it'll serve as a warning to their mangy kin."

Anika gripped her own skinning knife, carefully mimicking her father's movements as he cut around under a wolf's tail, all the way up its belly and chest to under its jaw. She copied his knife's precision on a phantom corpse as Bennik pulled the skin away from the dark bloody flesh underneath.

Usually, Bennik skinned with Gage, but it seemed more and more lately that Gage was too busy hunting and trapping to work with them. Thinking of Gage, Anika's hand went to the pouch on her belt, reaching in to feel the blue stone he had stolen that morning. Every time she touched the stone, she saw flashes of the creature from before. The visions were less intense now, but she could always see the winged shape in the pale green sky, calling to her—

"Anika?"

She shook the vision away to see her father, hands bloodied and face worried. He looked at her hand. Anika looked down and saw that she held her skinning knife in a white-knuckle grip. Relaxing, she slid the blade into the new sheath at her belt and released the stone.

"Sorry."

He gave her a sad smile. "It's all right, it's later than I realized." He grabbed the burning candle from the table and led Anika out of the large kitchen that was built behind their house. Closing the door behind him, he looked at the darkening sky—the sun was nearly set. "I should go find Gage."

Pepper yipped at Bennik's feet, the dog's tail flapping furiously.

"Let's go find him ourselves," Bennik said to the animal. He turned to Anika. "Sorry to make you work so late on your birthday." He reached into his own pouch and produced several queens, handing them to her.

"Why don't you head to the Mule and enjoy yourself. I'll make sure Gage picks up the slack tomorrow so you can sleep in."

Anika smiled, overcome with emotion for the second time that day. "Thanks, Father." As he made to go, she reached out a dark hand to grab his lighter one. "For everything."

He smiled and squeezed her hand. "You're worth everything, Ani." For a brief moment, his smile faded away and he looked as if he were about to say something else. But he just nodded and turned toward the darkening woods.

The Early Mule was busier than Anika ever remembered. The old yellow two-story building at the center of town had a few meager lodgings for travelers upstairs under its dark green roof, which were not nearly as accommodating as those at the Brook & Stable Inn at the edge of town. However, Ransil's establishment always stayed busier than the Evertrees' inn, which was a credit to Ransil Osbury's exceptional cooking, baking, and brewing abilities.

Anika pushed open the thick green door into a brightly lit common room where she saw many familiar faces, as well as a few strangers. Ransil himself was laughing behind the bar, handing Bruck a flagon of ale as the dwarf regaled the halfling with what must have been a colorful tale. Elza sat at a nearby table with a Karranese woman that Anika had never seen before; the stranger's skin was a deep chestnut color like her own. Matty Cullen and his two closest friends, the big-shouldered Esher Dell and Wesley Evertree, sat toward the back of the room, raising their tankards in a slurred song. Anika held her gaze on Matty, reveling in the joy she saw in his kind eyes.

"They've been singing all day," Jema Cullen said, appearing at Anika's side. "You would think they just won a battle or found a chest of jewels from the dragon lands of Vaina. But alas, their true heroics lie in selling a few extra sacks of grain and some eggs to a queen-pinching trader from Copera."

Anika covered her mouth to keep from laughing, and took Jema's hand as she led them to a table near the bar where their friend Wilma Evertree sat staring intently at Esher as the young man spilled more ale down his thick, muscled chest.

"It is Lady Anika Lawson's birthday today," Jema announced when they reached the table, drawing Wilma's attention. Jema made a lavish gesture for Anika to have a seat and turned to the proprietor. "Good Sir Osbury, perhaps you could favor her with your finest offerings?"

Ransil smiled wide, his face always a strange mixture of aged wisdom and boyish mischief. He slapped his small belly that was wrapped in a dirty apron. "I think I have just the thing to celebrate our Lady Lawson's special day." He turned toward the kitchen and called, "Robin!"

Elza turned toward Anika's table and smiled, drawing her Karranese companion's attention as well. Anika kept a tight smile as she nodded to Elza, reaching down to reassuringly pat the pouch that held the stolen stone. She avoided the stranger's gaze as best she could.

Cheers of "Anika!" and "Seventeen!" rang out through the Mule, with Matty and his friends leading the revelry. Matty smiled warmly at Anika and raised his ale in salute toward her. She blushed fiercely and was overcome with a sense of belonging that she could never remember feeling, even though this was a birthday tradition in Blakehurst.

Something about the way Matty noticed her tonight made her feel both changed and yet comfortably at home. *Perhaps this is just how it feels to become a woman*, she thought.

"I read in a book," Wilma leaned in to whisper to Anika, "that in Xe'dann, on their seventeenth birthday, ladies are expected to lay with a man of their choosing."

Anika gave Wilma a shocked look but then quickly joined the rising laughter.

"Robin!" Ransil shouted again amidst the merriment, leaping off the platform behind the bar that allowed him to serve patrons. The top of his head could be seen heading toward the kitchen.

Amongst the revelry, Anika heard a shrill cry like a ringing in her ear. It sounded like a bird of prey, only more sinister and frightening. Her eyes darted to the Karranese woman, who watched her intently. Anika shook her head to rid her mind of the sound and the woman's gaze.

"In that case," Jema said quietly to Wilma, motioning toward the kitchen, "I'll be hollering for Robin like Ransil there on my seventeenth birthday."

Laughing, none of them noticed when Ransil came back from the kitchen looking worried. "Has anyone seen him?"

Gage stoked the fire as Robin watched the dancing flames from a nearby log. The gentle sound of the creek filled the momentary silence. Normally, Gage hated sharing silences with people, even his own family. But ever since Robin had come into his life, he found that silence in the half-elf's company made his mind wander less and he could focus more on the present.

"So you just gave it to your sister?" Robin asked.

Gage shrugged. "It was her birthday. She may as well have asked me to take it. Last night and the night before, she woke me up in the middle of the night to remind me it was her birthday." He threw the twig into the fire and took a seat on the ground near Robin. "She said all she wanted was something called a skyshard. When I saw her fawning over it at the gnome's shop, I figured that's what she meant. Though, I don't know how she knew Elza would be coming to town."

Robin thought about that, turning to meet Gage's eyes. "Well, swiping it in broad daylight with an elf nearby—that's impressive. I'm sure the Guild would take you in."

Gage's heart quickened. "You think so?"

Robin nodded, looking back to their fire. "If you still wanted to go with me to Andelor, we could join the Guild, or stow away on a ship to Xe'dann or Caim." His dark eyes consumed the fire. "We could find my mother."

Mother. The word still stuck a spear through Gage's heart. It was a wound that he and Robin shared. As an orphan from Vale's capital city, Robin never knew his parents, and liked to remind Gage he was lucky to have a father. But neither of them knew their mothers.

Robin slid off the log, crossing his legs and taking a seat near Gage. Their knees touched slightly. "We could look for yours on the way."

"No," Gage said flatly. "She's dead. My father doesn't know, but I heard him tell Bruck the tale. The dwarf was building his shop when I was about nine, and I heard them at the Mule exchanging tales. My father said he went looking for my mother when she disappeared, leaving no trail behind. She was attacked by bandits while walking with me through the woods. I was just a babe then; would have died if she didn't hide me near the creek when the bandits came. Father found me before I drowned, and he found my mother's body, murdered by bandits. He told Bruck he buried her in the woods because he couldn't bear the thought of seeing her grave every day."

Gage threw another stick into the fire. "That's the only time I saw my father cry."

"Does Anika know?"

Shaking his head, Gage turned to Robin. "No. She wasn't her true mother. So I figured it's better she believes the lies my father tells us— that she went missing." He fought back the tears.

Robin stared deep into Gage's eyes. His delicate elven features framed very human eyes and human lips that parted to offer some sort of comfort. But nothing came.

For another brief moment, they shared the silence that Gage had fallen deeply in love with. Each one of them waited, trying to find the words that might explain their bond, finding none. Finally, Robin leaned forward and reached a hand up to rest comfortably on Gage's cheek. When their eyes met, Robin gently pulled Gage's mouth to his own.

Bennik stepped carefully away from the copse that overlooked the creek. He was not close enough to hear their exchange, but he had seen enough to know that Gage was certainly not in any kind of trouble at the moment. He turned to leave the two, smiling as he motioned for Pepper to follow.

As he made his way back to town, the deep silence of the night gave way to the sound of quick movements in the distance. Bennik drew the only weapon he had, his skinning knife. He crouched low and kept a hand on Pepper to steady her.

There was no sign of movement in the darkness. The moon was bright enough for him to see the outlines of the sparse trees and the space between—there were no shadows moving.

Then a shape fell from above, dropping down from a high tree. Pepper barked twice before Bennik was able to silence her, raising his knife to end the intruder. But a familiar voice stayed his hand.

"They're coming, Bennik." The crouched shadow threw back its cloak as it tried and failed to rise to its feet.

"Farrah!" Kneeling beside her, Bennik saw dark wetness and rough gouges across her decorative armor. "Who's coming?" He helped her up.

"Goblins. Their scouts disabled all your snares." She stood, leaning on her longbow. "I tracked them all the way to the hills outside of Buckley Woods. There were Green-necks from Lohkrest and Ash-hands all the way from Hollowood. They're gathering."

"Gathering?!" Bennik asked. "That's impossible!" Goblins were well known pests in the hinterlands throughout Vale, but they kept their distance from the settlements, scared of societal peoples that they didn't understand. They were more keen on raiding each other, forming dozens of rival clans that treated infighting as a culture and religion. "What in the Light could draw them together?"

Farrah's elven eyes gave Bennik a deep and knowing look. "Not the Light."

A distant sound echoed in the sky, almost like a hawk, but far more threatening.

Just then, curses could be heard toward the creek, followed by the blood-curdling screech of something wretched dying.

"Gage!"

Pepper leapt with Bennik as they raced back toward the boys' camp. Though wounded, Farrah kept pace with them, gracefully drawing and nocking an arrow as they leapt through the brush into the clearing near the creek.

Robin was laying on the ground, bleeding from his shoulder where he gripped a crude arrow. Gage had his own bow drawn, aiming at his father and the elf as Pepper raced to his side. The dog sniffed the diminutive corpse at Gage's feet, gnawing on the dead hand so it released its short bow.

Gage lowered his bow and knelt by his companion. "Father! It shot Robin!"

Before Bennik could answer or move, Farrah unleashed a silent missile into the trees. It found its mark and something fell bodily into the leaves. "There's no time!" Farrah warned as she drew and nocked. "I can see nearly a dozen closing in."

Bennik rushed toward his son as a snarling goblin leaped out of the shadows to intercept. Even in the faint moonlight, Bennik could see its cloudy, Shadowtaken eyes, cruelly looking for a victim.

Without hesitation, he barreled into the monster, using his skinning knife to gut the thing as he easily threw it over his shoulder. He reached Robin and effortlessly lifted the half-elf boy, cradling him in his arms as if he were his own child. A goblin died behind him as Farrah found another mark.

"To town!" Bennik cried, motioning for Gage to follow. The boy hesitated briefly as he caught a glimpse of Pepper leaping at a goblin's throat, but a wicked goblin arrow struck the dog above the hind leg, sending her sprawling with the remains of a goblin's bloody throat in its jaw.

"Pepper!" Gage shouted uselessly as he was pulled to follow, several other slobbering goblins leaping on the fresh kill.

The bird sound came again, cutting through the night, closer.

As Farrah continued releasing arrows, Bennik and Gage quickened their stride and raced toward Blakehurst to warn their community of the coming attack.

"Hang on, Robin," Gage said through broken breaths. There was no response.

"Robin?!"

"To the Nethering with him!" Ransil cursed in a mocking, gruff voice as he set the cake down on Anika's table. "Robin was supposed to add the last layer, but he must have gotten distracted somewhere. We'll just have to make sure we don't save him a piece!"

The patrons in The Early Mule crowded around Anika's table to sing songs and wait for a piece of Ransil's delicious cake. The halfling himself slipped away, Anika noticed, the jovial expression on his face fading away to one of genuine concern.

Amidst the chatter near her table, Anika turned to see the Karranese stranger approach. "You don't belong here," she said, looking deep into Anika's eyes—suddenly it felt as if Anika were looking at herself as an older woman. The woman's hand slipped into Anika's pouch where the blue stone was kept. "This is not who you are."

Anika couldn't move; her throat seized up and she couldn't breathe. "Mother?"

"What's that, dear?" Elza asked from behind.

Unthinking, Anika spun around. She held the blue stone in her hand, and the Karranese woman was nowhere to be seen.

"Is that—?"

The gnome's query was lost in a chilling shriek from Wilma, who fell away from the dark window. Two pairs of red eyes peered through; the muffled sound of chattering could be heard behind the glass.

"Goblins!" warned Matty, leaping to put himself between Anika's table and the door. He put a protective arm in front of his sister, Jema, who was reeling to get away from the window. At that moment, the door was thrown open and a gray-green goblin in ill-fitting armor slammed his jagged sword against his wooden shield.

The goblin set his eyes on Anika's open hand that still held the stone, gnashing its teeth and charging toward her.

Anika closed her fist and reached for her knife. Before she could draw it, a spray of dark blood spurted from the goblin's neck as it fell bodily to the floor. The handle of a small knife protruded from its neck.

"Matty, get the door!" Ransil called, leaping over the bar, surprising Anika with his sudden agility. He flipped his hand to reveal another small knife that then disappeared through the door, followed by a wet thud and a choking rasp. Bruck barreled into the kitchen to drive back several snarling goblins.

Matty slammed the door shut just in time for the windows to crash in. Two goblins tumbled over each other into the Mule, each one armed with a cruel dagger and scrambling toward Anika. Ransil rolled over to bury a knife in one of the goblins' backs as Matty's friend Esher stomped heavily on the other one's head until it finally ceased its thrashing.

"They're coming from the back!" Wesley cried, reaching for a nearby table where a small knife was thrust into a cheese wheel. He wrapped his fist around it just in time for a crude goblin sword to cleave his hand off at the wrist. Elza threw a small bag at the attacker that exploded in a puff of gray smoke. The goblin screamed as its head caught fire.

"No!" Matty screamed, abandoning the door to rush to his friend's aid. The front door was thrown open again, but this time Anika had her knife out and slashed in a blind panic as a fat goblin tried to force its way in. Her broad blade caught it across the face, sending it sprawling back outside.

"Go!" Ransil shouted, pointing toward the door. The sounds of goblins overtaking the back of The Early Mule drove the rest of the patrons outside, Matty covering their escape as he kicked goblins back from Wesley, who was slung over his shoulder.

"Anika!" Bennik rushed to his daughter's side, Farrah limping to lean against a tree after firing her last arrow at a goblin trying to escape The Early Mule. A fire could be seen inside, steadily growing.

"Everyone's out! Matty, cover that door!" Ransil ordered as he helped Gage with Robin. "Let the vile bastards cook in there!"

Jema and Wilma wept, clutching each other.

"Are you all right?" Bennik asked, inspecting his daughter.

Anika couldn't fight the tears. She held the stone out to her father. "I'm sorry... I should have told you. I think they're after this."

Bennik looked at the blue stone in confusion.

"Then hide it!" Elza shouted, turning to look at the otherwise deserted town. "Guards! Someone wake up the reeve!"

Bennik closed Anika's fist around the stone. A sudden chill wind blew, causing the flames inside The Early Mule to rise higher.

Torches appeared from several buildings throughout the town as the sounds of battle carried. The reeve's house was near the eastern edge of the square, on the hill that overlooked Lohkrest Woods. They all looked in that direction, where the night's chaos had not yet reached.

"We should go to the reeve," Ransil suggested, looking up from Robin's wound. "He has at least twenty swords, and we can take the wounded to the temple."

More guttural cries came from the darkness—goblin reinforcements.

Bennik nodded. "Farrah, can you escort everyone to the temple? Ransil and I will draw them away."

Ransil nodded, whispering something to the half-conscious Robin before rising to his feet and producing two daggers as if from nowhere. The halfling spun the blades flawlessly as he assumed a battle stance.

A deafening shriek split the night, coming from not very far above them. There was a gust of wind, and a winged shadow landed near them, making a cloud of dust.

The creature spread its wings to reveal a twisted form that was part woman and part bird—huge feathered wings and scaly flesh. The woman stood on massive vulture-like talons and reached out a similarly wicked hand toward Anika.

"You have something that belongs to Corvanna, child."

Bennik stepped in front of Anika, pointing his knife at the creature. "Back, harpy! You will have to go through us first."

Frozen in fear, Anika couldn't take her eyes off the harpy. Its face had a beautiful quality to it, but its eyes were murderous and cruel. She saw Ransil at the edge of her vision, moving to flank the intruder, but everyone else stood still, waiting.

"Very well," the harpy said, flapping one of her wings to send what looked like darts at Ransil.

The halfling cried out as he shielded his face from them, the sharp feathers embedding in his arm, blood spraying across the dark grass.

Matty and Esher charged the harpy, but her other wing easily threw them to the ground before she raised up both wings to take flight and dive at Bennik. Anika went sprawling as her father threw her out of the way. She could only watch in horror as the monster lifted her father into the air, the harpy's claws digging into Bennik's shoulders as its wings dragged them skyward.

"Father!"

Bennik struggled in the creature's grasp, disrupting the harpy's flight but not preventing their ascent. The harpy heaved with both legs that held the man, then released. Bennik went flying into the burning Early Mule. Not hesitating, the harpy smoothly spun, dove, and landed again in front of Anika.

Seeing her father disappear into the blazing tavern, fury replaced fear as Anika got to her feet. She gripped the knife her father had given her in one hand and the stone in the other, gritting her teeth. Something coursed through her body—it could have been the battlelust that she read warriors would experience when death was on the line, but Anika somehow knew it was something else. Something old and forgotten. Something she had always felt, waiting to be harnessed.

Elza gasped as she watched Anika lift herself into the sky, dust swirling below her as the air bent to her will. Only momentarily shocked, the harpy screamed and folded its wings, taking flight as well and watching her prey cautiously. Both women were held suspended in the air for a long moment before the harpy bared its sharp teeth again, ready to attack.

"Give Corvanna what is hers and you might live, stupid girl!" it warned. "You do not know what you have."

Anika closed her eyes, feeling the wind merge with her, turning into a storm that was dying to be released. She opened her eyes and narrowed them on the harpy.

"Yes, I do."

Opening her hand, a brilliant blue light exploded, illuminating the entire village. Anika breathed deep and the swirling wind below her strengthened, causing the harpy to buffet in the air. Its wings flapped wildly to maintain control.

"No!" the harpy shrieked as it tried to dive toward Anika. But the powerful winds grew into a concentrated storm.

Anika lifted up the stone, bringing the winds with it, and pushed everything toward the harpy. A massive gust of wind blew the harpy away, sending the creature spinning violently beyond the Bracing River in a cloud of shed feathers.

As the winds died down, Anika floated softly down to the earth and immediately collapsed.

CHAPTER FIVE

Awakened Fears

Footsteps echoed loudly throughout Valiant Keep as the moonlight coming in from the tall windows cast long shadows from a small figure. Archmage Fainly Lopke quickened his pace, his little old legs still cramping from his three-day-long feysleep, but he trusted no one else with his latest findings except the queen. While he had his doubts about the queen's full understanding concerning the severity of unsanctioned magic in Vale—despite his best efforts to keep her informed—she was the Arcania's best hope against the coming storm.

But the storm has already come, Fainly thought, cursing himself for letting his reverie last as long as it did. Many gnomes and elves practiced the feysleep—the act of projecting one's slumbering consciousness to the Fey Domain, from whence fey creatures originally came—but none had extended their mortal lives as long as Fainly had through such dangerous means. The Fey Domain was no peaceful haven anymore, and leaving an unconscious mortal vessel for such a long period of time came with extraordinary risks. But as the highest-ranking mage in the Arcania, Fainly had the means to protect himself as he continued his insatiable pursuit of magic well past his natural life.

"High Mage Lopkey," the queen's hulking half-orc guard addressed him as the gnome reached her private quarters. "Her Majesty has retired for the evening."

"Archmage!" Fainly corrected, glaring up at the halfbreed with contempt. "I am not a sorcerous lapdog for you to turn away when such pressing matters demand the queen's attention! Awaken her, or face her wrath when Andelor falls to rogue witches and warlocks!"

The guard glared at the diminutive figure from beneath an ornate silver helm which displayed the proud purple plumage of Andelor. After a long moment, the half-orc shifted his gray-green eyes to give a questioning look to his fellow guard.

On the other side of the queen's doors, a slender human woman in matching armor shrugged and gave Fainly a resigned look. "Please wait one moment...Archmage."

Fainly sneered at the woman as she turned to open the great doors, despising the way she mocked his title. He absently reached a hand into one of the dozens of pockets that lined the inside of his robe, feeling the components he would need to quickly cast a spell to listen in on the queen's quarters. Taking control of his emotions, Fainly resisted the urge and watched as the guard stepped into the queen's antechamber where her majesty's councilor and husband sat pouring over documents that were scattered across a table.

"The King of Vale" was a hollow title, as was the man that held it. Thin and plain, Markus Durrask was unremarkable in every way, except for his piercing gaze. His limp graying hair was tucked neatly behind the circlet he wore to mark his powerless station, but his cunning blue eyes held secrets that made Fainly wary.

The Archmage watched through the cracked door as the guard conversed with the king, motioning to Fainly. Markus' eyes held the gnome as he rose from his table and approached.

"Your Majesty," Fainly offered reluctantly, inclining his head only slightly. "I bring pressing news for the queen."

"Given the time, Archmage Lopkey, I would suspect it is of great urgency." Markus' cold eyes didn't change as he opened the door and motioned to the table. "Please, have a seat."

Fainly declined to climb up the tall chair to sit like a child at the king's table. Instead he waited while Markus motioned for the guard to resume her post and opened the door to the queen's private chambers. Only the briefest moment passed before Queen Sopheena herself emerged, still wearing a simple and elegant gown of purple tied at the waist by a yellow silk belt. The queen's preference for the fashions from Fehir'whin was only one of the ways she upset the traditions in Valiant Keep.

"Archmage Lopkey," the young elven queen began, making long strides to cross the room and meet him. "I understand you carry urgent tidings."

Fainly kept his mouth tight as he regarded the skeptical concern on Sopheena's annoyingly perfect face, which was free from blemish and age. As a gnome, Fainly was similarly touched by the Fey Domain, but his kind was not born from it like the elves, thus his own age showed in the wrinkles around his eyes and the wispy hair that barely covered his spotted pate.

"Yes, Your Majesty," Fainly began, clasping his hands together. "I can only assume that you have not spoken with any of your personal mages tonight?"

"Layla and Desmond are away on official matters," Sopheena said without hesitation. "What is this concerning?" She took a seat at the table, the king standing with his arms crossed near the fireplace. The enormous painting of Sopheena's predecessor, King Aberheim III, loomed over their small council, his eternal scowl disapproving of Fainly even in death.

"That is most unfortunate," the Archmage continued. "I would be curious to ask them if they experienced the same disturbance as I tonight—especially Layla. I was awoken by a sudden…shifting during my feysleep—"

"I have expressed my concern with your growing dependency on the feysleep," Sopheena interrupted, inclining her head slightly to emphasize the point. "You know very well that my dear sister, Nipheena, was lost to it, and I cannot afford to let the Arcania suffer the loss of its Archmage—not with the threats Vale currently faces."

Fainly bit his lip as he forced a nod of understanding. "I will take your concerns to heart, Your Majesty. But were I not sleeping, I do not know if I would have…well…" He reached into his robes and produced two stones, one in each of his small and wrinkled hands. One was red like a ruby with a burning fire in it, and the other was a dull blue. "Here." He stepped forward and held them out for the queen to inspect.

"Keyshards," Sopheena said, regarding the stones with disinterest. "I have been to the Arcania and seen your collections, Fainly."

"Then I suspect you know the difference between a drained keyshard a peddling merchant might foist on a farmer for a few queens and a keyshard that still channels the power of the old gods."

"Of course," the queen said, almost defensively.

"What are you going on about, Lopkey?" Markus asked with all the impatience of a human. "Is this a lesson in magic or are you going to get to the news?"

"To fully appreciate the gravity of the news I bring," Fainly said methodically, annunciating for dramatic effect, "you must understand some things that may not be common knowledge regarding the keyshards. There are secrets in the Arcania that even queens are not privy to, Your Majesty." Fainly raised his hand that held the red keyshard. "This is a greater keyshard, and only our Adepts are able to wield them—they do not leave the High Sanctum without my consent."

Markus and Sopheena listened with newfound interest—it wasn't every night that the secrets of the Arcania were divulged.

Fainly spoke an unintelligible word of power and a flame appeared above the red stone in his hand. "This keyshard still channels the power of Wick, the Kindler. If it were a lesser keyshard, it would have been extinguished long ago, as a sword made of cruddy iron will eventually rust regardless of the care it receives."

Sopheena opened her mouth to ask a question, but the gnome pressed on.

"It is believed that the legendary artifacts—the Keys—that the Purveyors of Light used to bind the old gods to the world were shattered into a million pieces, creating the keyshards we all know." Fainly spun the red keyshard and the flame went out in a puff of smoke. "But that's not entirely true. In reality, when the gods were bound to the Keys, their power retreated into every holy relic scattered throughout the world—little pieces of the gods' magic, filling any item used to worship them or crafted using their power." Fainly snapped his fingers and the red stone disappeared up his sleeve. "Poof! All those holy relics also shattered with the Keys, and those pieces are what we know as keyshards."

The king and queen were staring, both of their mouths agape.

"And the Keys," Fainly said, flourishing his hand to reveal Wick's stone again, "are the greater keyshards. And these do not diminish in power, I can attest to that."

Markus uncrossed his arms and stepped angrily forward. "You have kept this knowledge locked up in your tower?! That is treason! We—"

Sopheena silenced her husband by casually raising a hand, keeping her narrowed eyes on the gnome. "Something has happened to the other, hasn't it?"

Fainly's arrogant mask faded away as he raised the dead blue stone in the other hand. "Two months ago, this shard called to me, waking me from a troubled feysleep—I dreamt of a storm falling over the world, covering all in Shadow—a storm much like the one we have heard about in Rathen.

"When I held the stone," he continued, "I knew Eyen was being used for vile purposes. My last message from High Mage Hassok confirms my suspicion that the harpies are involved—they were always the worst of Eyen's disciples. But his and Kasia's investigation in Rathen is still ongoing. But whatever the harpies stirred, this keyshard responded, so I suspect there is another piece of Eyen's Key near Rathen."

"What woke you tonight, Archmage?" Sopheena asked in a tone that implied she already knew the answer.

Fainly considered the question a moment, then tossed the dull blue stone onto the table. "This keyshard is drained, which should not be possible. I have exhausted my spells on it just to be sure, and no magic remains—it may as well be a common child's trinket." He pointed to the shard for effect. "I am confident that this is indeed a piece of Skythe, the very Key that Luishen used during the Unthroning to bind Eyen to our world. The storm in Rathen could be felt through this, because I suspect another piece of Skythe was used to call the storm—the shards of Skythe must be more directly connected to Eyen than any lesser keyshards." He gave the queen a solemn glare. "And whatever woke me up tonight was more powerful than anything I have ever felt—as if Eyen himself had broken free and taken back his power, bleeding his keyshards dry."

Markus stared into the fire that was slowly dying in the hearth, his high boots clicking on the marble floor as he paced back to the mantel. The queen calmly collected herself before speaking. "What do you suppose this means?"

Breathing deep, Fainly shook his head and shrugged. "Something is stirring, clearly. There is magic in the world that my order still does not understand, but the Arcania has spent its entire existence devoted to studying and mastering the keyshards. I have already set the high mages to scouring the archives for any information regarding any phenomenon like this, though certainly I would recall such a momentous occurrence." He held up a stern finger. "My best guess currently is that there is an unaccounted shard of Skythe that is bigger than its other parts, and someone or something has gotten ahold of that. Though I cannot say how that would allow them to drain the other shards, it is the only thing that makes sense to me at this time. Which is why I have come to you."

Fainly could sense the king and queen stiffen.

"The Oathers," the queen said, her tone betraying her annoyance.

The gnome nodded. "Your Majesty, I understand your concern with setting them upon our own people—"

"Do you, Fainly?" Markus asked angrily. "Do you truly understand how quickly the people can turn against their rulers when witch hunters are given the queen's authority to ransack their homes and terrify their children?"

"It has happened before," the queen said, her voice less angry than Markus' but no less stern. "The Arcania's vast stores of keyshards did not come without a price. Vale nearly fell apart when the first Aberheim tried to wash it clean of magic. You convinced me on Rathen, and I conceded. But I cannot in good conscience give the Oathers full authority again. Especially not when I need them for the excavations on Suthek."

Fainly held up a single finger again in response. "Just give me one."

"One?" the king asked, incredulous. "What for?"

Walking to the table with the king's documents, Fainly climbed up on the chair suited for taller folk. A map of all of Noveth covered the table, from the Far Reach to the lower peninsulas of Karrane. Fainly pointed a finger to a small spot on the map near the Lohkrest Woods.

"What's there?" Markus asked, stepping to look over the gnome's shoulder.

The gnome looked up to stare into the queen's eyes that betrayed a hint of fear and confusion. "Whatever it is, we are going to need it."

Far to the east of Rathen were the Bone Hills, desolate and cruel. The civilized world stayed clear of those savage lands, but the orcs that survived the Nether Wars found themselves pulled there, drawn by the Shadow that cursed their entire kind. It was there, at the base of the Castreel Mountains that ringed the mighty Mount Myreth, that the largest remaining community of orcs—the Aggrot—found a home.

On a solitary hill overlooking the ragged plains sat Guluk, the Witch of Aggrot. She watched the black horizon; the Shadow that filled her eyes with rage and hatred also allowed her to see clearly at night. The sky above was blacker than normal; the unnatural storm continued to spread toward the mountains, growing stronger as her own power waned to nothing.

Guluk turned her eyes to her bent staff that held the great blue stone—the weakening source of her power. The staff, Thunderbranch, was the only thing that kept her in command of the Aggrot. With it, she had done the unthinkable: she had united orcs that would have been just as happy warring with each other. She had devoted them to a cause that they all had felt but couldn't name—Shadow. The Shadow led Guluk to the stone, and with it she had served its cause.

But now her stone looked powerless. She could no longer feel command over the wind or the dark clouds that carried lightning. Guluk felt nothing but Shadow that night, and it did not feel like enough to rule the Aggrot.

A harpy's painful, echoing shriek broke the night's silence.

"Guluk!"

The witch turned to see one of her mates, Nusk, carrying his signature scythe that he had stolen from a farmer.

"The harpy. Ready to talk."

Together, Nusk and Guluk descended the hill and made their way to a cave mouth that spilled firelight across the rocky ravine. Inside the cave were a dozen other Aggrot warriors. Two orcs held up limp, severed wings, presenting them to the cheers of the gathered. Between them was the harpy, tied to a post and bleeding heavily from her back where her wings had been torn off.

The warriors cheered and clashed their weapons together to celebrate the harpy's agony. But the harpy just gritted her teeth angrily, refusing to give up any more screams.

"Stop blood," Nusk ordered as Guluk approached the harpy. The two orcs that displayed the wings set them aside to retrieve burning brands, shoving the flames to the harpy's back to cauterize the wounds. This time the harpy did scream.

Guluk approached her prisoner warily, suspecting this creature was somehow responsible for her power failing. The witch stared into Shadow-taken eyes like her own, looking for some sort of deception, but the harpy only smiled as she stared back.

"Were you not warned," Guluk asked, "that the Bone Hills were ours? All treasure here ours." She presented her Thunderbranch. "Everything belong to Aggrot. Vulture-girl not welcome."

This brought another cheer from the gathered Aggrot, with some chants in favor of roasting the intruder. And the call that Guluk dreaded: "Give her thunder!"

"Thunder! Thunder!" The chanting had begun.

The harpy laughed quietly, just so Guluk could hear. Her beady eyes fixed on the witch as she whispered, "You can't."

Guluk's eyes widened. Fury overcame her. "It was you!" She grabbed the harpy by the neck and the cheers in the cave intensified.

"Look," the harpy said through her tightened throat, nodding to the stone. She closed her eyes as if concentrating.

Guluk peered at the dead stone in her staff, which began to give off a weak blue glow. As she looked deeper into the stone, a vision came to her of a massive, mutated harpy spreading her wings of dagger-like feathers. Her head was like the harpy prisoner's, only twisted with horns and spiked bone spurs protruding from scaled flesh. She was both hideous and glorious, overwhelming in presence. The creature spread her wings wider and then closed them.

A blast of wind erupted from the staff, sending all the gathered Aggrot orcs flying, their bodies breaking against the cave walls. All but the harpy and Guluk were dead inside the cave, and the blue stone faded again.

Guluk breathed heavily, looking at her dead kin, then turned toward the harpy with fear and meekness in her eyes. The harpy opened her eyes and smiled again.

"You will serve Corvanna," the harpy said. It was not a question or an offer, just a statement.

Guluk swallowed, feeling all the power of the stone slipping away again. The Shadow that connected her with the harpy told her that Corvanna—whoever that was—now held the power she once had. She nodded.

"The Aggrot serve Corvanna."

The wingless harpy spat up blood, her smiling face now becoming a death mask. "Gather your warriors, witch. And march for Rathen."

Chapter Six

The Graystone

Deina belched loudly as she left The Fourth Eagle, looking for a darker part of the city to relieve herself. It wasn't hard. The sky above was no longer sickly green, it was darker than anything Deina had ever seen—and she had spent much of her youth working in the deep mines of New Hold where a single torch was a luxury. All of Rathen was shrouded in shadow, with only small pools of light provided by the lanterns along the city walls and outside the wealthier establishments.

No wind disturbed the flames.

A large dark shape followed Deina out of The Fourth Eagle as the nearly drunk dwarf found a particularly inconspicuous place to drop her pants. As she squatted down, she belched again and asked the shadow, "You fancying a show, friend?"

"You travel with the priest?" The voice was low and gruff, and Deina knew it was the half-orc woman who had been watching her share drinks with the halflings.

Deina chuckled while she finished her business. "If you're looking for someone to warm your bed tonight, you'd have more luck with me than with that man. He's here on church business, and he's the type that don't let nothin' interfere with his affair with the Light." She dried herself with her hand, wiping it on her pants as she stood back up. "A future Archbeacon, that one is."

The half-orc stepped closer. "Can we talk somewhere?" She looked over her shoulder as a distant figure hunched over to empty their stomach in the middle of the road. "Your companion might be in trouble."

Percy's eyes stared lifelessly at the wood-planked ceiling in his quarters. Sweat dotted his brow and dried blood still crusted the corners of his mouth, which continued to spew a never-ending stream of curses in tongues foreign to Avrim.

"How long has he been like this?" Avrim asked the duke, who sat at his son's bedside. Avrim flipped through his luminary, looking for any other helpful passages that might pertain to Shadowlords escaping from the Abyss.

"Since the storm came," the duke responded. The man was covered in spittle and specks of dried blood.

Since Avrim had arrived, they had both been locked in Percy's quarters, the duke ordering his men to watch the door and leave them be unless otherwise instructed. It had been a harrowing afternoon and evening of shouted obscenities, vomiting, thrashing, and warnings about the Shadow coming.

Avrim had been present for a small handful of so-called demonic possessions at his own temple, but only one of them struck him as a legitimate case of a Shadowlord taking root in a mortal. The afflicted woman had died from her thrashings, but not before injuring several priests, Avrim included.

As Avrim nervously continued scouring the book for guidance, he tried to ignore the whispers of the late duchess who relentlessly tried to convince him to give up.

"The Light will burn him, Brother," the ghostly voice echoed through his mind. "Do not burn my son, Avrim. You were meant to heal, not to torture. Look at my dear, tortured boy. Leave him be."

"Begone, you wicked spirit!" The duke seemed to only occasionally hear his dead wife's voice, but it coursed through Avrim's mind continuously. The duke reached out to smooth his son's hair back.

As Avrim watched the father's tenderness, a thought came to him. "Your wife's illness was a ruse, wasn't it? To keep the Oather from discovering your son's condition."

The duke stiffened, not looking at the priest. "I've heard stories of the Arcania. Back in the days of the first Aberheim, entire villages would be put to the torch if there was even just a rumor of unsanctioned witchcraft. The Oathers are more likely to kill anyone doing things they don't understand than to ask questions, because magic and its secrets die with its wielder." Now Petrik looked at Avrim, his weary eyes brimmed with tears. "He's still my son, isn't he? Even if he already killed his mother?"

"He is," Avrim said firmly, not doubting it, but beginning to doubt his ability to help. Communion with a Shadowlord was not something enough priests had survived to share any sort of expertise on the matter. Stories existed within the Luminaura of those that did survive either turning from the Light after such encounters or giving their own sanity to the demon in exchange for abandoning the host.

Could I make that trade? Avrim wondered, hoping it wouldn't come to that, but desperately trying to convince himself that he could.

An idea struck Avrim then, and he frantically flipped toward the end of the luminary where Archbeacon Alluna Sorentha wrote about her account with the Disciples of Stane.

"What is it?" Petrik asked eagerly.

Avrim ran his finger down a particular page, looking for a phrase that struck him as an acolyte. "After the Unthroning, when the old gods were given back to the world they made by the Purveyors, the keyshards held pieces of celestial beings that tried to escape the heavenly realms when the Shadow came. Those beings became Shadowlords, tied to the keyshards of their former masters. Some believe the old gods were evil, but they were neither good nor evil— they were unable to discern good from evil, which is why they were Unthroned by the Light." His finger stopped at a certain passage.

The duke stood up and walked over to see what Avrim had found.

"Shadowlords are among us, but unable to possess us while their prisons hold," Avrim read. "The old gods stand vigilant over us, their creations, their physical nature now binds them to us, and they must protect us from Shadow as they protect themselves. The Six Seals binding the Nethering Gates are forged of them and by them, thus the old gods serve the Light as we do. Their dark prisons are the only place the Shadowlords can hope to hide from the Light."

Petrik was silent for a moment as he reread the words himself. "What does it mean?"

Avrim stared at Percy's vacant eyes and mumbling mouth, looking for any connection. "It means if a Shadowlord has taken him, it came from its prison. If we can find it," Avrim closed the luminary and rose to stand over the Shadowlord that had taken Percy Ambrose, "I can exorcise your son."

⟩———◇———⟨

"My name is Melaine, from Wickham," the half-orc whispered as she checked her bow. The small tusks that protruded from her lower jaw made her frown look more angry than she probably intended, but Deina was already warming up to the woman's directness. "I was a scout for a small company of rangers that operated out of an old temple of Wick in the Ashwood. We set out several months ago to hunt the harpies that had grown bolder in raiding—they had taken to attacking Wickham directly instead of just the occasional farmstead."

Deina knew very well the threat of harpies, even before hearing the stories from Suzy and Chera about the recent increase in attacks since the storm came. The dwarves of New Hold had an entire regiment of crossbows assigned to watching the hills for harpies from the coast, stealing livestock or even unsuspecting commoners. Deina hated the wretched things, and liked Melaine even more after hearing that she was devoted to hunting them.

"We tracked the harpies to Graymount, just to the north," Melaine said, motioning that direction with a thumb over her shoulder. She ran a hand through the black hair that fell from the top of her head, the sides of her scalp shaved to its dark green flesh. Perhaps she had been traveling with a dried-up priest of the Light too long, but Deina found the woman quite stunning. "The beasts had taken up in a high cave. I scouted ahead to make sure, then reported back to our leader, Jonah. He wanted to ambush them as they tried to take to the sky from that cave—we had enough bows to take all of them down before they knew what hit them."

Deina nodded with a grin. "Wish I coulda been there."

Melaine's shifting eyes finally settled on Deina's. She shook her head. "It was a slaughter, but not the kind we had planned. Like I said, I was a scout, so I went ahead while the others planned their ascent toward the caves. I found my own cave, which I had hoped might lead up to the harpy lair from below. I found a twisting labyrinth that finally brought me to the harpies' hoard."

Deina's eyes widened. She hadn't suspected such a gripping tale when she followed this woman into a dark alley.

"The cave I found was filled with treasure—coins, silk, gems, exotic weapons, and bottles of strange liquids. And keyshards. Lots of keyshards. I've heard that some keyshards hold magic, glowing brightly, while others are as dull as broken glass. These all seemed to be the latter," Melaine said with a dismissive hand, then raised a single finger. "All except one."

"And you took it, of course," Deina said with a raised eyebrow.

Melaine nodded. "I can't explain—it called to me. It was gray like a broken stone, but seemed to shimmer as if it were layered in some sort of glass. And I could see into it. Things moved inside of it. So, yes, I took it." Melaine looked down. "That's when the slaughter began. Once I touched that damn stone, I heard a deafening screech from above, and echoing shouts of the other rangers as they unleashed their attack. I rushed back out of that cave, but I was too late."

"The harpies?" Deina asked, doubtful. "Must have been a whole mountain filled with those she-devils."

"The harpies were all slain by my company," Melaine said morosely, "all but one. When I finally found the cave's exit, I saw the broken bodies of dead harpies all around, each one sporting at least a few arrows. The ambush worked. But I also saw something else. Something...huge."

"What else would live or fight alongside harpies?" Deina asked, finding the very idea ridiculous. "Some other breed of wicked, winged bitch-bird?"

Melaine's eyes were wide with remembered horror. "It was like a harpy, but much bigger. With wings that had dagger-like feathers, and these spikes coming from its devil-bird head. Long arms and legs that had talons the size of the hooked swords from Xe'dann." She drew the crescent moon shape in the darkness between her and Deina. "The stone seemed to speak to me, telling me that the creature's name was Corvanna, and I should not take what was hers."

"A speaking stone?" Deina said. "I heard stories of such things, but never encountered one meself, despite spending my entire life in the mines surrounded by stones."

Melaine nodded agreement. "I still don't believe it myself—I don't know if I heard anything that night, but I trusted what I felt. And I felt that Corvanna would come for me after she finished slaughtering my company. I unleashed a few arrows that seemed to veer away from the creature before finding their mark. My aim is true, always has been. Something unnatural protected that monster." Melaine looked down at her feet, resting her arms on her knees. "I ran. I didn't know what else to do, but I knew I had to keep that stone away from Corvanna. So I ran all through the night, through the warg-infested hills of Tultha Ridge. I don't remember stopping until I reached the ruins of Northlund Point outside of this city."

"Did Corvanna pursue?" Deina asked, eager to hear of the monster's demise, while secretly hoping it had yet lived so she may join in destroying it.

"I felt her following me, but never saw her. The stone had grown silent on me, almost like it was disappointed in me, but I convinced myself Corvanna was coming for it. So I planned a trap there in that ruined tower. I placed the stone in clear view and found a nearby ridge to watch for any sign of the devil.

"Two days I waited, chewing caffleaf to stay awake. I could feel Corvanna coming; every instinct I had said she was near. But she never came. When sleep finally took me, I awoke to the sounds of children laughing. I drew my bow, but could only watch as a noble boy and two of his friends tossed that stone back and forth. A regiment of armored men wearing the three eagles of Rathen accompanied the boys, escorting them back to the city. I had nothing to do but follow."

"The duke's boy?" Deina asked. "You think the stone is doing this?" The dwarf pointed to the blackness above.

Melaine shook her head, and even in the dark Deina could see the fear the half-orc tried to keep from her eyes. "I think whatever was in that stone has gotten out. I think whatever it is, the duke is hiding it. The city watch is under the Arcania's control now, so I can't go to them. They're more likely to kill me on the spot if they heard my tale, suspecting me of dark magicks."

The half-orc stood up, checking her bowstring. "I don't have answers, but I do know that your priest is in the heart of the storm right now."

Deina stood up too, feeling much more sober. "Well, let's go have a chat with the duke. Though I must say, I'd much rather be warming your bed."

For the first time in a long time, Melaine almost smiled.

In his dark study on the top floor of the city watch's barracks, Blane Hassok set the dull blue keyshard in a pile with the others. It seemed

Eyen was more popular in the north than either Wick or Oakus. He'd found seven new lesser blue keyshards littered around Rathen and its outlying holds, making his piles of red and green shards look meager by comparison. All of them were drained or almost drained, with only the faintest of gleams casting a pale rainbow across the wooden desk.

The gray one sat alone, drawing Blane's curious gaze.

As the elf stared deep into those foggy depths, Kasia walked in, stretching her neck as she began removing her white platemail gauntlets. Her young squire, Roy Warner, hurried to help with the straps along her sides.

"This place might be a lost cause," the Oather said as she shifted her head the other way. "We've been through every establishment now, and aside from your collection of trivial knickknacks, there is no witch that I can find." As Roy unlatched the buckles of Kasia's breastplate, Blane reached up to rub his temples.

"Why do you have to wear that in here?" He turned slightly to give her armor a glare of loathing. The black arcane markings on the white-enameled steel seemed to writhe in response to the discomfort coursing through Blane's head.

Kasia gave him a disinterested look, her eyes shifting between his bare neck and the crystal necklace that sat on the table near his keyshards. "If you wore your mark as intended, you would not be so afflicted. Unlike you, I take my station quite seriously, and I am not to entrust the care of the Arcania's armaments to the likes of Rathen's city watch."

Blane felt instant relief as he slid the Arcanian mark back around his neck. But he felt Fainly's presence as well, ever waiting for a member of his order to misstep while away from his direct control. The mark shimmered as it responded to the magic-dampening energy that Kasia's armor gave off. Any mage channeling—or often even thinking about channeling—magic in an Oather's presence could only do so if they could concentrate with a splitting headache or extreme nausea, unless they possessed one of Fainly's Arcanian marks that signified their endorsement by the order and thus negating the effects of the antimagic wielded by Oathers.

"So, what is our next move?" Blane asked, as Roy finished with the lower pieces of Kasia's armor.

The Oather pulled the sweat-covered wool padding over her head, revealing a bare muscled torso that rivaled a Coperan pit-fighter's. Her flat chest was riddled with scars as well as some fresh bruises from embarrassing some of the city watch during her morning sparring. "We report to the tower," she said, staring at him in a way that made Blane wonder if she expected some sort of argument.

"Very well," Blane said, moving to put his things away, hoping to avoid any questions regarding his growing collection.

As Roy struggled with the last few straps on Katia's greaves, the sound of fluttering wings came from the open window as a raven found a perch on the sill. It squawked loudly at Blane, who dropped a few keyshards in surprise. He turned to look at Kasia, looking for some sign that she summoned the Archmage's favored familiar.

The Oather betrayed an uncharacteristic look of confusion and waved Roy away from his work. She walked over to her own desk that was neatly organized and opened one of the drawers, producing a long wooden box. Blane moved to join her as Kasia opened the box and set the mirror it contained on a high shelf so that it was at eye level for both of them.

They stared into the mirror, watching their own reflections with anticipation—Blane wearing a lazy look of impatience and Kasia's face returning to a mask of stern concentration. Their visages faded slowly as mists began to creep along the edges of the mirror, which was framed in rather plain wood with no decoration or markings.

The face of an old gnome appeared through those mists. Archmage Fainly Lopke looked ragged, more so than usual. His expression of urgency faded as his image became more clear, and his eyes went from Kasia's naked torso to the elf's casually insolent face.

"We have policies against mages and Oathers…" Fainly began, his voice sounding ethereal through the magical mirror.

Blane smiled, rolling his eyes. "Trust me, Archmage, she's not my type."

"I apologize, Archmage," Kasia said with a nod, crossing her arms across her breasts—for expediency rather than modesty. "I thought it urgent seeing as you sent your familiar. If this can wait, then I shall dress."

"It cannot," Fainly said. "I need you in Blakehurst, Dame Strallow. Immediately. It's a backwater town to the east of Caffrey's holdings."

Kasia nodded. "I know of it. Knife has an agent she's trying to hide there, I believe. And Rathen?" she asked. "We were planning on reporting in the morning that this may be a lost cause. Whatever this storm is, it doesn't seem like mere witchcraft. Yet it does seem confined to the skies above the city, so a presence here would be wise."

"Blane, you can manage," Fainly said, "though if your investigations yield nothing in the next two weeks, you're to return to Andelor at once. There have been developments here that make Rathen's own plight rather insignificant as far as the Arcania is concerned." He gave a dismissive wave of his hand. "Let the free city be truly free from Vale. It has been a burden on all of the Joined Realms, if you ask me."

"Understood," Blane said with a nod.

"What can you tell me about Blakehurst?" Kasia asked. "Reports of witchery?"

"I believe there is a keyshard there," Fainly began, pausing as he considered his next words. "It should be a dead shard, one of Eyen's. But I felt a disturbance during my feysleep. I just need some eyes there to make sure all is in order." His arcane visage gave Kasia a stern look. "Give no quarter, Oather. I feel a shift coming, and we cannot allow any hedge wizards running amok."

"I will leave at dawn," Kasia added, wiping sweat from her brow. "It will be nice to feel the wind on my face again. The Shadow can have this place."

Fainly's face faded from the mirror, and the Oather and mage turned to see Roy holding Blane's gray shard in both hands, staring intently into its depths.

"Put that down!" Blane commanded, taking a step forward to slap the boy over the head. But he paused as Roy looked up. The young boy's dark eyes were as pale as the shard and wider than should be natural.

"Of course you couldn't hear me. Ithakan always preyed on young boys," Roy said in a voice that was not his own. He looked around the room in a panic. "Where is the duke's son? Take me to him!"

"Stop this, Roy," Kasia said, stepping forward with tightened fists. "Put the keyshard down."

"That's not a keyshard," Blane corrected, pointing. The stone began to give off a cloudy aura, similar to the very sky above Rathen. "It's the source of the storm!"

"Listen!" Roy said. "My name is Kartha, and I don't have much time! Take me to the host before Ithakan consumes him!"

Kasia casually drew the broadsword from the sheath on her hip. Its silver blade was worked with the same black arcane etchings as her armor and seemed to drink the essence emanating from the graystone.

"I need to find Ruke's stone before—"

The Oather's blade swept out in a quick arc.

Roy finally did drop the stone then as his body collapsed, his severed head rolling into a dark corner of the room. "Strallow!" Blane shouted, hands raised to shield his face from the spray of blood.

Kasia knelt to wipe her blade on her squire's tunic. "Kartha is a witch's name from not so long ago. I will not abide her wickedness, regardless of its form."

Blane gritted his teeth. "I have been wrestling with that stone since the duke gave it to us on our arrival. I wanted to hear what the boy had to say."

"I won't listen to blasphemy. But now you have something further to discuss with the duke," Kasia said as she stood and sheathed her sword, her bare chest splattered with blood. "His boy. Percy. Question him about this Ithakan." She wiped a spot of blood from her lip. "I need a bath." She walked calmly out of the room wearing only greaves, boots, and her sated sword. "Clean this place up."

Not knowing if she meant their quarters or the city itself, Blane knew he had his work cut out for him.

CHAPTER SEVEN

Taking Flight

Gage rubbed his eyes, fighting off the sleep that had been clawing at him since the last of the goblins were driven off last night. Faint sunlight streamed into the small room on the upper floor of the reeve's home. Gage sat on the floor next to the bed, watching Robin's chest rise and fall slowly, waiting for those beautiful eyes to finally reopen. His shoulder was covered in bloodied linen, and beads of reddish fluid still rested on his unmoving lips.

Standing up, Gage grabbed a cloth to dab at Robin's lips gently, wiping away the remains of the potion Elza had given him. The gnome said it was all she could do while Farrah was still suffering from the vile poison that the Hollowood goblins had often used to coat their blades. Despite being assured that the arrow that struck Robin was not poisoned, Gage still gritted his teeth as he remembered watching Farrah thrash about violently last night as the poison ravaged her. She would probably die this morning.

Feeling tears well up in his eyes, Gage bent over Robin and touched his lips gently to the half-elf's, whispering, "We're going to Andelor. Together."

At the sounds of boots on stairs, Gage turned to see a hunched figure limping toward his room supported by old Lana. "Careful, Geddy. Oh, Gage, do you suppose Geddy could rest on the other bed there?"

Gage nodded, motioning to the other bed in the small room. The reeve's twin sons, Jak and Roy, had gone to squire in Andelor. They had been Gage's closest friends before Ransil had brought Robin to Blakehurst.

"Ah!" Geddy gritted his teeth against the pain as his wife eased him onto the bed. "Rotten greenskins," the old man spat, trying to lift his leg into the bed. Gage helped Lana get him into as comfortable a position as possible while Geddy cursed. "Those monsters broke it. I knows a broked bone, that's no lie!"

"Shh, Geddy." Lana patted his hand. "Let me get help."

Gage gave Robin one last look as he followed Lana. The half-elf slept peacefully.

As Lana disappeared down the hall looking for help, Gage stretched and looked out the window to see sunlight breaking through the distant trees surrounding his family's home. Normally the town would be buzzing with activity at this time, but he saw no movement aside from the reeve's guards still on their patrols, looking for any remaining goblins.

"She knows."

Gage snapped his head around to look into the dark room near the window. A shadow stepped into the sunlight. "Anika! You're awake!" He made to go to her, but something held him in place.

Anika's dark skin reflected the sunlight like polished wood, her eyes fixed on Gage in the same unsettling way they had yesterday morning when she told him about the stone. He noticed she was not holding the stone now, even though no one could pry it out of her hands last night—not even Bruck's iron grip could force her fingers from that stone.

Hurried footsteps came behind him and Gage turned to see Elza being led by Lana toward Geddy and Robin's room. He looked back at Anika. "Knows what?"

"She knows the stone was stolen," Anika said. "It won't be long until she suspects you, or someone associated with the Guild." She let out a nervous breath. "Like Robin."

Gage shook his head, feeling the exhaustion overcome him.

"It won't matter if we tell her the truth," Anika said sadly. "We know Baron Oakworth will hang anyone and everyone associated with the Guild here should a robbery be reported."

Darkness flooded Gage's thoughts, shadows forming Robin's execution, his own body hanging from the gallows, and Anika struggling for breath as a rope tore into the flesh of her neck. The shadow visions continued until Gage's chest began to tighten and he thought he might lose consciousness. He shielded his eyes with clenched fists.

"I'm sorry, Gage."

Anger flooded him. "This is your fault!" Gage shouted, throwing his fists away from his eyes to see that the dark room in front of him was empty. He turned to see Elza poke her head out of the room down the hall; something about the look of concern she gave him seemed accusatory. But he shook his head and walked back to be by Robin's side.

"Now this should help with the mending," Elza said, her small hands gently dumping a flask into Geddy's mouth. The old man chugged the potion eagerly.

"Thank you, lass," Lana said graciously. "We are in your debt!"

Elza smiled and made to leave, but Geddy's hand shot out to take hers. Gage saw the old man blinking back tears. "Thank you," he said with shame and humility.

The gnome just gave him a wink and looked at Gage as she reached the door. "Your friend seems to be mending, my young Lord Lawson." She smiled warmly. "I look forward to seeing him awake."

Gage smiled warmly at Elza until she turned and left, then his eyes narrowed. Behind him, Robin stirred awake.

"This just doesn't make sense," Ransil said, kneeling down to inspect the goblin corpse. It had one of the halfling's small throwing knives lodged in its neck, and Ransil pulled it out, wiping its dark blood on the bandage that covered the wounds on his arm left by the harpy's razor-like quills. "This pale one came from Lohkrest, I know it. And this one here is from Hollowood—you can tell by the poison dirtying its blade. One bite from that and—"

Ransil caught himself and looked up at Bennik's weary face. "Sorry, Ben."

Bennik averted his eyes, checking his bow—Farrah's bow. "Elza's doing what she can. Farrah knew the risks of chasing goblins in the woods. Even elven blood can't fight off the cruel venom of Hollowood."

"I'm sure Elza will find something to help it," Ransil offered hopefully. "Too many have died here."

"Not enough of them," Bennik said with a nod toward the goblins that lay strewn about the deserted town square.

"The harpy brought them here," Ransil said, looking at the distinctly different goblin corpses as he stood up and sheathed his knife. "But why? Whoever this Corvanna is, they must wield some unique power to inspire such camaraderie amongst such a motley assortment of Shadowfiends."

"The Shadow claimed many creatures as its own during the Unthroning."

Ransil and Bennik turned to see Mother Beatrim from Brightstar Sanctuary approach, followed by several women and two of the reeve's personal guards flanking their procession. One of the women from the church carried a decorative brazier that burned brighter than any normal fire, and each other woman carried a collection of tallow candles.

"Unlike the Light," Beatrim continued with a stern face, stopping before a goblin corpse, "the Shadow takes who it pleases, those without the devotion or means to resist its preying on the basest of mortal urges." One of the Mother's followers lit a candle from the brazier and knelt, cautiously placing it near a dead goblin, as if afraid it might jump to life and bite her. It was a common tradition in the Joined Realms—where most followed the Light—to either burn the dead or at least cast the Light on their bodies so that the Shadow might not escape its vessel and take root.

"The Shadow brings them together," Beatrim said to Ransil, as if it were a fact that would brook no discussion. "Goblins, orcs, harpies, kobolds. These base creatures stood no chance against the Shadow when it was born, and as the Archbeacon Alluna Sorentha wrote, the Shadow's forces cannot stand against the Light without union." She gave Bennik a look of warning, her old elven features making her look more human than elf, for most elves devoted to the Light abstained from the rejuvenating feysleep. "I fear that union is upon us."

Bennik and Ransil watched in silence as they finished their ceremony of banishing Shadow from Blakehurst. The reeve arrived as the procession made its way farther into town to tend to more dead Shadowfiends.

"I'm sorry, Ransil," the heavyset man said as he rubbed his hands and surveyed the destruction of The Early Mule. His voice was thick with emotion. "Your establishment was a hallmark of our community, and it shall be rebuilt."

"I appreciate the concern, Reeve Warner," Ransil said with a curt nod, "but I fear we have more pressing concerns. Such as what has drawn these monsters here."

"Your daughter," the reeve said, looking toward Bennik.

The tanner stiffened, giving the man a cold look.

"Where did she come by it?"

Bennik considered that for a moment before shaking his head. He thought back to last night when he had tried to pry the stone from Anika's sleeping grip. The gust of wind that had thrown him back had felt like magic—which he had thankfully not felt since his days in the Westerra invasions. Everyone else that tried to inspect the blue stone in his daughter's grip had been treated with the same gust of arcane wind.

"It was dull when I found it," Elza had explained that night, staring at the glowing blue stone as Bennik had been recovering from his injuries in the fire. "It must be a keyshard, but that's just impossible— the elves would have found it... I would have felt it." The gnome looked warningly at Bennik. "This is what they're after. Whoever Corvanna is. This must be what they seek."

Bennik blinked away the memory. "I don't know," he responded sternly. "But it's hers now."

"I cannot allow it to stay here," the reeve began, stepping authoritatively toward Bennik. "If we cannot take it from her, then perhaps—"

"Perhaps what, Rupert?" Bennik asked, taking his own step forward. "You want to exile my daughter? Perhaps cut off her hand to take the stone?"

"Now you listen, Ben," the reeve's face reddening, "I kept the peace when you brought that child here from Karrane, despite the questions it aroused. I turned my head during the trouble that followed, and your wife's... Well, I kept your secrets, dammit!"

"Enough!" Ransil said, stepping between them. Despite the halfling only standing to their waists, both men parted. "Rupert, we understand your concern. We will find a way to part her from the stone. I'll take the thing myself to the Arcania if it needs done. We know it can't stay here—right, Ben?"

Bennik's anger fell away. He ran a hand through his wild hair. "I need to go check on her. Maybe when she wakes up—"

"Goblins!"

The reeve gasped, covering his fine doublet with a hand over his heart, near falling over to rush back to his house.

A knife spun into Ransil's hand as he dashed toward the shout, Bennik notching an arrow as he followed, his tattered cloak swirling in his wake. Two of the reeve's guards answered the call as well, rushing past Bruck's shop and splashing through the creek into the woods. The sounds of a skirmish greeted the party as a shrieking group of goblins were hacking at a downed guard. The woman did her best to parry the blows as their rusted blades rained down on her. One dead guard pinned a struggling goblin underneath him, and a dying guard thrashed around as he grasped the black arrow sprouting from his neck.

Bennik's arrow took one of the monsters through the chest, carrying the goblin into the air before falling limp to the ground. Ransil gracefully rolled under the wild swing of a goblin's sword, thrusting his knife into a gap in the goblin's armor. The two guards rescued their companion by lopping off one goblin's head and scaring off the other two.

Ransil hastily threw a knife after a fleeing goblin, finding its mark in the monster's back. With a hiss and a curse in its gibberish tongue, the wounded goblin kept fleeing, but the blood it trailed satisfied the halfling. "They should be easy to track back to their hiding spot now."

"We'll go after them," Bennik told the guards. "Head back to town and make sure the reeve's house is closely watched. My children are there." The guards nodded and Bennik drew another arrow, sparing a quick look back toward where Anika slept. He felt a sudden dread wash over him, but at the halfling's urging, he shook it away and disappeared into the woods with Ransil to track the goblins.

Anika flew. The ground below was a blur of greens and blues rushing past at blinding speed, but as she rose higher and higher into the sky, the view became clearer. The Lohkrest Woods sprawled far into the misty horizon of Eastlund and the Bracing River wound its way through the verdant lands of Vale, all the way to the Wane Coast where Andelor and the ports of Merithian held wonders and mysteries that were completely foreign to a girl who spent all of her short life in a place like Blakehurst.

She turned her head north, seeing the acrid sky that hung over a dark city—the same storm that she had seen in the depths of the stone.

The stone.

She opened her hand to see the stone, casting blue light across her sandy-colored palm. The sunlight ran across the relic's smooth edges. Anika stared deep into its depths once more, transfixed by a power that felt impossibly familiar.

It was the power of belonging, and it pulled on emotions deep within Anika that she had never felt before. She had felt love—within the arms of her father, in her cherished memories of her mother, and in the corner of Gage's crooked smile. But this was something more.

She felt her destiny, beyond the comfort of her home.

The stone was calling to her alone, no one else.

"Anika."

The breeze whipped her long, thin hair as she peered into the stone. The ethereal voice was riding the wind from every angle, but the stone focused it. Inside its depths, she fell into a world of light, as if the sun had swallowed her. It was blinding for a moment, and when her vision returned, the Karranese woman from The Early Mule floated before her.

Anika looked at herself—how she imagined she might look as an older woman. Dressed in plain Karranese wool and leather that seemed resistant to the wind, the woman opened her mouth to speak and the wind carried Anika's name again.

"Where are we?" was the first question that came to Anika's mind as she looked into the bright void surrounding them.

"This is where you came from, daughter," the woman said. "We are in the Light."

Her eyes shot back to the woman. "Daughter?"

Anika fell, the light fading, the Karranese woman's silhouette lost as darkness closed in all around her. She lost her grip on the stone and it twirled away from her in the rush of wind now parting to let her descend farther into darkness. Anika screamed, reaching for the stone, willing it to once more give her command of the wind.

"Mother!" she cried in vain, her voice stolen by the rush of air that had betrayed her. She continued falling until she awoke, her heart racing and her brow sheened in sweat. Anika jolted up in an unfamiliar bed as she sucked in what felt like the first breath she had taken since watching her father get thrown into the fire.

"Mother!"

"Easy," a raspy voice said from the dimly lit room. The curtains were closed to the morning sunlight, but Anika could make out elven features on a face that had very little life left.

"Farrah!" Anika tried to get out of the bed, but her entire body ached and she was barely able to brace herself enough to avoid tumbling to the floor.

"I said easy, dammit," the elf cursed, a coughing fit overtaking her. Farrah was lying in a makeshift cot constructed out of some overturned crates and pillows. "I don't have much time; the poison is resisting Elza's medicine. She is out looking for more of her herbs, but I told her she has better luck finding a bag of gold in these weeded woods than anything strong enough to fight hollower poison." She coughed again.

Anika tried again to rise, slowly this time. Using one hand to pull her as-good-as-dead legs over the edge of the bed and the other hand—

She opened her closed fist to see the stone.

"I warned Elza that it was from Skythe."

The word shot visions of the harpy monstrosity and the woman who claimed to be her mother through Anika's mind. She looked at the elf.

Farrah's eyes were cold. "Elza told me you had it. To be honest, I suspected the half-elf living with Ruse—I mean Ransil. All these small towns have Guild agents lurking around sniffing for trinkets." The elf's eyes narrowed and she gritted her teeth as she tried to rise. She coughed violently, wiping the blood from her mouth.

"It was dead when we found it," Farrah said, struggling for breath. "The lesser shards become useless if wielded by a greedy mage—they sap the magic right out without putting anything back in. They die all the time, then they're just gems for collectors." She looked back into Anika's eyes. "But the Keys—those never die. And I felt something different about that stone the moment I saw it amongst Elza's wares. But anyone who saw it could see it had no magic about it." She tried to laugh but coughed again, spitting up more blood. "I should have trusted my instincts, instead of my eyes.

"But there is something about you." The elf's eyes bore into Anika. "What you did with that stone—that came from within you, not the stone. It merely channeled you. I think you may be the Child of—" Farrah doubled over as a fit of coughing made her collapse to the floor.

Anika finally found her strength and went to the elf's side in a panic. "What do I do?" she asked as confusion, fear, and helplessness purged all logical thoughts from her mind. "Help me! We need help!" No one answered.

"Find…Elza," Farrah managed between violent coughs, her body thrashing as it fought the slow poison that crept steadily toward her heart.

Despite the ache in her limbs, Anika dashed out the door, realizing she was in the reeve's home. She bolted down the stairs past a panicked guard that had come in to see what the shouting was about.

"Where's the gnome?! Has anyone seen her?"

Two guards near the reeve's door both directed Anika toward the creek. "She was picking herbs o'er there," one of them offered.

Anika sprinted as fast as she could, still gripping the stone, but no longer feeling the power it gave her last night. She tried to draw on it to hopefully quicken her pace, but it was useless—she sprinted in her bare feet toward the trees. She was so focused on finding Elza and saving Farrah that she didn't even hear the harpy's screech overhead.

"It's back!" Bennik warned in a quiet hiss, turning from the trail that Ransil crept along with knives bared. "Sounds like two this time!" He looked back at the halfling. "If they're after the stone—" He turned and sprinted away without finishing the thought.

Ransil followed like a wolf bounding silently through the leaves. Together they followed the shrill cries overhead back to Blakehurst, emerging into the sunlight to see several guards loosing arrows at two harpies, screaming their fury. One of the harpies fell to the ground with several arrows sprouting from its chest. The other flew haphazardly in circles to avoid the fire, but not striking.

Bennik was taking careful aim at the harrying creature before he heard a distant, familiar shout. "Please! Help!"

"Anika!" Bennik took off at another dead run toward his daughter.

A primal voice screamed, "Skraw, now!"

Ransil cursed a warning as the trees rustled behind Bennik. The harpy descended like a giant arrow, digging its razor claws into Bennik's shoulders. It lifted him up into the air easily, wrapping its bony limbs around the man as if he were a precious newborn child. Farrah's bow was thrown to the ground in the struggle, and Bennik thrashed wildly to free himself despite the height—he knew he would not survive such a fall, but would rather die than be stolen away.

"Corvanna would like to meet you," the creature named Skraw

hissed wickedly in Bennik's ear.

Ransil shouted, but as the world below fell away and the wind enveloped him, Bennik could only hear his own echoing voice calling his daughter's name.

Anika thought she could hear her name, somewhere far away, but the pounding of her own blood pumping was the only sound she could be sure of at that moment. She pushed through the trees, calling the gnome's name desperately. She burst into a clearing near the creek.

It was there that Anika found Elza's body. The gnome's wide, lifeless eyes were fixed on her hand that was gripping what Anika could only imagine were the herbs she needed to cure the poison that was killing Farrah. The secrets of that cure died with the gnome.

As she fell to her knees, Anika finally heard the distant laughter of a harpy.

CHAPTER EIGHT

The Witch's Legacy

The port city of Caraby may not have been as sprawling as Andelor or Merithian in Vale, but against the hilly forests and mountains, it looked like a majestic metropolis carved into the very cliffs of Jath's coast.

"So you've been here before?" Layla asked, tucking her short hair behind her elven ears as her pale pink robes flapped in the sea breeze. Their ship neared the coast of Jath, and her keen eyes could see the mountains rising from the dense trees of the isle. She smiled warmly at the beautiful cherry blossom trees she saw along the coast that matched the shade of her robes.

"Once." Desmond was her dark human counterpart—long, spidery black hair that blew away from his corpse-like face to reveal dark eyes made all the darker by the ash he liked to smear around them. His own black robes flew wilder than Layla's in the ocean spray, since they hung from his waist like thin belts. He leaned against the ship's railing as if bored by the sight, looking every bit like a lazy ghoul.

Layla laughed, her mood lightened by her companion's dourness. "Well, I hope you remember Caraby's streets well enough. I don't care to get lost in the city while looking for our contact."

"We won't," Desmond assured her. "They know our ship."

"They?" Layla asked, giving him a raised eyebrow. "He or she? You haven't even told me who our contact is."

"Neither," Desmond said. "They don't like to be pinned down. Their name is Maze. And the queen trusts them with her life."

"Land ho!" The ship became a bustle of activity as they neared the port.

Desmond straightened, giving Layla a familiar look of indifference. "We won't be able to disembark for a while. We should go to our cabin and make use of the time." His eyes went to one of the elf's legs, left exposed by her blowing robes.

Layla wiggled her eyebrows in response, giving the morose man a smile as she walked teasingly toward the stairs that led below deck.

The Variance was Queen Sopheena's fastest and least extravagant ship. Its small purple sails were adorned with the most modest heraldry— the Vale's symbolic silver mailed fist with a dove perched on it taking flight, representing the land's beauty and the might of its people when called to defend it.

The light vessel navigated the crowded Caraby harbor with ease, turning tightly around anchored galleys and departing trade ships until it was clear to dock. The Coperan navy still occupied the northern shores of Jath, hoping to eventually pressure the isle's unofficial ruler, Admiral Florin Bournay, to align with the Copera throne as opposed to the upstart rebels that sought to overthrow their cruel king, Malcolmry Sulm.

Caraby itself was a sight to behold. The younger members of the crew on *The Variance* were awestruck by their first visions of Jath's iconic port. The city was built into Jath's cliff face, thousands of homes and businesses set into a series of ascending steps that rose in a semicircle of high towers. Those towers framed the rising sun, and colorful banners ran down the length of those smooth cylinders to mark all the various kingdoms and empires that openly traded with Caraby's network of renown seafaring merchants.

What the city lacked in size it made up for in concentrated activity. The docks themselves were a flood of people—sailors singing songs as they accompanied men or women of pleasure, traders shouting out prices for the day's catch, citizens going about their morning routines. There didn't seem to be room to breathe in those bustling streets, but it did not seem to bother the milling bodies that piled on top of one another.

"Anchors!" a sailor called out as *The Variance* reached its destination.

"Wow," Layla said as she stepped onto the solid ground of the dock, nearly stumbling as she adjusted to the steadiness of dry land. She tried to fix her wild hair, disheveled by the sea breeze and a quick moment of passion.

The other mage stepped off the ship's plank beside her, his thin pale hands inside his dark robes. Desmond's hood was drawn as well to keep the sun off flesh that had spent most of its time in the lower levels of the Arcania studying darker lore. "Maze will meet us for lunch," Desmond instructed. "The queen arranged lodging for us at that unremarkable establishment."

Layla followed Desmond's bony finger, looking over the hundreds of heads that separated them from their destination—a three-story building that looked to be leaning to one side. A crude sign named it The Wresting Tide, although the painted scene of a muscled woman in scaled blue flesh pulling an anchor from the crashing sea was quite faded from years of sun and saltwater.

The queen's mages shouldered their way through the bustling docks toward the market district of Caraby. Layla's young eyes were wide with wonder as she watched the citizenry. There were fair-skinned Eastlunder explorers, gruff dwarf sea maidens that spewed some of the most foul curses Layla had ever heard, and halfling fishers scrambling about to hawk their catches or stock up for their kitchens. Here she saw dark-skinned Karranese wayfarers making their circuit from home, Jath, to Xe'dann, and there she saw the self-styled high elves in their pearl-enameled armor and sapphire cloaks making port on their way across the Racivic Sea to Layla's own ancestral home of Fehir'whin.

"This place is amazing," the elf said.

Desmond carried on without turning his hooded head from their destination. "It certainly draws a crowd," he said, unimpressed.

The Wresting Tide sat on the edge of the city's first raised tier, overlooking the harbor, the lower coast, and the Underdocks, where Jath's most desperate survivors eked out a life under the certain doom of a high tide.

Layla and Desmond stepped inside the meager establishment, greeted with a welcoming silence. Desmond lowered his hood, his face betraying emotion as he found relief from the rising sun. "Find our rooms," he said to the queen's own escorts that carried their supplies from the ship.

"My oh my," came a raspy voice from a dark corner of the common room.

Both mages jerked their heads in either direction, looking for the speaker. However, all they saw was a rotund man that stood like a statue behind the bar, watching them. He turned to retreat back into the back room before the voice came again.

"What is the queen feeding you, Lord Skeleton?"

"It's Everton," Desmond said flatly. "Desmond Everton. I thought you had a better memory than that, Maze."

A hearty, choking laugh followed as the sound of ungreased wheels brought a large shadow into the dim light of the Tide's many lanterns. "How could I have expected you to know a jest if it up and bit you in the face like a Bright Bay crab claw, you macabre man you?"

Maze sat in a wheeled chair, their legs swollen with some sort of malady, but discreetly covered by an exotic woven shawl. Tightly muscled arms pushed the wheels on the chair forward as they approached the mages.

Layla smiled at the stranger, mesmerized by such a presence. She found Maze's face intoxicating to behold—elegant makeup brought out their distinct features, which were framed by short, straight hair dyed silver and earthy green. There were a myriad of mysteries about this person that Layla desperately wanted to solve, but for now she settled for pleasantry.

"A pleasure, Maze," Layla said, offering a hand in greeting.

Maze looked at her with raised eyebrows. "And what have we here?" Gently grabbing Layla's hand, Maze gave it a soft kiss. "Where did our dear queen find such a lovely and gracious elf witch?"

Layla's smile soured slightly. "I'm no witch." She took her hand back and reached it into her robes to present the Arcanian mark hanging around her neck as proof.

"Oh, we're all witches, honey," Maze said with a wink. "Fainly's little coven included."

"You're early," Desmond said. "Or do the Jathi eat lunch before the sun finishes rising?" He produced a small notebook from his robes, opening it to flip through pages containing detailed agendas. He found today's agenda. "No. Early." He closed the book and returned it to his robes.

Maze gave him a condescending smile. "My deepest apologies for threatening to upend your busy schedule, Desmond. But you just happened to catch me finishing up a morning appointment. I am happy to come back." Maze turned one wheel of their chair to move away.

"What do you have for us?" Desmond stepped toward one of the many empty tables in the vacant common room.

"Oh, just the usual," Maze said, stifling a yawn, "secrets to kill for."

The joke made Layla look around nervously. "Where is everyone?" She regarded the deep shadows that surrounded them—all the windows were covered, not letting any daylight in, and the three of them were completely alone now that the barkeep had vanished. She took a seat next to Desmond.

"Do not fret," Maze said as they rolled their chair to the table. "Roswald is on retainer with Bournay—and the admiral likes to make sure my business is discreet, especially when your queen comes knocking."

"Where is the book?" Desmond asked plainly.

Maze gave Layla a feigned look of shock, motioning to Desmond. "I hope he doesn't just try to get straight to the point with you as well, lovely. No romance with this one, eh?"

Layla couldn't help but blush and giggle, softening the tension a bit.

"The queen isn't the only one looking for the book," Maze said, their face turning serious, leaning toward the mages. "While Sopheena has been sicking her Guild on every rumor of the Keys, there has predictably been a renewed interest in…how should I say?" Maze stroked their chin. "Items of historical value."

Layla glanced nervously at Desmond, who returned a look but betrayed no such obvious emotion on his stiff face.

"Relax," Maze said. "No one besides myself and the admiral know that the queen and Knife are in league, or at least taking advantage of each other's current desires. But after we sent our man to Andelor with our message regarding the book, he didn't survive the trip home. Which tells me he was intercepted and likely questioned."

While Maze was speaking, Desmond swiftly produced a compact writing kit and his notebook. He opened to a page, dipped his quill in the small ink pot, and began his notes. "So you suspect someone else is looking to get the book to gain leverage over Sopheena or the Guild?"

"If only it were that simple," Maze said, knocking on the table. "A round, Roswald!" Almost immediately the heavyset bartender hobbled out with a tray of drinks. He walked on a wooden peg in place of his lower left leg, moving rather deftly for a man of his size and age.

"So the book is not here?" Layla asked, her head spinning from this flood of information. She had secretly expected that they were just picking up a dusty old tome for the queen and heading back to sea.

Maze laughed, taking one of the mugs. "Oh the *Book of Stane* is on Jath, but it's not in Caraby—certainly not in Roswald's humble establishment here. But that's not necessarily the complication."

"What would the complication be?" Desmond asked, still scribbling notes.

Maze took a long drink before asking, "What do you know of the Disciples of Stane?" Seeing the mages' silent reactions, Maze nodded. "I'm not surprised. They don't have any temples on Noveth that I'm aware of. They are an old cult, but still relatively secretive. I believe there is a sect here in the city, but the admiral forbids any action taken against them at this time.

"Stane is not a name you hear uttered much these days," Maze continued, "but I'm sure you know of his presence in ancient Vaustren, Desmond. With as much time as you spend in the depths of the Arcania."

Desmond looked up. "The prophet? From my understanding, his followers are mostly in Xe'dann."

"Mostly," nodded Maze. "But since the Unthroning, the Disciples have steadily found new members, especially among those foolish enough to sympathize with the Shadow—oh, write that down, there's a song there!"

Desmond was already writing furiously, while also ignoring the jest. "You suspect these Disciples have taken an interest in the queen's affairs?"

"Or she theirs," Maze said before taking another drink. "Tell me. Do you know why Sopheena seeks this book? Or her sudden interest in the Keys?"

Layla looked over her shoulder as if a royal spy was bearing witness to this possible treason. Looking back at Maze, she said, "We are the queen's court mages—it is not our place to question her decrees or motives."

Maze pursed their lips, nodding understanding. "Well, let me enlighten you. Dear Sopheena, and her late twin sister, Nipheena, were exiles from Caim, which I'm sure there is a fanciful story told throughout Vale about how that came to be. But here's the truth. The twin sisters were born to Delucar, a descendent of one of the Purveyors, and intended king of the high elves rebuilding the city.

"Well, Delucar would never live to ascend the throne, as the vampire lords on Caim that decimated most of Fehir'whin and Xoatia managed to sway him to join their ranks in death—becoming the first elven vampire…well, that we know of. Count Delucar has made quite a name for himself throughout Xoatia, chasing many communities from their homes, forcing them to cross the sea where he cannot follow, to find a life away from the horror that has claimed most of Caim—oh, I should have been a bard!"

Desmond flipped a page and dipped his quill again, his hand working furiously to keep up. "And what does the queen's father have to do with her interest in the book and the Keys? To me it seems she would just like to ensure they are kept in the right hands in Andelor, where the Arcania can protect them."

Maze chuckled. "The *right* hands. If you think Fainly has any interest in the noble protection of the land, I could tell you some stories. But I digress. The Disciples, the vampires, the queen, the Arcania, the Luminaura…they all have interest in finding the book, and it all comes down to one reason. Kartha."

"The witch?" Layla asked, raising her eyebrows. All children were raised on stories of the witch Kartha who defied death and spread curses throughout all the lands. She was featured in so many stories that many assumed Kartha was just a legend, while others firmly believed that many women assumed the name over the years to grow the witch's legend.

Maze pushed aside their empty drink, reaching for Desmond's that had been left untouched. "At least Fainly teaches some truths in that tower of his," they said with a wink. "Yes, the witch. Kartha had her little withered finger in many pots, but when she stole the only copy of the *Book of Stane* from the Disciples in Vaustren, she set about a chain of events that brought all these very different parties together in this desperate search you find yourselves in. Now, I know where the book is, but it won't be easy getting it. And I cannot guarantee that when you find it you won't be doing the exact thing necessary to complete the witch's legacy."

Layla watched Desmond continue his notes, still confused but also enchanted by the adventure unfolding in Maze's words.

"And what legacy is that?" Desmond asked, finally dropping his quill in the ink pot and looking up with genuine interest.

Maze smiled. "Well, the end of the world, of course."

Chapter Nine

Unwelcome Guests

Avrim looked from Deina's stern, scarred face to the half-orc's, waiting for one of them to provide more explanation. His own mind was already a torrent of concern, confusion, and doubt, and he was unsure how to digest Melaine's story. Yet his thoughts were fixated on this graystone that was somehow linked to both Percy's condition and the manor's hauntings. Finally, the Duke Petrik Ambrose broke the drawn-out silence, his red-rimmed eyes regarding the half-orc suspiciously.

"So the stone my boy found was yours? You're saying you brought this here? My city is dying because—"

Deina stood up. "Melaine did not bring this storm here, my lord." She spat the title out almost mockingly, as if to say she would just as gladly exchange blows with the town drunk as she would its ruler. "The creature Corvanna brought the storm. You should be grateful that this brave woman survived encountering the stormbringer so she could inform you of the threat."

Despite having the dwarf's defense, Melaine shamefully avoided the duke's gaze, looking at the floor as she said, "I don't know why the stone responded to your son. I have held keyshards, and the magic within is undeniable—you can feel it begging to be harnessed, released. This one," Melaine finally looked up. "Its power was locked away to me. I could tell it was there, but it would not respond to me. It must have responded to your son, or whoever else possessed it."

The duke thought on that, closing his eyes as if finally giving in to the sleep that eluded him for days. He sank into his chair in the dim light of his study. "We could not pry it from his hands. He had the strength of an ogre." He opened his eyes to look over his shoulder at the closed door to Percy's quarters. A soft, wicked cackling could barely be heard. "It was my wife that finally retrieved the stone from him."

As if summoned, the ghost of the duchess walked into the study, staying in the shadows of the candlelight. "Can I get anyone anything? Dear?"

Melaine gasped, nearly falling back out of her chair. She reached for the broad knife at her belt, as much good as it would do against a spirit. Deina, still standing, hunched down as if ready to pounce on the ethereal noblewoman.

Avrim stayed them with a raised hand, clutching his brightstar with his other hand. He whispered an invocation of the Light and turned his hand on the duchess. The dim glow in the room seemed to intensify until it flashed in a sudden blinding brilliance. The ghost hissed, the beautiful form of the duchess twisting into a serpentine horror that brandished impossibly long fangs at the priest before dissipating completely.

"The Shadow holds this house," Avrim told them all, almost ignoring the banishment that just took place as he thought out loud. "As long as the Shadowlord retains its possession of young Master Ambrose, the duchess' spirit will not rest."

"Where did your wife put the stone?" Deina asked the duke.

Petrik's eyes had closed, as if he had fallen asleep. But in response to the question, he looked at the dwarf with rising dread. "I gave it to the Oather."

Melaine's lower lip curled around the small tusks that protruded from the corners of her mouth as her brows furrowed. "Kasia Strallow."

It was not a question, but the duke shook his head. "Nay, her companion. The elf. He was collecting anything from my citizens that looked arcane in nature. I wanted them to go away until I could consult with a Luminaurian priest about Percy's condition—I knew they wouldn't wait for answers before stringing me and my son up. And I wanted that cursed stone out of this house anyway, so I offered it up to the mage as a way to buy myself some more time."

"So what you're saying is," Deina began, rubbing her temple with two broad fingers, "the stone that your son brought into your home held a Shadowlord, which he somehow freed. That Shadowlord possessed him, killed your wife when she took the stone, and then you gave the stone to the Arcania dogs, that would likely kill you and your son when they discover its nature?"

The duke's eyes were closed again. This time, it seemed like he had actually fallen asleep, slumped in his chair.

The dwarf turned to Avrim. "That really doesn't explain this storm though, does it, Brother?"

Avrim was quietly flipping through his luminary. He looked up at the dwarf and half-orc, his eyes wild with revelation. "We have to speak with Percy." He slammed the luminary shut before adding, "More precisely, the Shadowlord."

"What could possibly be the problem now!?" Blane snapped, gathering his belongings. He had decided on a course of action for the day, and this was already the third interruption he had encountered. He silently cursed both Fainly and Kasia for leaving him in charge of the city watch.

"Captain Greer has requested your presence on the East Gate," the soldier said, her voice shaking with fear speaking with an aggravated mage.

"I'm sure he has," Blane said, scooping the rest of his keyshards from the desk into his bag. "Go tell him I know about the storm—I've already been informed by the duke's treasurer and Earl Bolton."

It seemed the storm had expanded overnight, showing the first signs of activity in weeks as the gray-green void grew in all directions. The sudden change in the sky had caused panic amongst the nobles within the city; those who had the most to lose in the shadow of this phenomenon demanded the loudest.

"I...I don't believe this is about the storm, High Mage," the soldier replied. "Orcs have been seen gathering to the east, and the harpies have resumed their flights over the city."

Blane looked out the window to see the windless banners and flags hanging over Rathen, their limp forms a proper heraldry to the dying city. The faint hint of shadows streaked within the clouds and the elf narrowed his eyes. Blane's delicate pride was shattered at the thought of those vile bird-women not heeding the first warning he had sent them.

He heard the soldier gasp behind him. Looking at his hand, he saw the crackle of white lightning climbing his arm from his closed fist. Taking a deep breath, he relaxed his hand, knowing he should save his strength in case it came to battle once more with the winged nuisances.

"Prepare a dozen members of the watch to accompany us to the

East Gate," Blane instructed, putting the strap of his bag over his head so that it sat comfortably at his waist. He reached into his robes to produce the graystone, looking at it as if expecting it to possess him like it had Roy. When it didn't, he returned his eyes to the soldier. "Then you will accompany me to the duke's manor. He has some things to answer for."

"Ukarra, the Graveborn," Avrim said with all the conviction he could muster. "I summon thee. Reveal yourself!"

Percy's eyes remained fixed on an unseen void above his bed, an unblinking corpse whose mouth whispered in tongues.

Avrim watched a moment longer for any change, but returned to the pages of his luminary when Deina gave another loud sigh.

"How many more could there be?" the dwarf asked. Melaine watched the boy in studied silence, sitting in the duke's normal chair near the bedside table.

"Rile, the Plague Maiden, I name thee!"

"Lucretia, the Defiler! I name and command you!"

"Myriadas, the Shaper, the Light compels you! Come forth!"

"Avrim!" Deina slapped the holy book out of the priest's hands.

Clenching his fists, Avrim strained every muscle to contain the Light that was fighting to take over his body. He could feel its warmth, its cleansing, its fury. The names of the Shadowlords seemed to let the Shadow into him, and he instinctively channeled the Light to prevent being overtaken. It was a balance he was not sure he ever wanted to tempt again.

As the power subsided, Avrim looked at his companions. Deina's broad face wore a look of challenge, as if she expected to have to trade blows with the Shadow-taken priest that was attempting to summon demons in her presence.

Melaine's face was a mask, only her widened eyes betraying a sense of surprise at the proceedings.

"Sorry," Avrim offered, bending over to pick his luminary back up. "There is a theory in the Luminaura that during the Unthroning, when the Nethering Gates were weakened, demons poured into Aetha from the Abyss. However, much like the old gods, the demons were bound by the Keys that created Light and Shadow. When the Keys shattered, most demons died, but the most powerful ones found refuge in keyshards—creating the blackshards."

"The blackshards," Melaine repeated, her eyes distant.

Avrim watched Percy's restless mouth repeat blasphemies from the Abyss. "They are the prisons of the Shadowlords. And if we can determine which Shadowlord has escaped their prison and possessed this child, then perhaps we can trick it into telling us where the blackshard is—even though it is their prison, it is still a source of power for them, and they will want it, I suspect."

Melaine stood, eyes wide with realization. "Could this demon's shard be gray? Or is it black like night?"

Avrim's eyes shifted as he considered that. "I've only ever read or heard them described as black like onyx, enveloped in Shadow." He looked at the half-orc, his thoughts wandering. "The keyshards' appearances reflect their prisoner—verdant green for Oakus, sapphire for Eyen, earthly brown for Myretha, fiery red for Wick, aquamarine for Corsa, and cat's eye yellow for Syrina. Each of the old gods possess elements of Light and Shadow." Avrim's eyes settled on Percy. "The sign of the Shadow is black, the absence of Light, thus the blackshards contain only the essence of Shadow."

Deina followed the priest's logic. "But if something else were bound in one of those shards with a Shadowlord…"

"Archers! Fire!"

Blane quickened his pace up the stairs as the call to arms was sounded. He had no idea that the enemy was so near the city walls. As the mage reached the battlements, he was greeted with a symphony of bowstrings unleashing death into the fog that had settled over the ground below. Carefully peering over the stone wall, Blane could see shadows moving below in those foul mists—it seemed that the storm was spreading in every direction, enveloping the world below. There was an acrid taste in that air; something sorcerous but yet foreign to the high mage who prided himself on knowledge of all the arcane practices.

"Captain Greer!" Blane ducked low as a crude black shaft found its mark in the neck of a Rathen archer next to him. It was unmistakably an orc arrow, Blane noted, as the archer died loudly, thrashing for a few final breaths. "Captain Greer!"

"Mage!" a gruff voice called from elsewhere on the tower, from within the roiling mists that seemed to thicken every moment. "To arms! Orcs at the walls!"

Blane turned to the soldier behind him that had brought the message. "You told me they were gathering! Not that they were knocking on the damn gates!"

The soldier's eyes were wide with confusion and panic as she drew her sword and held her shield at the ready.

"Sorcery!" the captain's voice called in response. "One moment we see their camp in the distance, the next the sky fell and they were upon us!"

Bright green lights flashed in the mists below, drawing Blane's attention. Now he was certain he felt magic in the air, and for a moment he was concerned. *Shaman*, he thought with annoyance and sudden relief. He knew orc shamans to be untrained hedge wizards at best, counting themselves fortunate when they didn't tear their own bodies to shreds when channeling the magic that they did not fully comprehend.

"Archers!" Blane shouted, motioning to the display of green lights in the fog below. "Aim for their witch! The lights!" He took a deep breath of the pungent air, calling on the powers of air and propulsion to clear the clouds. There was no answer. He silently cursed the storm that seemed to deaden his ability to reach the wind in this cursed, arid city. Gritting his teeth, Blane thrust his hand into his pack to retrieve a blue keyshard—it glowed with eager magic. Using it, he easily found the footing for his spell and threw his arms wide.

Below, the mists parted to reveal an army of orcs, some loosing arrows up at the archers from their horned bows while others scaled the walls with their powerful hands. In the warriors' midst was the shaman Blane was looking for. "There!" he called, and in response a hail of arrows sped toward their mark.

But none found the blood they sought. Each arrow clattered away from an unseen barrier. Sickly green glimmering appeared where each arrow was intercepted, and behind that magic Blane could see the orc witch smile at him.

Fury overtook the high mage, unable to stomach being outmatched by such a lowly creature. Blane reached into his bag to pull out another blue shard, driven by a maddening need to bring the wind back to this city. Even while enraged, the poetry of such a display was not something the elf could easily ignore.

"You have come to the wrong city, orc witch!" Blane shouted as he performed the necessary hand motions for his spell, his knuckles white as he gripped the shimmering blue stones in each hand. His voice was amplified by the wind that gathered around him, nearly lifting him off the ground as his spell crescendoed. "I am Blane Hassok, High Mage of the Arcania, and I have come to give you a deadly lesson in the arts!"

The elf commanded the power that now swirled within him to be unleashed. But it did not obey. Instead, it continued to swell inside of him, threatening to tear his limbs from his body. His eyes widened, staring at the orc shaman below, disbelieving that crooked figure wielded the power to ward him against his own magic. But the orc looked just as confused as Blane.

It was then that a god-like shape appeared in the hazy sky. Part harpy, part dragon, all terrifying. Blane was held suspended as the giant creature's wings brought it down to perch on the walls of Rathen. Now that the thing was right before him, Blane could see a harpy's face on that hawk-like head, blue and black feathers falling like a great mane. Its humanoid body rippled with scaly muscle and was framed in features that seemed to have edges like razors.

The elf had never seen anything like it, and he prided himself on having read every book that came through the Arcania. Whatever this was, it was not of this world or any known plane.

"You have something that belongs to me," the creature said, its voice as overpowering as a tempest.

Blane's mind raced through a maze of arcane barriers within him, each one trying to prevent his control over the magic that now threatened to destroy him. His innate mental prowess and relentless study kept his mind sharper than any sword in Noveth, and he was determined to fight against this creature's magic, no matter how godly they seemed. Slowly, he found an opening, drawing more power from each keyshard than he ever normally would—he felt each one draining, and he returned no power to them. He was killing his precious keyshards in an effort to thwart this monster.

The gambit worked, and Blane felt the familiar ecstasy of magical release as he unleashed a torrent of air that threw the creature wildly into the air. In response, Blane's own body was hurled off the wall back into the city, landing roughly on a slanted roof from which he slid into a wagon that was thankfully carrying dried hay.

His respite was short-lived, as immediately Blane heard a shriek descending from above and felt agonizing pain as something sharp dug into his back.

"Give me Corvanna's stone, elf!" The harpy leaned close to Blane's face and he could feel her hot, rancid breath. "Or she will have to dig it out of my guts after I feast on your innards!" The harpy sank her sharp teeth into Blane's neck.

Blane screamed in agony, digging for any magic remaining in the stones he gripped. But they were bled dry. He released them and drew on more familiar magic that the storm above had not weakened. Lightning exploded from Blane's hands as he gripped the harpy's arm. The creature was blasted away from the elf in a crackling, smoldering flail.

Blane felt rough hands grabbing his robes, and turned to unleash more magic when he saw an unfamiliar dwarf woman.

"Save your damn spells," she growled, hauling him out of the wagon and onto the road. As he regained his bearings, Blane could see the city had descended into chaos. Orcs had somehow breached the gates and now battled the city watch or cut down screaming civilians trying to flee. A figure behind the dwarf that looked like a slender orc fired an arrow at one of the ravaging orcs that was chasing down a woman and her two children. A priest of the Light stepped forward with a raised hand in warning—*The man from the duke's garden*, Blane thought.

"Do not use any spells that call upon the wind," the priest warned, pointing to the sky. "That is an incarnate of Eyen—it is feeding off any magic you use under Eyen's domain!"

Blane followed the priest's hand to see the giant creature called Corvanna spreading its wide wings above Rathen, ready to descend.

"Give us the graystone," the slender orc demanded in the common tongue. "I brought it here, and it is what Corvanna is after!"

Sudden fury blinded Blane, remembering Kasia beheading her squire and thinking of the accursed storm above. *Your fault*, Blane thought. He reached into his bag and drew out the graystone. "You shall not have it, Shadowfiend! Worshiper of Ithakan! You brought this scourge to Rathen and you shall answer for your blasphemy at the Arcania!" He began to weave a holding spell.

Sudden hideous laughter erupted from behind the priest, and Blane was distracted by the sight of Duke Ambrose carrying a boy. That boy now looked at Blane with blackened eyes, his mouth twisted in a cruel grin.

"You dare speak my name, puny elf!"

Percy leapt out of his father's arms, knocking the weary man down. His demonic laughter continued. The priest muttered a quick prayer, but only a dim light emanated from his hands. Percy pushed him aside as well, knocking the priest into the dwarf. The slender orc was now held by Blane's desperate holding spell—the elven mage's face twisted in terror.

"You name me, elf," Percy said, his body contorting with every step. "And here I am. You think that witch in that stone can hold me?! You think to send me back?! I will not be bound again! I will not serve the incarnate's will!" Percy thrust a hand around the elf's throat as Corvanna rapidly descended on the unfolding scene.

"Sorry, boy!" the dwarf said as she charged, her axe raised. She brought it down to sever Percy's hand at the wrist, releasing Blane just in time for him to speak the words of power that summoned a fiery blast. Ithakan's spirit screamed in pain, grasping Percy's bleeding stump as he fell to his knees. Corvanna shrieked as the fire consumed her, knocking her to the ground.

A wet *thunk* brought Blane's proud eyes from Corvanna's flaming landing to his chest, where an arrow now protruded from his heart. He looked up to the slender orc, who he now saw was a half-orc—his holding spell was released when he diverted his power to bring down Corvanna.

The high mage's hand fell limply, dropping the graystone to the ground. He slumped to his knees as his vision faded. He saw the dwarf, priest, and half-orc scoop up the possessed boy, thrashing wildly as he cradled his bloody ruin of a wrist. Blane saw the duke become surrounded by bloodthirsty orcs, the ravenous mob making short work of Rathen's gracious ruler.

Blane watched as the city fell, the acrid sky above now threatening to swallow the entire world. His last thought was of the wind, and how glorious it had felt that day, however brief it may have been.

CHAPTER TEN

The Beckoning

Anika felt the wind through her hair as she stood on the hill overlooking Blakehurst. She could see most of the town from up here, as well as the trees of Lohkrest to the east. She couldn't look anywhere without being overcome with grief. To the east she felt the sorrow of Elza and Farrah dying, and with them any hope of learning the truth about the blue stone that seemed to have ruined her life—yet she dared not relinquish it.

"Do not let it out of your sight," Ransil had warned while consoling her in the aftermath of Bennik's abduction. "The Shadow wants it, and for some reason that stone has chosen you as its protector. Keep it safe, as it might hold the key to rescuing your father."

She couldn't look to the west without thinking of home—of Gage and the growing distance she felt between them. He had not spoken to her much since the attack, but she sensed an anger about him, as if he blamed her for everything that had happened. Even though he had stolen it, he had done it for her. The guilt she felt over it was surprising and heavy, and the tension it created was very real.

To the south lay Karrane, her homeland that had never been her home. Anika thought of the woman who had come to her in her sleep—and in The Early Mule when she was very awake—who had claimed to be her mother. *Mother*, she thought, thinking of the kind and nervous woman who had tried to fill that role for her. That same woman who disappeared when Gage was barely walking. There was a mystery there that she thought she would never solve.

Anika looked to the north as tears began to fill her eyes. She gripped the stone in her hand tighter as she thought of her father being dragged through that beautiful sky toward some sinister fate. She closed her eyes, hoping some wild visions would come to her and let her know that her father was all right. But all she saw in that void was her father's kind face, smiling at her, telling her how proud she had made him.

"Anika," the face said to her, bringing her to openly weep.

She tensed when she felt a small hand on her arm. Ransil looked up with an empathetic smile. "Anika, it's time."

Nodding, Anika thrust the stone back into her pouch and rested a hand on the hilt of the ancestral knife her father had entrusted to her. Together they walked toward Brightstar's Rest, where the dead were buried.

Graves had been prepared for the villagers who had died in the attacks. Anika's friend Jema was laid to rest next to her mother and father—also lost in the attack—near the edge of the cemetery. Matty knelt by the graves, a sword thrust into the soft earth. He pressed his head against the hilt, tears streaming down his face as he whispered a secret oath to the dead. He had lost everything, and Anika's heart ached for him.

Anika saw Wilma Evertree hugging her parents near Wesley's grave, who had died after valiantly defending those in The Early Mule. Brave Esher Dell was buried next to Wesley, the Widow Dell weeping on both knees next to her only son's resting place.

It was all too much for Anika, but she was determined to stand alongside her people in their time of grief. She watched through watery eyes as several Brothers of the Light prepared the wagons that were loaded with Elza and Farrah's corpses, destined for Lefayra where they both would be properly laid to rest in the fey tradition. Part of her wanted to go with them, to see the fabled elven city, but she knew her path led elsewhere.

Mother Beatrim stepped up on the altar that was carved into the Brightstar statue in the center of the cemetery. Reeve Warner steadied her climb, taking a firm stance in front of the altar when the proceedings were ready to begin.

Anika could not hear the words that Beatrim spoke, though she was sure they were comforting and filled with glorification of the Light. Her eyes were fixed on the two figures on the opposite end of the cemetery. Gage supported Robin in the shadow of the Brightstar statue. Anika thought she saw her brother's eyes find her, but they seemed to look right past her, as if he were ashamed to even acknowledge her. She wanted to go to him, wanted to comfort him over their father—they both had lost their families, but she hoped they still had each other after all of this.

Gage was all she had left now.

Ransil stood by Anika, the halfling looking much older than she had ever seen him. While he had always had gray curls amongst the mess of brown ones on his head, he seemed to carry a heavy weight on his shoulders today. She could see two broad-bladed knives at Ransil's waist and a few smaller throwing daggers sticking out of his belt. He had become ever-vigilant since the attack, and without the Mule, Anika had a feeling that Ransil had lost as much sense of belonging as she had.

Detached from the reality of the ceremony playing out before her, Anika knelt down in the damp grass so she could comfortably put an arm around her friend. Together they observed the passing of their old lives in Blakehurst.

Gage and Robin crept warily toward their old spot near the creek as the sun began to set. The reeve's guards expanded their patrols outside of town, watching carefully for any sign of goblins or harpies or other wretched Shadowfiends. But since the harpies had taken Bennik, the attacks had ceased and an eerie calm had settled over Blakehurst.

It was as if the very stone they were after had somehow scared the Shadow away. Thoughts of that damned stone from that damned necklace sent a flurry of emotions through Gage's mind. Mostly, he felt guilt for ever having taken the accursed thing, but also anger that Anika had planted the thought in his head. Something was happening with her, and Gage had begun to worry about being near her. He did not doubt that he loved his sister, but after the morning of her birthday and then before Elza...

"Are you all right?" Robin asked, taking Gage's hand.

The warmth in the half-elf's eyes chased away thoughts of the gnome and his sister from Gage's burdened mind. He squeezed Robin's hand, pulling him forward. They kissed there in the same spot where they had shared their first kiss, afraid to let each other go until finally Robin broke away to look deep into Gage's eyes.

"Ransil has asked me to go to Andelor with him."

Gage's heart lurched, unsure of what that meant. "You can't leave—not now!"

Robin swallowed, his eyes darting to the trees as if he suspected someone may be listening. "Come with us—with your sister."

Gage looked down, the guilt coming back. "Someone needs to be here in case my father—"

"He's dead," Robin said flatly.

Gage looked at Robin, horrified. He dropped the half-elf's hand and took a step away from him.

Sighing, Robin reached for Gage's hand again. "I'm sorry, but there's nothing here for either of us, Gage. I'm sorry about your father. And your mother." He looked back toward Blakehurst. "And I'm sorry about what you had to do. But it's time for us to leave, like we always talked about."

"To join the Guild?" Gage asked, feeling the hint of a purpose returning to his shattered life. "Together?"

Robin reached a delicate hand up to wrap around the base of Gage's head, pulling him forward. "Together," he breathed softly as their lips touched.

Two sets of eyes watched them from the trees, their shadowed forms silently disappearing back into the growing dark as the sun descended.

Silence hung in the reeve's spacious den. The hearth was burning, chasing the early spring's evening chill away as Anika sipped her tea with one hand and spun the blue stone—*The keyshard*, she reminded herself—with the other. Visions still plagued her, but they remained at the back of her mind, where she could reasonably keep them at bay.

Ransil inspected the cheese and bread on the table before them, turning his nose up at the meager offering. "I miss my kitchen already," the halfling said as he leaned back, placing a hand on his small belly as if to guard it from either starvation or subpar meals.

The door opened behind them and Anika and Ransil turned, both of them surprised to see Matty Cullen step in. He wore an old suit of leather armor that matched the attire of the reeve's guards, with a tabard bearing Blakehurst's brown leaf on a split field of green and yellow. His family's sword with the bull-head pummel was sheathed at his waist.

Matty nodded to Ransil and gave Anika a faint smile. "Reeve Warner told me we were to meet here."

"Have a seat," Ransil said. "The bread is not mine though. And I cannot vouch for the cheese."

After Matty found a place to stand near the fire, looking every bit like a sentinel on watch, the door opened once more and Reeve Rupert Warner made his way into the room. He nodded to Ransil and gave Anika a look as if she might roast him alive.

"I have arranged for you to be escorted to Andelor at once," the reeve said to Anika, without any sort of greeting. "Young Master Cullen has entered my service and will accompany you on the road." The fat man rubbed his hands nervously, bowing his head as he spoke so Anika could not meet his eyes.

"Lord Warner," Ransil said sternly, struggling to lean forward in the chair that was built for a larger person. "I told you I would escort Anika to the Arcania myself *when she was ready* to depart." He pointed to the window overlooking the peaceful town. "Night is about to fall and Matty has just buried his whole family."

The reeve had no trouble meeting Ransil's narrowed eyes. "I said at once."

"Her father was just taken!" Ransil shouted, leaping off the chair to stand on the table. The tray of bread and cheese was sent flying to the floor. "Light burn you, man! Are you exiling her?!"

"Yes," the reeve said firmly, his face a reddening and wobbling mask, as if he struggled to show any real emotion in Anika's presence. "The monsters were clearly after her, or that accursed thing she carries. I will not have it or her in this town."

"I will guard her tonight," Matty offered, stepping forward. "We could leave on the morrow."

Anika appreciated the consideration, but she could not seem to quell the fury that was rising within her. Whether Ransil fueled it, or the reeve laying bare the guilt she had already felt over her unknowing role in the tragedy that would forever stain her home. Shame and confusion roiled together into a ball of rage. She gripped the keyshard tightly and felt the ecstasy of power course through her once again.

"I will not have that or her in my town another night," the reeve continued, still keeping his eyes on Ransil. "I cannot protect my people while she is here. This is not the first time she has brought danger upon my town!"

The fury fell away and Anika stood up. "What do you mean?"

The reeve finally looked at her and she could see the fear his eyes held.

"That Xe'danni cutthroat that came for you," the reeve said. "Did your father ever tell you how many that murderer killed while trying to get to you?" His lips trembled. "No, I suppose he didn't. He always thought he was doing the right thing—what a good man would do—but he put us all in danger by bringing you here. I warned him!"

Ransil looked at Anika, then back to the reeve. "That's enough, Rupert!" Any remaining sense of decorum or formality between the two fell away. "You shut your Netherdamned mouth right now!"

The reeve pointed at Ransil. "That is enough, rogue! I gave you refuge too! How many years now have I kept my lips sealed about that half-elf? I'll have no more deadly secrets here! Begone, all of you!" The reeve openly wept now, tears running down his furious face.

Ransil looked from the crying lord to Anika, who stared at the ground in shock, trying to process the information.

"We will go," Anika said, looking up to Ransil. "I have nothing left here. I need to go find my father." She looked at the reeve, who tried to discreetly wipe the tears from his jowls. A vision came to her as she stared at Rupert Warner, the pain on his face came from afar—she flew through the skies in her vision, into a dark storm, into a different night. She saw Roy Warner, the reeve's son, beheaded in a strange tower by a figure that was bathed in Shadow.

Tears came to Anika's eyes as she stepped toward the reeve. "Your son. Roy."

The reeve looked at her, terrified and heartbroken, his brows furrowing as if he suspected she was involved.

"I saw something—"

She didn't know how to explain what she saw, as she didn't even understand it. But she understood the pain, and she suspected that was how the vision came to her. "I am truly sorry for your loss, Reeve Warner." She bowed her head, forgiving the man for making her feel like an outsider, but determined to find answers to his claims.

Ransil looked confused. "What happened to Roy?"

The reeve finally sat down, more tears coming. "The bird came this afternoon. The city of Rathen is under siege. Roy was a squire to Dame Kasia Strallow, an Oather—Lady Commander, no less." He wiped a tear away. "The letter said that he died a hero's death. Defending the Oath of Sorcery." His red eyes looked up at Anika nervously, as if she had killed him with her own witchcraft.

Ransil placed a small hand on the reeve's broad shoulder. "May he find the Light, Rupert." He turned and nodded to Matty. "We will be on our way."

As the three of them reached the door, the reeve stood up. "Ransil."

The halfling turned around.

"When you come back, I'll have a new kitchen waiting for you."

Smiling, Ransil said, "One way or another, old friend, I do not expect we will be back." He looked up at Matty and Anika. "Sometimes you just can't go home."

They went out into the fading light.

CHAPTER ELEVEN

Deep Understanding

The night sky was clear, revealing thousands of stars that stretched from one horizon to the other. Renay looked east, always drawn to the past. She had escaped the visions of her old life throughout the day, but the night seemed to be when they clawed at her, desperate to take hold and fester.

Renay turned around, looking into the baron's chambers where Vivian and Alburn slept peacefully in the enormous bed. She was always thankful for them, but even more when the sun set. They kept the visions away. Turning back to the sky—anywhere but east—she wondered, *Why now?* It had been so long since she had run away from that life, why was it coming back to haunt her now?

Looking at the stars, she thought of the glowery, where hundreds of candles bathed her in Light. The Shadow could not take hold. But was it truly the Shadow chasing her still? Or something else?

Guilt.

Fear.

Love.

The face came to her again, as if formed from the stars. It was the face of the man who taught Renay what love was, long ago. He was a rugged warrior when they met, an Eastlunder who had spent much of his youth as a ranger fighting in Westerra when the monsters from Guyen threatened the borders. She heard all the stories from him, and was swept away by the adventure he brought to her small town nestled in the peaceful borders of the Acreage in Westerra.

Those were the fondest memories of her life.

Before the Shadow came. It had taken root inside of her after less than a year of marriage, and she could feel its presence growing. That was when the visions were the worst. She had intricate dreams of stories she had read as a child, about life before the Unthroning, when the old gods still reigned and there was no evil in the world.

Wickedness always existed, but it was driven by confusion and fear. Pure evil came with the Shadow, and the Light. When the Shadow took her, she could no longer find rest—her dreams were horrible and filled her with every negative emotion she could imagine. It was all she could do not to give in and end her life.

Then the child came, and the visions were gone. Joy had returned to her life, and her marriage became once more everything that she could have hoped for. It wasn't until a year after her child was born that the Shadow returned, but this time it found a home in her baby.

Renay could not be near her child without feeling that sickening presence of Shadow. She tried taking it to the church, but the Shadow only hid, waiting for night or whenever the Light faded. It called for her to kill for her child, demanding sacrifices. That was when she began praying to the Light for answers. And then new visions came—new requests for blood, but now for the blood of her child.

She must kill the Shadowspawn.

The Light cannot let the child live.

It was her duty as the mother to purify it through death.

Bring the child to the Light by ending its life.

Renay heard all the commands, and they had driven her to the brink of her sanity. There were several times when she gave in to the Light and nearly killed her child, only to be stopped by her husband, who thought she had gone mad.

There was nothing to do except run.

Run and never look back.

But Renay didn't run far, and she could not stop looking back.

As her eyes were fixed on the eastern horizon where her old home lay, a hand on her shoulder startled her.

"It's all right, child," Vivian's soothing voice said, her other hand running through Renay's hair. In the privacy of her own chambers, especially around the baron, Vivian was always the tender caretaker. When alone with Renay, she was a lioness. Renay was glad for the former now.

"I couldn't sleep," Renay said, hugging her arms tightly to her body.

"I would think not," Vivian said with raised eyebrows as she regarded Renay's naked body covered in goosebumps. She reached to the nearby chair and grabbed a blanket to throw over Renay's shoulders. "Bad dreams?"

Renay gave her a faint smile. "Something like that." She let Vivian wrap her arms around her and rest a chin on her shoulder. "When you carried your children, did you ever…feel different?"

"Yes," Vivian said without hesitation. "I felt like a cow, and am thankful that I am unable to have any more of the wretches."

Renay chuckled. "You know what I mean."

"I think so," Vivian said. "I'll tell you, when I was carrying Viktor, I felt like a warrior." She clenched her fist in front of Renay's face. "That boy left something in me that chased away any meekness I may have felt as a noble lady. Even after birth, I still felt his strength, and I always tell him he's going to be a powerful knight when he grows up."

Renay smiled. "I could definitely see that." She thought of what her own child may have left in her and shuddered.

"But Lenora," Vivian continued, "that one is different. While carrying her, I remember being compelled to read much more. I never spent much time in libraries, but I had Alburn chase down many books during those final months of carrying her. I seemed to only want to read and learn."

Both women stared up at the stars, sharing a long silence.

"What about your child?"

Renay stiffened. She had never told the Cafferys about her old life, or the child she had birthed and abandoned. "What do you mean?"

"Come now," Vivian said. "I'm not here to cast judgments or pry any details you don't care to share, but surely you have been with child. At least once." Her hands moved to Renay's stomach. "Otherwise, why would you have asked me about carrying mine?"

"Perhaps I would like to one day," Renay said, hoping the coy tone of her voice might steer the conversation in a different direction.

"You have had a child," Vivian said with certainty. "I can tell. I also know about the tonic you acquired from Naya two years ago, so you won't be carrying any children anymore." Her firm hands grabbed Renay's shoulders and spun her around to face her. "Just like me."

Renay's eyes fell to the curves of Vivian's body, framed by the open robe she wore. The mothers shared many similar marks on their bodies, and Renay felt a closeness to the baroness that exceeded their carnal habits. "I did carry a child. A long time ago."

Vivian nodded. "Whether you gave birth or not does not interest me. Tell me how it felt carrying the child."

Tears welled up in Renay's eyes. "Dark," she replied. "I only remember the darkness. There was nothing good I felt during that time."

Vivian reached up to caress Renay's cheek. "We don't always get to choose what grows within us, Renay. I'm sorry for your loss, whatever it was." She kissed her forehead. "Whatever it was, I know it wasn't easy. It never is."

Renay fell into Vivian's arms and the women wept together as a star fell across the sky, disappearing behind the eastern horizon.

Deep under the baron's keep were the ancient twisting passages of the Oakhold, where Naya Lahmoud worked tirelessly in a massive study that looked as if it had been carved from the hollow of a tree. She rarely slept these past few weeks, as the power of the Shadow began to awaken from nearly a decade's slumber.

Exhaustion weighed heavily on Naya, who was much too young to have so many gray hairs and those withered cracks in the skin around her eyes. They were not wrinkles born from smiles of joy, but rather exaltation. Her ear lobes were stretched around hammered bronze ornaments, which were common amongst her people, as were the dangling earrings that hung from other parts of her ears.

Two lumbering tree golems that were twice the size of the Xe'danni woman ambled slowly from one side of the stone room to the other, each hauling large crates of books and scrolls.

"There," Naya directed one, pointing toward a shelf. "I want all of these crates emptied and everything categorized on that shelf there."

Neither of the golems responded, but went about their work regardless.

"Ye think they know how to do that?"

Naya turned to see her only resident disciple, Mosby Penkle. The dwarf leaned casually against the archway leading into the study; behind him ran a dark hallway of twisting vine-walls and dim dancing green lights.

The Shadow priestess narrowed her eyes on the stump where his right arm had once been and mouthed a familiar incantation. The dwarf watched with a bored expression as an animated tree branch began to grow from his stump, slowly creaking and sprouting more smaller branches that wrapped around it until Mosby had a muscled vine-arm that was a close match to his other natural arm.

"I am actually quite uncertain," Naya said, her Xe'danni accent wrapping itself around the common tongue like an intoxicating song, "which is why you are here to assist them in learning."

Sighing, Mosby pushed himself off the wall and trudged toward Naya's indentured tree golem. The dwarf watched as the golem picked up a massive dusty tome and placed it upside down on the shelf. "Where's the big guy?"

Naya reached into her dark robe and produced a large, jagged green stone. It pulsated with an emerald light against her coppery skin. "Resting. I may have pushed him a little too hard this afternoon during our training, but we are running out of time. He needs to be ready." She put the stone back into her robes.

Mosby blew the dust off of a dozen scrolls, inspecting them. They all bore the seal of House Monteague in Westerra, the elk's head crowned with a golden wreath on a field of crimson. "Well, at least you are finding some new friends." He shoved the scrolls on the shelf, noting dozens of royal seals from Eastlund, Vale, Westerra, and even Karrane and Guyen. "Are all these from the baron's new recruits? If so, it seems the Shrouded have enough high lords in their ranks now to maybe call the Guild's bluff. I told ye the gold would work—nothing brings the lords and ladies like gold mines. If I were ye, I'd send these boys down to find some more veins and have the baron open up a mine near New Hold, bring the dwarves into the fold."

Naya scoffed. "Don't take these offerings as pledges of loyalty. They are nothing more than the coppers a scared victim offers up when being robbed at knifepoint. We are being placated by rich lords that try to buy their way out of any sort of true conviction." She motioned to the crates. "No doubt the Luminaura receives more than just ancient texts collecting dust as offerings." Naya ran a long-nailed hand through her thin black hair. "Highshroud Fahid is convinced that we will need a display to truly sway the Joined Realms to the Shadow."

"As I keep tellin' ye," Mosby said, using his summoned branch arm to lift a massive text from the crate, "me kin down in Guyen will answer the call of the Shroud. The Shadow hangs heavy there, but they fight petty civil wars over that accursed land. All's they need is a cause to unite them."

"I've heeded your words on the matter, Mosby, and will take your counsel under advisement." Naya walked toward the great table in the center of the study where she had books stacked taller than her golem servants, and candles burning with unnatural green flames. She poured herself a large glass of wine from a decanter and sipped it while looking over a map of the world. "Xe'dann and Caim are almost entirely sworn to Shadow, in one way or another. Those wild elves on Laustreal don't know the difference—they're as good as the beasts they live amongst. And Vaina... Well, dragons can't be trusted anyway." Naya took another long drink. "Noveth stands as the most divided people of the world, and our dear baron," she rolled her eyes at Mosby, "is the lynchpin to our goals."

"Remind me why we don't just kill him," Mosby said, flipping over the empty crate to dump out a cloud of dust and a few broken talismans. "The way he's going about this war with the Guild, he's going to draw much more ire from the throne than we would if we just cut his throat and be done with it." The dwarf smiled and pointed to one of the golems. "Put one of your boys here on his seat—who's gon' know the difference?"

Naya answered the dwarf's jest with a leveled stare as she downed the rest of her wine. "Amusing," she said flatly. "We need the Cafferys. The queen would never upset balance in Vale when she is secretly trying to prevent a war on Noveth as well as start one on Caim. She has too much to lose, and so do we." She motioned to their surroundings. "How many years have we spent preparing this stronghold, Mosby? These tunnels run throughout the entirety of Vale, if not farther, for all we know. Imagine what the Shrouded could do from an underworld that we controlled."

"Would be like me kin's early days," Mosby said with a smile. "Ye think we could even find Myrethold?" The dwarf turned northward, looking fondly toward the glorious history of the dwarves.

Naya reached into her robes and drew out Ruke's stone once more. It still glowed strongly. "Once I master this," she said, mesmerized by the stone's depths, "I don't think there is a limit on what we can do." Deep inside the green stone, she saw the massive tree-form of Oakus being poisoned by Shadow, consumed by the forces of the Abyss, until he was a glorious natural monstrosity entirely free from the Light.

"Once I find Ruke," Naya said in a trance, "she will tell me how to command all the forces of Elysun." She blinked and turned to Mosby, who watched the golems nervously. The creatures had ceased their work and stood tall, their glowing green eyes fixed on an unseen enemy.

Naya lowered the stone and the golems returned to their work.

"Then, Mosby, we can kill the baron. But for now, he is our greatest ally. His patronage allows me to continue my work." She motioned to the golems. "The realm of Elysun holds an army of them, and you have seen the incarnate under our command. I have felt Ruke's presence in this stone—the only Purveyor to survive the Unthroning. Her cleverness will be our salvation," she smiled wickedly, "and the Light's damnation."

From deeper within the Oakhold, the fading sound of a crying woman died within the growing darkness.

CHAPTER TWELVE

To the Dragonpeak

The Jathi Plains were relatively peaceful, but much less exotic and exciting than Layla had imagined. The morning sun hid behind an overcast sky, for which the mages were thankful, as there wasn't much shade along the road toward the mountains. There were some farms littered across the plains, but instead of rows of plowed fields, most of them had trellises built to support small fruit trees and grape-bearing vines. A fortified keep could be seen on a distant hill overlooking the farms. Thick forests ran along a wide river to the south.

Layla tried to focus on the farms, watching distant figures go about their morning routines. She envied their simple lives as dread continued to draw her eyes toward the looming mountain in the distance—the awaiting doom of Dragonpeak. There was nothing remarkable about the mountain—she had seen higher ones when traveling across Copera in her youth—but its reputation was greater than any other mountain, aside from maybe Mount Myreth. Her mind wandered back to their meeting with Maze.

"You know the legends of Synderok," Maze had said, while they worked on their third round the day before in The Wresting Tide. "Even if you don't know you've heard it, you've heard it."

"Of course. The dragon." Desmond stifled a yawn as time waned on well into the evening. "My wetnurse probably sang me a few rhymes about it when I was a babe."

Maze touched their nose, giving Desmond a narrowed look. "Every fanciful story we hear as children was born from a truth, small as it may be. Besides, Fainly is no fool—neither of you escaped the Arcania without learning a bit about the dragons on Vaina, yes?"

"Sure," Layla said, hoping to get to the point. Even the memory of that night made her weary, as Maze continually avoided finishing a single thought.

Maze nodded. "Well, most of what you have certainly heard or read about Synderok is the stuff of fancy, I am sure. She is not the queen of all dragons, nor is she a Shadowlord made flesh. She is a dragon—a big, nasty, hateful dragon, but a dragon nonetheless.

"Nearly three hundred years ago, that destructive bitch nearly brought ruin to Jath. She found a home in those accursed mountains—"

"Dragonpeak," Desmond interjected.

"Aptly named," Maze said, raising their drink in a small salute to the mage before tossing the dregs back. "She tried to burn the entire island down, but back then the ogres that stomped around the wilds here put up quite a fight. Those brutes took it upon themselves to bring down the dragon, but it was a Gryphon Lord from Copera that is said to have slain Synderok, if his people's legends can be believed." Maze pointed up. "The songs all say Lord Salzair pierced the dragon's heart in the sky, riding his golden gryphon. Synderok fell dead into her home—Dragonpeak. She was never heard from again. But, do dragons really die?"

For a drawn-out moment, Layla and Desmond stared in silence as Maze picked something out of their fingernail.

"And?" Desmond asked.

"Fire and ash," Maze said, biting their nails now to get whatever it was out. "For nearly twenty years, the volcanoes turned the mountains into a fiery wasteland. Wiped out most of the ogres—thank the Light—and kept any adventurers seeking the dragon's treasure hoard at bay."

"You think the book is there?" Layla asked, swallowing as if it would stay the fear she felt roiling in her stomach. Never would she have expected to have to journey to a dragon's tomb to find a stupid book!

"What are you basing all this on?" Desmond asked, raising a questioning eyebrow. "Certainly this is not just a guess."

"Oh, you know me better than that," Maze said. "You think your queen pays me for guesswork? I have contacts in every bit of land on Aetha, even the ones you won't find on a map. While I don't dare ask about the *Book of Stane* directly—the Disciples have assassins and spies everywhere—we have our own language when it comes to these things.

"Problem is," Maze said with a shrug, "the translation can

sometimes be tricky. But we have a seer in Velcarthe down on Xe'dann named Sauthorn. He's an ancient elf, gets these visions in the feysleep—he's quite the master, been doing it longer than your Fainly has. Anyway, he speaks in more riddles than me—"

Desmond coughed, but kept his face passive.

"—so Sauthorn says that Eyen, the old storm god, stirred him awake from a dream in which he saw the dragon Synderok arise from a pit during the Unthroning—could tell it was Synderok from her cracked red flesh and such, like molten rock. Says one of her claws was wrapped around that book o' yours as if it were a prized treasure." Maze spread their hands, palms up. "And what do dragons do with their gains, children?"

"So," Desmond responded, leaning back in his chair, "we are to stride into a dragon's tomb based on the dream of some Xe'danni elf?"

Maze laughed. "You can do whatever in the Abyss you want, friend. I'm here to deliver the information your queen paid me handsomely for. And let me tell you," Maze leaned forward, looking over to Layla, "she paid very, *very* handsomely. If you doubt my word, or the judgement of your liege, then by all means, I can arrange your swift passage home this very night."

Desmond looked at Layla, and those normally empty, ash-rimmed eyes now held something that stopped Layla's heart—he was afraid. Just like her.

Layla let the memory fade as she watched the black spike on the horizon, feeling just as much dread now as she had yesterday. She turned in her saddle to look into Desmond's eyes; the fear from yesterday was gone, replaced now with determination.

"We could be there before nightfall," Desmond said, urging his own mount to catch up to Layla's. "But it might be better to camp in the hills and proceed in the morning so we don't have to share the mountains with any foul nightbeasts."

"How could she not tell us?" Layla asked, desperation and fear in her voice. It was all she could do not to openly cry as the situation continued to overwhelm her.

"The queen?" Desmond asked, eyes forward. "She did not know. That is why she sent us. This is why we came."

"To storm a dragon's lair?!" Layla took a deep breath to calm herself. "She had to have known that the book was not in Caraby, that we would be put into some kind of danger. A warning would have been nice."

"When was the last time we were *not* put into danger on one of the queen's errands?" Desmond asked, eyeing her with a tilt of his head. "I seem to remember a certain elven mage setting fire to an army of troglodytes along the Wane Coast."

Layla forced a small smile. "Yes, and we knew exactly what we were getting into. When the king laid out his plan, he never mentioned anything other than following up the lead in Caraby."

"Well, we could take Maze's advice and return to the queen empty-handed to see how that goes. Me? I'd rather brave a dead dragon's lair than face that fate."

Layla looked back at Dragonpeak. "It's never easy, is it?"

"If it were," Desmond asked the road ahead, "would it be worth doing?"

Even though they traveled on in silence, neither of them heard the screech of a harpy as it descended upon Dragonpeak.

Near the foothills of Dragonpeak was the entrance of a cave, high on a steep cliff and hidden by overgrowth. Inside that cave was a tunnel that wound down into the bowels of the mountain where lava once flowed. Following that twisting passage led to many chambers; one such chamber was a dark alcove adorned with rune markings that looked like sharp, flowing scripture of a long-forgotten language.

Those rune markings began to glow with a dim orange light, tracing each character like a quick-burning wick. The alcove was alight with long-dead magic, now reawakened. Soon, an archway formed from the scripture, and within that archway the stone turned into a shimmering surface like rippling water.

Two shadowy shapes formed in that mystical doorway, and out stepped a slender woman with a shaved head. Swirling tattoos adorned her scalp, cascading down to trace the edges of her sharp facial features. The woman deposited a whimpering elf that looked older than the room they entered.

"This better be it," the woman spat, surveying the glowing arcane runes. "If you've led us astray, my associates have strict orders to slash the throats of your sons and daughters."

"I swear," the old elf groaned in a strong Xe'danni accent. "I have been here before, and my visions have yet to lead me astray."

"Which way to the dragon's lair, seer?" The woman stepped into the winding tunnel, looking down either way. She flourished her hand and a purple orb of light appeared to throw back the darkness, casting shadows across her pale flesh.

"Please," the old elf begged in between wracking coughs. "Give me a moment, Disciple. You awoke me from the feysleep and my strength does not return as quickly as it did when I was younger." He tried to rise to his feet and failed.

"Which way?" the woman demanded again, her deadly tone unchanging.

The elf managed to point a finger down the deeper path.

"Very well." She motioned quickly with her hands and ethereal black spikes shot up from the ground around the elf, twisting to become barbed hooks of arcane energy that converged on him.

"No," the elf managed, reaching up desperately toward the woman. "My visions—you'll need them here—"

She spread her fingers wide, releasing the Shadow incantation, and the hooks were pulled violently back into the earth, taking large pieces of the old elf's leathery flesh with them.

"Stane thanks you for your service, elf," the Disciple said as she made her way down the tunnel toward her unholy destiny. "But he is all I need now."

The old elven seer gurgled and died slowly as his blood ran freely through the cracks in the ground toward the slumbering flames beneath Dragonpeak.

Somewhere deep underground, Synderok's slumber became restless.

That night, Desmond lay awake in their sheltered camp. They had found a remote cave with only a single discernable entrance. The two mages worked into the evening to ward that entrance, giving them both the peace of mind needed to get the rest their bodies certainly required for what remained of their journey.

After a bit more physical exertion—more so on the part of Layla, who was relentless in her desires of the flesh—the elven mage was deep in sleep while Desmond watched the dying embers of their campfire. His thoughts were darkening as well.

Turning to his companion, he made sure she was well asleep before he reached into his discarded robes, finding the secret pocket sewn inside.

The notebook he drew out was blacker than the night sky outside. He opened it to a marked page and began whispering the incantation. Dark wind blew inside the cave, and the fire was given new life, but it gave off no heat.

Layla sat up limply, her eyes open but her pupils lolled back in her head as she still slumbered. "Yes, my dear Desmond," she said in a slurred voice.

"You need me," Desmond said, looking up from his book.

"I need you, Desmond."

"You crave me more than you crave anything else in this world."

"I crave you more than anything, sweet Desmond."

"You do not remember ever being repulsed by me," Desmond said, emotion lining his normally graven face. "You regret ever rejecting me."

"I would never reject you, my Desmond," Layla said, her voice a distant trance. Her head lolled to one side as her dreams became disturbed.

Satisfied, Desmond reached over and cradled her beautiful head, guiding it back down to the rolled-up pack she had used for her pillow.

He gently pushed her hair out of her face, a cruel and loving smile touching his Shadow-tinged lips.

Hoping the spell would hold for the rest of the journey, Desmond lay down next to his unknowing lover. Sleep came to him as he returned to the dark thoughts of a past when Layla and her spoiled friends in the Arcania used to mock him. None of them understood his brilliance or the vast knowledge he could memorize perfectly to the smallest of details.

He was born to be worshiped, not reviled. Until they learned, he would be happy to teach them all, just like he was teaching Layla.

Desmond's dreams were pleasantly wicked.

CHAPTER THIRTEEN

The Demon's Name

Avrim looked over his shoulder as they rode from Rathen, their escape harried by harpies and orcs that pursued any survivors looking to escape the storm's clutches. They rode hard on horses taken in the chaos of the siege. Avrim led the way, pushing his mount harder, guiding the way to Rathaway Priory that he prayed was not yet under the storm. Deina followed close behind, struggling to keep in check a horse that was almost two times too big for her, made all the more difficult by the flailing Shadow-taken boy she shared a saddle with. Melaine covered their rear, twisting in her saddle to fire arrows at their pursuers as best she could.

"How much farther?" Melaine shouted as one of her arrows struck a harpy out of the sky. "My quiver is near empty!" The winged succubus fell in a rolling heap into the forest alongside the wide road known as the Rathaway.

"An' this saddle is near empty as well!" Deina cried as she steadied herself against another of Percy's thrashings.

"Let me fall!" Percy's demonic voice taunted. "I will serve as a mighty feast for your pursuers, mortals! This boy's meager life will buy your valiant escape. Blood must be shed to stay this storm, brave warriors! Do not let it be your own!" He laughed wickedly.

Avrim knew the trick well. If Percy were killed, the demon's spirit that possessed him would be passed on to any that shed the boy's blood with intended malice. He kicked his mount harder, trying not to think of the terrible havoc Ithakan could cause in the body of a harpy or orc, or any other Shadowfiend that pursued them for that matter.

"Just ahead," Avrim called back. But even as the hopeful sight of the priory's walls came into view, the priest's heart sank deeply. The storm he hoped to outrun was now hanging over the priory and its surroundings, with no end in sight. *Corvanna*, Avrim thought. *She will darken the whole world if she is not stopped.* He heard Percy—*Ithakan*—

cackle again then, and he silently wondered what the Shadowlord's role in Corvanna's plans was.

"Riders from Rathen!" a distant voice shouted from beyond the priory's walls. "To arms! The wretched succubi travel with them!"

Almost immediately after the call, Avrim could hear the loud twang of several crossbows. Fortunately, the quarrels were meant for the harpies, and from the scream and the sound of a body crashing violently into the underbrush, they had found their mark.

"We ride with the Light!" Avrim shouted as loud as he could, beseeching as much of the holy power as he could under the Shadow-spawned clouds. His voice rang out with a thunderous echo.

"Now that's a useful trick," Melaine said, unleashing her final arrow. She shouldered her bow and returned both her hands to the reins as they wheeled about toward the gates.

As the party slowed, they heard the distant hooves of the orcs riding stolen mounts from the city. The untrained riders were far enough in the distance to not be an immediate threat, but the gates to the priory were not opening.

Deina dismounted, roughly depositing Percy to the ground. As the boy tried to claw his way away from the bastion of the Light, Deina planted her sizable buttocks on the boy's head as she unshouldered her bag to produce a coil of rope.

"Be still, demon," the dwarf commanded gruffly. She went to work binding the boy's wrists and feet so he could not get away, which proved difficult with his bleeding stump where she had cut off his hand.

"I vill kush jor soul en da Aviss," Ithakan tried to say through Percy's smashed mouth, but the threat was entirely lost.

Melaine dismounted as well, drawing two curved short swords in place of her bow. The blades were from Suthek, barbarian-forged and designed more for hacking than finesse. However, Melaine spun them delicately in her large hands, watching for any dangers. But no harpies could be seen or heard.

Avrim slid off his own horse and banged on the gates. "Father Josaiah! Sister Rashene! It is I, Avrim Kaust, from the Temple of Dawn in Sathford! We seek sanctuary! Please!" His fist punctuated each statement with a series of knocks that shook the heavy gates.

At the sounds of wood sliding against wood beyond the gates, Avrim stopped and took a step back to let them open. The old hinges groaned loudly as a heavy Coperan man shoved one open while the other was pushed by a burly dwarf whose face was almost completely hidden by a bushy red beard. Both men were armed with crossbows and watched Avrim's company with wary eyes.

"Brother," said an older Coperan man in priest's robes with swarthy, wrinkled skin. He motioned welcomingly with both hands. "My apologies," Josaiah said, "but there have been attacks. We needed to take precautions."

Sister Rashene appeared behind Josaiah, covering her mouth at the sight—a disheveled Brother of the Light, a frowning dwarf woman sitting on a thrashing boy, and a hulking, armed half-orc woman ready for battle.

"Your blood will run freely through the halls of the Abyss," Ithakan decreed through Percy's twisted mouth. The boy's black eyes flashed wildly between the Coperans and the bearded dwarf. "Behold my chosen warriors come to bleed your filthy flesh husks dry in the name of the Shadowlords!"

Avrim turned from Percy to Josaiah, smiling weakly.

"Ye gon' welcome us in, or what?" Deina spat.

"An incarnate?" Josaiah asked the burning flames of the candles in the glowery. The old priest stared deep into the dancing lights, looking for reason amongst the madness he was hearing. "Are you sure?"

Avrim nodded, taking a drink of wine while trying to let the Light of the candle-filled room wash the Shadow from him. It felt oppressive even here, as the clouds reached farther overhead, not allowing him to escape. "I have never been more sure of anything in my life. When I saw it—Corvanna, she calls herself—everything else started to make sense." Avrim flipped through his luminary, finding the passage. *"The acrid sky shall mark the Shadow's hold on Eyen, where the wind will yield to a dry storm to give the old god's fury form,"* he read. He looked up to Josaiah. "It was hidden amongst our own prayers. I should have known something was not right when I was called—not a single priest of the Light remained in that city, as if they were drawn away." He paused in thought, looking to the older priest. "And you were not called either." It was not a question, but a revelation.

Josaiah looked up into Avrim's eyes nervously. "Ah, yes," the old man began, looking down at his wringing hands to collect himself. "I mean, no, I was not."

"Father?" Avrim closed his luminary and returned it to the strap at his belt.

"It's just…" Josaiah stood up, turning away from Avrim to face the rows of candles. "It's a lot to take in." He turned back to Avrim. "So, you suspect that this incarnate is the one that started the storm? And she manifested Eyen's spirit by restoring the Skythe?"

"Well," Avrim said, "that's why I need to speak with Percy, with your assistance, I hope. The demon possessing him is named Ithakan, and he comes from a keyshard that the boy found in the hinterlands north of Rathen—not a blackshard though. This one is gray, meaning it not only contains Shadow, but perhaps some answers. At least," Avrim rubbed his head, "that is my best guess."

"You are weary," Josaiah said, the nervousness fading from his voice. "Perhaps you should rest. I can tend to the boy and your companions' injuries. Please, take one of the beds upstairs, Avrim."

The door creaked open then, revealing Deina's flushed face. She nearly spilled her sloshing wine as she nodded to Josaiah. "Father." She said to Avrim, "The boy has fallen asleep. Seems whatever be inside 'em don' want any of this Light." She motioned to the candlelight.

Avrim stood up. "There is no time for rest right now, Father. Will you assist me?"

Sighing in defeat, Josaiah nodded, moving to extinguish the candles as Avrim made his way out into the priory's main hall. Deina returned to converse with the red-haired dwarf that looked old enough to be her father. Melaine reclined on a pew that faced the priory's nave, also partaking of wine with the two dwarves. Deina laughed heartily at something the dwarf said to her, and Avrim felt a small reprieve from his inner struggles.

"Why don't you both get some rest," Avrim said to his companions. "I must speak with Percy, and it is probably better if there were less of an audience." He reached out a hand to Melaine. "I will need the stone."

Melaine arose, digging the graystone out of the pack at her side. She thrust it into Avrim's hand, but did not release it. "Be careful, Brother."

Avrim nodded, and the half-orc loosened her grip on it.

"Where ye goin'?" the red-bearded dwarf asked as Deina appeared next to Melaine and put her arm around the half-orc's waist to lead her toward the stairs.

"Beauty sleep calls," Deina said to the other dwarf, raising him a toast over her shoulder before she took another drink.

As he made his own way to the other stairs leading into the crypts, Avrim heard his friend whisper to Melaine, "But I ain't too tired for you." Deina snorted again as she elbowed Melaine's thigh, and as the two ascended the stairs, Avrim thought he saw the half-orc almost crack a smile in the faint candlelight.

Sighing, Avrim found a moment of calm before descending into the awaiting darkness below the priory where the demon rested.

Bennik awoke to blinding pain as he was violently deposited onto the broken steps. He let out a cry as he tried to shift his leg, which felt broken. Favoring his other leg, he managed to sit up and observe his surroundings. As his vision returned, he saw that he had been brought to a ruined world.

The sky overhead was a sickening shade of green and the air itself tasted of dried bones and acrid blood. Wind did not cool his face, and he felt almost no moisture in those arid ruins.

Fighting the pain in his shoulders where the harpy's claws had dug deep, he turned his head to survey the wreckage around him. Hunched figures moved about the city, between the husks of some buildings that had been burned and over the ruins of others that had been completely demolished. They were big figures with heavy jaws and massive arms that seemed to reach their knees.

Orcs, he thought, remembering those that he had slain in the Westerra invasions, or those that he had seen as a child, strung up in Kulthair's Keep on the western edges of Eastlund. They were the first monsters Bennik had ever seen. "Born into Shadow," his father had always said, "orcs don't think like people do. They just hate everything—they are driven by it. The Shadow consumes them and makes them live only for cruelty."

Instinctively, Bennik pushed himself back, hoping none of the orcs had already seen him. But as his hand reached for something to hold onto, he felt something move. He turned to see a halfling in piecemeal armor with a crude winged form drawn with ash on their chestpiece.

Kasper's eyes were filled with pity and fear, but he held his spear firmly pointed at Bennik. "The duchess will see you now."

Confused, Bennik could only stare at the halfling, not even having the words to question where he was or why he was here.

"Empress! You fool!" The booming voice came from within the dark manor. "I am no mere duchess!"

"I am sorry, Your Highness," Kasper stammered, turning to bow to the unseen voice in the manor. "Empress! Of course! All hail Empress Corvanna!"

"You have ruined the moment, Kasper," the echoing voice from beyond roared.

There was the sound of heavy cloth being whipped, and then several sword-like blades burst through the manor's walls, driving through the halfling and sending the man flailing to the ground. Bennik cringed and shielded his face from the splash of blood. When he opened his eyes, he saw the grisly display of the halfling guard impaled upon shining blue feathers the size of Jathi sabers.

"Bring the father in," the voice called.

The rustle of feathers finally alerted Bennik to Skraw's presence—the harpy that had abducted him—on the roof above. She leapt down and gently shoved her claws under Bennik's arms to drag him inside. He was surprised by the harpy's strength, but not nearly as surprised as when he saw what occupied the main hall of that manor.

As his vision adjusted to the darkness inside the stuffy building, Bennik gasped at the sight of a giant harpy, nearly four times the size of Skraw. It had shimmering blue feathers on its wings that wrapped defensively around its body. Its forehead sloped into the shape of a beak that shadowed its wicked bird-like eyes. As terrible as the beast was, Bennik could not deny the grandeur of it—even amongst the bodies of dead naked men that littered the floor around its great clawed feet.

"As you can see," the empress began when Skraw deposited Bennik on the stained entryway rug, "men tend to disappoint me. There was a time when men were eager to please me." She unfurled a giant wing and used its feathers to caress the curves of Skraw's body. The harpy smiled mischievously at Bennik.

Corvanna continued, "Before I was called to a higher purpose, men pleased me eagerly and thoroughly, to their dying breaths." She looked at Bennik with those dark eagle eyes. "But now—well, let's just say I have much less patience. So do keep that in mind when the opportunity to displease me arises."

Bennik swallowed, feeling like he was about to lose consciousness again.

Corvanna spread both wings wide now as she leaned toward Bennik. "Now. Tell me about your daughter, little man."

Soon after, if there were any winds blowing over Rathen, Bennik's agonized screams would have been carried far and wide across northern Vale.

Josaiah finished lighting the candles around the bed that Percy was bound to, the boy still sleeping peacefully, safe in the Light. Avrim sat near the head of the bed clutching the graystone as if it were an egg that might fall and crack. His eyes followed its rough contours as he wondered about its origins and intended purpose—he prayed it held the answers he needed.

Lifting up his oversized luminary, Josaiah gave Avrim a nod. "The priory's fighting Brothers and Sisters watch the gates with crossbows, Avrim. We should not be disturbed. Are you ready?"

Avrim nodded firmly, leaning forward in his chair to hold the stone above Percy's head. Sweat dotted the priest's brow as he licked his dry lips, casting a glance back at Josaiah. "Once you start, do not stop, Father. I will draw him out, whatever it takes. Just do not stop."

The older priest grasped the jeweled Brightstar that hung around his neck and pulled it up to his forehead, whispering a silent prayer with closed eyes before he began reading from the book. "Light of mercy, Light of justice, do stay the Shadow as we gather in your radiance…"

Josaiah's voice droned on melodically as Avrim focused on the graystone, preparing his own words. His lips trembled and the hand that held the stone above Percy's head wavered slightly, but he found his strength as Josaiah's prayers enveloped him. The Light was certainly present here, despite the storm's best effort to hide it from the world below. That thought gave Avrim a sudden burst of conviction.

"Ithakan!" Avrim nearly frightened himself out of his chair as his voice echoed throughout the crypts. "Shadowlord of Deception and Defiler of Youth! I name you!"

Percy let out a howl of pain as his back arched, his waist rising as if a rope around his torso pulled him against the bindings on his arms and legs. "Noooo! Too bright!" Demonic cries came from the boy's mouth.

Avrim cast a panicked look at Josaiah, but the man held his nerve and did not falter in his prayer, despite his wide and terrified eyes.

"Kill me!" Percy begged with Ithakan's words, looking for any escape from the searing pain of the Light. "Name your price, mortal! Aaaahhh!" Wide black eyes pleaded with Avrim. "You dare name me, now name your price!"

Avrim felt something pushing against the stone, repelling it from the boy's head. The priest stood up and applied his other hand to keep it in place. At that point, an unfamiliar voice pierced through his mind, drawing his eyes from Percy to the graystone.

"It's working, priest," came a mysterious voice. "I can feel him opening the way! Touch its flesh! Do not falter! Ithakan will try to deceive you!"

Avrim looked around the room, but it was just him, the boy, and Josaiah, who continued reading from his luminary, perpetually flooding the room with the Light so no Shadow could survive.

Percy's screams became so bestial that Avrim was afraid the boy would not survive, but he heeded those words in his head and did not falter. He pushed with all his might, whispering his own prayers to the Light, forcing the graystone to Percy's head where the answers might lie.

"I can bring you things the Light cannot," Ithakan begged, trying every tactic to avoid returning to his prison. "You will regret banishing me, priest. I never forget!"

Avrim gritted his teeth and channeled all of his faith and mortal strength. Light exploded from his hands as he forced the graystone onto Percy's brow, where it sizzled and burned the flesh.

"AAAAAAAGGGGHHHH!!!" Ithakan screamed.

"There!" The voice in Avrim's head became more distant as Percy's screams pierced both priests' ears. "The fool is showing me the way…"

Avrim clutched his ears against Percy's screams, falling to the floor as all his strength left him. He heard Josaiah collapse too, and the graystone clattered to the stone floor next to Avrim. Then, the screaming ceased.

There was a long moment of silence that followed before Avrim let himself uncover his ears. He heard Percy's heavy breathing, which sounded unnatural. His heart sank as he began to suspect that the exorcism did not work.

"It's been a while since I've been this young," Percy said in a voice that was certainly not Ithakan's.

Avrim struggled to his feet, standing over a familiar body on the bed that regarded him with much different eyes.

"You did it." Percy smiled weakly, a searing scar on his forehead. "You will want to do whatever it is the church does with those things," he said, nodding to the stone on the floor—which had turned from gray to pitch black. It was now a blackshard, containing only a Shadowlord.

Avrim looked from the blackshard to Percy. *Then what are you?* he asked himself.

"I'm an old dead woman," Percy said, as if in response. "My name is Kartha. And I may have some answers for you." Percy's eyes closed. "But first, I need some sleep. Get that shard away from me before you let yourselves out."

Avrim looked at Josaiah, but neither priest had any words left.

CHAPTER FOURTEEN

Thieves in the Night

There were several roads leading out of Blakehurst. The eastern road was rarely used by Vale travelers, as it led directly into Lohkrest Woods by way of unguarded divergent paths riddled with lurking monsters that were incessantly drawn to the mystical sprawling forest. The northern road served mostly as a direct path to the Bracing River, where it curved and led travelers on the long trek to Sathford and the Valeway. A southern road followed the edges of Lohkrest all the way down to distant Hambury, with nothing but wilderness and the occasional lonely farm along the way.

Anika's company set out from Blakehurst on the well-traveled westward road that wrapped around Buckley Woods and the Oak Hills, leading them toward Oakworth.

"I have a cousin there," Ransil assured Anika before they began their journey. "She's not as good a cook as me, but she should be able to get us comfortable enough accommodations." He looked into the setting sun. "We'll have to make camp tonight, but if we cover a bit of ground first, we should be there by midday tomorrow."

Anika looked over her shoulder now as she kept pace with Matty's long strides, barely seeing the roof of her home over the trees. She turned away from the place before the growing distance stole the sight of it from her, giving the knife at her side a reassuring pat. *I will find you, Father.* She hefted her heavy pack, the whitewood bow that had been Farrah's resting on her shoulder along with a quiver on her hip.

The party traveled in relative silence while the last rays of sunlight fell behind the trees of Buckley Woods in the distance. None of them had mounts, as most of the horses in Blakehurst were either slaughtered by the goblins or had fled in terror during the fighting. Ransil traveled a good distance behind his companions, partly because his short legs were easily outpaced, but also because he insisted on watching their rear while Robin scouted ahead. The halfling was not fully convinced that the goblin menace had been fully routed by the reeve's patrols.

Anika walked in stride with Matty, finding his company a welcome distraction to her dark thoughts. Although they did not spend the time conversing, she was able to occasionally steal a glance of the handsome face framed by that leather helm. Fawning over the boy— *Oh, but he is certainly a man now*, she thought—gave Anika something familiar and simple to dwell on, and she allowed herself the pleasure rather than fretting about the stone, Farrah's dying words, her father...any of it.

Matty himself strode like a guard pacing the streets of a great city, tall, proud, and commanding. The reeve's armor suited him, and he had taken his charge quite seriously. He carried a small round shield that bore the green, yellow, and brown colors of old House Warner, whose seat used to reside on the borders of Blakehurst before it was ruined in the Nether War. Anika thought he looked like a wandering knight straight out of an Eastlund legend, undertaking noble quests before pledging himself to a great lord in a sprawling castle. When he turned and gave Anika the slightest of smiles, it was as if nothing else mattered at the moment.

But it was just a moment.

Anika turned away awkwardly, realizing she had been staring at Matty. She fixed her eyes on Gage in the distance, scouting with Robin. They still had barely spoken since everything had happened, but her brother had shown her no anger or hurt. He merely kept to himself, which somehow bothered Anika more. She wanted to go to him, to ask him how he was coping, but it felt selfish somehow. Who was she to tell her brother how to deal with losing his last remaining parent? She wasn't even sure how she should cope with it.

Anika had lost so many parents, she should be an expert by now. But that thought alone nearly drove her to her knees to weep on the road.

She looked at Matty again, who glanced back at her with a softer smile than before, sadness in his eyes. *He has lost more than me*, Anika thought. She instinctively reached a hand out to him and he took hold of it. The silence they shared then was more comforting than anything Anika could think to say to Gage.

Robin's eyes darted from tree to tree as if he had seen something, his hand slowly and silently drawing his dagger. Gage tried to find what the half-elf saw, but the trees ahead were dark and motionless for him.

"What is it?" Gage whispered, stepping silently over to Robin as the half-elf began to creep off the road. "Should I ready the others?" He nocked an arrow to his bow as silently as he could.

Robin held up a hand to silence Gage, but after the briefest moment the half-elf relaxed and straightened, letting the dagger fall back into its sheath. "I thought I saw something—two shapes in the trees. But they're gone, whatever they were." He gave Gage a grin. "Keep that bow ready just in case."

Gage nodded, relaxing the string on his bow but keeping the arrow nocked. Aside from the full quiver on his back, he traveled light, much like Robin. Neither of them had much to bring from Blakehurst, and Robin assured him they would find anything they needed for the road in Oakworth.

"I have plenty of queens set aside," Robin had said proudly before they departed Blakehurst. "And you better believe I wasn't hiding them in Ransil's kitchen." He had buried his wealth in the spot that he and Gage had named their own. When Robin had dug it up to show him, Gage no longer held any doubt that he loved the half-elf completely. "Oakworth is quite a place," Robin had said with a smile. "It should prepare you for Andelor."

As they continued on the road now, Gage spared a quick look over his shoulder to see Anika walking close to Matty and holding his hand. He smiled warmly, feeling a coldness toward his sister melt away. His worry for her had driven him away from her, and he knew that. But there was something inside of him that kept trying to reject her—something he couldn't explain or make sense of.

It has to be that damned stone, he thought bitterly, thinking back to that morning of her birthday when she had woken him before the sun—before even their father had stirred from his sleep—and put thoughts of that stone in his mind. *How had she known about it? Why did she want it?* He had thought about confronting her regarding these questions, but it was almost like he knew she would not have any answers—as if it wasn't even her.

That thought sent a dark dagger into Gage's stomach. *What if it wasn't her? What if it was that stone? Did it want to get away from Elza? Did it want Elza to—*

"Gage?"

Shaking the thoughts away, Gage looked at Robin, who was several strides ahead of him. It was then that he noticed he had stopped walking, his jaw dropped and his eyes widened with fear.

"Did you see something?" Robin asked, his own eyes darting into the growing darkness around them.

"Are you all right?"

Gage turned around to see Anika, concern and empathy in her eyes. His sister—not a vision or a trick—stepped toward him with genuine concern.

He smiled at her. "I'm fine, Anika."

She smiled, the glow of the day's sunlight glimmering from a tear in her eye.

"Let's camp before it gets too dark," Ransil announced as he caught up to his companions. "We'll find a place amongst the trees."

Nearby, in Buckley Woods, a dark figure smiled from the shadows, fading back into the deadly trees.

Ransil pulled the long spoon from his pack and stirred the boiling broth, leaning his bulbous nose over the pot to take a deep whiff of the aroma. "Gonna need some herbs. Spices only do so much."

Matty looked up from rubbing his sword with an oilcloth. "I'm sure we will all take what we can get, Ransil. This ain't exactly The Early Mule." He motioned to the trees that surrounded their clearing.

Anika and Gage both looked up from skinning and butchering the two rabbits they had managed to track. Anika smiled. "A little bit of meat will be enough for me." She brought the meat over to Ransil's boiling pot hanging over the roaring campfire. "A stew's a stew," she said as she dropped the meat into the bubbling spiced wine that already cooked the onions and carrots.

"Nonsense," Ransil said, stirring the meat in. "Robin, keep an eye out with Matty." The halfling pulled out a carving knife and motioned toward the woods. "I'll see if I can't dig up a few mushrooms, maybe a few herbs—I think there might be some nettle or elderberries."

"You think that wise?" Robin asked with a worried look. "Remember the figures I saw?"

Ransil stepped into the trees, saying over his shoulder, "If anything is lurking about, they'll be drawn to the fire. I trust you and Matty to keep a tight watch, and I'll be near enough to—" A hand over his mouth cut him off as strong and surprisingly silent hands pulled him into the thicket. Ransil's struggles were easily restrained by the powerful figure that was much larger than him.

He was carried—still, ever so silently—into another clearing, but with no firelight, he could not make out all of his surroundings. His breath was taken out of him as he was pushed up against a tree. As his vision began to adjust to the darkness, he saw a dark face leaning into his own, and as the hand was removed from his mouth, he felt that looming face's lips embrace his own forcefully.

Finally Ransil was able to lash out, using his hands to grasp the figure's shoulders, push them away, and slam his head into their face. A grunt of pain from the figure told Ransil that he had barely dazed the assailant, despite the sharp pain on the top of his own head.

He took a deep breath to cry out, but the hand returned over his mouth.

"Is that any way to greet an old lover?" a familiar voice asked.

"Enough games, Grip," a different, yet also familiar voice from below said. "Let him down."

Ransil's vision finally settled on a bloodied face from his past, a beautiful face that caused him nothing but pain and heartbreak. He stopped struggling and narrowed his eyes on the dark elf, waiting for her to grow tired of her little show.

Grip smiled, licking the blood from her lips. Her nose was clearly broken, but it did little to spoil her beauty. "I think we need to have a little chat, just the three of us." She loosened her gloved hand from Ransil's mouth. "What do you say?" She lowered her hand.

Ransil held her gaze firmly and asked in a tight whisper, "What do you want?"

Grip leaned in, smiling wickedly and seductively biting her lower lip. "What if I said you, Ransil?" Her lips were only a hair away from his. "Would you like that?"

"No," Ransil hissed, not moving.

As Grip made to lean closer, the distinct sound of a blade being drawn broke the tense silence.

"The man said no," Brood said threateningly. "I know ye don' like to hear no, Grip, but I won't stand fer this type a' business. Put me cousin down."

Grip turned menacingly toward the other halfling. "You've never been as fun as this one, Brood." She eventually lowered Ransil so his feet touched the ground. Grip was on one knee when she let him go, returning her eyes to Ransil. "But then again, no one has ever measured up to Ransil Osbury." She let out a timid breath.

Ransil turned coldly away from Grip to regard his cousin. "What are you doing here, Rosh? Has Knife already heard about what happened in Blakehurst?"

Brood was taken aback by that, but shook his head. "No, we're here for your boy. The half-elf. We need him for a job."

"What job?" Ransil demanded.

"The kind of job you don't say no to," Grip said. "Not even you, Ruse."

"Don't call me that," Ransil said, giving the elf a flat stare. "Ruse is dead. And Robin doesn't answer to Knife anymore; the Guild spat him out."

"But will he answer to the queen?" Brood asked.

Ransil gave him a long, silent look. "I guess we'll see." He held out his hand and Brood gave him the carving knife he had dropped during the scuffle. "Make yourselves useful and find me some mushrooms and herbs, or you're not invited to dinner." He gave Grip the faintest of smiles as he spun his knife. "You're still a terrible kisser, Your Highness."

Grip ran a gloved finger over her smiling, bloody lips in response.

Anika drank the last of her stew—which turned out to be quite remarkable—as the newcomers finished their cryptic tale. They spoke as if in a second language, using code words that only Ransil and Robin seemed to understand. But Anika caught enough to learn that something important was held below the baron's keep in Oakworth, only Robin knew how to find it, and they desperately needed it.

Matty scowled during the entire conversation, his newfound position giving him a sense of justice and duty that made cavorting with criminals more than uncomfortable.

"What is it?" Gage asked, looking at the halfling named Brood.

"That's none of your affair, boy."

"Yes it is," Robin said, standing and putting a hand on Gage's shoulder. Gage reached up and grabbed his hand.

Brood scoffed. "We ain't invitin' your lover, Robin. We just need you."

"He's certainly not going alone," Ransil interjected. "This is your job—your responsibility. I won't see you foist it upon him."

"Easy," the dark-skinned elf said, raising her gloved hands defensively. "Look, we know what your company is about."

Anika straightened, instinctively reaching for her pouch where the shard was.

"Honestly," Grip continued, "we don't care. We have a job, and that is all that matters to us at the moment. However, it seems you are all trusting Ransil here on a fleeting hope that Knife will even agree to see him in Andelor. The Guild is not known to be welcoming to anyone looking to them for help."

Ransil glared at Grip as the rest of the company turned to him.

"What does she mean, Ransil?" Anika felt a sense of panic rising. "You said we were going to the Arcania…"

Ransil didn't look at her, his eyes cast downward in shame. "We were never going to the Arcania. Your father meant to, knowing full well that an Oather would most likely kill him before hearing his tale—but he would never want you to go there." He sighed. "I had hoped to meet with Knife. She has a direct line to the queen, who would be more helpful to our cause than Fainly Lopke." He looked at Grip. "But she's right. It is a gambit."

"We can help ye, coz," Brood said. "If you help us—help Robin in this, we can get you to Knife. Grip's word carries weight with her."

Grip winked at Ransil.

"I'll go with him," Ransil said firmly. "Both of you will stay out of it. Caffery will be looking for any reason to get his hands on notable Guild members. Robin will find your piece and I will help him get it back to you." He looked at Brood. "And in return, you will accompany us to Andelor on your return journey so that we may meet with Knife."

"Seems fair," said Brood, tossing back the rest of his stew. "This be crackin', coz. Ye haven' lost yer touch."

"I'll take first watch," Matty said, eager to be done with all this talk of stealing and skulking around a baron's keep.

"Yeah, let's try to get some sleep," Ransil said. "I'll join Matty. Robin, you take next watch with Brood. We should make for Oakworth at first light."

Anika found a place to lay down where she could see Matty.

"Oh, he's a handsome one," a husky voice said. Anika didn't even see the dark elf lay down near her, silent as a snake.

"Does he know you are the Child of Light?"

Anika's breath caught as she fixed her terrified eyes on Grip.

The elf laid a finger over her bloodied lips. "Your secret is safe with me, child. But trust me, if you want to unbuckle his sword belt, let him know sooner rather than later." She winked and then closed her eyes.

Unable to speak, Anika thought about Farrah's final words to her, looking for any possible way that the truth she knew in her heart was somehow a deceit.

As Anika watched the fire burn down to embers, she thought of all the tales she had heard of the Child of Light—a holy destiny laid out before her to find and slay the Child of Shadow. It was thankfully an exhausting thought, and she quickly fell into a dreadful sleep.

CHAPTER FIFTEEN

Oaths and Offerings

As morning broke over Oakworth, Dame Kasia Strallow made her way across the keep's courtyard, regarding the dead thieves that adorned the gallows to either side of her path. She found their presence reassuring—it seemed Baron Caffery was a just man who enforced his laws openly here, demanding respect and giving no quarter.

That should make her work that much easier. She didn't mean to approach Blakehurst without some sort of a company, the keep's guards would serve her well. Most high lords were eager to cooperate with the Arcania in such requests, but some were paranoid when it came to their personal militia. She suspected Baron Caffery might be of the latter sort, but by appealing to his sense of justice she suspected he would bend easily enough.

The guards directed Kasia toward the baron's audience chamber beyond the great doors in the main hall. She could hear the baron's voice through those doors as he engaged in a heated debate. The two guards flanking the doors looked at her nervously, as if unsure if they should stop her. Both of them looked at her unmistakable armor and froze in place as she strode toward them. Not wanting to drag the situation out unnecessarily, Kasia chose not to revel in the discomfort her position inspired, as much as she enjoyed it.

"I am sure the baron would be quite displeased if he heard the Lady Commander of the Oathers was accosted at his doors on official business from the Arcania—an institution that the baron himself is an accredited member of."

The larger guard, a young woman with a strong grip on her halberd, made to open the great doors. The other guard quickly followed, bowing his head in acknowledgement.

The baron's voice carried clearly now into the main hall. "—and I will not tolerate such blatant conspiring with the known brigands and knaves of the Guild in my own holdings!"

Baron Alburn Caffery was standing, red-faced and spitting as he thrust a large finger down at what looked like a child kneeling before him.

"Yes, m'lord," the figure said with an older woman's voice. It was a halfling commoner, wearing a soiled apron and a white kerchief over her graying hair. "I meant nothin' by givin' them a meal and a—"

The halfling turned slightly to regard Kasia Strallow striding in, losing her words as her eyes widened in horror. Kasia smiled in delightful recognition.

The baron recognized the Oather with a knowing look and a slight nod as he continued his business. "Consorting with such criminals is punishable by death." His furious eyes challenged the halfling woman to defy him. "You have served my house, fed me, fed my wife, fed my children! This is betrayal—betrayal, I say! Those thieves tried to openly rob me in this very room, and then you give them shelter?! Give them food from my markets?!" He stepped down the dais now, towering over the halfling. "Did you conspire with them? Did you share with them the details of my keep? Are you aligned with the Guild?!"

"No!" the halfling sobbed, trying to keep control of her voice as she lied. "Please, m'lord. I am just a cook. Just a halfling trying to raise my two girls. I never wanted any trouble, and I don't know much about no Guild. Have mercy, m'lord!" She bowed her head, wringing her hands together in supplication.

Kasia was highly entertained by the display, never thinking she'd see the arrogant Scratch fall so far, but kept her face passive, curious to see how this baron dealt with such affronts in his keep or if he would somehow reveal her identity.

She found a place to stand near the back of the chamber, regarding the Cafferys' aesthetic choices. Large tapestries hung from the high ceilings depicting the wealth of the land around them—lumberjacks felling trees, shepherds tending their flocks, farmers harvesting their yields. It was clear that this was a proud family that cherished their holdings, which Kasia found rather charming. A good escape from the warlike imagery Rathen displayed, or the ancient honors of Andelor. Kasia herself was raised amongst the farms of Westerra and still had fond memories of laboring in the sun.

The baron spun on his heels, motioning to one of the guards that waited on either side of his raised seat on the dais. "Perhaps a few nights in the pens shall give you some time to reflect on the choice of company you keep," Auburn said dismissively, his rage fading. "Lock her up."

"Please!" the woman begged, crawling on her knees toward the baron. "My daughters, please let me see to my daughters! Then you can lock me up as long as you need. Please—"

"Oh! Can I?!" The baron spun back on her, finding his rage again. "How kind of the halfling scullion to allow me to carry out my own decrees!" He kicked his leg out, his polished leather boot smacking the woman in the face. The halfling's head violently whipped back as she was sent sprawling. "Get her out of here!"

Kasia heard an audible gasp from the other side of the chambers. She saw a beautiful woman, dressed like a servant but with more presence than most highborn ladies. The noble features of her face were framed in long red hair, and she clasped a delicate hand over her mouth as a guard dragged the dazed halfling woman off to the pens.

The gasping woman disappeared through a side door in the chambers. Baron Alburn Caffery didn't even notice.

"My apologies, Lady Oather. A nasty bit of business I had to clean up."

Kasia pushed herself off the wall she was leaning on and stepped toward the center of the chamber where business was done. "I have had my own troubles with the Guild, Lord Baron. You seemed to handle it justly."

Auburn seemed to puff up at that.

Oh, this one will be easy, Kasia thought as she gave him an uncharacteristic smile. She was emboldened by the fact that even if he would not be swayed by her flattery, she had information regarding his new prisoner that would certainly be enticing to such an openly defiant enemy of the Guild.

"What brings you so far from Andelor, Lady Commander Strallow?" Alburn asked in a more demanding tone than Kasia cared for.

She began carefully. "My presence is needed in Blakehurst for a quest of the utmost importance to the Archmage. There may be trouble brewing in your eastern borders."

Alburn perked up at the mention of trouble in regard to the Arcania. He was a man that knew well what that would mean, so Kasia kept the details unspoken. But she noted his reaction. "Well, uh," he adjusted himself in his raised seat—*A loftier throne that the queen's*, Kasia thought—and gave the Oather a strained look, "it is good to have the Arcania vigilant. As you can see, I have enough problems here within my own walls."

Yes, you do, Kasia thought, wondering why the Guild had agents here in Oakworth, especially with Knife keeping her spies at work in Caim and Xe'dann. Regardless, she kept her face a mask of duty, waiting for the baron to let something slip in his discomfort.

"I suppose you require some arms to march with you," Alburn said eagerly—*a little too eagerly*—as he motioned to one of his guards. "Blakehurst does not keep much of a militia, beyond the reeve's guards. I can arrange a company to travel with you—I suspect you'll be wanting to leave immediately to reach Blakehurst by dusk."

Kasia regarded him silently, forcing herself not to smile even though the power she now felt over the man was invigorating—it aroused in her the familiar desire to dominate a person with nothing but her gaze.

Alburn averted his eyes during that silence, clearing his throat before looking back to her for a response. The nervous sweat on his high brow made Kasia bite the inside of her lip, drawing blood—it would do for now, but she would need much more of a release later.

"No," Kasia finally said, "I think I will rest here for the day, and leave first thing on the morrow." She gave the baron a condescending smile. "I would like to enjoy the exquisite charm that your town is so well known for, Lord Baron."

Kasia violently rocked the bed in her room on the third floor of The Harvest Breeze, keeping a steady and straight face on the nervous lad below her as he tried to hide the fear, pleasure, and awe that threatened to break him.

He lay perfectly still as Kasia had commanded while she finished what had started in the baron's audience chamber. She thought of that terrified man's face, drenched in sweat—the sweat got thicker and heavier as his fear of her grew. Whatever secrets he hid instilled him with a deathly fear of the Oather, and she held onto the memory of the power it gave her.

"Not yet," Kasia said, her voice betraying no sense of pleasure or concern. She had a task to accomplish, and nothing would stand in her way. "Wait."

Jak's face twisted finally, as if he were about to disappoint his master. Kasia wrapped one of her powerful hands around his throat. "No," she commanded dryly. Sweat sheened her muscled body in the rising morning sun. They had been at it since before dawn, and she knew the boy would not last much longer. But she would finish her task.

Jak let out a choking sound as he struggled for breath, but his body did not give in. Kasia appreciated that, and quickened her gait, ready to finish.

She thought about the baron's face, drenched in sweat, his nervous eyes searching hers for relief. Kasia ran her free hand over her own sweaty body, finding every muscled contour, finally allowing herself to accept the release she had craved since that meeting.

"Now." She released Jak's throat so she could grab the headboard, wrapping her strong thighs around the young boy. He wheezed for breath as he obeyed, his body convulsing, lifted off the bed by Kasia's crushing grip.

As her body recovered from the exertion, she stood up, crossing the room to find a towel to clean herself up. "That was satisfactory," she said to Jak, who rolled over, still struggling for air. "You are much better than your brother." She remembered chopping off Roy's possessed head, which only added to the pleasure that still ached through her body.

"Thank you, Dame Strallow," Jak managed, reaching for his clothes. "I look forward to serving as your new squire."

He may have been Roy's twin, but he somehow looked younger. Kasia didn't mind; they were grown men where it counted, even if they had plump, boyish faces.

Kasia strode to the window, surveying the town below while letting the sun warm her body. "We will stay here for the day. I have a prisoner to chat with in the baron's keep."

"One of the Guild?" Jak asked excitedly. The boy was much too interested in Andelor politics, and was exceptionally intrigued by the baron's war on Knife's cabal.

"It seems," Kasia said. "I suspect our baron is hiding something—something he doesn't want me around to sniff out. If he's locking up his own citizens on wild suspicions, I think my answers lie somewhere in those dungeons."

"Shall I accompany you?" Jak asked.

Kasia shook her head, motioning to her armor in the corner. "You're to clean my armor and prepare it for the morrow. And be prepared on my return in case I need," she looked sternly at him, "further assistance."

He averted his eyes. "Yes, dame."

"For now though," Kasia threw the towel at Jak and presented her glistening body to him, "clean up your mess."

"Vivian, please!" Renay begged. "We cannot leave them to fend for themselves." She held the halfling children, both of them sobbing quietly as if afraid any sound they made might result in angering the highborn lady staring at them. "They cannot be held responsible for their mother's mistakes."

Vivian looked over her shoulder. The door to the dining hall was closed and guarded, and the baron had already left on his morning ride of the Oak Hills. She gave Renay a look of angry surrender. "Fine, but you keep them in the servants' quarters, woman. They are your responsibility—I'll have no part in this."

A tear streamed down Renay's face. "Thank you, my lady. I will take care of it." She hurried toward the door, looking over her shoulder one more time at Vivian, who held a hand to her mouth as she watched the halfling girls weep, calling quietly for their "momma."

"Lady Commander." Scratch's voice sounded weak from the shadows of her cell. "You do me a great honor."

Kasia stood near the bars of the cell, her arms held behind her back. She wore a simple tunic that stretched against her firm body, her broad shoulders draped with a simple white cloak that bore the four crystals of the Arcania on it in threaded silks of blue, green, yellow, and red.

"I believe this was how we met before," Kasia said to the shadows. It took a good amount of willpower not to smile, but she wanted to maintain her composure to take measure of the halfling's mood. Scratch was no single-minded buffoon like the baron. "But your accommodations here seem much better than the dungeons below Merithian, no?"

"Oh, they're pleasant enough now that you're here, my big strong knight," Scratch teased, her old attitude resurfacing. "Why don't you come on in and join me? We won't have the sailors to play with this time, but maybe I can make you smile." The halfling stepped into the faint torchlight, her face bruised and bloodied, showing her age. But her smile also showed that she would be as immune as ever to the Oather's intimidation tactics. "I always said you should smile more."

Kasia kept her mask on. "Dolly, was it? Tell me about the baron's feud with the Guild. Those children of yours don't want to wake up with a stolen keyshard under their pillows."

Scratch's facade fell away, but Dolly still kept her cool, smiling as she said, "Oh, I'm sure the baron's plaything has snatched up my girls. She was always fond of the young ones. I think she lost hers some years back." Her smile faded. "But I suppose you've got me stuck between the Light and the Shadow here. What do you want to know?"

"You were harboring Knife's lackeys here. Why?"

Dolly leaned in close, looking at the jailer that was far enough away not to hear her whisper. "Seems your baron here has some unsavory friends, meddling in Shadow. From what I hear."

"That matters little to me." Kasia kept out of religious matters, unless they pertained to any magical affairs that conflicted with the oaths she upheld. "He can worship who he pleases."

Dolly shook her head. "Not who—what. His war with the Guild has to do with his family's worship of Ruke's stone. Not Oakus, but the old halfling's stone itself. Knife's not much of a friend of mine these days, even if she tries to keep trouble outta my hair. So I don't mind telling you that Knife wants that stone, and has tried sixteen ways short of the Abyss to get her hands on it."

Kasia ground her teeth thinking about the baron hiding this from the Arcania. Ruke's stone was not something that Fainly seemed to care much about—it was a particular keyshard that he believed to essentially be powerless, containing Ruke's meandering and dreadful thoughts on Elysun, the domain of Oakus. The Archmage's outright dismissive attitude toward Ruke always made Kasia suspect that maybe Fainly had been involved with the halfling during her mortal life. She was almost certain he had been alive during that time.

"Kasia." Dolly's voice lost its arrogance. "For old time's sake—

knowing I will tell you all I know regarding the baron and his war with the Guild, please. Keep my brother out of this."

"He is not my concern," Kasia said, her eyes distant, considering her next move given this revelation. "Though if he has been sent by Knife to acquire Ruke's stone, you better hope it is not him that acquires it." Her eyes now fell on Dolly. She knelt so the halfling could see her face clearly.

"Heed my words, Scratch," she whispered. "I will kill any unsworn that has a keyshard and call it justice. It doesn't matter if that person is a friend, lover, or family member. I swore an oath and, live or die, I will uphold it. Whatever it takes." Her brows furrowed slightly, betraying the hint of an emotion. "You may live your pathetic life free from any shackles of responsibility or honor, but there are those of us who take matters seriously. It is hard and can be cruel, but someone has to maintain order in this world. Someone has to punish those who would thrust the land into the chaos your precious Guild profits from."

Kasia watched Dolly's eyes try to hide the fear, hide the powerlessness that she inspired, and she now felt the need to return to The Harvest Breeze once more. She arose, letting the weight of her words press down on Dolly.

But the halfling merely looked up. "May I offer you some advice, Kasia?" In that moment, the fear that Kasia thought she saw in Dolly's eyes looked more like contained rage. "Do be careful meddling with Knife's affairs. I really did enjoy your company in Merithian. We did some great things in that city, before either of us swore our lives away. I would hate to see you suffer."

Kasia turned to leave, eager to be back on her way to Blakehurst. The baron wasn't going anywhere—she could deal with all of this later.

Chapter Sixteen

A Place Without Light

The Archbeacon of the Luminaura was not accustomed to being summoned by the Archmage of the Arcania—the two rarely had to even interact outside of courtly affairs. But this was not a royal summons from the queen. The letter came directly from Fainly Lopke himself, placed in Luriah's own hands by a high mage who made sure she understood the urgency of the summons.

Luriah Vaughn's palanquin now made its way through the crowded trade district, weaving through the morning hawkers and tradespeople trying to make their fortunes in the royal city. Andelor was a sight to behold, even for Luriah, who had been born into its sprawling embrace. The five districts that made up Vale's capital city blossomed from the walls of the Valiant Keep like the petals of a flower, with the queen's tower rising like a wheel's spoke keeping the bustling city turning.

The financial hub of Vale was Andelor's trade district, which resided between the arts district—where the Arcania's towers stood in the shadows of Valiant Keep—and the manor district—where the Lighthold was built amongst the most elegant living quarters for high lords and traveling dignitaries. Most common citizens of Andelor made their meager homes in the tightly packed apartment rows of the trade district, or nestled safely in the utilitarian living quarters in the law district.

Although she made an effort to connect with the commoners of the various districts in Andelor, Luriah was always kept on edge when she had to leave the manor district. She felt anxious around peasants that scampered about chasing coins and carnal pleasures, something Luriah was certainly glad to never have to do. She was born into nobility, the eldest daughter of the previous Archbeacon and rightful heir to the Lighthold. She spent her youth in the luxurious comforts of Andelor's manor district, studying the Light and how it would guide her life, caring for little else and sparing no time for friends or personal affairs. While her every basic need was met, and her life's path had been laid out before her, she did not have to make any hard decisions—there was Light and there was Shadow, and she saw no need to complicate her life beyond those simple facts.

There was a sudden jerk that lurched Luriah's palanquin, nearly spilling her out the door. But with a white-gloved hand, she caught herself on the vessel's frame and kept her seat. She placed her other hand on her chest, bracing the holy star that dangled between the tops of her breasts. The elaborate gown she wore made bending over to peer outside awkward, but she managed to steal a glance at her loyal paladin, Sir Darrance Moore, shoving a burly half-orc man aside. The sandy-colored man shouted a curse at Sir Moore as he struggled to collect the scattered fish carcasses from the cobbled road. The fish had brought a dozen dirty commoners flocking, hoping to sneak one of the things away before the fisherman recovered his haul.

"Sir Moore?" Luriah whispered, keeping her face hidden behind the curtains.

"Bless us, Lightmother!" a shout cried out from the distance. Another. "The Light shine on our dear Archbeacon!"

Darrance looked over his shoulder, the visor of his helm raised to show his handsome, stern face. He had striking blue eyes, and a shock of his sweaty blond hair was plastered across his brow. "Your Luminous, he stepped too close and did not heed our warning. Shall we alert the guards?"

Luriah waved a hand. "No, Sir Moore, let us just make haste." She looked around nervously as more cries took up her name, begging for a wave or a simple greeting. She did not give it, instead closing the curtains and praying to the Light that she did not suffer the same fate of the second Archbeacon—strung up on the city walls during the Fading Rebellion. She shook those thoughts away, reassuring herself that the Shadow had not grown that strong again.

Not yet, she thought. But she also knew that the Light must be ready.

At that moment, she leaned forward and threw back the curtains to her palanquin. She was instantly greeted with a gasp and roaring applause accompanied by piercing whistles. They all praised her, and the Light forgive, Luriah reveled in it.

Let them see, she thought. *Let them see the beauty of the Light*. She knew the time would come soon that they would need her strength and conviction.

They would all need the Light.

Each of the Arcania's four towers were devoted to a different level of study, all surrounding the great Hall of Sorcery where the arcane council convened. The shortest tower was the one adorned with green banners, where most one-term wizards swore their oaths to the Hall of Sorcery before setting back off into the world. These were the "green" wizards who were privy to the simplest incantations but were not allowed to train others in their craft, scribe spells, or otherwise consult. Being called a green wizard was a bit of a slight amongst the more accomplished wizards.

The yellow tower trained wizards in increasingly complex magicks and prepared the more committed students of the Arcania for a life of service. Most who completed their studies as a yellow mage went on to serve as the personal mages for high lords and ladies.

Blue wizards earned their status by enduring all but the most complex lessons that the high mages endured, and most that made it through the blue tower were committed enough to their craft to remain at the Arcania until they reached the elite status of high mage by surviving the red tower's wrath. There were so few high mages at the Arcania that the red tower was in fact only slightly taller than the green tower, but each structure was tall enough to give a sweeping view of not only the arts district within Andelor, but even of the verdant lands surrounding the city.

Luriah stood now at a tall window in the red tower as she waited for the Archmage. She stared over the gabled roofs of the arts district, where scholars, painters, sculptors, and writers added to the complex tapestry that was Vale's intertwined culture. She saw many robed figures walking the cobbled streets below, not shouting, pushing, or rushing around—these were the shapers of the land's history and future moving at a pace she admired.

She was a slow and steady woman, and did not mind waiting for the Archmage to finally appear.

Fainly Lopke stepped through the heavy curtains of the archway that connected the chamber to the tower's entrance. Beyond those curtains, Luriah's stomach turned slightly at the smoky haze of magic that allowed them to step through an arcane dimension and travel nearly fifteen stories up in a single step. It was not a comfortable experience, and she was glad for the Lighthold and its lack of such unnecessary elevation.

It was not that Luriah disliked magic—in fact, she found it fascinating and somewhat exhilarating. But she did not like to depend on it. Magic was so closely aligned with the old gods that it made a wizard's reliance on spells almost a weakness to a devotee of the Light.

"My apologies, Archbeacon Vaughn," Fainly said. His voice was raspy and high-pitched, but carried authority and the weight of decades. "I did not intend to keep you waiting, but it seems there has been trouble reported in Rathen."

Luriah did her best to look surprised and genuinely concerned. "Oh, I do hope the storm has not worsened—it is already unnatural enough."

"I'm afraid it has," Fainly said, motioning to the long table that stretched out between them. The gnome took a chair at the head of the table, leaving only the top of his head visible. But with a snap of his fingers, the chair began to rise, bringing him to a comfortable position. "I have scouts from Harkand that tell me the city has fallen and the storm is moving, now covering most of the old Northlund holdings. Those foul clouds can be seen from Wickham and Harkand now, still creeping, with no wind to carry them."

Luriah delicately placed a hand to her mouth in a show of shock as she found a seat of her own at the other end of the table. Her own scouts had more detailed reports for her, with Father Josaiah sending a steady stream of Light-guided doves bearing direct updates on the fall of Rathen. "Light have mercy."

Fainly gave her a flat stare. "Indeed. It seems the Light is needed desperately in the north. It is an ill omen indeed. Perhaps you might have some insight into this phenomenon?" He raised a questioning eyebrow, but there was something more there than just curiosity.

Does he know? Luriah banished the thought, maintaining her composure. "I'm afraid I don't know what you mean."

"I have lost contact with High Mage Hassok," Fainly continued, holding his gaze on the Archbeacon. "He was holding the harpies that were raiding Rathen at bay, but neither he nor my Oather—Dame Kasia Strallow, no less—could find any cause for the storm within the city." His eyes seemed to narrow slightly on Luriah. "But they did find it odd that Duke Ambrose's priests had abandoned the city, called away by your own decree. Perhaps the Light may have swayed the battle or found a connection between that storm and the forces that assailed the city?"

Luriah kept her face passive as she remembered her mother's skill at disarming her father with innocent looks and misleading words. "I do appreciate your concern, Archmage. Your knowledge and guidance shall surely help us get to the bottom of this dark omen. It is the Shadow's work, of that I have no doubt. Which is exactly why I had sent word to my priests to—"

"Your priests were dealing in keyshards, Archbeacon," Fainly interjected. "Of that, I have no doubt. I was just hoping you might be able to tell me why."

The Archbeacon's heart stopped. Terror seized her mind and she had no response as the gnome's cold eyes pierced through her deception.

Fainly leaned forward. "I am not looking to expose you, Vaughn. My Oathers may go about the land confiscating keyshards from peasants, but I honestly care little for the things—any true mage knows they are but a crutch, holding the refuse of the old gods' power, nothing more." He leaned back, easing the tension slightly. "I care not how the church profits off these old relics. But they do fall within my domain, yes?"

Luriah offered a stiff nod, doing everything in her power to keep a straight face. She resented how childish this little man had made her feel. She may have been the youngest Archbeacon that the Luminaura had ever seen, but she was determined to not let that be her legacy. She sat a little straighter. "They do, Archmage."

"Good," Fainly said. "Perhaps you might enlighten me as to what your priests were doing up in Rathen."

Luriah took a moment to collect her thoughts, avoiding the gnome's awaiting gaze. She wondered who had betrayed her—her plans had been discreet, patient, and subtle, leaving what she thought was no room for failure. Yet, either her faith had been misplaced in one of her co-conspirators or Fainly Lopke was indeed the ancient, all-knowing wizard that he outwardly projected.

"The Shadow has been growing this past year," Luriah began, carefully considering her words. "You never struck me as a person of faith, but surely you can feel the shifting in powers."

Something passed over Fainly's face that Luriah took as admission.

"You do not have to worship the Light to feel its ebb and flow," she continued, "empowered or weakened by the strength of our communal faith. The Light cannot exist without Shadow, Archmage. It took me many years to come to terms with this simple fact, but as many philosophers have pointed out—what is good without evil?"

"Good and evil are relative," Fainly said impatiently. "I want to know specifically how the Luminaura is involved in what happened in Rathen."

It was Luriah's turn to narrow her eyes. "I am getting to that, Lopke."

The gnome bristled at that, but waited for her to continue.

"It is important that you understand the stakes here, regardless of your beliefs." Luriah stood up so she could look down on the gnome. "The Light needs the Shadow, but we need the Light to fight the Shadow—it is the unending conflict we must accept. Yet the Light is losing the war with the Shadow. Do you know how many Shadow cults plague Eastlund, Archmage? Or how much of Xe'dann has fallen under the control of those blasphemous Disciples? Even here in Vale, the old gods still hold more sway than the Light amongst the common folk!"

The Archmage kept his composure while Luriah's emotions began to deteriorate her own. Even in realizing that, Luriah refused to calm herself.

"The Luminaura is failing," the Archbeacon admitted. "The Prophetess has had visions of the Shadow overtaking the world as the Light fades. Meanwhile, the rich high lords sit on their wealth instead of donating to the church, growing complacent as the Light keeps the Shadow at bay—but for how long?! The people do not see the threat, because the Light has been too strong for too long. We will not survive its waning!"

Fainly opened his mouth to reply then, but held his tongue, waiting for her to continue.

"It was decided during the last Bright Council," Luriah said, her voice calming. She clasped her hands together behind her back, assuming her most courtly pose as she paced down the length of the table toward Fainly. "The people of Vale needed a discernible threat so they might truly appreciate how much they need the Light—how deadly the Shadow can be. One of my high priests in Wickham found the first piece of Eyen's shard near the mountains, as he accompanied a party of adventurers chasing a rumor of a foul harpy queen gathering forces."

"The one they call Corvanna," Fainly offered, making sure the Archbeacon remembered the reach of his vast knowledge.

"The very one. They say the harpies were the daughters of Eyen, elven battle maids known as the Valkyra—fanatical disciples as chaotic as the wind. They were cursed by the Shadow during the Unthroning, and now carry out Eyen's darker desires."

"I know my history, Archbeacon," Fainly said, motioning to get on with it.

"Corvanna made herself known to the Luminaura long before I was born," Luriah said, ignoring Fainly's impatience. "She is a being of Shadow, wholly evil and purely devoted to Eyen. She was trying to collect the pieces of Skythe, Eyen's Key; for what, we did not know. But she had claimed the one my priest found, as well as several others in the north where Eyen's worship was most common." Luriah gave Fainly a look of guilt. "We merely led her to the final pieces—she would have found them eventually."

"So you aided the Shadowfiend?" Fainly asked, more entertained than shocked. He clearly had not expected this twist.

Luriah's lips tightened. "As I said—the Light needs Shadow. I have no doubt that the Light will smite down whatever wicked plans Corvanna concocts with the Skythe. I have no doubt that the storm is Corvanna's work—"

"It's yours, from the sound of it," Fainly said, betraying a smirk.

"—and killing the beast will put an end to it," Luriah continued as she glared at the arrogant gnome. "Your mage may have failed in that charge, Lopke, but you know as well as I that no Shadowfiend can stand against the might of the Lighthold. My paladins stand ready to ride and meet the winged heathens when the time is right—when the need is right."

Silence hung between them for a long moment. Fainly let his eyes drift to the view through the windows. It was a perfect day outside, only a smattering of clouds amongst an otherwise pristine blue sky.

"I must say, Archbeacon, it's quite a scheme. I do not doubt your abilities in smacking down a few rogue harpies, but have you considered how your holy warriors will fare against an incarnate of Eyen?"

Luriah's eyes widened at the word.

Fainly set a blue keyshard on the table. "This used to be a greater keyshard, believed to be a very piece of Skythe." He laid out the same information that he had shared with the queen and the king, relishing the shock that slowly spread over Luriah's youthful, lovely face.

Fainly spread his hands. "It seems you have assisted in creating the first incarnate, your Luminous." He inclined his head and put up his hands defensively. "Now, do not mistake this for mockery. I am indeed impressed and—dare I say—intrigued by this turn of events."

"How do you know?" Luriah asked, her wide eyes distant, looking for ways in which she had overlooked this possibility. The incarnation of the old gods was a long-theorized possibility, but should not be possible without—

"The Children," they said in unison.

Fainly actually laughed. "Yes, the Children. My own records in the archives describe many strange phenomena when one—or both—of the Children come of age. I had my suspicions, but your ingenious scheme confirms it. Now, please tell me," he leaned forward, "for all that is holy, tell me—does the church know who the Child is?" Fainly's eyes looked wild now as he held them on the Archbeacon.

Luriah shook her head, still making sense of everything. "There are theories within the most sacred circles of the Luminaura who the Children are—we even have records of all of the false Children exposed throughout the years. The only solid lead we had on the Child of Light's lineage was lost in Karrane during the Xe'danni invasion about a hundred years ago."

"Has the trail gone cold?" Fainly asked. "I have those I can trust in Karrane."

Luriah shrugged, biting a lip. "I don't know, I—" She paused and looked at the Archmage. "Are we conspiring together now, Fainly Lopke?" Luriah allowed herself the smallest of grins.

Fainly returned the look. "It seems to me that together we should be able figure out the Rathen situation, but neither you nor I know the methods or repercussions of slaying an incarnate—*can* it be killed, truly? If so, does Eyen die?" He put his chin on his fist thoughtfully. "These are questions I would be much more comfortable asking the Child of Light, if we can find them. If they're even real."

"They are real," Luriah said with full conviction. "The Child of Shadow killed my father before my very eyes. And he swore he would slay the Child of Light."

Fainly gave her a long look before sliding off his chair. "Then, my dear Archbeacon, we have our work cut out for us."

CHAPTER SEVENTEEN

Some Rest for the Wicked

Avrim awoke from a troubled sleep to the welcome sound of laughter downstairs. His dreams were haunted by the Duchess of Rathen, as if her ghost still lingered so near Ithakan's blackshard. Pushing himself out of bed, Avrim stepped over to the basin near the stairs and splashed some water on his face. His body still ached from yesterday's exorcism—as well as from the hard ride out of Rathen—but the ache in his stomach from lack of food would not allow him any further rest.

As he went downstairs, he heard Sister Rashene laugh heartily as she tried to reprimand Deina. "Oh, you scandalous lass! You keep those stories for the ale houses, not my place of worship!"

There was a long table at the back of the nave, behind the pews. Hot breakfast lined its surface, and most of the priory's inhabitants were either helping themselves or reclining on the pews. Melaine, who looked quite different to Avrim without her leathers, cloak, and cowl, was stacking her plate with biscuits, eggs, and sausages, making Avrim's mouth water. As he finished descending the stairs, he was struck by a notable change in not only the half-orc's appearance, but her demeanor as well. She looked…happy.

Everyone did. He smiled as he nodded to the gathered. Deina raised a mug to the priest as she shoved a whole biscuit in her mouth, the butter glistening on her lips. Sister Rashene, who Avrim had assumed was Josaiah's partner, was a lovely middle-aged woman with kind green eyes that sparkled with the incoming morning sunlight that lit the nave from the high windows.

"Good morning, Brother," Sister Rashene said, still catching her breath from laughing. She stood up. "May I get you a plate?"

Avrim waved a hand. "Let me," he said with a smile. "You stay there and make sure our Lady Brasson there doesn't drink her weight before the day even begins."

Laughter followed as the Coperan man that had opened the gates of the priory during their arrival stood up. "That would be my fault," the man said, motioning to two huge casks near the breakfast table. "The ale was bound for Rathen, and I did not want it to go to waste."

The mention of Rathen brought a sobering silence to the meal, as those who were laughing found food or drink to fill their mouths. The man looked abashed, but quickly wiped his hand on his fine vest before presenting it to Avrim.

"We did not get a chance to meet during yesterday's excitement. My name is Nephillip Draunon—most of my trading partners call me Neff. It's easier on the southern tongues." He smiled, a mint stem clenched between his bright white teeth.

Avrim shook his hand with a smile of his own. "It is good to meet you, Neff. As a man who has become enslaved by his appetite, I believe I have you mostly to thank for this feast." He motioned to the walls of the priory. "And I thank the Light for guiding your path here in our time of need. And you as well," Avrim said to the bearded dwarf who lounged in one of the pews, a heavy crossbow leaning against his seat as he fashioned quarrels for his quiver. He had opened the other gate for them when they faced pursuing orcs and harpies.

"Kolin," the dwarf grunted with a wink of his eye. "I be a simple hunter that often finds sanctuary here. 'Twas the least me could do in return. 'Sides, I never turn down a fight wi' d'orcs! I kilt two before the sun went down—an' I think we turned dems away now."

Melaine stepped near Avrim, chewing a whole sausage in one side of her mouth. Quietly she said, "I been keeping watch too, Brother. The storm still creeps southward, ever so slowly. But the harpies seem to have gone to lick their wounds. I do not doubt they have claimed Rathen."

The thought of the once mighty free city being reduced to ruin was dreadful enough, but imagining it becoming a refuge for those vile creatures infuriated Avrim. But it made perfect sense as well. The storm seemed to have been centered on Rathen or its nearby surroundings, for whatever reason.

"Thank you, Melaine," Avrim said, noticing that the half-orc had been waiting for some sort of response. It was then that he noticed everyone looking at him, as if he held some sort of guidance for them all—as if he had answers.

He made his way toward the food, wondering what he could say to his companions, to the current residents of the priory, that might ease their minds or give them hope as the wind died outside and the storm continued to consume the world.

Avrim knew he didn't have answers. He just hoped *she* did.

Kartha awoke from her long, deep sleep. Her unfamiliar eyes adjusted to the candlelit tomb, immediately wondering if she had awoken from some death she could not recall. But the bed was no coffin—it was a comfortable mattress with smooth satin sheets, cool on her flesh.

Her flesh.

She raised her hands—or one hand and a bloody, bandaged stump where the other should be—to her adjusting eyes, seeing young fingers without any of the leathery, wrinkled flesh that she last remembered seeing.

The memory came back like a blow to the head. She closed her eyes tightly as her mind was thrown into a different time and place. She held a rough gray gemstone in the palm of her withered, skeletal hand. A whispered incantation echoed in a deep, underground chamber. The exact words were lost to her, unimportant. But she remembered the visage of Ithakan that appeared in the shadows of that cave, framed by unnatural light coming from the stone she held.

A pact was being made, and that was the last she remembered of mortal life.

The present came rushing back to her when she opened her eyes, reaching up to touch the young features of her face with her remaining hand. Her mind struggled to maintain a single thought as the echoing cries of a young boy begged for release—begged her to leave his body.

She tried to sit up, but the body did not respond to her will. Not yet.

"You are not the boy I was hoping to speak with."

Kartha turned to see an old man with tanned flesh sitting next to the bed, a golden chain hanging from his closed fist. Through the labyrinth of her thoughts, she recalled the man's face, remembering scattered details about her escape from the graystone.

How long was I inside there? she wondered, amongst a thousand other things.

"I'm sorry, Father," Kartha said in a boy's wavering voice. *Yes,* she thought, *a priest of the Light. Oh, the Light.* The thought made her feel blinded by the faint candlelight in the dim chamber. She instinctively shielded her eyes, knowing the priest was calling to the Light with that holy symbol in his clutch.

"You are not a Shadowlord," the priest said. "But it seems the Light still compels you."

"As does the Shadow," Kartha managed against the pain. "I don't suppose either like me so much."

"What are you?"

Kartha forced herself to look at the priest, hoping his face might trigger more memories—hoping she could buy herself some more time to remember why she was here. "Just a spurned woman, Father. Seeking divine justice."

Pain crept down her limbs as the priest's lips moved in silent prayer. She gritted her teeth, the boy's body already wrecked from Ithakan's presence.

"You think you can lie in the presence of the Light, witch?"

The word sent another flurry of memories through Kartha's mind—memories of Velcarthe and the sprawling dungeons of Vaustren, the *Book of Stane*, the Unthroning. The events of her long life began to fall like shattered glass as she tried to make a larger picture out of them. But the priest's holy grip on her would not let her concentrate.

"Mercy, Father," she begged. "Please. A moment."

The pain subsided, but when Kartha opened her eyes, she saw that it was not sympathy that stayed the old man's wrath. Another figure stepped into the room—a younger priest. Behind him, a dwarf and a hulking woman with a broad jaw and pale green skin.

The priest—*Avrim*, she remembered, *the exorcist*—regarded Kartha coldly. His companions watched her with less trepidation, obviously disarmed by the body she possessed.

"Father, thank you for keeping watch," Avrim said, turning to the older priest. "I am even further in your debt. Would you mind giving us a moment with... Well?" He motioned to Kartha, who struggled to push herself up to a seated position with her one remaining hand.

The old priest's cautious glare held onto Kartha as he stood out of his chair, finally softening as he turned to Avrim with a nod. "Of course, Brother. I shall retire to my chambers." He cast Kartha another dreadful look. "To pray."

With that, the old man departed and the half-orc woman closed the door securely behind him. Avrim took the departed priest's chair and leaned toward Kartha, unafraid.

"With whom do I speak?"

Kartha licked her lips. "Kartha the Cursed, so they once called me." She gave a weak grin. "Seems fitting, all things considered."

"You are not a Shadowlord," Avrim said with certainty. "What are you?"

Kartha couldn't help but laugh.

"Do we amuse you?" the dwarf asked with arms crossed over the chain mail armor covering her barrel chest. Her arms were thick and corded with muscle.

"No," Kartha replied, composing herself. "I just— My memory is— Perhaps you could explain how you happened upon my stone, and we could go from there?"

Avrim considered that, looking to his companions. "Melaine."

The half-orc woman laid out her tale. As she spoke, thousands of memories returned to Kartha—not just since binding herself to the graystone, but hundreds of years of events flooded the young boy's mind. With all those lifetimes of dark happenings poisoning the young boy's own memories, Kartha wondered if there would be any hope for the boy's sanity after her possession—but the thought was chased away by more pressing matters.

"Ruke's stone," Kartha said, "of course."

"What does that stone have to do with the storm?" the dwarf demanded.

"Deina," Avrim said, raising a hand. "Please." He regarded Kartha. "We've told our tale. Now yours."

"As I said," she said flatly, "I am Kartha the Cursed, or Kartha the Cruel, depending on who you ask. And I created both Light and Shadow."

The priest, dwarf, and half-orc all stared blankly.

"Well, maybe not created," she continued. "Found? Revealed? I don't think any of the other Purveyors even fully understood what we were doing besides stopping a dark prophecy from destroying the world."

"Kartha was— I mean, you were one of the Purveyors of Light?" Avrim raised his eyebrows in disbelief.

"Yes, as was my friend Ruke, which is really what is pertinent at the moment. You see, during the Unthroning, each of the Purveyors that was aligned to one of the old gods perished—all except Ruke. She figured out how to bind herself within the stone of her staff, a trick I used myself in making the deal with Ithakan." The memory of that fateful day gave Kartha renewed vigor, and she found the strength to lean forward, emphasizing the dramatic moments with her hand.

"So, when Light and Shadow split the world and the Purveyors were consumed by their old gods, Ruke," Kartha smiled, holding up a finger, "my clever Ruke retreated into her stone, waiting to be freed."

"How do ye know?" Deina asked. "How do ye know she wasn't just consumed too like the others?"

"The storm," Kartha said, pointing up. "Everything in this world is tied together. Light, Shadow, the old gods, the Nethering, the Abyss… It's all connected. That storm is the work of Shadow, but the Light," she snapped her fingers, "brought it into being. I could feel it. It's what woke me up—woke Ithakan up. That is when I heard Ruke's call."

"Are you saying the Light is responsible for that storm?" Avrim asked, a hint of fury in his voice. "Perhaps we should take you outside to see that storm—to see a land denied the Light!" He stood up, thrusting a finger upward. "You claim the Light is responsible for that?"

"In a way," Kartha said calmly, recognizing the man's wounded faith, "but there is much more at play. Do not confuse my words. The Shadow is the enemy here; it threatens to kill everything under these clouds."

"And the incarnate?" Avrim responded, his fury not sated. "Was that the Light?"

Kartha nodded. "An incarnate is a god made flesh—at least in part. And the old gods were born of Creation, from both Light and Shadow." She inclined Percy's head. "But you know that, Brother, despite how much you would wish not to acknowledge it. That harpy may have been twisted by Eyen's rage, but it is made of Light and Shadow."

"How do we kill it?" Melaine asked.

Kartha turned to her and said, "I do not know—not easily, that is for sure. But Ruke will know—she is tied to the Nethering and will know what made the incarnate and what can unmake it. I am certain."

"What of this Ruke?" Melaine asked, taking a menacing step forward. "You said you heard her call. Is that why you seek this stone?"

"Yes," Kartha said. "I have known Ruke longer than any other living being, and she is devoted to preserving the natural world. She will have answers for us, but I need her stone."

"Where can we find it?" Deina asked. "I'm not saying we believe ye," she added, "but enlighten us, if ye will."

"Her temple was south of here," Kartha said. "It was deep underground—sprawling tunnels that ran through all of Noveth, all connected to the temple she built. The Oakhold."

Deina stepped toward Avrim. "Me kin speak of such a place. They say it is where foul beasts dwell, driven mad by the old god Oakus' furious wrath."

Kartha nodded. "Your kin does not lie, proud lady. But I would not call them foul—they are possessed by nature and its shifts between wrath and nourishment. Regardless, it is not a safe place." She smiled sadly. "Ruke would not have made it so easy to find her resting place. She knew her knowledge would be needed to protect this world from the powers that seek to ruin or enslave it."

"Is that why you bound yourself?" Avrim scowled. "Making deals with Shadowlords. To *save* the world?"

Kartha gave him a sorrowful look. "I do not expect you to believe me, but yes, I seek to undo a terrible injustice—one that I had a hand in."

Finding strength returning to the boy's limbs, Kartha stood up, ignoring Deina and Melaine taking defensive stances, both resting their hands on their weapons. Her eyes were fixed on Avrim.

"There is much I can tell you, and even more that I must atone for, Brother." Kartha wiped a tear from her eye, not knowing if it was hers or Percy's. "But there is no time now. You must find Ruke's stone before the Shadow does. I fear they may already be upon it."

Avrim's eyes remained narrowed as he considered the words, turning toward Deina and Melaine. Both women nodded to him.

"Tell us then," Avrim said to Kartha. "How can we find this place?"

"I'll show you."

"This is a tree," Deina said, holding her axe as her nervous eyes surveyed the forest for any signs of orcs or harpies. The tree before the gathered figures had the widest trunk that Deina had ever seen, but it was just a tree.

Melaine watched Kartha intently as the possessed boy paced the ground surrounding the tree.

"I can still feel it," Kartha whispered, as if to herself. "She hid it well though…"

There was a harpy's screech far to the north, and both Kolin and Neff raised their crossbows, watching the darkened sky warily. "This be madness," Kolin huffed.

"Brother Kaust," Josaiah whispered, "you cannot be trusting this troubled boy. Clearly he's succumbed to delusions and madness. We must take him to your temple."

"Let us see," Avrim said, hefting the mace Neff had given him when they left the safety of the priory. He also wore pieces of scaled armor over his robes, courtesy of the trader. "I must see this through."

Kartha finished pacing the tree and turned to both priests, approaching cautiously. "I can open the way, but it will most certainly exhaust me. My power has not returned, but as I said—there is no time to waste."

Avrim nodded.

Kartha turned back to the tree, falling to her knees. She lowered her head and began whispering unintelligible words. After a moment, she raised her remaining hand slightly and the boy's fingers began contorting along with the erratic rhythm of her words. The acrid taste of the stagnant air around them was replaced with a foul breeze carrying foreign scents of burning things.

Deina gasped as the tree visibly shuddered, its roots creaking in response to Kartha's incantation. Bark began to splinter from the trunk as a crack ran down the middle of the tree, splitting it wider and wider, revealing a gaping darkness from whence a subtle green glow began to pulsate.

"Light protect!" Father Josaiah gasped, a hand going to his mouth.

Soon the tree finished shifting and an arched doorway had been formed—as if it had always been there. From the darkness inside the tree, a subtle green glow seemed to beckon them in.

Percy's body collapsed into the leaves on the ground.

"Burn me eyes!" cursed Kolin.

"The path to Oakhold," Deina said with absolute wonder. Her eyes were wide with both terror and excitement. She gripped her axe tightly.

Melaine held her bow taut, aiming it at the opening as if a monster might burst forth. But only silence followed.

Avrim knelt down next to Percy's body, rolling him over. Kartha looked up at him, barely able to keep her eyes from rolling back in Percy's head.

"Go, Brother. Hurry. Follow the light, but be wary. Oakus can deceive. Bring Ruke's stone and we will stop this storm."

With that, Percy's body went limp.

Avrim let the boy's body rest, standing up to face Father Josaiah. "Can you keep him safe, Father? We are going."

Josaiah opened his mouth to protest, but when he saw Avrim's eyes, he simply nodded. "I will attend to the boy. Please," he reached out to take Avrim's hand, "be safe and return to us."

Deina and Melaine already approached the tree and looked down its depths as Avrim joined them. The errant priest spared Father Josaiah one last look before he and his companions disappeared into the Old Ways.

Percy woke up in a strange forest, the sky above shrouded in bruised green clouds. His body ached and his mind was twisted by horrendous nightmares that felt like they had lasted for years. He tried to get up, but struggled as he clumsily discovered the bandaged stump that used to be his hand.

"Easy, my son," an unfamiliar voice said.

Turning his head, Percy saw an old dark-skinned priest sitting on the ground nearby, cutting a sharp piece of wood with a knife.

"The witch is gone, yes?"

"What witch?" Percy asked. "Where am I? Where is my father? My mother? What happened to my hand?" Tears were welling up in Percy's eyes.

"Shhhh," the priest said, sliding over to him. "You are safe in the Light, my boy. I will see that the witch suffers for what she has done."

Percy was confused and scared, but somehow reassured by the man's voice. Pieces of his dreams came back to him then—visions of him doing horrible things. He searched the priest's eyes for some sort of forgiveness.

"Have I done wrong, Father?" Percy asked.

There was a tear in the priest's eye now as well. "No, boy." In a blinding movement, the old priest leaned over and buried the sharpened stick into Percy's heart. "You did nothing wrong."

Percy coughed, his vision fading. Kartha tried to reach for any lingering power, to no avail—she was out of options. As her borrowed body died, she looked deep into the old priest's eyes, giving him a wicked smile.

"It was…the Light…"

Percy's body died, and Kartha fell forever into the Abyss.

CHAPTER EIGHTEEN

An Unexpected Prophecy

They arrived at Oakworth in early afternoon, having made good time on the road at the urging of Grip and Brood, who were on a much tighter schedule than their new companions. The Guild agents drew their hoods as they passed the first set of guards patrolling the town's stone walls.

Anika remembered coming to Oakworth once when she was younger, but the town looked much larger than she recalled—it was a proper city to her eyes, with people of all shapes, sizes, and colors bustling through the cobbled streets. High lords in colorful satin doublets, noble women in exquisite dresses, young drifters in dirty leathers with swords on their hips and bows on their backs, artists, laborers, peasants—Anika felt like she had stepped into a fanciful tale of adventure.

"We shall convene at the Breeze," Grip whispered to Ransil as she made discreet hand signs to Brood. "It is best that we not be seen together. Take time to acquire whatever provisions you need." Anika saw her produce a small cloth bag of clinking coins and toss it to Ransil, who expertly snatched it and tucked it away. "Our contact is at the inn. Just blend in and don't draw any attention to yourselves."

Grip gave Anika a knowing grin from the shadows of her hood. "Especially you, child."

Anika hated the woman, looking away rather than giving in to her cruel teasing. She looked to Matty instead, who also seemed to be caught up in the excitement of Oakworth. He walked beside her, craning his neck to take in his surroundings. Just days ago he had been a mere farmer in one of the smallest villages in Vale. Now he was thrust into an unexpected adventure. That reminded Anika of his dead family, and her own abducted father, and just like that the enchantment of the town turned to fear, as if every person walking by her on those cobbled streets was a potential villain.

Brood and Grip disappeared into the milling populace.

"I could use a meal and a bath," Robin said, rubbing his neck. A couple drunk men passed by, laughing about something they had probably said in their cups. Robin threw an arm around Gage. "She said to try to blend in," he said to Matty with a wink.

Matty looked down into Anika's eyes, giving her a shrug. He stuck out his elbow so Anika could hook her arm through his.

Ransil nodded between the couples. "Sure. It's better you don't look like a prisoner anyway." He assumed a much more casual walk, as if he were just going to town to stock up on some kitchen supplies.

Anika forgot her troubles for a moment and let her heart flutter as she pulled herself closer to Matty's arm. As her group stepped into the market, two giggling halfling girls scurried behind them with a red-haired human woman laughing as she chased after them. Several guards followed.

The five travelers went from market stall to market stall, acquiring some necessary provisions for travel with Grip's coin: some flint and tinder, candles, dried berries with nuts, rope, additional water skins, and other sundries.

"Child," came a thickly accented Xe'danni voice.

Anika looked up from an arrow she was inspecting at a fletcher's stall. A woman with skin nearly as dark as her own stared at her with equally dark eyes. Her head was wrapped in a tight scarf that left her decorated ears visible, dangling bronze ornaments hanging from them.

"Yes?" Gage answered from behind, startling Anika.

Gage's voice drew a smile from the woman, distinctive wrinkles forming around her eyes, belying her youthfulness. Her dark eyes fell on Anika. "Sorry. For a moment I thought you looked familiar." She inclined her head slightly. "What brings you to Oakworth?"

"Visiting family," Ransil said, stepping next to Anika.

The stranger's eyes went to the halfling, then to Anika, and then to Gage, as if considering which family he meant. She opened her mouth to reply, but was distracted by a short figure that appeared at her side. "Ah, Mosby," she said.

A one-armed dwarf gave her a curt nod, and offered Anika's party a hesitant smile.

"Oh, I must away," the woman said, patting the dwarf on the shoulder. "Do enjoy your stay, Child." She turned away, but the last pointed word she said seemed to echo cruelly in Anika's mind. Turning to Gage, Anika saw that he was disturbed as well. Matty glared at the departing woman as if he meant to follow her.

"We should get to the Breeze," Ransil said, shouldering his now heavier pack. "It may be a busy night for us."

"What is it?" Naya hissed under her breath, keeping her eyes on the retreating figures—specifically the Child.

"There's been a…disturbance," Mosby said through clenched teeth. "Your…faithful servants have abandoned their work."

She spun on the dwarf, fury in her eyes. "What happened? Where are they?"

Mosby shrugged. "I woke up and found your study deserted, several crates turned over as if the— Your servants vanished."

Naya reached into her robes and felt the shard, cool to the touch. It had not been her who had commanded the golems elsewhere. But what would—

She spun around to look for the Child, but the company had already disappeared into the throng of people moving through the marketplace. "Dammit, Mosby! Do you realize how— The Child is here!" Naya spun back to Mosby, lowering herself to level her eyes with his. "The prophecy! That is why the Shadow has stirred here! The Child has come!"

Mosby blinked at the priestess' growing excitement, straining his head to try to catch a glimpse of the Karranese girl she had been speaking with. "Is that why the gol—servants have fled? Does this *Child* command them?"

Ignoring the question, Naya stood up, turning the dwarf around by his shoulders. "Come, Mosby. I have much to tell you!" She shuffled them toward the walls to the baron's keep, where the secret entrance to her domain was hidden in the rear gardens. "Destiny has fallen into our laps, dear friend. The Child must embrace the Shadow to fulfill the prophecy."

Mosby quickened his pace to keep up with the eager priestess. "And which prophecy are we talking about?" He kept his voice lower than a whisper as a group of fishermen passed by.

Naya smiled, wrinkling the flesh around her cruel eyes. "The final one."

Anika's breath caught in her throat as she looked into their room. A single bed sat against the wall, its head under a curtained window that let in rays of the afternoon sun. She stared at that bed nervously, her hands clasped together and fidgeting. Biting her lip, she turned to look at Matty, who stood with her in the doorway. He also looked at the bed, shifting his eyes between it and Anika, his lips twisting around some words that he struggled to say.

"You two take that room," Ransil said behind them. He motioned down the hall. "Robin and Gage will take that one." Pointing behind him to a third door, he said, "I'll take that one with Brood and Grip—lock your doors just in case, but I will keep an eye on them."

As the halfling made his way to his room to deposit his things, Matty motioned to let Anika in.

"I can take the floor," Matty said, scratching his neck as he looked at the hardwood under their feet. "Wouldn't be the first time." He smiled sadly at unspoken memories.

"Oh," Anika stiffened as she set down her pack and the white bow that had belonged to Farrah, "all right." Relief and disappointment made a mess of her stomach, which was already growling for food. *Of course he doesn't want to share your bed*, her racing mind told her. *You are his charge, not his lady.* She didn't know what else to say as she smoothed her hair with her hands, cleaning out the dust from the road.

"What do you think it is?" Matty asked.

Anika gave him a puzzled look as Matty unshouldered his own pack, which was much lighter than hers or any of her companions'—he was clearly a man of small needs.

He nodded to the pouch at her waist. "The gnome's necklace. I heard whispers that it was a dead keyshard. But I saw what you did that night—to that harpy. There's something left in it, isn't there? Maybe not the magic like they train in the towers, but—something?"

"I don't know," she said, struggling with Farrah's final words and Grip's mockery, unsure if she should burden Matty with her wild thoughts. "I think there are still things in the world that we don't know." She looked into Matty's eyes, feeling a strange confidence coming over her. "I don't think there are easy answers to everything that happens—even if we feel like we need those answers." She took a step toward him, overcome with a desperate desire.

"I remember when I first touched it," Anika continued, as if in a trance, "there was a sense of freedom that I never knew I wanted. Something called to me—something bigger than Blakehurst, bigger than any king or queen or story I heard when I was a girl."

She took another step toward him.

"I don't know what it is, but I know it's part of something bigger—and it called to me, Matty. Gage may have stolen it from that cart, but when I look back on it, it *feels* like I asked him to—as if I needed it."

She took another step toward him, reaching out a hand to his waist.

"It felt like a part of me that I was always missing."

She reached her other hand up to the back of his neck, feeling the sweat that dampened his hair, twisting her fingers through it to take hold.

"I just knew that I needed it, and it needed me."

Matty swallowed, his lips slightly parting as he leaned toward her.

"Anika!"

Startled by the voice from the hall, Anika let go of Matty and straightened, blinking away whatever it was that had come over her. She glared at Gage. "What?"

"Downstairs," her brother said. "Food."

Matty smiled, motioning for her to go ahead, the redness slowly fading from his blushed face. Anika quickly fled into the hall with Robin and Gage, feeling embarrassed and avoiding the boys' eyes. The four companions descended the stairs into a buzzing common room where they found Ransil in a raised seat at a table suitable to their heights.

Anika's mouth was watering as they joined the halfling's table. Five bowls of steaming, creamy chowder were waiting for them, as well as a basket of smoking bread fresh from the oven. There was also a large bowl of hot vegetables in the center of the table, and five mugs filled with cider.

"It's decent," Ransil said of the chowder with an upturned nose. "It seems my cousin, Dolly, is not in the kitchens today, and the fare here is definitely telling."

As they ate, Anika observed the common room. She was relieved to see that they had not drawn any particular attention. There were many prospecting miners sharing stories of their finds in the hills, toasting to their successes. A few unscrupulous eyes observed those conversations from the darker parts of the room, and Anika feared that the bragging miners might be setting themselves up to be robbed of their yields. Through one of the windows, she saw a human woman on the porch with vibrant red hair tossing a squealing halfling girl up into the air and catching her.

Something about the woman drew Anika's eyes—a distant sense of nostalgia or familiarity that she could not explain. But the two hooded figures that discreetly entered the common room from the main doors quickly made Anika forget the woman.

"There's trouble," Brood said as he climbed up the other raised seat to join the table. "Where's me chowder?!"

Ransil slid his bowl to his cousin. "What trouble?"

Grip leaned against the table, squatting rather than sitting in a seat to join them. "Does the name Kasia Strallow ring a bell?"

Anika did not recognize the name, but from the look Ransil gave Grip, it was not a good name.

"Bleh!" Brood said, dropping his spoon back into the chowder's bowl. "Dolly would never serve this swill—there's almost no cream!"

"Dolly isn't here," Ransil said dismissively before turning back to Grip. "The Lady Commander is here? I'm guessing for the same reason you're here? Ruke's stone?"

Grip shook her head, casting a quick glance at Anika. "It seems she is preparing a company of the baron's finest to ride to Blakehurst on the morrow."

Grumbling, Brood slid down to make his way to the bartop where the innkeeper was refilling the drained mugs of a couple dwarf miners. Anika watched him distractedly. "Ella, where is Dolly? Who ye got in the kitchen?" His voice was lost in the mill of conversation, and Anika returned her attention to her table.

All eyes were on her.

"What?" Anika looked at Gage, who looked more confused than her.

Ransil leaned in, looking directly at Anika. "It seems the Lady Commander of the Oathers knows about you." He turned to Grip. "We cannot stay here."

Anika's heart raced; she was not entirely sure why, but Ransil's nervous demeanor unsettled her greatly—usually nothing seemed to rattle the old halfling.

Grip shook her head. "We cannot leave without that stone.

Especially if the Oathers are after it. Knife will gut us if the gnome manages to snatch something up before her."

"If the baron has the stone," Ransil hissed, "*and* is in league with Strallow, it's as good as hers! What makes you think she doesn't already have it?"

"You think she'd be worried about a Blakehurst witch if she found Ruke's stone?" Grip asked with venom in her eyes, motioning to Anika with a nod of her head.

Being called a witch didn't sit well with Anika, but her head was racing too much to interject in the argument.

"Grip," Brood hissed, the halfling appearing as if from nowhere. His eyes were wide. "The baron. He has Scratch."

"What does that mean?" demanded Ransil, sliding off his seat to face Brood. Grip took a knee to hear her smaller companion.

"She's locked up," Brood said, fear in his eyes—eyes that darted in all directions to ensure they weren't being watched or eavesdropped on. "Me sis is in irons, in the baron's keep."

Grip tightened a fist. "If that's true, then we do not have much time." She turned to Robin. "We need to go tonight."

Robin nodded. "Dolly was like a mother to me," he said. "I will not let her rot in a cell." He looked at Ransil. "You know the dungeons as well as I do. We can get her out before we look for the stone."

Ransil scowled. "Do you even have a hint where that stone may be? I thought we'd have a day or two to scout the place, not leap in blind! And with an Oather about, no less?!"

Anika nervously twitched her leg as the conversation heated up. She didn't realize she was reaching into her pouch until her hand was already around the stone.

The common room disappeared as a wave of energy rushed through her body. Darkness enshrouded her and she felt as if she were falling. Slowly, a faint green glow lit her surroundings and she saw earthen hallways speeding by. The landscape continued to rush past her as the fall—no, her forward momentum, carried her onward through the maze into a brilliant green light at the end of the tunnel. She sensed a vast chamber surrounding her, and then she was lifted upward into the darkness above. Higher and higher she climbed until the mists around her parted and she saw Oakworth far below.

Anika gasped as she felt Matty's hand take hers, his touch like a bucket of water on the weak flames of the vision.

"I know where it is," Anika said.

All eyes turned to her.

Grip smiled. "I thought you might."

"Then it's settled," Brood said, taking Anika's sudden claim as an undeniable fact.

Does he know as well? Anika wondered, looking from the hooded halfling to the hooded dark elf. *Certainly she would have told him.* She rubbed her eyes, taking a deep breath. Desperately, she looked to her brother to make sure he didn't suspect something of her based on this revelation.

But Gage's eyes were fixed on the window, his face slack with disbelief. Anika turned to see what he was looking at, but all she saw was the back of the red-headed woman as she walked the halfling children toward the baron's keep.

CHAPTER NINETEEN

The Stained Pages

Desmond regarded the impressive mountains surrounding the mages with as much enthusiasm as he regarded most things—which was almost none at all. He occasionally produced his notebook to flip through its pages until he was satisfied with a particular passage, putting it away to pass the time in more silence.

For the briefest of moments, Layla wished Desmond were not with her, despite the aching love she felt for him and the constant pleasures he provided—pleasures that she found herself craving even more today. If she were to be honest with herself in that passing moment, she wanted nothing more than to flee—wanted little else than the comfort of the queen's ship taking her back to the ports of Merithian.

The moment passed into distant memory when she turned her gaze back to Desmond. She desired him as always, and wouldn't dream of leaving him. As she fell back in love with her dark companion all over again, their journey toward the dragon's tomb continued on into the craggy terrain of Dragonpeak.

The sun was still high as the shadows grew, tall rock spires blocking out the light on their path. Dragonpeak itself was within reach, its blackened surface looking almost as if it were encased in glass.

"The volcano," Desmond said, as if reading Layla's thoughts. He was idly flipping through his notebook as he spoke, looking for a particular entry. "They say it erupted during the Unthroning. Completely buried the only dwarven stronghold on Jath that was called First Forge." He looked up to the black mountain again. "Many think that's why the dragon chose this as her home—a deadly catastrophe of fire." His eyes were blank slits in the pools of ash that circled them. "Quite the metaphor."

"How are we supposed to find it in there?" Layla asked.

"As Maze said, it'll be in the dragon's hoard. Probably deep below the mountain." He gave her a look that might have been amusement.

"At least we won't have to scale that terrible hill."

Layla allowed herself to smile. "That is—"

She was interrupted by a bone-chilling shriek from the distance. The mages looked to the sky, following the sound. Several winged forms descended from the clouds.

Dragons! Layla thought immediately, but the shapes were not right. They looked like women on the wings of vultures.

"Harpies," Desmond hissed. Layla heard the crackle of fire from behind her and she made the motion for arcane energy to gather into her hands, ready for battle.

Both mages slid off their horses, knowing the beasts would probably bolt once the fight commenced. Desmond stalked forward, waving his hands around the ball of fire that grew in size before him. Layla followed more apprehensively, watching the figures—four of them—grow in size as they descended.

Their eyes were so focused on the harpies that neither of them saw or heard the lumbering shape to their left, emerging from a collection of huge rocks.

"Ogre!" Desmond cried, the fiery orb he summoned dissipating as his concentration was broken.

Layla kept her mind focused as she turned her attention to the fat, disgusting monster bearing down on them. She unleashed the arcane torrents coursing through her fingers, sending dozens of purple lights shaped like darts toward the monstrosity.

The ogre shielded its eyes as magical explosions erupted all over its brown-green flesh. It carried a tree trunk with a boulder crudely tied to it to serve as a club suitable to its size. But as Layla's spell riddled its body with painful sears, it dropped the weapon to swat away the pesky magic.

Desmond recovered and held out a contorted hand that told Layla he was attempting to befuddle the ogre's mind—an easy task, she figured—but before the spell could be cast, a harpy's shriek sent him to the ground for cover.

Layla turned her attention from the stunned ogre to an incoming harpy, readying to blast it out of the sky. But the ground shook then, and she saw a second ogre barreling toward her, surprisingly fast. She had little time to react and, when Desmond cried out for help, she saw that a harpy was swooping low toward him.

Her attention divided, Layla couldn't wrap her head around the simplest of spells, and she turned toward the charging ogre that was mere steps away from her. She froze and closed her eyes, awaiting her demise.

Time slowed as Layla felt stones pelt her body; the ogre's next step would crush her. She felt rough flesh brush against her, followed by a strong shove throwing her to the ground. Rocks tore her flesh, but did not break her bones or end her life. Coughing, she opened her eyes to see dust left in the ogre's wake as it chased something up a hill.

It was then that she realized the harpies had passed over them, descending on a dark figure in the distance.

A raspy voice shouted, "The book, the book! You worthless brutes! Corvanna will not abide failure in her empire!"

Magic erupted on the horizon, and a smoking harpy crashed to the ground in front of that fleeing figure. The stunned ogre had recovered and joined the other one in pursuit, egged on by the shrill voices of the commanding harpy.

Layla looked at Desmond, who was brushing himself off and watching the distant battle as well.

"The book," Desmond said, realization washing over his face. He looked at Layla. "Someone beat us here."

Before she could respond, Desmond broke into a sprint, moving faster than Layla would ever have imagined the man capable of. She joined his pursuit, clearing her mind for any spells she might need when they crested the hill.

The sounds of dying and the unmistakable taste of sorcery greeted Desmond and Layla as they approached the battle. The figure was a woman, bald and wielding a long whip of glowing Shadow energy. She lashed it around an ogre's neck as a harpy wheeled overhead, having missed its last dive. The mysterious woman yanked her arm and spoke an incantation, freeing her magical whip and the ogre's head from its shoulders. The massive body collapsed on top of the other ogre that had died before the mages arrived.

The bald sorceress was hunched over, visibly winded from the power she wielded against her foes.

"Give us the book, witch," one of the two remaining harpies screeched. The other two were smoldering heaps on the ground near the whip wielder.

"Look," whispered Layla, pointing to the heavy tome the woman carried under her other arm.

"Corvanna has served her purpose," the woman said mockingly through broken gasps, lashing her summoned weapon to keep the hovering birds at bay. "Stane does not need her anymore. She may rule over the Joined Realms as she sees fit, but the Disciples only answer to one lord."

"Your Shadow magic won't protect you from her," the harpy mocked. "The Empress *is* the Shadow's chosen, and you will obey her!"

The stranger laughed in response, lashing her whip again. She barely kept her balance as she continually channeled such volatile power.

Layla began the workings of her own spell to disorient all three of them, but something shook the ground violently—a tremor that ran under them as if a giant worm were burrowing below their feet, nearly knocking them all to the ground.

Turning, Layla saw smoke billowing out of Dragonpeak. "That wasn't there before, was it?" she whispered to Desmond. He shook his head in response, also staring at the source of the tremor.

"We will return," one of the harpies croaked, flapping its wings harder to gain altitude. "Perhaps the dragon will recognize its new master, and bring your smoking corpse before the Empress!"

The harpies disappeared into the clouds.

Turning to the mages, the bookkeeper scowled. "Do you quarrel?"

Desmond stepped toward her. "You're weakened, clearly. The Shadow may be inexhaustible, but you certainly are not. And you've expended more than you expected, yes?"

She cracked her whip, but Desmond reacted like lightning, snapping his fingers to snuff the whip out of existence.

The woman fell to her knees, as if the weapon were the only thing keeping her from collapsing.

She glared at them as the earth shook again. "The dragon comes. It will come for the book, and only its words can stop it." Looking at Layla, she snapped, "Do you know how to read it, elf? Or you, boy?"

"I'm certain the queen can figure that part out," Desmond said, taking another calm step forward.

A loud rumble drew Layla's eyes back to Dragonpeak, and she saw more smoke than before coming out in bursting plumes.

"Desmond," she said, trying to maintain her composure in front of an enemy. "We have to go." She clicked her tongue and whistled for the horses, who were nervously sauntering along the path a good distance away from the site of the battle.

Desmond looked at her, then back at the stranger who struggled to stand back up, hugging the book with arms that were wrapped in tight black bands. He threw his arms wide and motioned toward her. Arcane energy thrust the woman's arms behind her back, dropping the book. "Coming," he told the elf mage.

Layla watched him walk over toward her, kneeling down to look her in the eyes as he traced one of his fingers over the book. "Though, now that you mention it, Disciple—it seems you may be of use to us if you can indeed read the old Ghultan scripts." He gave her a faint smile. "The queen might have need of you."

Picking up the book under one arm, Desmond stood up and whispered another incantation.

"You will regret this, boy," the woman warned. "My people lie in every dark shadow in every city. You will not—"

Her warnings were cut short as Desmond's spell took effect, wrapping an invisible noose around her and sending her sprawling as arcane energy dragged her in his wake.

"We will try to ride slow," Desmond said as the earth shook again, "but we must make haste if we are to outpace this dragon you speak of. I apologize for any discomfort."

The woman's neck was corded with veins and muscle as she tried to breathe against the cruel magic. A hint of fear washed over her face as Desmond mounted his horse, still dragging her behind.

Her last vision before passing out was of the boy with ashen eyes smiling wickedly at her while the young elf mage gave her a look of horrendous sympathy as she was dragged across the rumbling terrain.

They rode slowly back to Caraby so as not to kill their dragged captive. Night fell before they reached the end of the Jathi Plains, forcing them to rest. They made camp as soon as the ground stopped rumbling, finding shelter in one of the burned-out ruined towers that dotted the lands outside of the mountains. Layla looked at the strange woman's injuries, healing what she could, but she was no priestess.

"If you wanted to make use of her, why would you drag her behind your horse?"

Desmond didn't look up from the large black book, flipping

through the nonsensical scripture as if he could somehow decipher it. "She will be fine. I felt her wards—they may have drained her, but they kept her alive. I've never seen this language." He flipped another page of the *Book of Stane*. "I heard it was written in obscure Ghultan dialects, but this looks nothing like any of the Ghultan texts I've read. And I've read them all, I thought.".

The woman moaned as Layla finished another healing spell—her last one for the day. The elf's mind was aching and her body was weary from magical exertion. "I need to rest—we both do, Desmond."

He looked up from the book. "You rest. I'll keep an eye on her. I need to maintain my holding spell on her anyway."

Layla was too weary to argue. She curled up near the fire, falling almost instantly asleep.

Desmond flipped another page of the book, unable to discern any of the text, but mesmerized by it regardless. He turned another twenty pages before their prisoner began to stir awake.

"What is your name?" Desmond asked, feeling his spell still at work, restraining the woman from the magic she already struggled for. He didn't look up from the book to see her glaring at him with cold, dark eyes.

"Valix." Her voice was an icy dagger.

Desmond closed the book to look at her. "Tell me why the Disciples want this book, Valix." He reached into his robes to produce his notebook and his quills. "Enlighten me."

She held his gaze for a long moment before responding. "What do you even know about the Disciples?"

Desmond raised a hand and Valix's head was pulled slightly forward—the mystical noose still around her neck.

"It holds the secrets of Stane's Four Comings," she said, straining against the pain. "It contains all of Stane's prophecies, not just the Unthroning." The noose slackened and the fury in her eyes subsided as she sized the opposing mage up. "May I ask you a question now?" Valix gave Desmond the smallest of smiles.

Desmond nodded. "Tread carefully."

"Did you not think to shield me from your own Shadow magic?"

Confusion washed over Desmond's face as his heart skipped a beat. He tightened the noose, but it didn't respond—the spell was broken.

Valix didn't move, she just shifted her eyes to the sounds of Layla stirring.

Desmond looked to his companion, who was rubbing her temples, groaning against some phantom force. He looked back at Valix, desperate. "Please, leave her alone."

"Funny," Valix said, smiling wickedly. "I was going to ask you to do the same. She's nothing more than a prisoner as well."

"Desmond."

There was no love or longing in Layla's voice—there was only painful realization. Desmond looked at the elven mage as she stood up, her hands falling from her head. Furious understanding was in her eyes.

"Layla," Desmond begged, reaching desperately into his robes and groping for the little black book that held his salvation. "Wait, I can explain. I—"

His excuses were cut short as his throat tightened, Layla reaching up a hand, newfound power surging through her.

"Allow me to explain, you pathetic fucking coward." Layla lifted her other arm up and Desmond was raised into the air, his legs kicking wildly as he struggled for air. "You raped me for months because no one in this world could ever love such a narcissistic, empty shell of a person."

Valix watched in ecstasy, weaving her hands to empower Layla with the darkest Shadow magic she could channel from the discarded *Book of Stane*. Its pages flipped wildly as Valix looked for the necessary incantations to whisper, feeding that malicious witchery into Layla's own furious ritual.

Desmond spat up blood as the magic strangled him, his insides being shredded from within by cruel and ancient magic. Bloody tears ran down his ashen eyes. He mouthed the word "please" over and over again.

The *Book of Stane*'s pages finally finished flipping, and Valix whispered the words shown.

Layla screamed as the Shadow shuddered through her, igniting memories of Desmond thrusting himself into her like an insatiable dagger. She felt all that pain and pleasure, coalescing into violent magic that begged to be released. Her eyes bore into her abuser, wanting to see him endure the mental agony assailing her.

But she wanted more—she wanted to see that agony made flesh. She shrieked again and tightened every muscle in her body as she finished the spell.

Desmond's skin was slowly stretched against his contorted limbs. His agonizing scream was only a bloody gurgle as his bones began to break. Blood sprayed from his mouth, eyes, ears, and everywhere else as he was completely eviscerated, his insides staining the pages of that ancient book.

Valix stood up, free from the dead mage's spell now. She bent over and closed the bloody book, turning to Layla, who was now on her knees weeping.

The Disciple knelt down next to Layla, putting a gentle arm around her. "You are not the only one to have suffered at the hands of a man like this," she said softly.

Layla looked up into the stranger's eyes. "You—you saved me."

Valix shook her head, taking Layla's hand and placing it on the book, letting the elf feel its power.

"I did not save you, friend." She wiped the tears from Layla's eyes as tears ran down her own cheeks. "Stane saved you, just as he saved me."

Layla stared at the book in horror and reverence, letting her fingers feel its legacy while its celestial magic coursed through her, giving her visions of the inevitable being that would one day be the one true god of Aetha.

Overwhelmed, Layla collapsed into Valix's arms, sobbing in the gruesome remains of her former tormentor.

Valix ran a soft hand over Layla's hair, confident that the Disciples had just gained a powerful new recruit.

CHAPTER TWENTY

The Eye of the Storm

"Do not let him die."

Bennik heard the distant and cruel voice on the edge of a dream—a nightmare, he remembered now—as the pain returned ever so gradually with his consciousness.

"He will tell us his tale," the voice continued, sounding partly like a roll of thunder and partly like a bird of prey's echoing call.

The searing pain grew to an almost unbearable agony before it subsided into an ache that left him limp and moaning. Bennik was lost in memories of his past, each one passing through his mind in little drawn-out lifetimes.

On a day when he was no older than six, he remembered his father kneeling down and grabbing him by the shoulders. The old man pulled Bennik's chin up so that their eyes met.

"You mustn't let failure prevail," Lord Jarrod Lawson told his son in encouraging tones. He lifted up the small bow, showing Bennik how to properly draw back the string this time. "We can accomplish nothing in life if we do not learn from our mistakes and press on."

Jarrod drew another arrow from Bennik's quiver and helped the boy knock it, guiding his aim at the stuffed deer that watched them with lifeless button eyes from the depths of the woods.

Young Bennik gritted his teeth as he drew back the string, feeling his father's warm breath behind his ear. "Hold your breath while you find your mark," he whispered. "And then be still as you release."

The arrow found its mark in the deer's head.

"Excellent shot, Lawson!" a voice that was not his father's echoed in Bennik's head. The forest was replaced by a walled village, with the flames of several burning homes lighting the night. "There's more on the wall!"

Bennik drew another arrow, his taut bowstring rubbing the side of his rough face—no longer a boy's smooth, red cheeks, but now a man's with the shadow of a beard. He lined up the tip of his arrow with the wretched lizard-like face of the kobold that threw another torch onto a roof. He released, splitting the monster's skull and sending it back over the wall.

"For Westerra!" Folk-at-arms rushed forward, wielding whatever tools and weapons they could find, rallied by the Eastlund ranger's impeccable aim and stalwart presence. "Hold! Do not let Grandridge fall!" The rabble of militia charged into the fray as a fiery yellow orb crashed into Bennik and threw him to the ground, disarming him and blackening the world.

Bennik opened his eyes to see the ruined manor in Rathen, his blurry vision focusing on the present. An elderly orc towered over him, still muscled and deadly, but covered in leathers with a beaded hood and rattling bones hanging from its clothing.

The orc carried a staff with a blue stone weakly glowing in its crooked top. With its other hand, the orc made intricate motions over Bennik, and he knew the monster was working magic—it was healing him. *But why?*

The voice of another harpy came from the haze, the one who had escorted him to this hell. "We have found the shards, Empress Corvanna."

"Good. Show me." A ruffle of feathers. "Make sure he is ready for more questioning when I return."

Bennik turned his head to see his captor, Corvanna, spread her impossibly wide wings into the sky—which the duke's manor had been opened up to beyond the great hall that served as Bennik's prison. He hardly needed one in his current condition—he wasn't going anywhere with his leg still broken.

As if in response to that, Bennik felt a sharp pain, forcing him to cry out. He tried to reach for his leg, but he couldn't sit up or move his arms. His body was beyond any level of exhaustion he had ever felt. The pain in his leg continued, but less sharply. He opened his blurry, watery eyes to see the orc continuing her work, a bony, sickly colored green hand contorting over his leg.

He was surprised to see the orc was resetting the bone. That realization brought back the memories, and the dire world around him fell away, replaced by a cozy, candlelit chapel.

"Lay still, warrior," a gentle voice begged. "Let the priestess finish her work."

Laying on a soft bed in a room flooded with candlelight, Bennik turned to the red-haired woman that held one of his hands tightly. His grip could have crushed her bones as his seared flesh wracked his body with waves of pain. But still she held on, desperately. He gritted his teeth, begging for it to end.

Another voice whispered a constant prayer to the Light, asking for its healing powers to make whole the man that had saved their village. The priestess touched Bennik's brow and the Light consumed him, soft and tender. He felt the cool relief of the healing like a soft breath on his neck, coursing through his entire body. The unbearable pain from the burns was replaced by pleasant aches, and Bennik relaxed his grip on the red-headed woman's hand.

Bennik looked up at the woman who would one day be his wife, and her face contorted into the ugly visage of a leathery-faced orc, with yellow tusks protruding from its downturned lips. The pleasant aches from Bennik's memory were replaced by twisting discomfort. This was not healing magic that the Light provided—this was dark magic prolonging a painful life.

The Shadow coursed through him, preventing him from dying so his body could endure even more pain.

"Stop," Bennik grunted between clenched teeth, knowing he would not be able to reason with an orc, but growing desperate. "Let me die."

"Guluk heal," the orc said, its voice like a dog's growl. "So Corvanna can kill. Guluk obey. You obey."

"Why?"

Guluk went about her work, not answering.

Bennik's eyes wandered, looking for any escape from the pain. The distant cries of harpies in the unseen sky beyond kindled more memories, and Guluk and the duke's ruined home fell away once more, replaced by a clear blue sky and the open road.

"Refugees," the fellow soldier said, whose name had been lost to time, but Bennik remembered his curly blond hair and the southern lilt to his voice as if he were a close relation.

Bennik reined in his horse in response. Turning to his left, he saw the two dark-skinned figures approaching, looking road-weary and desperate. "From Karrane, it looks," Bennik told his nameless companion.

Dismounting, Bennik shouldered his bow but kept his hand near his blade as he approached. "Peace, travelers. Do you come from the war?"

They did not respond, walking as if in a trance. It was a man and a woman. The man held his side, blood staining his robes and his face scratched as if goblins or kobolds had accosted them. The woman carried a bundle to her breast.

"Vhar'ai," Bennik greeted in Karranese, then asked them if they were injured in their native tongue.

The man nodded, stumbling to a knee as he approached. The woman struggled to lift him up as Bennik cautiously approached to help him. The man managed to sit down, but looked as if he were ready to die.

"We were attacked at Deerun," she said in the common tongue, looking at Bennik with desperate eyes. "My husband is mute. He is dying. It comes for me next." She thrust the bundle toward Bennik. "Please, you must get her away. She is too precious."

Bennik saw a baby, sleeping peacefully in its wraps, despite the desperate situation at hand.

"I cannot," Bennik said nervously, holding up his hands in defense. "I am a soldier from Eastlund—a ranger in the king's army. I am no wet nurse."

"She does not need a wet nurse," the woman pleaded, tears in her eyes. "She needs a soldier—a protector. She must live. He must not get her!"

As if commanded by an unseen force, Bennik reached out his hands to take the child, watching as her small eyes flicked open. The girl did not cry or stir when she gazed up into Bennik's eyes—she smiled, and Bennik's resolve melted.

Once more, the world shifted, and the blue sky and open road were replaced by a cozy room softly lit by a burning hearth.

"She's perfect," his wife said, cradling Anika in their new home tucked in the trees surrounding Blakehurst. The war was over, and Bennik had deserted his honor and his king, absconding to a paradise that he never knew he wanted.

He blinked and he was outside among familiar trees.

"Careful!" his wife shouted as she raced over to catch Anika. The child almost fell off a rock before her mother snatched her up just in time.

"You be careful," Bennik teased as he went over and scooped Anika up out of his wife's hands. He looked down at her swollen belly. "Lana said you were to take it easy, remember." He patted his wife's stomach gently, and rustled Anika's hair with his other hand.

The three of them all smiled as they continued walking through the woods, not seeing the shadowy figure that followed. An unnatural shroud concealed that creeping figure, and his steps made no sound despite the leaves on the forest floor.

"You think you could hide her from me?!"

The memory of that voice burned in his ears even now in the present as the orc continued its cruel magic. But he was still in the past.

"She is my destiny!"

Bennik grappled with the spindly figure wrapped in black shrouds and a mask that only revealed their eyes. "Get out of my house!"

Finding his footing, Bennik summoned all his strength and turned the assassin's weight against them, throwing them out the window. His wife shrieked and his daughter cried, but Bennik kept his focus on the assassin, following them out into the night.

Blood stained the ground as the assassin flipped to their feet, a twisted silver dagger appearing in their hand. In the blink of an eye, they flipped the dagger over Bennik's shoulder. Knowing his daughter was behind him, Bennik shifted as the dagger neared him, using his shoulder to catch the blade. He screamed as it tore his flesh, but found relief that it did not hit its mark.

"You will die for that!" He ran toward the assassin, who was fumbling for another weapon.

"You cannot kill me!" the assassin screamed, even as Bennik barreled into them, knocking them to the floor. The larger man began brutally beating the assailant, cursing them for bringing terror to his home.

"You come to my home," Bennik grunted, bloodying his fists on the assassin's face. "How many innocents have you killed here?!" Another blow. "And now you come for my daughter?!" Three more crushing blows.

"Bennik!" his wife called through her sobs. "Please stop."

Turning to see his terrified pregnant wife and wide-eyed child, he pointed to their house. "Take Anika inside. Now."

Both of them went back in and Bennik drew his skinning knife. He turned back to the barely conscious assassin, kneeling astride them.

"Who are you?" He stabbed the blade into the assassin's shoulder, driving it to the bone.

Screaming in agony, the assassin thrashed against the pain. After a moment, the figure reached up to remove their mask, revealing an unremarkable face that could have been a young man or woman.

"I am the Child of Shadow," they said. "If I don't kill your daughter, she will destroy the world." They raised a surrendering hand. "Not just for the Shadow—she will destroy the Light and the Shadow, and everything we know will fall apart." Tears streamed down the assassin's face now. "She cannot live, Bennik. I think you've always felt something wrong with her, haven't you?"

Bennik kept his heavy breathing steady, gripping his knife tightly but ever so still. "No," he said with certainty. "You're wrong."

"If you kill me," the assassin warned, "the Shadow will follow her until it finishes my work. It will be done—must be done." Their voice wavered. "I'm sorry, Bennik—truly. But she cannot live."

Bennik removed the knife, his eyes fixed on the assassin's, looking for any sign of deceit. He saw none. Regardless, he fluidly drove the knife into the assassin's heart.

As their body went limp, Bennik felt something leave their body that was not just their life. Something dark.

A gust of wind brought Bennik back to the present, where the constant pain continued to grip his body. He watched as Corvanna descended through the torn-away roof, flanked by several harpies on either side of her, each one fluttering their wings to find purchase on various broken pieces of the duke's manor.

The orc stopped her magic and Bennik felt the flooding relief left in the healing's wake. He was still unable to move, but the pain had finally subsided.

"Guluk, attend me," Corvanna demanded, her thunderous voice shaking the remains of the house. "Have you earned your keep?"

The orc turned away from Bennik and lifted up a fetish from the folds of her clothes. "He told all," the orc barked, holding the talisman up for Corvanna to see.

The god-like bird creature let out a cawing laugh as Bennik struggled to understand. But when the orc turned back to him, a broad hooked finger tapping on the scaly flesh of her head, Bennik felt the ice-cold grip of dread around his heart.

"He think too much," the orc said through a twisted smile. "Always think too much."

The memories, he thought. *The spell.*

The orc had not just been keeping him alive, she had been trapping his memories in her rattling bone fetish. It was an old practice that shamans used to remove nightmares from paying customers. Old, primal magic.

Gods no, he thought. "Anika..."

Corvanna laughed wickedly again. "Oh yes, Anika. Let us see about Anika, shall we?" The ruined manor shook with the cruel laughter of the harpies. Corvanna raised a bag that glimmered with the glow of various colored keyshards.

A flash of green eldritch light bathed the ruins, and a peal of thunder echoed through the growing storm above.

"You cannot mean to do this." King Markus Durrask pointed to the closed doors that stood between the royal couple and their throne room. "I understand the threat, and I agree that it must be addressed, but if you send out the Luminaura—you may as well surrender the crown now."

Sopheena gave her husband a cutting glare, her cold eyes chilling his fiery temper. "Who is queen of the realm, dear husband?"

He sighed, letting his hand fall. "I do not mean to suggest you have not thought this through, Sopheena, but we both know what is at stake—and if it's not one impending doom, it's another. Each one more threatening than the last."

"Your point?"

He took a deep breath. "I would rather lose a thousand cities than see your reign cut short." With softening eyes, he added, "I am scared, Sopheena."

"What now?"

The king and queen turned toward the third voice that came from the shadows under a winding stair that led up to the queen's study.

A slender figure stepped out, dressed in dark violet—almost black—with dozens of knives sheathed at waist, legs, boots, and across a bandolier that hung between small breasts.

The figure wore a violet lacquered mask, with only slits for eyes and flowing blade-like patterns carved into it. Stringy black hair hung over her shoulders.

Sopheena looked over her shoulder to make sure the door to the throne room was still closed and then scowled at the figure. "What are you doing here?"

A sound that could have been laughter came from behind the mask, but Knife's raspy voice sounded dead serious. "I'm always here." The elf crossed her arms casually.

"Perhaps you can speak reason to the queen, Knife," Markus said, turning away to take a seat in a cushioned chair nearby. "She would give the realm to the church at the behest of a gnome."

Sopheena gave him another glare before facing the masked figure. "What have you heard?"

"Probably as much as you," Knife said, shifting to rest a hand on her hip. "The storm is coming, the gnome is scheming, and the church is—well, that one is a mystery to me even. But they are in the game, that's for sure." She gave a little shrug. "Yet, no Ruke. The book?"

Sopheena shook her head. "No word. We are being pressed from all sides, and I see no other option." She gave her husband a side eye. "The paladins can tend to whatever Shadowfiends are behind this storm—I trust the Guild's assessment that the Shadow must be behind that, and the church is the best weapon we have against it right now. I dare not make our play yet on account of some clouds."

Markus sniffed, but he kept his words to himself.

"And the Oathers?" Knife asked. "We need them in Suthek if we hope to find the blackshards."

Sopheena smiled. "You ruined my surprise, Sister. I was going to wait until Markus burst a vein in his neck before telling him the best part."

The king stood up. "What's this now?"

Sopheena betrayed a small chuckle, taking her husband's hands. "It seems the Arcania and the Luminaura have taken a mutual interest in chasing tales of the Child of Light in Karrane.

"However, they will be too swept up in celebrating the leverage they've won over the throne by taking credit for ending this storm, that poor Fainly won't realize we'll have stripped him of his military might here in Andelor—sending his Oathers to Suthek to dig in the dirt for us and his new paladin friends riding for Rathen. Meanwhile, the Guild will lay false clues for his investigations in Karrane."

The king's smile grew wider and wider as the plan was laid out. He began to laugh, before asking, "The Child of Light?"

Knife waved a hand. "We'll find them first. They don't pertain to our plans, but if Fainly and Luriah want them, you better believe I want them more."

Sopheena made a show of motioning toward the throne room.

"Shall we go give the command then, my husband?"

Markus smiled, holding out an arm for the queen. "I don't remember ever being this excited to see that gnome in my life."

CHAPTER TWENTY-ONE

The Old Ways

Avrim swung his mace with both hands, asking the Light for guidance as the weapon struck true, bursting flesh and shattering bone. The huge worm let out a gurgling groan as it shuddered and thrashed, its grimy hide running slick with dark blood.

"Back!" Deina cried as she pushed the priest out of the way, bringing her axe around in a sweeping arc. The broad blade cleaved the thing apart, both ends of its body thrashing wildly for a moment before laying still.

Melaine approached cautiously with her bow drawn, the light from the holy symbol around Avrim's neck casting ominous shadows of the monstrous corpse down their path forward. The eldritch green glow of the earthen halls only provided low light, which allowed the worm to ambush them.

"Remind me why we came down here," Melaine asked in a dry voice, narrowing her eyes to watch for any creeping shadows in the distance.

"To save that boy, me thinks," Deina said, kicking the worm roughly to make sure it was, in fact, dead. "Maybe a bit o' curiosity as well."

Melaine looked to Avrim, who stared at his bloodied mace with distant eyes, his lips moving in prayer. She stepped toward Deina and lowered her voice so as not to disturb the priest.

"I know why I have come—I will see this through to avenge my order. I will kill Corvanna before I draw my last breath." Melaine motioned to Avrim, who was still in a trance, not hearing them. "He is bound by the Light. But what about you? Are you bound by the Light?"

Deina wiped her axe on the dead monster, smearing its gore along its rough hide, letting out an exhausted sigh. "In a way, I suppose."

Melaine checked her bow, keeping a raised eye on the dwarf to continue.

"Me oath to the Light ain't the same as the Brother's," she said, her voice a gruff whisper like the groan of a bear. "When Avrim found me, I was good as dead—not talking like I was at Mural's Gate, more like I was takin' me first step through." Deina leaned against the wall, looking toward the darkness behind them. "I traveled all over Vale— on up from Westerra where I spent some time with the halflings in the Acreage, fattenin' meself up.

"After a short stint in New Hold with me kin," Deina continued, "I decided to make the journey down the Valeway to Eastlund—soldiers never go hungry there, I hear. But it's always just been me on the road. Been betrayed more times than I can count—me dead husband was just the first of many—so I slept alone much easier.

"Anyway, the Valeway ain't what it once was." She put a finger to her throat, giving Melaine a small shrug. "I got a knife in me neck while I was camping, down near Sathford."

Melaine winced.

Deina nodded. "Was me own fault—got a bit sure o' meself after so many years camping alone, thinkin' I might not get pounced. But it was a messy job—managed to slay the wretched halfling before she got away with me coin." She laughed. "Her companion didn't stay long after I took off her head—he bolted into the woods and I was left bleeding, unable to shout for help. Limped all the way to Sathford where our Brother's church be."

Deina turned to Avrim, who was on a knee now, eyes closed in deeper prayer. He was clearly more and more disturbed by this place.

"He brought me back," Deina said, turning back to Melaine, holding up her axe. "And this is his until I am able to repay that debt. Or until we find enough gold that I can buy a castle and get back to fattenin' up."

Melaine allowed herself a smile before turning back toward their destination.

"Something is wrong."

Both women turned to Avrim, who stared wide-eyed at the dead worm—eyes still distant but regarding something imminently dangerous. Without looking away from the dead monstrosity, he spoke.

"I prayed to the Light for guidance. There was no answer. The Light has never abandoned me—my entire life, I could feel its presence. Its warmth." He blinked, looking at the women who now approached him. "I feel Shadow—cold and terrible. I've never felt it before, not like this. It *touched* me through the blood of this creature—through these walls."

He stood up, taking a step away from the worm, not touching the walls. Overwhelming fear guided his every movement, and his mouth twitched, unable to find words to express the conflict inside of him.

"Kartha," he said finally. "She said the old gods were of both Light and Shadow— What if—" He swallowed, his gaze growing distant again. "What if the Shadow has already found Ruke's stone?"

Melaine's mouth opened to respond, but closed as her narrowed eyes fell on the worm. Silence hung between the three of them as they each considered the foes they had encountered since entering this strange web of enchanted tunnels—the great worm, the living plants, the shambling tree figures.

"The Shadow grips this place," Avrim said. "I can feel it, but I dare not reach into it to learn more—it wants me to. A voice calls to me, begging me to take hold of the Shadow so it may speak directly to me."

"Ruke?" Deina asked.

Avrim looked at her, not responding but nodding slightly.

"It is guiding me," Avrim said, looking up into the dark abyss above. "Should we follow?"

Melaine looked to Deina, unsure who Avrim was asking. But the dwarf had turned to face whatever lay ahead.

"Yes."

Naya threw another heavy volume over her shoulder as she continued her hurried search for the text. The book landed in a noisy heap on the ground, along with the other discarded tomes.

Mosby sucked air through his bared teeth, clenching his fist. He knew he would have to clean this mess up, unless the priestess somehow found out what happened to her golems. "Can I help?"

"Quiet, Mosby!" Naya snapped. "I just saw it— Ah! Here!"

The priestess hefted a huge tome with both hands, slamming it down on one of the tables. "The Shrouded have several prophecies involving the Children," Naya explained, opening the huge book and running her fingers over the various passages. "If I can just find the reference—"

The slam of the door jolted them both from the book. Hurried steps came from the stairs leading up to the baron's secret passages to the chamber. Naya moved several other books to cover up the one they had been reading, moving to greet their most prickly host.

Baron Alburn Caffery waved dust and cobwebs out his face as he descended the last of the stairs, his face a mix of annoyance and concern.

"The Oather is still here!"

Naya nodded. "Yes, I saw. I do not suspect she will be a problem. It seems there is something most pressing for her in Blakehurst."

"But what about when she returns from Blakehurst?" Alburn growled, stepping angrily toward his guests. "I can deal with the Guild so long as my standing with the throne holds, but the Arcania is a different matter, Nayamere."

Naya cringed inwardly as the fool uttered her full name. Novethans didn't understand the full power of names like the Xe'danni—if the wrong person heard him speak her full name, she would be susceptible to magic that she cared not to endure. She bit back what she wanted to say and nodded her understanding.

"We have a few days to prepare for that," she said. "Rest assured, the Shrouded do not want the Oathers interfering with their business just as you do not want them suspecting you of involvement. Neither serve our order any purpose, and all will be done to keep the Arcania out of our mutual affairs."

The baron considered that with a frown, looking to Mosby as if the dwarf had something to add. He looked down, almost abashed. When he looked up, his demeanor had changed almost completely. "Perhaps it is time we conclude our business. Certainly the Dark One would feel more comfortable knowing the Shrouded did not keep its seat in one place for too long."

A long foreboding silence fell between the three of them then.

Naya felt fury rising inside of her, trying to comprehend how this pathetic man thought he could somehow kick her out of his bed as if she were a portside doxy. The Shrouded was a lifetime commitment— a devotion not to be undertaken lightly. It took every ounce of fortitude she had not to reach into her robes and reduce this absolute coward to the pile of vermin refuse that he truly was.

Instead, she took a calm breath and smiled at the baron, who she knew was at her mercy now. "Tell me, Alburn, have you grown weary of the riches provided to your family by the Shrouded over the years? Are your coffers so full that you seek to send away the woman who has kept your mines full, your harvests fruitful, and your people's bellies near to bursting?" She raised her eyebrows in expectation.

Alburn chewed on his lip, trying to maintain his composure.

"If you would be so inclined to cut ties with the Shrouded," she continued, "then perhaps I should just fade into the Shadow so you don't have to worry about the potential fallout you might endure due to our profitable operation ceasing." She stepped toward him. "You might be forced to answer some difficult questions regarding the sudden decline in your holdings."

The baron stiffened. "I spoke hastily, Nayamere."

"Naya," she corrected, feeling emboldened.

"Yes, Naya," he said, "of course. My apologies. I am concerned, that is all."

"Your concerns have been noted, Baron Caffery. Now, I need to continue my work so I may prepare for the Oather's departure and inevitable return."

Bowing his head ever so slightly, the baron turned to retreat back up the stairs, his pace quickened.

Mosby chuckled when the door slammed above. "The Dark One chose a unique devotee there."

"The Cafferys have not always been so craven," Naya commented, moving the books and parchment to continue her search in the tome. "Alburn's father was a true believer. It's a shame he did not live to see the Child come to his very town."

"Pardon my ignorance on these matters, Naya," Mosby began, "but ye know I'm relatively new to these teachings. I don't remember much mention of the Children in the Dark One's tenets."

"The Dark One doesn't concern himself with the Children, mostly. But in his constant quest to darken the world in Shadow, he is concerned with corrupting the Light—that which cannot be destroyed must be corrupted." She ran her fingers through a long passage, stopping at a line. "Here!"

Mosby leaned in as she began to read.

"The Children of Light and Shadow may be the eternal reasons why the Light outshines the Shadow, until such time as the Child of Shadow shall slay the Child of Light to tip the scales the other way. But the cycle will never end, only shifting the balance for at least a generation. The Shrouded shall not play this game, as it has no discernible end."

Naya's voice became more lively as she continued reading. "Yet the first Dark One claimed to be the second Child of Shadow and was born with visions of these prophecies." She ran a hand down the list. "These have all come to pass," she said to Mosby, her finger stopping on the seventh and last one.

"When the Child of Light can be swayed to Shadow rather than slain, the cycle will end as the Children unite in darkness."

Mosby looked up. "Sway to Shadow?"

Naya smiled. "The Child of Light is here, Mosby. I saw her." She produced Ruke's stone. "The stone has never lied to me, and it assured me as well. The Karranese girl is the Child of Light."

"And how do you plan to sway her to Shadow?"

Naya couldn't help but laugh. "The Shadow travels among her, dear Mosby! I felt it as pure as I felt her presence. One of her companions is in league with Shadow—must be deeply devoted with how much darkness I felt around her."

"So," Mosby said, still slightly confused, "how do we sway her?"

"We don't," Naya said wickedly. "They do. We just help."

The halls began to glimmer with tiny green shimmers as they delved farther down into the earth, as if a thousand emeralds exploded and embedded their shards in the walls. Avrim wondered if that wasn't exactly what had happened. Their passage had not been further impeded since the worm, and now the relative peace and quiet let Avrim's mind wander to the history of this place.

"Kartha said Ruke created these ways," Avrim said aloud. Melaine did not turn to acknowledge the musing, her bow slightly drawn with an arrow nocked as she surveyed the shadows ahead.

Deina hefted her axe, but gave the priest a side eye. "Rather impressive work for an old halfling witch."

"Ruke was no mere witch," Avrim said. "She was a powerful priestess. And if she was in fact the oldest living devotee of Oakus in her time, as Kartha described, then I suppose this is the place where an incarnate might emerge—the oldest and most devoted shrine to the old god."

Melaine turned to the priest, the emerald gleam of the place making her skin glow green. Understanding flashed in her eyes. "The harpies were the most devoted worshippers of Eyen."

"And we be among the most devoted of Oakus, I be guessin'," Deina said with a dark laugh.

Avrim swallowed, hefting his mace to make sure he felt comfortable with its weight next time he would have to use it. "We should quicken our pace. The deeper we go, the less of the Light I can feel. It's as if we are descending into the Abyss itself."

As if in response, the earth shifted and groaned under their feet, and the sound of creaking roots echoed down the hall—not so far away.

Melaine drew her bow tighter and crept farther ahead, eager to be at the end of this tunnel, wherever it would lead them. Avrim continued reaching out for the Light as they went deeper, determined not to lose his hold on it.

The hall turned and the three of them neared a pool of green light where the tunnel opened up. Melaine held a hand up, signaling for Deina and Avrim to hold position while she crept to see what lay ahead.

Avrim knelt down slightly, listening to the continuing groan of what sounded like huge plants growing. Melaine motioned for them to approach quietly, turning fearful eyes on them, chilling Avrim's heart.

Deina took the rear as Avrim took position next to the ranger, peering ever so carefully around the earthen wall. The lights beyond illuminated a bizarre and shocking scene.

Plant-like figures with skin made from tree bark moved slowly about the chamber, their branch-like limbs carrying bundles of dirt, roots, and other growing things to a pack onto a larger, unmoving figure.

It was as if they were building a monster out of foliage.

An incarnate.

Deina gripped her axe, its leather grip creaking slightly. Melaine motioned for her to stay. The half-orc pointed at the figures, jerking her head so Deina would watch. That was when Avrim realized what she saw. The plant golems seemed to be ignoring any bundles they dropped, and did not respond to the critters that scampered around the floor of that chamber, their homes disturbed by the work.

Melaine reached down and grabbed a stone, tossing it at one of the golems. It bounced off the thing's head without interrupting its work. Looking at Deina, Melaine raised her bow. The dwarf nodded.

Taking a deep breath, Melaine drew and fired, her arrow thunking perfectly into the head of one of the golems. Again, it did not falter or take notice.

Avrim said a quick prayer to the Light, and did not wait for his companions. He stepped into that chamber, walking tall and unbothered by the busy monsters.

Deina gasped, but held her breath as Avrim crossed the chamber without drawing the attention of a single golem. They were completely engrossed in their business of building Oakus a deserving vessel.

Melaine and Deina looked at each other, shrugged, and followed Avrim's lead. While Deina had to step out of the way of two golems, they crossed the chamber unobstructed and joined Avrim on the other side, where the hallways seemed to shine even brighter than the one they came from.

"This must be the way," Melaine whispered, nodding.

Avrim looked back at the incarnate being constructed, afraid that she was right. He whispered a prayer to the Light, asking for courage, but the Shadow grew heavy down here.

He would have to find the courage himself.

CHAPTER TWENTY-TWO

The Heist

The sun began to descend as Anika watched the figures below. Ransil, Brood, Grip, and Robin made their way toward the halfling Dolly's apartment. She stood alone in her room, wondering how she had gotten to this point.

Why me? she thought, feeling ashamed even as the question formed in her mind. It was a pitying thought, the type of thinking she was not prone to doing. Her entire life seemed to be a series of sporadic tragedies of different severities, but she was not one to dwell on them.

How would pitying herself solve the mystery of the stone in her pouch? How would it save her father? How would it protect her friends? While she may not know how to solve these problems, she certainly knew that wishing it had all happened to someone else would help nothing.

She didn't hear the footsteps approaching from behind or the hand on her shoulder that made her start violently. Soothing calm came over her when she turned to see Matty.

"Sorry," he said with a small smile. "I just wanted to let you know. Gage is in his room—said he was going to try and sleep so he wouldn't pace the room worrying about Robin." He looked toward the disappearing figures that were going to make their plans. "I'm not saying I would go with them on this unscrupulous task, but it's hard knowing that we can't do anything while we wait."

Anika nodded, letting her eyes wander to the busy streets of Oakworth. The evening crowd seemed even bigger than the afternoon one, which at that time had been the largest collection of people that Anika had ever seen.

"I might go walk the streets," Matty said, turning to retrieve his sword belt. "Maybe I can keep an eye on this Oather that is roaming about."

"My mother used to tell me stories about this place." Anika's eyes were distant now, staring into the past. "She always told me that we would move here someday." She turned to face Matty. "Gage was a baby then, and I only have vague memories. But I always remember how she spoke about Oakworth." She smiled sadly. "She made it sound like a magical kingdom where anything was possible. And she told me that we would leave the darkness of Blakehurst together, as a family."

Matty shifted uncomfortably, considering for a long moment before looking into Anika's eyes. "I remember your mother, Anika. She always seemed sad, or scared—I couldn't tell which. It was her eyes I remember the most. It made me—I don't know, sad for you." He took a step toward her. "I worried that she would look at you with those sad eyes, inflicting whatever troubled her onto you." He reached out to take her hand.

Trembling now, Anika gazed into his kind, caring eyes.

"You deserve to be happy," he said. "I may have sworn my blade to the reeve, but I will break that oath in a heartbeat if needed to see you through this. I am yours, Anika. You are all I have left of home."

Anika kissed him, letting him pick her up with his powerful arms to lay her on the bed, both of them forgetting the desperate plot unfolding that night.

In the stillness of their room, a light breeze was unknowingly summoned, enveloping them.

Kasia Strallow ascended the stairs to her room in The Harvest Breeze, Jak close behind. As she reached the second floor, rounding the banister to take the next flight of stairs, she felt something unusual.

It was a faint ripple that washed over her, stirring to life the antimagic enchantments of her armor.

"Dame?" Jak asked, looking around the balcony for any sign of trouble. All was quiet. "Is everything all right?"

Kasia narrowed her eyes on the three closed doors down the hall. The urge to kick each of them down nearly overcame her, but she reminded herself there were more pressing concerns than some hedge witch passing through Oakworth.

Besides—she turned to Jak, thinking of the additional leverage she had gained over the baron by meeting with Scratch—she meant to make use of their third-floor bed before setting out for Blakehurst tomorrow.

She gave Jak a long and silent look, making the squire visibly uncomfortable. "No, Jak. Everything is not all right." Kasia motioned up the stairs. "You have a long night ahead of you."

Jak swallowed nervously as he hurried up the stairs.

"She still has 'em," Brood said, producing a set of grapples and coils of thin rope from a chest that had been hidden beneath his sister's bed. "Plenty of lockpicks in here too if we need 'em."

"Pack them," Ransil said over his shoulder, keeping his attention on the layout of the baron's keep, "in case we can't find the key for Dolly's cell. Where would it be, Robin?"

The half-elf pointed toward the northeastern part of the keep. "Under here. I remember taking two flights of stairs, but the dungeons go down several levels. I'd assume Dolly is being held on one of the top levels—the baron can't think she's much of a threat yet."

Grip leaned in. "She'll be close to the surface. Two of our agents escaped the dungeons before and reported that the baron kept the lower levels reserved for more long-term prisoners." The elf's shadowy face held uncharacteristic sympathy. "Depending on what he knows about Dolly, she will either be released in a few days or be hanged on the morrow."

Ransil gave the elf a look of understanding, turning to his cousin who now joined the table. "We'll get her out tonight, Rosh."

Brood nodded.

Turning back to the drawn map of the keep, Ransil pointed to the southwestern wall. "We grapple here, where Robin says there is a patrol between this crenellation and the tower. We wait for them to pass, grapple up, and silently subdue the patrol." Ransil looked at Grip. "No killing."

"Relax," she said with a wink. "I have more vials of ether than I know what to do with."

"That goes for everyone," Ransil added. "We risk much by infiltrating the keep, but if any deaths are laid at our feet, we implicate more than ourselves in this operation. Absolute discretion is key."

The conspirators all nodded in agreement.

"Brood," Ransil instructed, "you hold position at the grapples, bring them up so no one notices them on the walls. Then you wait for me and Robin to bring Dolly back. You bring her straight back here and pack her things for Andelor.

"Grip, you will stick to the shadows behind us, making sure no patrols interfere. Once we free Dolly and escort her back to Brood, the three of us will go for the stone. Agreed?"

After the plan was settled on, they individually made their way to the Breeze to wait for dark.

"I'm so sorry!" Renay scooped up the halfling girls as the two men who guarded the drawbridge helped a trader pick up her scattered produce. Apples rolled across the road, several falling into the moat.

"The road is no place for such small children running about!" The trader was on her knees scooping up her lost fruit, her tipped-over cart's wheels spinning uselessly. "It is dangerous!"

Renay nodded, consoling the scared child that almost got ran over by the cart. "I know, I'm very sorry. I will take them inside now."

"It's all right," one of the guards said, offering Renay a sympathetic smile. She bent down to help the other guard turn the cart upright. "We'll take care of this."

"Thank you," Renay said with a slight bow, her face reddening. "Come, children." She moved into the keep's courtyard.

As the guards were focused on righting the cart and cleaning up the apples, a shadow slipped behind them through the gate, following Renay. It was like a shimmering in the air itself, faint mists obscuring it as it crept along the wall into the courtyard.

Aching from pains and pleasures that were all new to her, Anika sat up in the bed, looking for her discarded clothes. Matty sat up as well, stiffly and clumsily.

"Anika."

She turned toward him, instinctively covering her breasts, horrified by what he might be about to say to her. *Did I do something wrong?* she wondered. She felt the slight touch of the same power from the night Blakehurst was attacked. Something stirred within her, aside from the echoes of passion. *Did he feel it too?*

"I'm sorry if—" A flush crept onto his face. "I didn't hurt you, did I?"

Smiling in relief, Anika let her hands fall from her chest as she leaned over to kiss him. "Yes," she said, with a teasing smile, "but in a good way."

She turned to get dressed.

"I should check on the others," Matty said, pulling his own pants on. "Will you be okay? I won't be long."

Anika smiled, her face beginning to hurt from the repeated act. "I'll be fine."

As he finished dressing and left the room, Anika felt a pull toward the stone. She drew it out as she finished dressing. Looking into its depths, she awaited the visions, but a knock at the door interrupted. She got up to answer, opening the door to see Robin with a concerned look.

"Have you seen Gage?"

She looked out in the hall to see her brother's door open. "He wasn't in there?"

Robin shook his head. "I was meeting with Ransil, Grip, and Brood. But when I got back to the room he was gone. You didn't see him pass by here?"

Anika shook her head, feeling slightly guilty that she had been so indisposed that she wouldn't have heard anything. "He never tells me where he goes." She turned to get her things. "I'll go look for him with Matty. When are you leaving?"

Robin gave her a scared look. "Now. It's dark."

Anika reached out to grab his shoulder. "Are you sure you want to do this, Robin? What if we don't need the Guild? What if there's another way?"

Robin shook his head. "Even if there was, I can't leave Scratch in there. I know something bad will happen to her. And with that Oather here—it's just asking for trouble. Just thinking about her hanging from those gallows…" He shuddered visibly.

She shook her head. "I'll go look for Gage, I'm sure he's fine." For some reason, Anika had trouble believing those words. Something felt wrong. But she kept that suspicion to herself. "You just focus on what needs to be done, Robin."

He nodded and turned to join the others downstairs.

Gripping the stone, Anika followed, hoping Matty hadn't gone far.

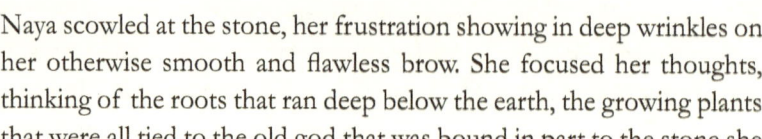

Naya scowled at the stone, her frustration showing in deep wrinkles on her otherwise smooth and flawless brow. She focused her thoughts, thinking of the roots that ran deep below the earth, the growing plants that were all tied to the old god that was bound in part to the stone she held.

There was no response. Something had changed since yesterday, and she felt no command over the golems that had served her up until now. Mosby was scouring the halls, trying to learn where they went.

She was alone in the vast study, feeling more isolated than she had in her entire life. Although the Shrouded grew in number all across the Joined Realms, here in the heart of Vale, she felt adrift. Oakus had given her the warmth she needed to stay her course, furthering the Shadow's grip on the world. Oakus was her companion in that quest, more so than Mosby or any other mortal.

Oakus was the closest thing she had to love, aside from her unending devotion to the Shadow. She reached out again, but felt nothing.

She had been abandoned. And she knew why.

The Child, she thought, Anika's face looming in her thoughts like a lifelong nemesis that had come to ruin her plans—her only purpose. Her fingers tightened around Ruke's stone, struggling to keep wrath from her mind. She needed the Child as much as she needed Oakus. But her purpose was more clear.

Reaching out in her mind with all of her conviction, she called for dark guidance from the Shadow's deepest reaches—beyond any reckoning.

A path was laid for her and she got up to follow.

The guard looked over the pools of torchlight that marked intersecting roads and the steady paths of the watch's patrols. All was in order, despite the recent excitement caused by the Oather's presence. Both the watch and the keep's guards were numbered fewer tonight, as a force was being prepared to march to Blakehurst on urgent Arcania business.

Diligently keeping their pace, the guard shifted to move toward the westernmost tower. Once they passed through the archway, the sound of the heavy door shutting covered the clattering of metal hooks finding purchase on the wall's rough edges.

Renay closed the door gently so as not to disturb Kadie and Sadie's slumber. The exhausted halflings were unconscious before Renay had finished the first story, and she was overcome with affection for the sweet, adventurous girls as she spent a few precious moments watching them dream.

As the door clicked closed, she heard a scrape of stone behind her and she spun, her heart caught in her throat. She saw only dancing shadows from a torch in the servants' hall. There was no other sound or movement, and she took a deep breath to steady her nerves. Ever since she had seen the baron lock up the halflings' mother, Renay had been on edge. Something frightened her about Alburn's sense of justice in that matter, but she dared not question him.

Not again.

She made her way out of the servants' hall, not noticing the shadowy figure that followed her every step, her thoughts focused now only on keeping the Shadow's visions away—which she had remarkably evaded throughout the day.

The shimmering mists stalked her as she walked the baron's empty halls, the guards all called away on important Arcania business. Renay's footsteps echoed like a scratching heartbeat, quickening as dark thoughts began to push her toward the baron's chambers where she would find the security she needed.

She made her way to the baron's children's rooms, finding them both laughing from within Lenora's chambers.

"...and I'm an orc! Coming to chop off your head," Victor bellowed, waving a wooden sword over his head.

"No!" Lenora cried with glee. "You need to be the knight, because I need rescued! I'm the princess trapped by the ogre!"

"Princesses don't need rescued," Renay said with a laugh. "Especially when they have wits like yours, my dear Lenora."

The children chased each other, laughing breathlessly until Renay managed to calm them down.

"It's bedtime for you two," Renay said.

"Tell us a story then," Victor said, pointing his sword and assuming a soldier's erect stance. "The Lord of Oakworth commands it!"

"Well," Renay said, tickling the boy, "if the lord commands it."

The three of them fell back on the bed laughing as the children attacked Renay with wiggling fingers.

The shimmering mists wavered for a moment in the dark corner of the room.

Tears ran down Gage's cheeks as he watched, but his face was a contorted mask of fury behind the shroud that concealed him. A volatile mix of emotions turned his stomach. He felt overwhelming relief, seeing his mother alive after all these years. It was a miracle. But the rage he felt toward his father, lying to them about her death—*He said he buried her!* Gage couldn't breathe as hatred and malice found purchase in the chaos of his heart.

He drew his dagger from its sheath, eyes narrowed on the children that had somehow stolen his mother. His blood pumped the growing rage throughout his body and it painted his vision red. He took a step toward his no-longer-dead mother; the magical shroud he somehow commanded followed, hiding him from the world.

Matty and Anika convened near the drawbridge leading toward the baron's keep. Her eyes searched his for any hope, finding none as Matty shook his head.

"No sign of him," Matty said. "I can't imagine where he would have gone."

Anika looked to the baron's keep, thinking of Robin and Ransil creeping along the shadows inside the walls. Something told her Gage was in there—it wasn't a hunch, it was a certainty.

"He's inside the keep."

Matty looked at the two guards flanking the only way into the gates. "How do you know?" But when her eyes found his, he saw she knew—somehow, she had no doubt, and he did not question it. He would never question her after witnessing what she was capable of that night in Blakehurst.

"We need to figure out how to get in." Anika looked up on the walls and saw archers on watch, pacing the length of the wall. It seemed impossible.

Matty bent over, digging something out of his pack. "How do you feel about being my prisoner?"

Anika stared at the manacles curiously.

Ransil and Robin shuffled across the courtyard, the half-elf leading the halfling toward an unguarded doorway. Above them they heard a faint rustle, and they both knew that Grip had incapacitated another guard.

"If she keeps this up," Robin whispered to Ransil, "there won't be any guards to avoid on the way out."

Ransil nodded, giving a reluctant smile as he glanced upward.

"Why do you call her *Your Majesty*?" Robin asked.

"That's a long story best reserved for telling over celebratory drinks once this business is settled."

Robin nodded and led them to the dungeon stairs, both figures moving in practiced silence toward Dolly's prison. They stopped when they heard a commotion near the gates. Ransil gasped as they saw Anika in chains, being led by Matty, who spoke to the guards. The halfling started to rush toward them, but Robin held him back.

"We can't," Robin whispered.

"What is he doing?" Ransil growled. "I told him to stay in the Breeze! If he means to betray us, I will cut out his damn heart!"

After a brief moment, the guards motioned across the courtyard to where Ransil and Robin were hiding. Matty gave the chain attached to Anika's wrists a tug and they walked toward them, Anika keeping her head down.

When they neared, Ransil moved forward with a raised dagger. "Matty!" he hissed. "Release her!"

"Shhhh," Anika said, looking over her shoulder. She moved toward the door with Matty. "They'll hear you. They think I'm a prisoner."

"What are you doing?" Ransil's eyes were wild with confusion and rage.

While Anika explained, Robin and Ransil both cursed Gage.

"All right," Ransil said, waving his hands to silence everyone. "Let's go free Dolly and be done with that, then we'll worry about Gage."

The four of them descended the stairs into the dungeon.

Naya watched from outside the chamber, peering at the shadow that hid near the curtains in the child's room. She felt the Shadow's presence pulling her toward that shrouded figure lurking in the mists, urging her in ways she had never experienced.

Could it be? she wondered, moving forward, seeing a blade in the shrouded figure's hand. But a sudden movement made her seek refuge in the room across the hall.

She saw the baron's doxy, the red-haired servant that warmed the lord and lady's bed, leading Viktor back to his room across the hall. Waiting for Renay to pass her by, Naya crept back into the hall to approach the shadowy figure, smiling when she peered into the dimly lit room.

"Who are you?" the little girl asked the shrouded figure, unafraid— as if she wanted to keep her new friend to herself.

Naya whispered her own words, summoning a field of silence around her and the two other figures in the room, ensuring that no outsider could hear. She allowed herself to move into the room under heavy shadows, unseen to the girl or her strange new friend near the window.

"I am her son," the figure said in a trembling voice, fighting back an anguish that Naya could feel in her bones. She smiled, knowing the Shadow would take hold easily in this one, and knowing that it must. Because she now saw with her Shadowsight that this was one of the Child's companions—the Eastlund boy with thick, dark hair.

He was her key to swaying the Child of Light.

"She is *my* mother," the boy continued. "Not yours." He stepped out of the magical aura, his knife shimmering in the moonlight.

The girl shivered in her bed; terror had gripped her now and she was unable to move. Her confused eyes were fixed on the older boy with the blade, knowing he intended some malice toward her, but not knowing why.

The Eastlund boy stopped, his own body trembling.

Naya stiffened, feeling the boy resisting the Shadow. She felt his internal struggle, threatening to awaken some sympathy within her that had died a long time ago. But she would not allow it. She listened to the story of his emotions so that she could manipulate them through the Shadow to her own ends.

She felt the betrayal, the hatred, the sadness, the confusion, all at war within him—it was overwhelming, even for a husk like Naya to endure. But she persevered, knowing the stakes were just too high. The tragedy of a mother who abandoned her family for fear of the Shadow was quite poetic.

"Are you going to hurt me?" Lenora's voice was choked, as if she feared crying might force the stranger's blade.

The intruder didn't outwardly move, but a dark claw reached up into his heart, gripping it in cold, hateful certainty. Naya's face watched from the shadows, delighting in the dire serendipity playing out before her. She was reassured that the prophecy was at hand.

The Eastlunder gripped his blade tighter, the Shadow taking hold. "You stole her from me." His voice was reluctantly dripping venom. He took another step, Naya urging him to give in to the Shadow, to take his vengeance.

It was then that Naya had a sudden realization. She felt the Shadow's urging, but it was not her who prodded this boy forward. Her mastery of the Shadow gave her an unbreakable connection to it, and it tied her to this boy—to feel his anguish. She was meant to be here, that was undeniable. But she was not here to drive the boy.

She was here to witness.

She was here to worship.

She was here to usher in the chosen one.

The boy took another step toward the cowering girl, his blade now raised and steady. "Why did she choose you?" His voice cracked with emotion. "She left me, for you. Why?!" His raised voice was amplified in the field of silence surrounding them.

The girl wept. "Please don't hurt me," she managed through desperate sobs. But she did not scream, as if she knew it would be futile.

"I don't want to hurt you," the boy said, stepping next to the bed with murder in his eyes. "But I must—to hurt her." He slashed, spraying blood across the room.

Naya watched in pure reverence, witnessing the Child of Shadow's coming.

"Hurry," Dolly hissed, nervously watching the torchlight coming around the long hall's corner. The jailer was only steps away. She turned back to Ransil's frantic fingers, working the cell's lock deftly.

It clicked, the door creaking open with only the faintest of a sound as the halfling slipped out to join her rescuers.

"Come on," Ransil said, leading them down the hall.

But Anika stood frozen against the wall, her eyes distant and a hand on her stomach. Dread knotted in her gut like spoiled food.

"Gage," she said to the shadows.

"Anika," Matty whispered, taking her hand.

She followed, but her eyes held on the unseen tragedy that she felt like a dagger through her heart.

For the first time in her life, she felt the Shadow's touch.

Chapter Twenty-Three

Somewhere Gray

As Bennik's life bled from his countless wounds, he dreamed of home.

It wasn't the rolling hills, lush forests, and majestic castles of Eastlund that he dreamed of—that was the home of Bannerlord Lawson, a life he had abandoned when he deserted the king's army in Westerra. No, he dreamed of peaceful and dark Blakehurst, where he had lived a simple life with his one and only love, Renay.

Their shared life played out in his mind like a slow-burning candle as he dipped in and out of consciousness. One moment he saw the burned ruins of the duke's manor in Rathen, and the next he would be in his tanning shed, the visceral smells of brutal, thankless labor keeping his heart beating with a fading will to live.

He saw Renay's face, smiling at him with that shyness she possessed from the night he had met her—when she had helped bring him back from death. He pleaded for her to do so again, wanting to forgive her but knowing that there was no forgiveness because there was no fault.

There was only cruel fate.

He dreamed of the times he had hated her as much as he had loved her. The furious nights when he watched their children sleep, letting himself weep as he struggled to understand what could have driven her away.

It was then that he learned the truth.

That night, many years after Renay had abandoned them, Bennik sat sleepless as he nursed a tankard of ale that had long gone stale. Watching his children rest after a hard day's work, he drank to his sorrows, thinking of his lost love as he did far too often. Sitting outside the doors to both his children's rooms, he watched as Gage sat up stiffly, sitting on the edge of his bed and facing a shadowed wall.

Bennik set down his drink and started to rise, but stopped as he heard his son give a soft chuckle.

"It is not yet time," Gage said in a low whisper. "You will see, sister.

The Light cannot burn forever."

Frozen in fear, Bennik mouthed his son's name, but no sound escaped his lips.

"Oh, you think so?" Gage gave another slight chuckle. "I think not. She still has a part to play. Unless you strike first, sweet sister." Another soft laugh. "Do you think you can? Kill your own brother? Why not, you aren't true kin. Come take me while I sleep. I will be back. Your father killed me once and I took his only born." The laugh came again, gentle and ancient.

Bennik stood up, a dream within the dream played out—as he killed the Child of Shadow, black mists drained from that figure and slithered across the earth toward his home.

Renay, he said presently, but only in his mind, as his mouth was far too parched to make any sound aside from a wheeze. *No. Not Renay. Not my son. Take me. Take me, take me! I shall be your damned Shadowlord!*

His mind continued its descent into madness as he went back to that horrible dream, watching his son commune with dark forces—seeing visions of Anika that were not there. Bennik knew he watched the unending battle between Light and Shadow that night, though he had no words or even thoughts to comprehend it at that time.

He wept in his dream, because he had no tears left in the present. Cursing himself for not doing something with the forbidden knowledge he would not allow himself to say or even put down in writing—that his Children were doomed from birth, and he could do nothing to prevent them from killing each other.

Bennik remembered his frantic thoughts that night, wanting to flee, but knowing there was nowhere he could take his children to escape their cruel fate. He wanted to take them somewhere gray, where Light and Shadow did not control every aspect of the world.

He thought of Renay, and his heart broke for her plight. She was a fervent follower of the Light, raised in the Luminaura to object to Shadow's stain on the world, opposing its very existence wherever and whenever possible. To know she birthed the Shadow itself, to know the Light would call on her to extinguish the life she had made— Bennik knew it had ruined her.

Bennik groaned into the night under the storm in Rathen, his heart breaking all over again. *Renay*, he thought, as blackness overcame him, devouring thought and dream into silent oblivion.

Renay felt the Shadow pass over her as she walked toward her own quarters. It wasn't a vision this time, but a dark wind that chilled her to the core—a foreboding that felt familiar but terrifyingly alien. Something crept beside her, unseen. She knew it, but refused to openly acknowledge it—as if that would somehow give it strength and a foothold in her world.

She stopped suddenly, turning toward the baron's chambers before continuing on her way, not wanting to be alone with this Shadow.

She needed her escape, but still it followed, unyielding and merciless.

The halls were eerily empty, much like the rest of the keep, with many of the guards preparing for their journey east with the Oather. She found that oddly reassuring, as the Oather's presence had put her on edge—not just because of the timely episode with Dolly, but also because she feared the knight might sense the Shadow's stain on her.

She quickened her pace. The deathly terror that followed her seemed to get worse, as if it were closing in on her. It was all she could do not to run up the last flight of stairs that would take her to the oblivion she sought.

"Renay," Vivian said when she opened the door, motioning for the flanking guards to be at ease. "What brings—"

Once the doors shut, Renay kissed the woman deeply, her terror turning into unbridled passion. Her mouth worked as furiously as an animal that had been dying of thirst and had finally found water.

"Take me," Renay breathed, holding back the tears so as not to ruin her escape. "Please. Both of you, take me."

The baroness obliged, leading her to bed where the baron was waiting. None of them saw the small figure cloaked in Shadow that lurked in the corner of the room, bloodstained and watching with black slits for eyes.

Mosby paced about nervously, waiting for Naya to return. His footsteps echoed mystically in the vast chamber of roots and packed earth, where sound should not carry so—not naturally, at least. It was not like his master to be late. Something must have gone wrong. He knew he should not have let her go alone, but she was far too caught up in the excitement of her discovery.

The dwarf's frantic pacing made it easy for the intruders to sneak up on him.

"Gah!" Mosby tried to cry out as the massive, muscled arm around his neck cut off his air supply, silencing him. The figure that grappled him spun him easily around to see a red-faced dwarf woman and a priest of the Light holding a bloodied mace. Both of them were glaring, determined fury in their eyes.

"Who are ye and where are we?" The dwarf woman hefted an axe threateningly, taking a step toward the grappled servant of Shadow.

Mosby felt the arm around his neck loosen slightly so he could respond.

"Ye don't want to be here when me master gets back—"

The rest of the threat was cut off as the arm tightened again. He let out a pitiful croak as his face turned red again under the monstrous figure's strength.

"You won't be here when your master returns if we don't get answers," the priest said, hefting his bloody mace. "Tell us."

The arm loosened once more.

"Under Oakworth," Mosby coughed, sucking in another gulp of precious air. "The baron's keep. Yer in the baron's private library, and he won't be happy if he comes down them stairs to find ye trespassing."

The priest gave the dwarf woman a look, and then they nodded slightly toward each other, confirming a suspicion most likely. An idea came to Mosby.

"I'm the baron's personal assistant," he said, assuming a more dignified pattern to his speech, hoping they wouldn't notice. "He'll lock ye up if ye don't let me go."

The huge figure holding Mosby let out a gruff snort. "The day a high lord like Oakworth takes a one-armed dwarf Shadow priest into his service is the day I become an Oather."

Mosby had forgotten the volumes of Shadow-worshipping texts that lined the shelves, cursing Naya for not keeping them locked away somewhere instead of displayed proudly, even in the privacy of her own library.

The priest took a step toward Mosby, holding his flanged mace a few hairs away from the dwarf's face. "If this is in fact the baron's keep, then he will not be baron for long when the Lighthold discovers he secretly worships the Shadow. I fear not his wrath—but you should fear mine."

In a blink, the priest swung that mace down low, burying it painfully into Mosby's knee. The dwarf howled in agony as his body went limp, held up by his powerful captor. Excruciating pain blinded Mosby. Unable to think or reason, he cursed any Shadow prayer he could think of, but none took hold.

As if in response, the priest whispered a prayer to the Light and knelt down to touch the wounded knee. Mosby felt a warm touch followed by coolness easing the unbearable pain—he felt his bones mending and flesh healing as the power of the Light undid the priest's brutal attack.

"I can do that again," the priest said with restrained fury. "And again. As much as it takes for you to tell us the truth."

"Aye," Mosby said, surrendering his very life to avoid that pain again, "I'll tell ye what ye want to know."

"Who are you?"

"Mosby. Ain't got no clan name no more. Exiled from New Hold for consorting with the Shadow."

"Who is your master?" the priest asked, his face contorted with rage.

"A Xe'danni Shadow priestess," Mosby said, leaving out the Shrouded in hopes that maybe, just maybe, he could avoid their wrath if he should escape this. He had already accepted that Naya might not survive the night with how things were going. "In league with the baron. She uses the baron's stone to keep his coffers stocked and he gives her sanctuary."

The priest turned back to the dwarf woman, whose eyes were narrowed on Mosby in fury that nearly rivaled the priest's. She nodded to him, seeming to be satisfied, and the priest returned his cold gaze to Mosby. "She has the stone?"

Mosby nodded. "Aye. I can help ye get it."

"No need." The priest spoke the last words that Mosby would ever hear with almost no anger—he spoke like a priest leading a congregation, with calm divine purpose. He lifted the mace with both hands and brought it down to cave in Mosby's skull before the dwarf could utter a sound. He slumped to the floor in a dead heap, his head nothing but a bloody ruin.

The Shadow retreated from the room as Avrim's holy symbol began to glow.

Under a gray hood, Lexeth watched the ruins of Rathen with gray-green eyes that almost matched the hue of the clouds overhead. The cursed storm had come to Lohkrest two days ago. It could be seen from the tree spires of Lefayra, and the Eldercrowns had sent their rangers to investigate.

Lexeth spat, unable to get the rancid taste of the air out of his mouth. Seeing the ruined city with his own eyes reassured him of his purpose here. When word of his sister's death reached Lefayra, he wanted to ride immediately to Blakehurst—not to honor her death or her dying duty, but to avenge her. Yet the Eldercrowns assured him that Farrah's death was tied to the storm in Rathen somehow. When the Eldercrowns spoke, every elf in Lohkrest was expected to listen and obey, else they could go live amongst the city elves. So he resigned himself to joining his fellow rangers in an effort to not let his sister die in vain.

"Orcs," Geneva said, sniffing the air. How she could discern any smell in this putrid, dying air was beyond Lexeth, but his eyes confirmed her suspicions. Even from the distance, he could make out the hulking forms of orcs moving about the city ruins. The winged wretches still patrolled the skies.

"With harpies?" Lexeth asked. "What could unite such creatures?"

Geneva gave him a knowing look. "Shadow."

Lexeth shook his head, unconvinced. "The Shadow has already taken them, as well as hundreds of other monsters that are at war with one another. But this union," he motioned to the city, "and this storm—it's something more. The Dreamers won't tell us, but I know they saw something in the Domain. The Eldercrowns won't tell us either, they just expect us to solve the riddles they don't understand or don't want to speculate with us."

"Does it matter?" Geneva asked, motioning to the city. "We were told to scout and report back what we see. Do you want to worry about the old ones back at home sitting on their self-important asses, or do you want to see what is going on down there?"

Lexeth grinned, despite the state of affairs. "Let's go and see." He made a series of hand motions to the stale air behind him before turning to follow Geneva.

The elves made their way silently down the hills, their gray cloaks blending in with the gray and dying world around Rathen.

In the sky above, the harpies continued their patrols, not seeing the party of elven rangers that followed Lexeth and Geneva. They numbered less than the orcs, but they moved with mastery that outmatched the monsters and their winged masters.

Once again, death marched on Rathen.

CHAPTER TWENTY-FOUR

The Inevitable Threads

The road back to Caraby was hard, and not just because the earth was shaking.

Layla walked in a trance, her horse probably sitting in an ogre's digestive tract now. Her legs ached and her feet blistered, but the hollow feeling in her chest was worse than anything else her body endured on that journey.

She felt ruined—somehow at fault for what had happened to her. In her mind, she knew there was no excuse for what Desmond had done to her, but her heart was not so easily controlled by reason. Something ached in her, and she wanted nothing more than to suffocate that ache in rage.

As the sun hung over her shoulder, warming her under her robes, she imagined Desmond being torn to shreds, and she tried to sustain herself on that imagery.

She wanted nothing more than to revel in that gruesome vision.

But other memories came to her in flashes. She remembered Desmond from her first few years at Raventhal Spire. He was not the type of person that occupied the thoughts of a young elf caught up in the hustle and bustle of Sathford for the first time. But she remembered him nonetheless. While in the green tower, she and her friends had ridiculed Desmond for his awkwardness and the little notebooks he carried.

Below her feet, the ground rumbled again.

"I know what you're thinking."

Layla turned to Valix, her eyes skeptical—both of the claim and of the woman in general. She had shown the elf kindness when it was needed most, but Layla was still not yet certain about her new companion.

"You think you did something wrong," Valix said, shifting the large book she carried to her other arm. "Killing that pathetic man. That was not wrong. I know what he did to you—it had been done to me when I first became a Disciple. It is an accursed thing, and even the most painful death is not an adequate enough price to pay for using the Shadow for such things."

"Isn't that what you do?" Layla asked. "Isn't that what the Shadow is for? Corrupting people, using monsters?"

Valix shook her head, a hint of what might have been anger washing over her features, but it was gone before Layla could be sure. "Just because you can do something doesn't mean you do that thing. The Shadow is a tool for my people, and yes, we use it. But only as a means to our lord's ends, and never to corrupt." She hefted the book, nodding to it with her tattooed head. "We do not accept anyone into our order, and certainly do not force anyone. The Disciples of Stane are true believers. Completely devoted."

Layla looked ahead as Caraby came into view. The earth shook again, and she whipped her head back to make sure the mountain had not erupted—it still plumed smoke into the sky, but nothing else.

"To what?" Layla asked the mountain.

Valix faced the road ahead. "You know. You felt Stane last night when you bloodied the pages of his book. I felt the conviction in you, accepting his inevitably."

"I want to hear you say it," Layla said, turning to her, waiting for the Disciple's eyes to meet her own. "I do not yet trust my own feelings."

Valix looked at her; sadness and understanding melted all the arrogance from her face. She nodded.

"Whatever you know of Stane is probably just fancy," the Disciple began. "Many people have claimed the name of Stane and deceitfully added falsehoods to his legend. But when you accept his inevitably, you can feel what is true and what is false.

"He is the First Born. Before Creation made the old gods, she made Stane to walk the lands she had molded." Valix's voice became distant and emotionless, as if she had begun a practiced ritual. "He is born of powers older than Light and Shadow, like the old gods. But unlike the old gods, he is not influenced by them. He was born to be the One God over all, uniting Light and Shadow under his domain.

"As Aetha's first prophet, Stane wrote of each of his Comings in this book. The First Coming was his making, son of Creation. He was the first mortal that built the great edifices in Xe'dann. He laid the first stones of Ghulta, the holy city, before sleeping for two thousand years in its labyrinthine tombs. When he emerged, he united the warring Ghultans to fight against the Sacrum Dominion."

Valix gave Layla a knowing smile. "Did they teach you this in the Arcania?"

Layla shrugged. "Some of it, I think. I never cared much for history."

"History paves the present and the future," Valix said, looking back to Caraby. "Stane was cursed in that war. A lich named Gravern made a pact with Mural in the Abyss. Stane was the only mortal able to elude the Death Maiden, and Mural was more than eager to pool her magic with Gravern's, cursing Stane to a mortal life.

"He spent the rest of his life writing this book." Valix shifted the tome to her other arm again, clearly struggling from its weight, which seemed to be increasing as the story unfolded. "Each of his Comings are detailed here, as well as his teachings. They are hidden in the various dialects of the Ghultan tongue. Only one person has ever been able to read its entirety, and that witch is burning in the Abyss, having gone mad doing so."

"Why do you need it if you can't read it?" It was a question Layla would have asked Queen Sopheena if she had been brazen enough, but she felt an unsuspecting comfort in the fact that she could ask such questions of her new companion without fear of wrath.

"Mostly to prevent others from reading it," Valix said. "But our master, Gravern, needs it to decipher the rest of Stane's Comings."

Layla stopped. "Wait. The lich who cursed Stane is your master? Of the Disciples?"

Valix turned on her and smiled softly. The earth rumbled again. "Stane is inevitable. Our master is proof of that. His greatest enemy becoming his most faithful servant? Could you imagine any stronger proof of Stane's foretold ascendancy?"

Layla had no answer for that, but she did know that the ache inside of her was almost already a faint memory. She felt insignificant by the magnitude of Valix's words, and she found remarkable comfort in that.

Valix continued toward Caraby and the elf followed.

"Where are we going?" Layla asked, convinced that she could not return to the queen, nor did she want to after Sopheena entrusted her to Desmond. Yet she was not convinced that she would follow Valix on whatever quest lay before the woman. All she knew was that she wanted to numb the pain—she wanted to forget the memory of

Desmond's cruel hands on her flesh, how she had opened her legs for those pitiful eyes drowning in ash.

"To find a ship to Velcarthe."

"What's there?" Layla asked, if only a little excitedly. She had never been to Xe'dann, but had always dreamed of seeing the legendary cities along the desert's coast. In her dreams, though, the circumstances were much less dire.

"The means to decipher this text. Gravern believes the Shrouded have the answer, but those Shadowsworn dogs are using it to play their own game. Their Dark One resides in the depths of Velcarthe, and I know her mistress, Naya, well."

"And this Naya can translate it?"

Valix gave Layla a considering eye. "You ask a lot of my business, my dear. I'm not sure I am comfortable discussing these matters more with an outsider." She gave her a smile. "Now…if it were *our* business…"

Layla held her gaze, drunk in the numbness that this woman provided her in light of such recent tragedies. "What would the Disciples require of me?"

"Only faith," Valix said, "and devotion to the cause."

"And how do I prove it?" A nervousness tingled through Layla, exciting her as another tremor shook the earth below their feet.

Valix stopped them again, turning on the packed dirt road to face her. "You've already begun," she said, opening the tome to reveal Desmond's blood on its pages. She placed the book down on the road and proceeded to undress, revealing muscled shoulders covered in scars and swirling tattoos. She pushed the robes down further, revealing small breasts that were also inked, with sharp designs that cascaded around her nipples.

Layla blushed; the nervousness tickling her limbs turned to a sweet burning of excitement. It wasn't attraction to the woman she felt—at least not in any way she was accustomed to—but rather a promise of certainty bared before her in flesh.

As Valix pushed the robes down further, Layla looked all around, not seeing any travelers that might happen upon the scene. The earth trembled again, and she thought that most travelers had probably taken shelter like reasonable people in reasonable times.

Her eyes fell back on Valix's exposed stomach; the tattoos continued, but new scars were revealed. Layla had seen scars like that on women that had to give birth the hard way. She imagined the woman before her as a mother, but could not hold the image. Meanwhile, her face flushed fully as Valix kicked away her robes, naked under the sun.

"If you wish to join us," Valix said, unbothered by the heat, the shaking ground, or her bare flesh. She nodded to Layla, looking at her clothes.

As if challenged, Layla lifted her chin and unbuckled the belt, tossing it to the ground. She lifted her own robes over her head in a fell swoop, letting the wind gently carry them to the dirt road. She felt free and soothed, bonded to this naked stranger before her in a way that she had never felt with another person.

It wasn't love or tenderness that hung between them, filling the silence. It was a desire for certainty—for some sort of absolution in this vile world they suffered in. It was the promise of violence on those that would oppress. It was divine purpose.

It was everything that Layla needed at that desperate moment.

Valix took in all of Layla, letting the silence linger as her eyes traced every exposed curve, blemish, and imperfection of the elf's young body, looking for a weakness. Layla did not give her one. She stood as unyielding as Valix, embodying the woman's calm and assured demeanor.

Seeming satisfied, Valix put her hands out for Layla, motioning for her to join her over the book. Layla took her hands, feeling their calloused but comforting fingers thread their way into her own.

"We bare ourselves to Creation," Valix said, holding Layla's gaze, "nothing of the world between us. As Stane was given, taken, and so shall return, we stand in flesh to promise ourselves to his Coming." Pausing, Valix's eyes widened, as if something had come over her. "Do you promise yourself, Layla Abrigale?"

I never gave her my full name, Layla thought while keeping her face as still as she could. There was power flowing through their intertwined fingers, she could feel it. But it did not trouble her—it continued to soothe her, despite her racing heart.

Yes, she thought, *I do*. Her thoughts were surprising, but relentless in their conviction.

"I do." Layla's voice did not falter, it carried a newfound purpose that this woman had somehow kindled inside of her.

Valix untangled one of her hands from Layla's, holding the other one tight, her fingers writhing like hungry serpents. Her free hand made a motion and shadows took form under the bright sun to forge a dagger. The summoned blade shifted and writhed like smoke, insubstantial in form, but Layla could feel its deadliness. Valix held the blade out in an open hand, presenting it to Layla.

The elf stared at the blade, knowing what was asked of her through its unspoken command. She took her own free hand and grasped the blade of Shadow, her hand wrapping around its ghostly hilt. It fit her grip perfectly, as if she had summoned it herself.

Valix turned their hands over, revealing their open palms that were linked together by their twined fingers. She gave the elf a look of vulnerability, which was only emphasized by her nakedness.

"You have to get us both to join us. That is the only way."

Layla's body shivered at that, but she clenched the blade as steadily as she could, finding resolve in the Disciple's eyes. She took a deep breath and set the Shadow's blade on Valix's palm—it took no pressure to pierce the flesh—then drew it across both of their palms.

Blood blossomed from their cuts, pooling together in the crevice of their joined hands. Valix exhaled a relieved breath, smiling at Layla as the united blood dripped down on the pages to join Desmond's dried stains.

Valix turned their linked hand back over, pressing their palms together. She flourished her other hand and the Shadow knife dissipated out of Layla's determined grip. The women stared into each other's eyes as their blood continued to drip.

"We are joined," Valix said, her warm breath smelling like an extinguished candle. She unlocked their fingers but took the elf's hand in both of hers, raising it to her mouth. Looking into Layla's eyes, she dragged her tongue slowly over Layla's wound.

The sensation that surged through Layla's body was unlike anything Desmond's filthy touch had given her—it wasn't sensual, but it was enlivening and enveloping. A fierce devotion that went deeper than mere love. She forced her eyes to stay fixed on Valix's as they otherwise tried to roll back into her head.

It was overpowering, and Layla welcomed it completely.

Valix took the blood into her mouth, licking her lips that seemed to blacken in the process. She whispered words that Layla could not hear over the quaking earth that had seemed to intensify throughout the ritual.

There was a roar in the far distance, but she ignored it, holding Valix's eyes.

Layla felt the wound on her palm tingle, but when she looked at her hand, it was completely healed. Valix licked another drop of blood from those blackening lips. The woman pulled Layla close, moving one hand to cradle her neck and the other to her hips, pulling them together.

"We are sisters now, Layla Abrigale, joined by blood under devotion to Stane's Fourth Coming." She pulled the elf to her face so their noses almost touched, their lips almost brushing as she whispered, "I will never let another man harm you. Not while I live. I will die before another Desmond even looks at you. My sister."

Layla's resolve gave way then, and she succumbed to the sadness born from the night before. She fell into Valix's strong arms, weeping in newfound joy, shed misery, and the promise of inevitability.

Valix brushed her hair lovingly, watching the clouds gather above Dragonpeak with expectant eyes as the mountain shot fire into the sky and a dragon spread its wings above the eruption.

Knowing the signs of Stane's Third Coming, Valix smiled and began to cry with her newfound, inevitable sister.

CHAPTER TWENTY-FIVE

The Light's Embrace

"Where are you going?" Ransil hissed at Anika as he helped Dolly up the last flight of stairs. "We have to get to Brood."

Anika looked up the stairs, seeing the shadow of a guard pacing by the hallway above. The pull had become undeniable. She *felt* Gage, reaching out to her—he needed her. She looked back to Ransil, unsure how to make the halfling understand. "It's Gage. He needs me. He's up there."

Without offering further explanation, she moved up the stairs, Matty close behind as he gave Ransil a futile shrug.

"If Gage is here, I need to help them," Robin said. "I've been through here before. They'll get caught wandering around."

Ransil hissed between his teeth as if he wanted to hit the boy.

"Go," Dolly insisted, catching her breath. "I'm weary but I'll make it. Just point me to where Brood is and I'll meet 'em."

Ransil did so as he gave his cousin a quick hug before motioning for Robin to go on after Anika. He whispered over his shoulder, "If you see Grip, tell her to hold her damn position until I can figure this out."

He joined Anika, Robin, and Matty as they crouched near the doorway, watching the guard disappear around a corner.

"Where is he?" Ransil asked.

"I—I don't know," Anika was forced to answer, shaking her head. "I can't explain it, but you'll have to trust me. I know he's here."

"How?" Robin asked.

She looked to each of her companions, desperate for some sort of explanation that would silence their doubts and give her their trust.

Without thinking, she drew out the stone. "Something is happening to me," she said, to the stone as much as to her companions. "I think this sought me out for something—I don't know what. But I'm different than—than everyone in Blakehurst. I've always felt different, but never wanted to dwell on why." Her eyes found Ransil, knowing he was more worldly than any of them. "I don't know why Gage took this, but maybe it did something to him too. I can feel him—he's in trouble."

Ransil held her gaze for a moment before nodding. "Well, let's go then. We cannot afford any more trouble. We get him, get that damned stone the Guild needs, and get out of this accursed town."

Anika smiled at the halfling, overcome with relief to have him by her side. "It's up there," she said, motioning to a set of wide carpeted stairs that were flanked by elegant standing candelabras.

"Are you sure?" Robin asked, his eyes wide.

Anika nodded.

Robin turned to Ransil. "That leads up to the baron's chambers."

Inside the baron's chambers, Gage watched his mother writhe naked in the bed, convulsing under the touch of the baroness and her husband. The Shadow hid him from the world, a hazy sphere of ancient magic silencing his presence and shielding him from untainted eyes.

Hot tears clouded Gage's vision more than the magic did, but he could see every painful detail of his mother's face. Her eyes were tightly shut against the world, losing herself in the sweaty flesh of simple passions. He wondered how long she had done this—how long she had given herself so freely to others nearly a world away from her own flesh and blood.

How long had she been so consumed in pleasure, living in a castle, and loving a new family? For as long as he had mourned her death?

The dagger in Gage's trembling grip splattered young Caffery blood onto the otherwise perfect rug. He let out a shuddering breath to steady himself, wanting to consume every drop of violent rage that this display provided. He didn't want the suffering inside of him, but he let it fester and grow into a raging monster.

When he inflicted that suffering on the world, a voice inside his head surmised, he must ensure that it is whole and complete, otherwise it may remain inside of him in part.

Gage blinked away the burning tears so he could focus on the wrathful sight, watching his mother arch her back in explosive pleasure. He imagined driving his dagger into her bare chest, hoping she would feel a fraction of the betrayal and insignificance that consumed him now.

She wanted me to believe she was dead, Gage thought, twisting the grip of his dagger, *then I can accommodate.*

As he was about to step forward, he felt a presence in his small blackened world. Time seemed to slow to a crawl in that moment; the baron, his wife, and Gage's mother were now figures in a slow-moving painting instead of a thrusting, groping sea of flesh.

"You are whole, Child," a whispering voice told him, deadened in the ensorcelled sphere but ringing in his ears as if carried by magic.

Gage turned to see a cloaked and hooded woman next to him—a beautiful Xe'danni with flawless ochre flesh that seemed to glow slightly within the Shadow. She motioned to the bed.

"Time yields to you. Tell me your name, Child, for I must know whom I serve with every breath of my remaining life."

Gage wiped his tears away with the back of a hand, glad to have a reprieve from the scene beyond the Shadow, but watching the woman skeptically. "Gage Lawson."

Recognition flashed in the woman's eyes, time still crawling on outside as she turned to regard Renay. "She is your mother." It was not a question, but an unholy revelation. "You are the Child." Her eyes returned to his—her worshipping, loving eyes. Her shoulders slumped in reverence as she reached out both hands to him.

Gage recoiled, feeling an uncertain relief from his misery, and the woman dropped her hands. She blinked away the trance but kept her smile.

"You are the Child of Shadow," she said, "the prophesied one. I am Naya, your loyal servant. I am yours, wholly yours, Child."

He shook his head, knowing it to be true, but not accepting it. He was just a simple thief from Blakehurst, abandoned by his mother so she could fuck high lords and ladies, and give her motherly love to their children.

The fury came back as if it had never abated. "Leave me," Gage commanded, readying his blade again.

Naya looked nervously at the slow-moving tryst on the bed. "Your mother betrayed you, and needs to suffer, Child. But spare the baron, as he will be your loyal servant as well. He is needed for our cause."

Gage gave her an angered look. "We have no cause!" Naya withdrew slightly from his shout, raising her hands defensively.

"She is your only way out, Gage."

A new voice.

Turning his head, Gage saw Anika in the sphere with him, smiling. He reached up instinctively, horrible memories beginning to stir at the sight of his sister here in the Shadow with him. His twitching hand touched Anika's cheek, and she reached up both her hands to lovingly take his own, her chestnut skin a deep contrast to his own pale flesh.

She was real.

"Remember," Anika said, smiling as she took Gage's hand and turned it over with her own, "you used to think I was the Child of Shadow when you used to hear those old stories. Because of my skin. Because I was different."

Abashed, Gage remembered. "You're not real," he said, tears came anew.

"I am real," Naya said. "I—"

The rest was cut off as Gage expelled her from the Shadow, throwing her from the sphere. Time slowed even more, and Naya's fall was frozen, holding the woman suspended in midair just as the Cafferys' and Renay's ecstasy was frozen.

"I am whatever you need me to be," Anika said. "I am you, Gage."

"You made me steal that stone."

She smiled. "It was always you, Gage. The Shadow is part of you, and you are the Shadow. Sometimes, it is not always easy to accept the enormous power—the responsibility of that power—but the Shadow has ways to…expedite the process."

Gage pulled his hand away from her.

Anika tilted her head. "You know your paths are joined. You could not become who you are, until she became who she is. That's why you had to steal the shard for her. She would not hear Eyen's call otherwise."

"You're not my sister," he said, holding the dagger up to keep her back.

The Shadow smiled, more wickedly than he imagined Anika ever could. "No, she is not your sister. But that is your mother." The thing that was not his sister pointed a finger at the bed, but Gage would not look. "She rejected us, tried to kill us! And when she couldn't, she fled. To love another father and his children—but not her own. Not us."

"You made me kill Elza," Gage said, his eyes distant.

The Shadow shook Anika's head, letting out a low chuckle. "That was just to get your hands dirty. To prepare you for this."

"Prepare me for what?!" Gage demanded. "What do you want from me?!"

The shadowed Anika smiled. "You are the Child of Shadow, Gage. It doesn't matter what anyone wants from you anymore." She stepped toward him, her face melting away and becoming Robin's. "What do you want?"

Gage's heart fluttered at the sight of Robin's face, and he ached to be with him. *That* was what he wanted—that was all he ever wanted. He turned to face his mother, raising his blade again. Time began to quicken ever so slightly.

"I want to be free of this," Gage said, taking a step out of the Shadow.

Derik stifled a yawn as he continued down the hall, enjoying the solitude that the keep's recent excitement had allowed him. Most of the other guards had been pulled into the Oather's service, leaving the keep's inner halls under the watch of only three guards, Derik included.

While Mandy covered the northern wing and Derik's brother, Cobb, paced the south halls, Derik relegated himself to the main hall and the master quarters. He hummed a little tune as his leather boots softly kept a steady rhythm on the carpet, oblivious to the dark-skinned elf that slipped into the shadows behind him.

As he turned a corner, a muffled whimper ceased his humming. Thinking of his soldier's training, he reached for his sword and tore it from its sheath, bending his knees slightly to prepare for any trouble.

None came. But the whimpering continued. His darting eyes went from door to door down the hallway, seeing nothing amiss, until they fell on young Lady Lenora's doorway. There was a glimmering streak on the stone, and the door was slightly opened.

Caught between the fear of intruding on the young lady's nocturnal games and the sheer terror of letting something ill befall the girl under his watch, Derik froze for a moment. But a similar groan from Viktor's room jolted him into action, and he dashed for the girl's door.

Throwing it open, Derik's hand seized and his blade clattered to the stone floor.

Tied to her bed and gagged, the young Lady Lenora struggled as her eyes lolled in her head. Blood was everywhere—*How can a little girl have so much blood in her?!*—and continued to run from several deep cuts on her young, innocent flesh.

"Aid!" Derik tore a dagger from his belt, struggling to find the words he needed to save the girl. "A priest! I need a priest! Oh, Light! Help! The children!"

His cries echoed down the hall, breaking the serene silence of his watch.

Avrim heard the cry—no, *felt* the cry—as they made their way up the hidden stairs. It wasn't the first time that the Light carried a desperate plea to him, but it was the first time that Avrim felt the actual words of a prayer, letting him know exactly how dire he was needed.

The Light, he thought, as he turned toward Deina and Melaine. Their faces were confused, not hearing the same desperate plea Avrim did. *The Light is here.*

"Hurry," he said, running up the stairs, compelled toward the door above.

"Quiet!" Melaine hissed, her own feet taking the stairs lightly as Avrim and Deina shook the entire staircase with their stomping feet.

The three got to the top of the stairs to a strange door with no handle. Avrim threw his shoulder into it and it flung open, spilling him into a great candlelit chamber—a lord's bedchamber.

A woman's scream was lost on his ears as he got up, looking for the door that led to the desperate cry. Three naked figures scrambled for clothing as Deina and Melaine entered, armed and nervously chasing Avrim into the room.

"Who are you?!" a bellowing voice from the bed demanded. "Guards!"

Avrim looked over his shoulder as he ran for the door. "Your children are dying! I am a priest of the Light! Come!"

"What?!" one of the women shrieked, her voice already heavy with emotion. "What do you mean?" She threw on her robe and chased after the newcomers. The man was close behind. The other woman scrambled for her clothing, Deina saw. But as the dwarf followed Melaine out the main doors, she saw the woman freeze in place as she stared into the shadows of the chamber's corner.

Uncaring, Deina charged forward, driven by her need to protect Avrim in the face of whatever foolery this was.

None of them saw or heard the body of the Xe'danni woman crumple violently to the floor in the baron's chambers.

Ransil held a stubby finger to his lips, motioning for Anika and Matty to stay silent in the shadows. The halfling and Robin hid behind a heavy curtain that hung from the wall as the figures rushed past them out of the bedroom.

Matty's arm was held out against Anika, keeping them out of sight. Anika watched as a priest barreled down the hall toward the stairs, followed by the baron and the baroness in heavy, golden-embroidered robes, and then a monstrous, green-skinned woman and a stout dwarf woman not far behind.

Anika and her companions watched as the strange procession made their way around the corner down a different hallway, toward the shouts.

"Their children," Robin whispered.

Before anyone could answer, the door to the baron's chambers was slammed shut with such force that it seemed to shake the stone walls.

Anika stepped out of the curtains and faced the door, feeling her brother close by, but feeling something else as well. Something dark and deadly—a secret beyond that door that she was not sure she wanted to know.

"Is Gage in there?" Ransil asked, stepping beside Anika, a knife in each hand.

Anika nodded.

Robin leapt forward at that, frantically grabbing at the door's handles. He pulled, jiggling the doors to no avail. "Locked."

"Here," Ransil said, tossing Robin the lockpicks from Dolly's house.

Robin caught them and got to work on the door as they watched his back. After only a few metallic clicks, the doors opened, and Anika's breath caught in her throat as her eyes adjusted to the awaiting shadows.

———◇———

Avrim found the guard cradling the girl on her bed, blood everywhere. The man looked up with desperate eyes, his hands fumbling with makeshift bandages, trying to stop the dying child's bleeding.

"Lay her down!" Avrim commanded, pointing to the carpeted floor.

"Lenora!" The baroness' voice was high and frantic as she tried to push the priest out of her way to get to her child.

"Back! I will heal her!" Avrim shouted, shoving the woman back violently. "Bring the boy! Now!" He produced his luminary from the pack that hung at his side, his eyes taking measure of the child's injuries.

Deina gasped. "What kind of monster would do this to children?"

"Viktor! My boy, answer me!" The baron's voice from across the hall sounded frantic.

"In here!" Avrim shouted. "Bring him to me, dammit!" He flipped through the pages of his luminary, knowing the words but needing them at hand should his mind fail him at the wrong moment. He thought of Percy Ambrose still possessed back at the Priory, and his conviction burned white hot.

He would not fail these children.

The baron carried his son into the room, laying him next to Lenora. His cuts looked deeper and more numerous. Unlike the girl, whose eyes still rolled in her head, the boy had lost consciousness from blood loss.

"I don't know who you are," the baron said, as he smoothed his son's hair away from his bloodied brow, "but please save my children. I'm a man of the Light. Do not let this devilry stand!" His face was furious but his eyes were pleading.

Avrim looked at the blood, reflecting on the healings he had done in the past. He had never brought anyone back from something like this. But the Shadow was at work here, he could feel it—he could taste the wretched taint.

He ripped the holy symbol from his neck, breaking the chain. "I can save them," he said through gritted teeth, already reaching out to the Light. The heavy cloud of the Shadow was hard to penetrate, but he pushed through, reaching for more power than he had ever tried to channel before.

Avrim's fury bathed the room in a warm glow as he reached his hands out to lay them on the dying children.

The Shadow fled, and Avrim undid its foul deeds.

Brood and Dolly hastily made their way back to her apartment under the dim moonlight. No guards accosted them, and Brood whispered his thanks to the Arcania for their impeccable timing in sending an Oather through.

He immediately regretted that thanks as they opened the door and found the armored woman sitting casually at Dolly's table, rubbing her sword with an oilcloth.

"Good evening, Scratch."

"Kasia?" Dolly gasped, catching her breath. "I thought you'd be gone by now."

The Oather took a measure of Brood. "So this is your brother? I can see the family resemblance." Her eyes remained on Brood. "Do you have the stone?"

Brood looked at Dolly, searching for an explanation.

"We don't have it," Dolly answered, shaking her head at Brood.

"Did the baron release you already?" The Oather reached into a bowl on the table and picked up an apple, biting into it.

"Kasia," Dolly pleaded, "what do you want? I'm just here to get a few things before fetching my daughters and getting out of this wretched town."

"No," Kasia said, taking another bite.

The halflings looked at each other, then back at the Oather.

"Your daughters are already on their way safely to Andelor," Kasia said, chewing the apple calmly. "My squire is accompanying them." She stood up, taking another bite, chewing casually, savoring the halflings' desperate need to hear her words. "I changed my mind, Scratch. I think I do want that stone. I felt something tonight, and I suspect the baron is up to something." She tossed the apple away. "You see, my armor only really affects magic in close proximity. But it responded to something tonight, something I know is happening in the keep. But I'm a busy woman, Scratch. So I need you to go ahead and acquire the stone with your brother, but bring it to the Arcania."

"Or your daughters will burn as witches."

"Witches?!" Brood made to take a step forward, but his sister held him back with an arm.

"Don't do this, Kasia," Dolly pleaded, her eyes seeking something in the Oather's. "What happened to you in those towers? How can you do this? They're just girls!"

Kasia licked the juice off one of her fingers, looking away from the woman. "It's business, Scratch. You should know not to take it personally.

"I am departing this evening in order to reach Blakehurst by the morning. I expect to have that stone on my way back through here, or when I get back to the Arcania."

She stepped toward the door, the halflings sliding away to avoid being kicked by her long legs. "Have a pleasant evening."

"Mother."

Anika stood in the doorway, mouth agape and arms hung limply at her sides. The woman on the bed was unmistakable, even in her current state of naked terror.

Renay's eyes moved from the shadows in the corner to her now teenaged daughter, seizing the shuddered breath she had sucked into her chest.

"Anika…"

Silence hung between the women. Anika stared blankly at her mother, happy memories at war with years of grief inside of her. There were no words to fill that insurmountable void. Renay sat on the bed, her legs curled under her, a thin robe draped over pale shoulders.

A rustling of movement caused Anika to jerk her head to her right, where a robed figure struggled to its feet. A Xe'danni woman, bleeding from the brow, her dark hair plastered to the slick wound.

"Naya," Renay said, moving slightly to the edge of the bed, "what are you doing here?" Her eyes went back to Anika, not waiting for the apothecary's answer.

Naya found her feet, looking toward Anika and her companions that were waiting in the doorway with her. Shouts continued to ring out down the hall behind them. She smiled, ignoring Renay.

"The Shadow has come," she said, drawing an emerald shard out of her robes. "I can feel it now. The deed has worked, and the Child has come." The stone pulsed in her hands, its faint green glow returning.

"I am not the Child!" Anika shouted, her voice a roll of thunder in that echoing room. Matty took a step back, his sword drawn and held toward the stranger.

The floor began to tremble to the rhythm of the Xe'danni's stone.

"It's Ruke's stone," Ransil whispered to Robin, shifting slightly on the balls of his feet as he crept around Anika, his eyes fixed on the Xe'danni's artifact.

"Oh, but you are," Naya laughed, turning toward the shadowed corner, "yet you are not the only one."

As Gage emerged from the Shadow, Renay was already weeping, as if she knew what came for her.

"Gage!" Robin cried, pushing past Anika to go toward the Shadow.

Raising a hand, Gage stopped his lover midstep. The half-elf lifted into the air as Gage motioned in that direction with his gloved hand. "Wait," he said calmly.

Anika's heart ceased beating as she stared at her brother, understanding worming its way into her broken mind. She drew out her own shard, seeing it pulse with a soft blue light to the same rhythm as the rumbling floor and the swaying levitation that held Robin aloft.

Gage looked at her, his red-rimmed eyes apologetic and yet unyielding.

"Only one of you shall leave," Naya said to Anika. "It is foretold. The Child of Shadow and the Child of Light—only one shall prevail, lest the other lives long enough to gather the powers necessary to usher in the Entity Wars."

The woman's babbling was lost on Anika, who only cared enough about the Child prophecies to know that the Child of Light was expected to slay the Child of Shadow to avoid an all-encompassing war.

This woman wanted Anika to kill her brother.

Gage stood with a bloodied dagger in his hand, raw eyes smoldering into his weeping mother. "She's been here," he said. "She left us to be fed Father's lies so she could play queen in a castle."

"No," Renay sobbed, reaching out a hand toward Gage.

Gage slashed at it with his blade, spraying blood. Renay shrieked in pain.

"No!" Anika cried, stepping forward, Matty ready to charge.

"Don't," Gage warned them, his blackened eyes boring into Matty.

"Take a step closer and I'll cut her throat here and now."

Renay wept, cradling her hand.

"Brother," Anika breathed, her own eyes reddening with tears.

Gage glared at her. "I'm not your brother anymore." He thrust the blade toward Renay. "She took that away! We were a family until she deceived us and left us for her new children—the ones I left dying in their beds after she sang to them, kissed them." His furious eyes returned to Renay. "Loved them."

Robin struggled against the corrupted air that held him. "Gage, this isn't you! Fight it! It's the Shadow!"

"I am the Shadow!" Gage screamed. Everyone in the room recoiled as a wave of black wind empowered his declaration. His face softened as he looked at Robin, the half-elf lowering slightly back to the ground as Gage said, "I can't fight it anymore. It's taking me." He turned back to Renay. "And it's her fault."

Naya whispered prayers to the Shadow, reveling in the scene playing out before her. The green stone in her hand pulsated quicker now, the floor quivering in response.

"Gage," Renay said through broken sobs. "Please, kill me. I know what hounds you—it hounded me since you were born." She looked toward Anika. "You were too young, but the Shadow has latched itself to me. It came to me when your father killed that assassin that came for you."

Naya licked her lips as the green light of the stone responded to her request for more power, draining all the Shadow from it to empower the Child's rage.

"It found you, Gage," Renay wept. "I prayed to the Light every day, asking to banish the Shadow that hung over my child, but it—it..."

Now is the time, Naya thought, *she can be swayed.* "It asked you to kill him," she finished. "The Light," she turned to Anika, "the Light *commanded* your mother to kill her only true child for your sake, Anika!"

Anika shook her head, looking back desperate to her mother, seeking any denial.

All she got was tears as Renay doubled over in grief, hiding her face.

"Come to the Shadow, Anika," Naya offered, taking a step forward. "Join your brother—you do not have to kill each other. Together you can fight the prophecy."

Naya pointed to Gage and Renay. "One of them will die, Child. Either your brother will avenge the children that woman abandoned, killing her and sealing your prophecies. Or the Light will continue hounding her until its bloodlust is sated by your brother's death."

Anika looked at Gage, hoping to see any resistance from him. But his eyes were set on death, and his blade was ready.

Naya motioned to the knife at Anika's waist. "Or you can save your brother. Join him, and let your mother rest, away from the Light's torment. Do not make her live in the grief that consumes her—in the memory of the baby she could not smother as the Light within you commanded."

Anika drew her blade.

"Mother. I am sorry."

CHAPTER TWENTY-SIX

The Sundered Gates

Fainly Lopke wandered the familiar dreams, staying on the lit paths of his memories, ignoring the beckoning magicks that tried to lure him into oblivion. His vision was fixed on the impossible figure that awaited him.

The Fey Domain was not a place one could trust, its power was deep and natural, drawn from Creation and not diluted by the mortal poison that plagued Aetha's own magic.

He felt the youthful vigor taking hold in his limbs, rejuvenating his mind and assuring his confidence that had only begun to waver slightly in the face of the recent unexplained events. Those events—the storm, the Light's deceit, the missing mage in Karrane—had him playing the dangerous game of doubt, which he spent his long years avoiding.

The impossible figure approached, and Fainly breathed deep of the fey atmosphere. Dread and anticipation froze him in place, waiting for the confrontation, but refusing to initiate it.

Shapes lurked along the path, Shadow trapped between worlds, looking for a vessel to corrupt and take hold on a plane more susceptible to their powers. The figure came closer, motes of light dancing around its dark form, but Fainly saw her face perfectly.

She was his lost love. His mother, his sister, his only partner—she was his counterpart in every way, and he would never feel love toward another mortal being because of her. His devotion to her went beyond mere lust; it was all-encompassing and confusing, which was what drove them apart in life. He frowned now at that thought.

"Ruke," he said as the halfling stepped into the light. His voice was a whisper from the grave, deadly even here in the realm of everlasting life.

Dark green robes hung from the youthful woman whose true years were beyond count. Her dazzling eyes caught the gnome's tight face.

"So sad to see me? After all these years."

"Shouldn't you be in Elysun?" Fainly asked, keeping his face firm despite the yearning ache in his chest. "Can you sleep there now?"

"I'm awake for the first time in a long time, Fainly." The look in her eyes was hidden fear laid bare. "The Child…"

"I felt it," Fainly said, assuming an uncaring demeanor as he gazed at the stalking Shadows. "We are on their trail."

"No, you're not, Fainly." She stepped forward. "How do you think I managed to come here, to our spot?"

"The powers shift," Fainly said dismissively, as if it were simple. "I can see it in the shards, can feel it here."

"The Nethering Gates are breaking, Fainly."

The gnome's uncaring guise fell away, exposed horror in his wide eyes.

A sound came from beyond the path, as if the shadows laughed mockingly at the small figures. A solitary mote of light withered and died between Ruke and Fainly, leaving only the smoke that would trail an extinguished candle.

The questions raced through Fainly's mind quicker than he could dismiss them, knowing the answer to each before the voice inside of him asked them. He knew the halfling spoke the truth, as much as he did not want to accept the reality or the consequences of that truth.

"The Children," Ruke said, her eyes now distant, looking into the gloom of the Fey Domain, beyond the dancing lights. "I know more than I care to about their fate, the burden they carry. But I do not have time to explain all; even this place is in danger as long as I'm here."

Fainly just stared, unable to conjure a single useful thought. "Tell me what you can, Ruke. I am yours to command in this."

The halfling took his hand, their flesh emitting a faint glow where it touched. "You know the prophecies, yes?"

He nodded, having studied them intently since Ruke's bindings.

"They do not apply to these Children. Never before have the Children been so closely tied—brother and sister, united in tragedy. Even now, my stone is being used as a conduit for the Shrouded to try to sway the Child of Light to Shadow."

The Shadow writhed excitedly beyond the path in response.

"The Gates have already been sundered," Ruke continued, gripping Fainly's hand tightly in both of hers. "They will break completely if the Child of Light is swayed—the Shadow's taint on the Nethering will be complete if the Light fails, and the Shadow held within each of the Nethering's Domains will be free to return to Aetha."

Visions flooded Fainly's mind of a world shrouded in Shadow—misery, suffering, unending death. He tried to let go of Ruke's hand, but her grip was unyielding. The visions continued—he saw the towers of the Arcania blackened, a robed skeleton atop his own tower, summoning smoky black wings that enveloped all of Andelor. He struck Ruke, but still the halfling held on. He saw the Lighthold crumble, and Queen Sopheena cackling with black eyes as she floated above the twisting shadows, ruling over her new empire of the damned.

"Enough!" Fainly cried.

Ruke released him. Tears were in her eyes. "I apologize, Fainly. Yet that is but a taste of what I have seen play out in Elysun. Those golden fields have slowly succumbed to the Shadow's poison, turning into acres of dry death. The storm over your world comes from the old gods' domains, Eyen yearns to be free of Shadow, expelling it on Aetha in hopes to be rid of it.

"The suffering has been a long time coming," Ruke said sadly, looking for something in Fainly's eyes.

Hope?

Answers?

Sympathy?

What do you want from me? Fainly's mind demanded.

"I just need you to see," Ruke said, feeling his thoughts. "I have to leave here, Fainly. And I cannot return. I must return to Elysun, but I will try to break through to my stone before the Gates fall. You must find me."

"Oakworth?" Fainly asked, knowing where she had resided, but always refusing to face the pain of feeling her again. Hers was the only shard that he taught his followers not to worry about.

Ruke nodded. "For now. If the Child is not swayed, I will do what I can to guide her. Only she can face the incarnates that come, but killing them will—"

"Incarnates?!" Fainly interrupted. "More than the one?" But Ruke was already fading. "Ruke!"

"Find me, Fainly," Ruke said, as her face disappeared. Her voice echoed, "Do not leave me again. Stane is coming—"

The halfling's voice was cut off by a piercing bark, then there was a sudden growl as a huge black shape leapt onto the path. The Shadow beast's infinitely deep maw opened and reached for Fainly.

The Archmage woke up in a sweat, immediately rolling out of his large bed and rushing for the door of his chambers.

The queen finished affixing her seal to the letter. The dove's wings spread wide over the mailed fist dried in the purple wax as Sopheena blew softly on it. The words within the letter would hopefully stay the brewing war in Copera long enough for her and Nipheena to carry out their plans. If not—well, this was no time for such dire thoughts.

She picked up her glass and sipped the sweet wine as she heard the muffled shouts and clamor from outside her study's doors. Swishing the wine in her mouth, she waited for those doors to be thrown open—she was no prophet, but the Archmage had certainly become predictable. *He has heard about his dead mage in Karrane*, she thought amusingly.

As if in response, her prophecy came true and the doors were violently thrown open as Fainly strode inside, one of the queen's guard crawling after him, struggling against the magic that seemed to choke him.

"Kindly release my guard and have a seat, Archmage."

The gnome made a gesture and the guard gasped for air. "Your Majesty—"

Sopheena raised her hand. "It's quite all right, Ellis, I don't expect you to meet our dear Archmage in fair combat." She motioned for Fainly to have a seat, but he kept walking until he was close enough to peer over her desk.

"Why do you want the *Book of Stane?*"

Sopheena kept her face as calm as she could. *Well*, she thought, *isn't this the twist?*

Fainly waved a hand. "Save your denials. I was here when this city was made—I am older than any of you scheming devils that rule this city by my permission, and I want to know *now* what game you are playing with that book!"

Footfalls thundered into the room as a group of guards led by the king flooded into the chambers. "What is the meaning of this?!" the king demanded.

Again, Sopheena raised a hand to stay them. "Markus, please join me. The Archmage has graced us with his presence."

The king stiffened, but nodded to the guards, who exited and closed the doors behind them. Markus watched the gnome cautiously as he found his place next to the queen.

"It seems Fainly has forgotten his place, husband," Sopheena said, smiling sweetly.

"I forget nothing," Fainly said, twisting his hands in fury. Ruke's dire words echoed in his mind, and he had to learn how Stane played into all of this.

"You forgot about Ruke," said a familiar voice from behind Fainly. The Archmage's shoulders slumped slightly as he turned to face the elusive master of the Guild.

Fainly narrowed his large eyes on that lacquered mask, knowing full well whose face hid behind it. But he kept that to himself for now.

"You left the poor woman waiting for you," Knife said, pacing from the dark curtains near the window that had hid her presence. "How long had she been the baron's doxy? Spreading the land's legs so he could take his fill?"

Fainly watched the rogue, waiting for a reason to strike her dead, consequences be damned. But Ruke's words stilled his rising fury—he would not risk her for petty revenge. "What of Ruke?"

Knife shrugged, leaning against Sopheena's desk. The king and queen caressed each other's hands in a show of uncomfortable affection. Fainly was not amused or bothered—his eyes held on Knife's mask.

"She should be in safe hands by now." Knife's voice was soothing and cruel, like the soft purr of a cat watching a caged mouse. "As long as you ask the right questions." She flipped her wrist and a knife appeared, spinning in the air. She caught it flawlessly by the blade, then twirled it through her fingers. "And avoid the wrong ones."

Fainly let out a resigned breath, his tightened face unchanged. "Keep your secrets then. But know this." He pointed to the window. "That storm—it has something to do with Stane. And I will find out what that is. You can take my damned Oathers across the sea, but you better hope your games do not interfere with my affairs. There are looming threats far outweighing your petty political games."

He gripped the desk and leaned forward, his eyes boring into the queen's. "You can gamble your throne all you want, but I will do everything in my power to protect this city. It means more to me than you know—you can fool the people of Vale all you want, but I see you, Sopheena—daughter of the vampire."

Fainly knew he risked much by showing his hand, but the look that soured Sopheena's beautiful face was worth abandoning answers here for now. He held onto the image of her sour expression as he departed the Valiant Keep, hoping to never return while Lord Delucar's daughters still held onto power.

CHAPTER TWENTY-SEVEN

The Keeper of the Wind

Bennik awoke to the sound of harpy chatter. He was unsure if it was night or day—the clouds had grown so putrid and stagnant that the world was an infinite gray-green haze. The familiar aches still kept him from moving much and reminded him of his new life as a plaything for a wrathful and insane demigoddess. Guluk dragged Bennik by one leg, the hunched shaman not even remotely struggling with the man's weight. Bennik would never have imagined that an orc with Guluk's hunched and withered frame would have such raw power, dragging him about as if he were a scarecrow made of brittle hay.

"...the book has been taken, Empress."

While his senses slowly returned, Bennik played dead and listened to the squawking conversation in the ruined hall that served as Corvanna's throne room.

"The ogres failed us, as you predicted."

"Of course they did," Corvanna replied. "Much like these orcs—such lowly beings cannot comprehend my significance, or our righteous cause. Oh, they respond to fear of the old gods' power well enough, but they are made for breaking empires, not building them."

Bennik heard the incarnate's wings flutter and he let one of his eyes open slightly enough to see Corvanna rise onto the ruined walls, surveying her new empire.

"I am tired of waiting," Corvanna continued. "We've wrung enough out of this man to know his daughter is no threat. And the shard she has *must* be the last piece of the Skythe... I know it—I can feel it."

"Without the book though..." a harpy began.

"There will be time for the book," Corvanna snapped back. "I need to be whole to show the world who keeps the wind." Bennik could see the incarnate look to the sky, proudly surveying the storm she had created—those wicked clouds seemed to move with the slow rise and fall of her breathing. "No one will worship what they do not fear."

Bennik could feel the storm abating, ever so slightly. The overpowering staleness of the air made it so even the slightest lessening of its oppressive weight could be felt. Whatever was urging Corvanna to take action was rooted in desperation.

The thought gave Bennik a small glimmer of hope that maybe his daughter had somehow found a way to fight against Corvanna, wherever she was.

"Bring me the shards," Corvanna commanded.

A harpy took flight to speak candidly with the incarnate. "Empress, the mage's shards are nearly depleted. Perhaps we should consider letting the storm wane until you are whole."

Corvanna turned her gaze on the creature. "Do you have any idea what it cost me to summon this storm, Ursel? You should remember, you helped pay the price. I will not pay it again. Nor will I endure any more insolence."

Corvanna casually grabbed the harpy in one of her massive talons. Ursel struggled in vain as the incarnate opened her beak and snapped shut. The insolent harpy's body went limp and Corvanna tossed it casually aside, where it crashed violently near Bennik.

"Bring me the shards," Corvanna repeated. Two harpies took flight without an argument.

As Corvanna watched them fly toward the watchtower where she kept her spoils, out of reach of the orcs, the shaman entered behind Bennik.

"Empress," the orc grunted. "Heal man?"

Bennik kept as still as he could.

"No," Corvanna said. "He has served his purpose. Maybe not as a ransom, but your magicks revealed something much more useful. I need his children now, not him."

"I take 'em?" Guluk asked, adding, "Empress."

Bennik couldn't see, but in the following silence he could *feel* Corvanna's gaze falling over the orc, considering. He had gone beyond caring about his own fate, but the quiet pause was dreadful— something about not knowing how he would die kept him eager to live.

The flutter of wings announced the harpies' return, and Bennik peeked once more, hoping their arrival kept attention away from him. The first harpy—his kidnapper, Skraw—carried one blue stone in each of her clawed hands, and the second carried a single larger blue stone.

"Only three remain, Empress," Skraw said, holding the shards out to her master. Their glow seemed to intensify as they fell into Corvanna's enormous hand, which immediately closed into a fist. The sound of grinding stone told Bennik that the incarnate had crushed the shards. He felt the heaviness of the air return as Corvanna absorbed the trapped magic.

A strong blue glow also came from the stone wrapped in the head of Guluk's crooked staff, causing the orc to gasp.

"A gift to you," Corvanna said as she spread her wings, head tilted back to the sky. The ecstasy of the power was clear to see, even with Bennik's squinted eyes. "For the gift you gave me—gave our new empire." She flapped her wings to lift her up into the sky. "And take the man to play with as you will. But kill him in the morning." She flew higher, her heavy breathing like thunder rolling across the ruins of Rathen.

"For in the morning," she said with a booming voice that came from the clouds above, "we march to take over this pathetic world."

As he struggled against the pain of being roughly pulled across hard earth and broken cobbled roads, Bennik tried to get a sense of his surroundings. The city of Rathen was the first Free City and the only one to survive the sackings of Mad King Lowry before the Unthroning.

The misery of his current predicament was slightly overshadowed by the sudden sadness that came over him as he surveyed the destruction. There were orcs roaming about, picking through the wreckage, looking for food or playthings. The Shadow drove its thralls to revel in vile pleasures, which Bennik saw firsthand during his time in Westerra when the swamp fiends from Guyen sought fresher game in the nearby rural plains.

Now he watched sobbing men, women, and children, those that survived the invasion, subjected to fates worse than death. He saw two massive orcs tossing a flailing, sobbing dwarf child back and forth as his father wept desperately on his knees for them to take him instead. He saw a screaming halfling woman stripped bare, her body bloody from lashings, an orc woman howling in pleasure as she swung a barbed lash over her head amidst the havoc.

This is her empire, Bennik thought, his dry and dying eyes desperate for tears that could not come. *This is the world Corvanna is building.*

Fury gave him the strength needed to survive the violent journey from Corvanna's throne room to Guluk's quarters, which looked like it had once been an apothecary shop. The orc roughly deposited her prisoner to the ground, making an intricate motion with her hand. A sudden gust of wind rose in the shop, blowing parchment and debris in small whirlwinds. Bennik felt his limbs pulled to the ground, his arms stretched out like wings and lashed down by the wind while his legs were pulled straight, similarly restrained.

"Just kill me, witch," Bennik said, his voice a dry, reedy whisper. Speaking was agony, and he couldn't even swallow to relieve his ragged throat.

"I will," the orc said, gathering various herbs, adding them to a nearby mortar and pestle. Her breath was heavy and gravelly as she ground up the herbs and reached for a bowl that had a long, rusty knife in it.

More screams outside made Bennik close his eyes, praying for oblivion to take him. Desperate, he reached out to the Light, seeing Anika's face in his mind.

"Leave him be," the dwarf begged, his voice a gruff sigh. He was nearly dead from lack of water, having given any fluids he had found to his son that now soared out of his reach. Futility was a sweet embrace, beckoning the dwarf to its cold arms.

"Father," the boy cried amidst the orc laughter, "please."

The painful innocence drove a knife into the dwarf's heart, and he let agony spur him, ignoring his broken leg. He leapt with his remaining good leg to reach the boy, but his ravaged body failed him. The father fell sobbing to the ground, fresh blood pouring from where the bone had now pierced its way through the flesh of his wounded leg.

"I'm sorry," he cried, his vision fading. His son flew through the air again, his tears falling on his father's dirty face. "I'm sorry, boy." As his vision began to fade, he saw a gray shadow consume his son from midflight—an enveloping shadow that stole the boy from a cruel fate. He heard the orc laughter turn into bloody chokes, and warm blood splashed over him, strangely comforting.

There were distant shouts and the ringing of swords. A battle had erupted. The father slowly drifted out of consciousness.

"Father!" his son cried.

A trembling hand touched his face, bringing the father back. He opened his eyes to see his son's tear-streaked face, a pair of delicate gloved hands on the boy's shoulders.

The dwarf found the strength to keep his eyes open, focusing on the gray shape that stood above him and his boy.

"Healer," the elf whispered over her shoulder.

The dwarf had no tears to shed, but his body trembled in relief as he desperately pulled his crying son to him. A gray cloak fell over them to shield them from the rising sounds of battle, and a water skin was placed in his hands.

Geneva spun away from the dwarves, feeling too exposed without her cloak, but finding cover behind a nearby building. She motioned with her hands to Shareena the healer, who would most likely have her work cut out for her by the look of things.

Grabbing her bow and flawlessly nocking an arrow, Geneva motioned for Lexeth and Rhenal to join her. Both elves wiped their bloody knives on the two orcs they had just dispatched and joined her, sheathing their blades and pulling out their own bows.

"The orcs are gathering near the front gates," she said. "Survivors first." She nodded toward the shrieking halfling woman about to be lashed again.

Without waiting, Rhenal fired an arrow that caught the halfling's tormentor through an ear. Rhenal had another arrow nocked before the orc crumpled lifelessly to the ground. Geneva nodded and Rhenal slipped away from the ruined building and made his way to the halfling, giving her his cloak as he motioned for Shareena.

"There was a man dragged there," Geneva whispered, motioning to the apothecary shop. Lexeth nodded and slipped away, his gray cloak billowing in his wake.

Surveying the ruined city and seeing the harpies flying overhead, Geneva worried that they had grown too bold in this attack. But she refused to let anyone in the city suffer if they could prevent it.

A piercing cry sounded overhead—the Shadowfiend. "There isn't much time," Geneva whispered to herself, praying the Eldercrowns would hear. "The incarnate joins the fray, Rhenal. We must end this swiftly."

Her companion nodded, rushing to retrieve arrows and follow Lexeth.

As the hulking Shadowfiend that flapped its wings over the center of the city let out an echoing war cry to assemble her army for march, Geneva wished she would have pushed the Eldercrowns to send the Glade Wings, envisioning the giant eagles lancing the cruel harpies out of the sky.

Their time will come, she thought, turning from the harpy scum as she looked for more survivors. *This will not be forgiven.*

Bennik didn't flinch as Guluk dragged the rusty knife across his forearm. He watched uselessly as his blood flowed from the wound into the orc's bowl. She sprinkled her crushed herbs into the blood, stirring it slowly with the knife as she grunted in some ancient tongue.

"You tell me your blood," Guluk said as she stood up, watching the blood flow. She straddled Bennik, lowering herself to sit on him as if she were a lover. "Your daughter. Your son."

"She's not my blood," Bennik said, thankful that the orc could not reach Anika through him with this blood magic. *But Gage...*

"Son," Guluk said, her heavy body crushing his thighs. "Tell me where your son be. Corvanna praise me if I know secrets."

"Rot in the Abyss, witch." Bennik tried to spit, but couldn't find the means to, as his tongue found only dryness in his mouth. "I won't tell you anything."

"Blood will," Guluk said.

Bennik struggled to keep his mind clear, but to no avail. His children were all he had in this world, and he held onto the memory of their faces as if it were a precious treasure that he would die for.

And he would, he knew, especially now as Guluk wormed her way into his mind. She swayed on her knees, rocking back and forth on Bennik's legs, calling on the most primal of magic to force her bond on him. He could almost feel her through the stream of blood that ran from his wound.

Unbidden, images came to Bennik of an unfamiliar room. His eyes lolled in his head, rolling back into a dream. He saw through someone else's eyes, surveying his new surroundings. He was in a lavish bedroom with a huge bed, four elegantly carved posts supporting a dark green canopy.

His already weak heart stopped when he saw his wife, cowering on the bed with a thin robe covering her nakedness. Her face was ravaged with emotion, tears still streaming down her face as she looked on toward—

Gage, Bennik thought. The boy held a bloody knife out toward his mother, his eyes were blackened orbs that seemed to smoke with smoldering hatred. *No*, he thought.

Yes, Guluk replied, their minds melding. Bennik could feel her eagerness, desperate for more of the vision. He tried to scream for his son to stay his blade, but he was only a visitor here, wherever he was.

Guluk's rocking grew faster.

Bennik's dream eyes shifted away from Gage and Renay, seeing a strange Xe'danni woman holding a glowing green stone. She looked hungrily at something out of Bennik's vision, but behind her he saw a small shape in the shadows.

Ransil, Bennik thought, but pain made him wince. The dream blinked away for a moment.

No, came Guluk's gruff voice. *Blood.*

Shifting again, he saw Anika. She cried as well, raising the knife that he had given her toward her mother. *No*, Bennik thought. *What is happening?! She saved your brother from the Light! Anika!*

"Mother, I am sorry," Anika said.

Bennik tried to wake up. *No!*

Guluk held him down. *Yes.*

Anika closed her eyes, raising her stone up to the knife. She held both together, gathering power. As she did, Bennik felt a weight lifting from his body, even though his consciousness was far from it. His daughter's body began to glow with a blue aura, a blinding light forming where the stone met the knife.

It was a blinding sun she held in her hands, and the dream began to fade away against its brilliant shine. He heard Guluk grunt in pain, her grip on him failing as the ruins of the apothecary shop replaced the nightmare.

Bennik felt the air around him become less biting, less stagnantly heavy. Corvanna cried out her decrees in the distance, the thunder of her voice faltering like a dying storm.

"No," Guluk said, fear in her red eyes. She reached for the rusty knife. Bennik struggled against his invisible bindings, but the stone on Guluk's staff flickered its resistance. She drew the knife up, ready to plunge into Bennik's heart.

He closed his eyes, ready to die.

Warm drops splattered on his face when he heard the smooth sound of something sharp and fast piercing flesh. He didn't know how the orc managed to bring the blade down that fast, or why he couldn't feel it bury into his heart, but he welcomed death.

But instead, his bindings fell away, and the orc on top of him slumped backward. Bennik opened his eyes to see an arrow protruding from Guluk's eye. He didn't hear the elf enter the room, but saw him pull out a knife and cleave the stone from Guluk's staff. The shard disappeared into the elf's gray cloak.

An eerily familiar face turned to Bennik.

"Can you walk, Eastlunder?"

Bennik let the darkness take him then.

Geneva recoiled as the massive creature thrashed in the air, losing its aerial equilibrium. It let out a thunderous caw as it extended its great clawed legs to find purchase on the ruins of the mansion on the hill.

Above, a ray of sunlight—*Is it morning?* Geneva wondered—pierced through the malign clouds. The monstrosity shrieked as it shielded its black eyes from the first ray of light that had graced Rathen in months.

"By Oakus," Geneva breathed, unsure of what she was witnessing but somehow understanding the gravity of it. She drew her bow, finding her shot in that sunlight as if it were calling to her. She unleashed and her arrow sped to its mark, burying itself into the monster's chest.

A howl threw the elf off balance as the master of these ruins and the skies above thrashed its wings, finding its center again. It ripped the arrow from its chest and its eyes fell on Geneva as the elf readied another shot.

"Intruders!" Corvanna shouted, thrusting her wings toward Geneva, sending razor-like feathers spinning toward her.

Geneva dove behind the building. She heard the projectiles thump into the stone wall, several of them breaking through; the force that threw the feathers was so great that not even solid stone could withstand its flight.

"Ware!" Geneva shouted to her rangers. "Watch the skies!"

The sounds of dozens of harpies shrieking followed the voice, rushing through the acrid sky to find the one who would dare assault their burgeoning empire. Elven arrows were quick to find several harpies' paths, sending them sprawling and dying in wildly spinning heaps.

Geneva rolled out of the way as one of the harpies landed where she had stood, its talons digging into the earth and already pivoting toward the elf's new position.

"Elf scum!" the harpy cawed, leaping back into the air with claws bared. An arrow took her in the neck, knocking her out of the sky. Geneva turned to see Rhenal leaping aside from a clumsy orc's axe, stabbing it in the neck with another arrow before nocking it and shooting another harpy out of the sky.

"Geneva!"

She turned to find Lexeth with a heavy Eastlunder slung over his shoulder. He nodded for her to follow. "We have to get the survivors out! Give command to Rhenal! We need to send word for the Wings!"

Geneva obeyed, making the necessary signs with her hands as she ducked into a ruined building. The harpies called for orc reinforcements as they pursued, diving toward the elven rangers that now spread throughout the ruined city to gain higher ground. Their bows would make short work of the orcs, but the threat of harpies assailing from above meant that storied buildings with windows would offer the best cover. She rushed up a set of stairs as she heard the thundering charge of orcs outside.

"For Corvanna!" the orcs cried. "For the empress!"

Geneva fired twice from the upstairs window, sending a harpy spiraling out of the air and an orc collapsing under the boots of its allies. She shouldered her bow and made her way down the backside of the building where Lexeth was fleeing toward the eastern walls.

As she sprinted between buildings, leaving the battle to her capable companions, Geneva heard the keeper of the winds give out a shrill cry.

"Kill them all!" Another ray of sunlight broke through the clouds. "I am going to end this! The Child is mine!"

Geneva spared a look over her shoulder. The empress fled her empire, flying south on wings that rivaled a dragon's. In its wake, rays of sunlight lit the battlefield as the elves of Lohkrest liberated the ruins of Rathen from its tyrannical storm.

CHAPTER TWENTY-EIGHT

Retribution

Lenora Caffery sobbed weakly, barely able to stay awake as the healing powers of the Light subsided within her. Her body had to do all the work of replacing its lost blood and mending its ravaged flesh, as the Light only gave it the means to do so. Only those who truly wanted to live could manage such a healing, and Avrim was grateful for the young girl's determination and resilience.

The priest smoothed her hair, releasing his breath. *Thank you*, he said, to her and to the Light. His faith had been shaken since Rathen, but he was glad for this affirmation, despite its harrowing circumstances.

"Thank you, Father," the baron said, his voice breaking Avrim's reverie. "I don't know who you are or how you came to be in my home, but you are most welcome. You saved my children from certain doom."

Avrim slowly took his hand away from the girl's brow. Trembling with rage, it tightened into a fist. The rage took him so unexpectedly that he had no notion at what angered him, only that it was a profane thing that must be punished. He stood up quickly, spinning on the baron and throwing all his might into his clenched fist. It smashed into the baron's shocked face, knocking the man back against the wall. Avrim was on him immediately, grabbing him by the throat and raising his fist again.

"You brought this on your house!" Avrim shouted, his eyes glowing with divine wrath. "You welcomed the Shadow into your home! We saw it, below your keep, the priestess' foul library! You did this to your children with your unholy dealings, heathen!" He drove his fist into the man's face again, the baron struggling to push the maddened priest away.

Vivian shrieked, cowering with her children. Viktor shook weariness from his face as he heard the commotion and felt his mother's trembling hands.

"Father!"

Derik, who was kneeling next to Viktor, made to stand up, reaching for his sword. But Deina shoved him down with her axe, shaking her head. Melaine raised her bow toward the doorway where another guard had arrived.

"Hold," the half-orc said. "Deina!"

The dwarf went over to Avrim and drove her shoulder into his side, the force of her smaller body still managing to knock him away from the baron. Wide-eyed, Avrim looked at her, tears welling in his furious eyes.

"I—I'm sorry," Avrim managed, releasing his bloody fist, his body going slack against the wall. "The Light…it knew."

"See to your lord," Melaine said, loosening her bow and returning the arrow to her quiver. "We will help you search the keep for whoever did this."

The baron was a crumpled, bloody mess as Vivian went to him, weeping. Viktor was on his feet now, fully healed, and Lenora leaned up on an elbow looking as if she had just woken up from an unexpected mid-day nap.

Avrim's eyes watched everything in a haze, his mouth struggling with the words. He finally looked up to Melaine. "I know who did this." His face was raw with terror and something else, like the desperate look of someone looking for some sort of lie within a hard truth. "The Light showed me who did this.

"I saw his face. The Child of Shadow."

Renay watched as the Light bathed her estranged daughter, driving away the oppressive darkness that had fallen on the room. Naya looked toward her maliciously, hungry for blood, although Renay still did not know why. The woman had always been so kind to her, empathizing with her when she sought to purge her womb.

She felt the Shadow hanging over that woman now, almost as much as it hung over Gage. Though Renay did not dare look at her son again, awaiting death rather than face that torment any longer. The Shadow had chased her since she ran away from her children, refusing to kill her only son as the power begged her to. But now, it was clear to Renay.

It was never the Shadow.

It was the Light that asked her to sacrifice her only son.

What kind of vile power would ask for such a thing? Renay wondered as she watched that same power gather in her daughter's hands.

Mother, she had said, Renay thought bitterly. She looked deep into Anika's dark eyes, feeling eternally grateful that it was her chosen—accepted—child that would put an end to her misery.

I am sorry, Renay thought, but instead, with a weak breath she said, "Thank you, my child."

Anika could not hear her mother. The Light was deafening, and her surroundings flickered between the poisoned sky of her dreams and the elegant bedroom that would be her new nightmare.

The visions in her head took over, and the bruised sky hung over her head, a black winged shape rising and growing above her.

"You cannot have it," the terrible shape said to her, a rushing wind that blew through that cold and desolate world within her mind. The only sound that followed was the heavy flap of wings cutting through a thick, windless sky. "The wind is mine, fool Child! I know you can feel me! We are joined, but I will consume you. I will consume all! I will leave you an empty husk like your father, to serve in my new empire however I choose!" There was a hint of fear in that voice. "The wind is mine!"

Blinking that world away, Anika opened her eyes to the real world.

She focused on the brilliance that came from holding the stone to the knife her father gave her. She thought of him—sorrow, joy, pride, longing, love, resentment—and each emotion she felt sent a surge of power through her arms into her hands, fueling the burning Light.

That Light held the answers to all of her problems, but each answer only spawned more questions. There was certainty within reach, but its consequences were what agonized her.

Kill Gage, she thought. *Kill the Shadow.* It was what the Light wanted most, and it took everything within her to resist that path. She refused it, denying it with her every thought and every quickened breath.

Kill my mother. She shuddered. *End her misery and save Gage from the Shadow consuming him completely.* She gritted her teeth. Could she resist the Shadow if she joined him in that struggle? She resisted the Light, which wanted her brother's blood more than anything in this moment.

I can resist, she thought, narrowing her eyes on her mother.

She pulled her hands apart, the keyshard now embedded in the knife's guard, between its blade and grip. The weapon still held a hint of the Light, but the stone gave it a blue aura.

Anika had never held a magic weapon before, nor had she ever considered how they were made, but she felt certain this wasn't the traditional method of forging. Regardless, she could feel its power and she knew it was fitting.

The knife belonged to the Lawson family.

Anika looked at her mother one final time, both of them crying but accepting. Anika drew back her hand in a quick jerk, knowing the blade would fly true. She flung the weapon toward her mother.

Time slowed as Renay gasped and closed her eyes, not watching the spinning blade fly toward her. Anika closed her eyes as well, a sudden gust of wind blowing her hair back.

The blackness receded from Gage's eyes slightly as they widened in shock, his mouth opening to let out a cry.

Naya's hand gripped her own keyshard tightly, eagerly awaiting Renay's blood to mark the Child of Light's first step toward Shadow. She did not see the figure behind her, or the glimmer of its blade poised above her wrist.

"Anika!" Matty shouted, reaching out for her. The summoned wind kept him back, blowing him nearly out the door in a sudden gust.

Robin was released from the power that held him and he fell to the floor, scrambling toward Gage.

Meanwhile, the knife that flew toward Renay slowed in its flight, but it spun quicker and quicker. A heavy breeze blew Renay's hair toward the spinning knife, and after a thousand rotations, the knife reversed course.

Anika pulled her arms back, using the wind to direct the enchanted knife back in her direction.

"No!" Naya cried as she tried to dive away, but the blade was too quick. It buried itself into her shoulder—where her heart would have been a moment earlier—knocking her back. Ransil's own blade came down then, severing her hand completely from her wrist. The halfling used his other hand to catch Ruke's stone as it fell from her grasp, then he rolled away toward his companions.

Anika made another motion, her hair blowing in a sudden breeze. The blade was ripped from the priestess' shoulder, the wind sending it spinning back toward the Child of Light. Anika caught it deftly, her eyes now smoldering on the Shadow priestess.

"I will not play your games," Anika said. "I am not your pawn, nor is my brother."

"He is not your brother," wailed Naya, cradling her bleeding stump.

"Yes. I am."

His blade clattered to the ground as Gage stepped toward Renay, falling to his knees. "Mother... I—"

Renay's chin quivered in a futile search for words as she stared down at the boy that almost killed her. Her breath came in ragged gasps. Before she could respond, a voice came from the doorway.

"You!"

Everyone turned to see a Luminaura priest, one of his hands gripping a mace and the other dripping blood.

"It's you," the priest said, falling to his knees, looking up at Anika. "The Light made flesh..."

Anika regarded him dismissively, along with the dwarf and half-orc woman that stood behind him with weapons ready. She looked to Matty and then Ransil, seeing the green keyshard in the halfling's hand, its glow intensifying.

"We need to go," Ransil said. His darting eyes went from the door blocked by the newcomers to the dark gap in the wall behind one of the curtains. "That looks like a way."

A shadow emerged from that hidden doorway as if in response, and Grip smiled at Ransil. "A good eye." She saw the stone he held. "Looks like our work is done." She beckoned them to join her with a nod of her head.

"Child," the priest said, his own gaze going from Ransil's keyshard to Anika, "we have come for Ruke's stone as well. Perhaps our purposes align—we seek to end the storm in Rathen and destroy the incarnate that made it."

Anika looked from the strangers to her own companions, her eyes resting on Matty. He stared at her in awe, or fear—she couldn't quite tell. But she felt a distance between them in that moment that truly affirmed her lifelong concern that she did not belong. She was different—more different than she could have ever imagined.

"Anika."

Turning to Ransil, she saw her friend's face aglow with green magic. The stone in his hands was shimmering in a way that paled the aura that still surrounded her. The halfling held it out toward her, looking up in expectation.

She bent to grab it, and when she did, the entire keep shook at its deep, deep foundations below.

CHAPTER TWENTY-NINE

An Entangling Fate

The Luminaurian army marched all day east along the Valeway, reaching Sathford before the sun began to set. Two blue banners, each adorned with six white stars—one star for each of the old gods that sacrificed themselves for the Light—flapped proudly at the head of the column as it neared the city's walls, while another two identical banners marked the rear of the army where the chaplains made up the main marching force.

At the head of the column were the acolytes, led by Chaplain Brace Cobbit, who now urged his horse to swiftly deliver his scouts' reports to the High Warpriest. The acolytes were the only part of the army that did not wear the church colors, as to more easily blend in when needed. Brace wore a dark green cloak with its hood pulled up over his long dark hair. He reined in his horse along the road, looking for his cousin, Hope Kandalot.

Instead, he found Sir Darrance Moore, who locked his mount's step with Brace's. The commander of the paladins nodded back to the rear of the force. "Hope is with the chaplains, praying." Darrance was almost the exact counterpart of Brace—a clean-shaven, handsome face with carefully cropped blond hair that fell easily across his brow. He searched Brace's stubbled scowl. "Any problems?"

Brace shook his head, looking up at the darkening sky to the north. "Looks like a storm," he said, his voice much more gruff than his age would suggest. "The Archbeacon said we should expect it, so I don't consider it a problem. Damned if it ain't unsettling though."

Darrance's blue eyes searched the sky for anything unnatural, but from this distance it appeared to just be another spring storm coming. "Better scout it out once we get settled," the paladin said. "Luriah's doves will arrive at sundown. Would be good to have a responding report for her by morning."

Brace nodded and spat. "Aye. I've already sent Jenore on ahead.

Told her to ride on to Rathaway Priory. We need to know what we're walking into here, Darrance. I don't like it."

"You're the one that said you'd go crazy if we spent another week in Andelor," Darrance said with a smirk. "Be careful what you pray for, friend." He spurred his mount forward as the gates to Sathford opened.

"Aye," Brace said, producing his pipe from a pouch at his waist. He raised the small red keyshard his father had passed down to him, spoke a single word, and lit the pipe with the flame produced by the stone, puffing smoke out the corner of his mouth. "I do think I'll pray for something different tonight."

He watched as the smoke from his pipe swirled in front of his face, mixing with the distant gray horizon, looking for something. What it was, he couldn't say, but he was certain it wasn't in the city that opened up before him.

Sathford was the second biggest city that Brace had seen with his own eyes, dwarfed only by Andelor itself. Raventhal Spire emerged from the heart of the city like a wicked dagger, looking even more sinister against the lifeless sky. Castle Tolle rose behind the tower, majestic and impenetrable by any army due to the steep hill it was built on. The Bracing River was abustle with flat merchant ships bound for Andelor or Eastlund or even far Copera. It was a glorious city, that was no doubt. But the sweeping sights did not settle the dread that festered in Brace's stomach as he rode through those gates under those heavy, still clouds.

Jenore rode hard alongside the Rathaway road, pushing herself to reach the priory before nightfall. Her auburn hair flew wildly behind her; the only wind under these foul clouds was the gust she left in her wake, and she felt no cool relief that normally accompanied such a hurried pace.

She watched the skies above, looking for any sign of movement but finding none. And yet those clouds continued to swallow the world.

It'll be covering Sathford by morning, she thought with sinking dread, kicking her horse harder. *Not much farther now. Father Josaiah will have doves ready to send word back to Brace and Hope.*

As she cleared another hill, she saw horses riding south—a heavy draft horse and a smaller beast that struggled to keep pace, a heavy rider astride the undersized mount. Jenore slowed her horse, but she knew that there was no hiding from the strangers. The trees had receded from the road and she had no time to divert her path.

Let them be merchants, she prayed to the Light, *or refugees from Rathen.* She patted her short sword reassuringly—if it came to a skirmish, she would not shy away.

"Ho!" a voice called out, the larger horse slowing slightly as the distance between riders closed. "Ho! Ware, rider! Ware!"

Jenore slowed her horse, seeing a tan Coperan and a dwarf with the bushiest beard she had ever seen. The man looked like a trader, while the dwarf looked like a grizzled forester.

"Light be with you, travelers," she greeted. "I am with the Luminaura paladins marching to relieve Rathen."

"Rathen be gone," the dwarf answered, "long gone. So be the priory up the road."

"The priory?" Jenore's heart sank. *Has it really gotten so dire in the north?* "Father Josaiah, is he—"

The Coperan man shook his head, true sadness in his eyes.

The dwarf replied, "He—he went mad, Sister. Killed a boy at the priory. That was before the orcs came. They did them in while he tried to give them a sermon."

"Damn you! Show some respect, Kolin," the Coperan barked at the dwarf. "The man saved your life, summoning the Light against those savages."

The dwarf merely nodded. "Aye, Neff, I meant no offense. Josaiah—he died a hero, he did. But that boy—"

Jenore stared, slack-jawed, unable to comprehend. *Josaiah was a good man*, she thought. *A kind man. He could never hurt a child. Unless they were Shadowthralled.* The thought sent a chill down her spine. *Maybe these men are Shadowfiends looking to cover up their wickedness.* She discreetly gripped her sword, slowly easing it out from its scabbard.

There was a sudden deafening shriek from above that reared all three of their horses, nearly tossing the riders.

Jenore did tear her sword free then. The dwarf produced a heavy club and the Copera man readied the crossbow that had rested on his saddle. A huge shape took to the sky.

Dragon! Jenore thought, her breath caught in her throat.

"It's the incarnate!" The Copera man kicked his horse, motioning for Jenore to follow. The dwarf reared his mount as well and made to ride southward at full speed.

Incarnate?! Jenore turned her own mount to follow, no option but to trust these strangers as the winged monstrosity soared over them, its screeching cry piercing their ears.

Jenore wasn't sure what an incarnate was, but the word conjured thoughts of blasphemy and unholy intent. It was as if she had heard the word in a sermon—which she had guiltily never paid much attention to, if she were to be honest—and the memory of it, inspired by the urgency of these strangers, terrified Jenore.

Whatever an incarnate was, it was flying straight for Sathford.

Hope Kandalot strode toward the Temple of Dawn, which was tucked away in a small wood to the northeast of Sathford's walls. She was armored in heavy mail, enameled in sky blue with polished white edges and brightstars. Under one arm she carried her helmet, leaving her round, flat face to be seen by worshippers leaving the church.

Four armored paladins walked with her, two on either side. They all wore blue cloaks trimmed in white with the large white brightstar displayed on their backs. With the rest of the church's army currently resting in the city, this small procession was a coordinated display of the Light's presence at one of Sathford's most popular places of worship.

The temple's remote location was a testament to just how little the city cared for the Luminaura. *They will see,* Hope thought as she continued her march, *they will certainly see the error of their ways.*

"Light be with you," she said to a pair of passing men with arms locked. She gave them only the hint of a smile, letting them know she was their protection and also their judge of conviction.

"And with you," both men said, almost in unison.

She heard pieces of their whispers as they passed. "…save us…the church won't leave us…like Rathen…"

Another woman leaving the temple took a moment to bow to Hope; terror filled her eyes, but her voice was low and restrained. "Does war come for our city, Dame? Are we doomed like Rathen?" She clearly wanted to avoid any sort of panic.

Loudly, Hope replied, "We are here to stop the Shadow in its tracks, luminant. Fear not."

The woman bowed again, satisfied with the response. None of the other temple patrons stopped her approach, which Hope found slightly bothersome. *They truly do not appreciate the Light here*, she thought angrily, her shadow of a smile turning to that of a frown. The birthmark on the left side of her face near her eyes—a patch of bruised flesh that ran from her hairline to the middle of her cheek—wrinkled as her eyes narrowed on the temple's doors.

"Wait here," Hope said, turning to her paladins. "I don't want anyone disturbing me."

"Yes, Dame Kandalot," they said in practiced unison, drawing their swords and raising their shields in a show of force. They turned their backs to Hope and made an armored line to secure her privacy.

Throwing open the doors, Hope heard several gasps as Sisters of the Light looked up from their work cleaning the temple after service. Vicar Tomen Shaw sat in a pew near the temple's decorative altar—the trunk of a massive tree that had been cut down after the Unthroning, representing the temple's shift from worshipping Oakus to the Light.

"Dame Kandalot," Tomen said with a smile, standing up. The vicar was a middle-aged elf with short, well-kept brown hair, going gray on the sides. Like most elves, his face was devoid of stubble, but his jaw had a shadowed look to it due to his defined cheekbones. "I had heard you would be arriving, but I did not expect you to honor our temple so soon."

Hope saw another figure stand up with Tomen, a younger woman in rough leathers and furs. She was much too young to need the support of the twisted wooden staff she carried. The girl shared many of the same physical qualities of the vicar.

Daughter? Hope thought, not knowing the vicar had been married. But the woman was certainly of the same blood.

"May we speak?" Hope asked sternly. She surveyed the temple, regarding the girl in their presence. "Alone?"

Tomen's smile faded slightly. "Certainly, Dame." He stepped down the dais toward Hope, looking to the temple's caretakers. "Sisters, perhaps my daughter could accompany you to the city to pick up the evening's offerings."

The Sisters obliged, bowing their heads slightly as they moved past Hope toward the temple's main doors. The vicar's daughter was the last to leave, giving her father a concerned look.

"It's all right, Fallon," he said with a warm smile. "We can continue our discussion when you return, after I meet with the most honorable Hope Kandalot, High Warpriest of the Luminaura."

As Fallon passed Hope, she gave the warpriest a bold stare. The elf had her hair shorn on the sides, so short Hope could see her scalp, which had swirling tattoos.

A druid, Hope thought, intrigued. *Is the vicar hiding a daughter devoted to Oakus?* Worship of the old gods was not necessarily noteworthy, but Tomen—the vicar of a temple of the Light that used to be devoted to Oakus—having a daughter still devoted to the old ways...

Hope gave the young woman a sidelong glance as she passed. Fallon was slightly shorter than Hope, which was surprising considering how accustomed the warpriest was to looking up to others, much to her disdain.

The doors to the temples closed and the vicar and warpriest were left alone.

"What brings you here so unexpectedly?" Tomen asked. "Not that it isn't an honor to have you in our place of worship."

Hope walked down the aisle toward Tomen, who stood waiting with his arms peacefully held in front of him, his hands hidden in his sleeves.

"Where is your errant priest?" Hope asked, letting her eyes wander around the temple's impressive architecture. Dwarf-built, if Hope had to guess, eager to preserve their kin's architecture since most was lost in Myrethold. "Avrim was his name?"

"Yet to return from Rathen," Tomen was quick to answer, no concern in his voice—which infuriated Hope already. "Though we all pray for his swift and safe return, as word from the Rathaway is that the city has fallen. I do not believe he perished though."

Hope nodded, stepping within reach of the vicar. She let her inquisitive green eyes settle on his oblivious gray ones.

There was no fear in those eyes. No reverence. No admission of guilt.

Hope smacked the vicar across the face with the back of her mailed hand.

The elf was thrown back by the force, crying out as he sprawled onto the carpeted aisle. When he landed, he spun his head around, eyes wide with confusion and unexpected anger. Blood dripped from his perfect mouth, which twitched as he struggled to find the right words.

"Were not all the chapels told to keep their errant priests at heel?" Hope asked with a leveled voice, looking down on the vicar as if he were a whipped dog. "Did the Archbeacon's decrees not reach your temple out here? Perhaps you have converted back to Oakus and do not believe the Luminaura's decrees apply to you?"

"No, Dame," he said, turning around to sit, but clearly afraid to rise. "I did not—Duke Ambrose requested aid. Are we not to protect those plagued by the Shadow?"

Hope adjusted her armored hand, her eyes fixed on Tomen. "You are to adhere to the commands of Her Luminous. We were to stay out of Rathen. Are you a fool?"

"Hope," formality forgotten, "what—"

"Did you not question why the duke requested aid? Did you not stop to think that maybe the Archbeacon called his own priests away from the city?"

Tomen blinked, his gaze lowering as he searched for meaning in her words.

"You have drawn unwanted attention to the church, Vicar." She drew her broadsword, a gleaming crystal in its cross-guard at the base of its blade. Lightshards were a rarity, even amongst the Luminaura's forces; it glowed with the light of a small sun as she raised the blade. "Her Luminous requires someone to pay the price."

Hope was surprised to see Tomen not beg for his life or make excuses for his deeds. He got to his knees and looked up into her eyes.

"If I am to die," he said, reaching his hands behind his back while he leaned forward to expose his neck, "perhaps you may enlighten me what the church wanted to hide in Rathen. Were they the cause of the storm?"

Smiling in appreciation of his honor in death, Hope hefted her blade and assumed an executioner's stance. "The Light is fading," she said. "Your temple is a sign of that—hidden out here in the woods, still under the yoke of Oakus. Most in the city can't bother to even bring you their offerings themselves, can they?"

Tomen's gaze fell as he nodded. When he looked back up to her, Hope saw understanding in his eyes.

"Faith is found in a common foe," the vicar said, quoting the Enlightened's words from the luminary. He smiled and let out a soft laugh. "Tell me, Hope. Do you know what common foe the church made for you to fight?"

"Does it matter?" Hope asked, raising the sword.

"No, I suppose not. May the Light forgive you all."

The sword slashed down, severing the vicar's head, silencing his treachery against the church.

As Hope watched the headless body slump to the ground, her heart stopped when she saw the glowing green keyshard drop from the vicar's limp hands. As the light from that stone faded, Hope imagined an identical keyshard in the druid's palm, glowing with the dangerous truth. The warpriest turned and sprinted for the door as fast as her armored legs could carry her.

Smashing the doors open, she shouted to her paladins. "Find the druid! Find the vicar's daughter!"

A piercing screech split the darkening sky as poisoned clouds rolled in from the north. Hope and her paladins forgot the elven woman and stared at the enormous, soaring enemy above—knowing it was sent to reaffirm the world's faith in the Light.

As if in response to that terrible thing's screech, the trees shook and goblins poured out to surround the paladins. Hope spun her bloodied blade and charged, never having been more eager for a battle.

Fallon stifled a cry with a hand to her mouth, dropping the small keyshard—a gift from her father when she had declared her intent to become a druid.

"This is so we can be together, even when we are apart," he had told her when she pledged to the Order of Oakus, kissing her forehead. "Our faiths bind us."

In her mind, her father's lips were fixed in a tight line as she pictured a sword cleaving through his neck. The vision played out slowly in her mind, over and over again, forever poisoning every memory she had of the kind man.

She fell to her knees outside the butcher's shop in Sathford, near the north gates. Her shoulders shook as she tried to contain her sobs, knowing that the zealots who had murdered her father were lurking throughout the city, maybe looking for her. There would be time for mourning later, she assured herself, wiping tears away. Her grief was terrible, but she found strength in the keyshard that she picked back up from the cobbled road.

"To arms! Ware the sky! The storm comes!"

Cries erupted from all directions. Fallon looked up and saw the tall torches along the city walls lighting a terrible foe, as big as a dragon but feathered like a bird of prey. She turned to run toward the only place she could think of to find shelter from the gargantuan beast that now perched on the north walls.

But even the mighty Raventhal Spire looked small in comparison to whatever that monstrosity was. She gripped the keyshard tightly, seeking its depths for some sort of escape from the hell that she had found herself in this night.

Darrance leapt on his horse, having only had time to put on his breastplate, greaves, and arm guards, his helmet still in his room in The Glad Tidings with his dirk and cloak. But he had his sword and shield, hoping it would be enough for whatever caused the alarm.

"The stormbringer has come," Brace said, rearing his own horse near Darrance's. "There!" He pointed toward the northern wall.

Darrance gasped as he saw a beast the size of a grown dragon perching on the north gate with clawed bird legs. Its feathered wings were extended threateningly as it let out another shrill cry.

"Bow before Corvanna," the booming voice called. Darrance winced as the command rolled over him like a wave of thunder. "I am the keeper of the wind and the master of your skies! You are under my domain now! Submit!"

Black shapes joined Corvanna—harpies appearing from the otherwise still storm—descending onto the city in open assault. Arrows from the city militia's archers flew toward the invaders, knocking a few creatures out of the sky.

"Light forbid!" Darrance cursed, wheeling his horse toward the city's courtyard, Brace following with wide, terrified eyes on Corvanna. "Your archers?"

"Joining the watch," Brace replied.

"Where is Hope?!"

As if in response, a flash of light erupted beyond the northern walls, and a giant lance of light pierced Corvanna's breast. Black blood and huge feathers erupted from the wound as the creature let out a shrill curse that summoned a crash of lightning. The unnatural storm rumbled angrily when Corvanna fell back off her perch, wings struggling to find purchase.

"The Light!" someone shouted from behind the men, followed by more cries of, "The Luminaura has come! The Shadowfiends shall not take Sathford!"

Emboldened by the rallying cries of the citizenry, in addition to Hope's Lightspear that had wounded the beast, Darrance and Brace kicked their mounts toward the north gate to meet the harpy threat. As their horses galloped across the great Sathler Bridge that spanned the Bracing River—from which Brace's father, a fisherman, had given him his name—Brace saw a hail of small black arrows arc over the walls.

"Goblins!"

Darrance spurred his mount faster, driven by fear and faith to smite the Shadow that had found its way to Sathford.

Fallon threw open the doors to Raventhal's northern vestibule, hundreds of candles flickering in the gust that followed. Two robed figures—a gnome girl in the green colors of a Novice and a human boy in the yellow colors of an Accepted that looked no older than nine—spun around at the clamor. No guards stood sentry outside the tower, as most knew better than to intrude and trigger the thousands of glyphtraps that riddled the premise—and those that didn't suffered the fatal consequences of breaching one of Vale's most prestigious arcane academies rivaled only by the Arcania itself.

"Quinn!" Fallon raced over to the boy who had been reading from a heavy tome, his hand now holding a glowing amber keyshard. Its light faded as Fallon neared. "The city is under attack!"

"The paladins?" The boy closed the book, his calm demeanor more fitting of an elderly man unconcerned with the world and not a pale Westerran boy yet to see his tenth year.

Fallon scowled, fighting tears at the mere thought of the Luminaura. "This city is not safe regardless. We need to leave. Now."

"Not safe?" The gnome girl stepped over to join them, looking even younger than Quinn. She had a round nose and big, bright golden eyes. "How can we not be safe here? The shardvault is here! High Mage Konrath is the Archmage's own Chosen! How can we not be safe here, with the Archbeacon's army as well?"

"See that Konrath knows of the attack then," Fallon said, nodding to the great stairs that lay beyond the vestibule's lounging chairs and desks.

A thunderous boom shook the walls of the spire, and the gnome girl gasped.

"Go, now!" Fallon commanded.

The boy made to follow, but Fallon caught his arm. "We need to find the Old Ways, Quinn. My father is dead—executed by the Archbeacon's decree."

Quinn's normally passive face stared at her in wide-eyed shock. "On what charges?"

Fallon shrugged, shaking her head. "I do not know exactly, I—My father's keyshard. He used it to show me what happened, but I don't know what it all means. All I know is that the church wants to cover up something that my father threatened to expose." She grabbed the boy's shoulders with both hands, tears now welling in her eyes.

"Quinn, I need your help. The High Warpriest knows about me—she knows what my father showed me. They will kill me next, if whatever is attacking this city doesn't kill them first."

The boy gave her a sympathetic look, but shrugged his shoulders helplessly. "Master Audreese is in Andelor, counseling with the Archmage. I do not have permission to use the—"

Fallon braced Quinn as the entire room shook, the ground beneath their feet buckled. The thundering shriek sounded right above them, forcing the druid and mage to cover their ears.

"We don't have time!" Fallon pulled the boy toward the stairs that led into the bowels of Raventhal. Stones began to fall from the upper levels, crashing violently into the main hall. As they raced down the stairs, Fallon could hear the screams of students and teachers, as well as the unmistakable sound of arcane energy being unleashed.

"Archers!" Brace shouted, rearing his horse, pointing toward the wave of goblins surging through the fallen northern gates. "Show them the Light!"

Hope and her paladins charged toward the eastern gate that was buckling under something massive banging against it. The main fighting force had fallen back to the bridge, determined to hold the invading infantry at the river—if the bridge fell, the city was as good as lost.

The thrum of bows was music to Brace's ears, as streaks of Light flew over his head toward the enemy. The blessed arrows hit with flashes of blinding light, the Shadowfiends shielding their eyes as their allies fell dead. Goblins screeched and scurried for cover from the holy assault, only to be urged to hold and continue their charge by the harpies overhead.

"What is it doing?" Brace heard several members of the city watch near him, and he turned to see them pointing toward Raventhal Spire that sat on the other end of the river, near Castle Tolle.

The creature that called itself Corvanna found a perch on one of the great eaves that protruded from the tower. Several harpy minions swarmed around their master, darting in and out the tower's windows. The ones that came out of the windows carried stones—*Keyshards*, Brace thought, recognizing the arcane glow—and produced them to Corvanna. The monster reached out her clawed hands to crush the stones, each time producing a lightning strike from above and sudden violent gusts of wind.

"You will bow before me, fools," Corvanna said with a voice that came from the gray skies now covering all of Sathford. "Serve me from the grounds while I rule the skies!"

Brace tried to calm his horse as goblin arrows fell uselessly from the sky, spinning haphazardly as the mighty winds began to create small funnel clouds of scattered debris and discarded weapons. The howling wind intensified, and buildings began to groan under its oppressive strength.

Goblins screamed as they were lifted into the sky near the northern gate, pulled into a funnel cloud that touched ground near those walls.

"Light preserve! Flee! Take shelter!"

The shouts of retreat started with the chaplains, who threw down their spears and joined the panicked citizenry that rushed to cross the bridge to the south side of the city—despite the invading beast that was descending from the mage's tower to block their path.

Unthinking, Brace rode hard toward the foe, fumbling for the small keyshard his father had given him—the one he had kept secret from his superiors in the Luminaura lest they think him a secret worshiper of Wick. As the great bird spread its wings to block the fleeing mob that he rode through, Brace remembered something his father had said when he had given him the stone he now gripped tightly in his hands.

If you can't get it to work, just find a good breeze. Wick's fire can never truly go out, so the stronger the wind, the stronger Wick's flame.

Brace held the stone in front of him, thinking of his father as he rode headlong into his doom. He spoke the word as thunder rolled again and Corvanna laughed wickedly, and the great storm that consumed all in its path gave power to the small gout of flame produced by Brace's small keyshard.

The summoned flame seemed to catch the very wind on fire, a burning wall that crashed over Corvanna like a tidal wave. The screech that followed was primal and godlike, knocking those that did not already dive out of the flame's way to the ground.

Brace was blown back from his saddle, his horse toppling and crushing several unfortunate soldiers. The wind seemed to die immediately, the deafening roar of the storm giving way to the agonized shriek of Corvanna and her burning harpy minions.

His vision blurry, Brace saw the incarnate—this was, he knew now, clearly an incarnate of Eyen—rising from its smoldering heap, spreading its terrible smoking wings. It retracted its bird-like head back to let out another cry, but a spear of Light once again pierced its chest. Brace turned to see Hope at the other end of the bridge, her eyes glowing with divine rage. Her arm was extended, the holy power of the summoned lance still shimmering across her blessed armor.

The sounds of heavy wings flapping marked Corvanna's difficult retreat, taking back to the sky that was now clearing. Her voice still rolled across the city like thunder. "I will return when the Child is dead, fools! You will regret this interference!"

Several harpies burst from Raventhal Spire then, keyshards in hand, retreating with their master. With each keyshard the incarnate claimed, it seemed to regain some of its stamina. No amount of enchanted arrows could prevent the abomination from ascending.

Cheers rang out all over the city. "The Light! Praise the Light!"

Brace watched as Hope began to glow—literally—in the worship that surrounded her. He pocketed his keyshard as he struggled to his feet.

A strong hand reached under his arm to help him, and Brace saw the bloodied face of Darrance, more disheveled than he had ever seen him.

"It's not done," the paladin said.

Brace nodded, turning to see Corvanna climb into the sky—something more pressing than conquest had called to the incarnate, but it would surely return to finish its work.

And Sathford must be made ready.

CHAPTER THIRTY

Secrets Sealed Away

Anika opened her eyes to oppressive darkness. There was no sound or movement for a long, drawn-out breath, but as she exhaled, she could see a faint green light at the edge of the oblivion. It pulsated, growing more vibrant as it drew closer to her—or she drew closer to it? She could not tell in this place, wherever she was. The baron's bedchambers had fallen away along with its inhabitants, and she was alone with a mysterious essence of life that grew brighter and brighter until—

"The Nethering," Valix said, pointing to a page in the great book that looked like it had been rubbed with charcoal. There were little dots of white in that blackness, where the charcoal hadn't adhered to the page quite right. *Or are they deliberate imperfections?* Layla wondered.

Valix pointed up into the darkened rafters of their quarters below deck. They swayed together with the steady rock of the ship on the calm waves of the Racivic Sea. "Beyond the sky," she continued, her eyes fixed on Layla's, "where I'm sure you've been taught to believe the Heavens reside."

"And the stars," Layla said, failing to restrain a teasing smile.

"It's the Shadow," Valix said firmly. "The Shadow came before the Creation, and Stane was born of that union. He is the original Nethering Lord."

"It is called the Nethering," Layla said, laying back on her bed, propped up on a single elbow, "as in the Nether...Ring. The Ring being the astral domains. I learned them all in cosmology at the Arcania—each one begat an old god or a mortal aspect. Which one do you think Stane came from?"

Valix closed the book. "He came before all, when Aetha was

formed yet before it could sustain life." She climbed onto the bed next to Layla, placing the book under her legs. She closed her eyes. "The Luminaura will teach that the Light spawned Creation, but Creation is chaos—it was not planned. The Light was created to keep Shadow at bay in the Nethering, but both were kept at bay by the Creation while Aetha was forged. Yet Stane walked its surface before either poisoned his providence.

"And he will walk it again," Valix said, turning to Layla. "We will learn how to break his seals and bring about his next Coming."

"To what end?" Layla asked, fearful of the answer.

Valix smiled.

—Ruke appeared.

The halfling was bathed in a soft green glow, the light behind her swallowing Anika as a landscape of breathtaking verdancy replaced the suffocating Shadow.

"Where am I?" Anika asked. She could not feel her body, but looking down it was still there. The green glow that enveloped the halfling was coming from the stone she held.

"You're in the keyshard," Ruke said, "only for a moment in your world, but here we have more time—not much, but hopefully enough."

"Enough time for what?"

"You know," Ruke said, giving Anika a nod while she bent down to pluck a long blade of grass from the green swaying sea that surrounded their path. "You are the Child of Light, and you will already know all I tell you—deep down. The knowledge is buried in your doubt and fears, but with each uncertainty you overcome, you will see your purpose that much clearer."

Ruke handed the blade of grass to Anika, the halfling's fingers child-like and yet ancient. Anika reached down to take the grass.

When she touched the blade, Anika saw the vibrant land around her transform into a barren wasteland of craggy, dry earth. There was no wind, just clouds of choking dust. No true light, but the faint illumination of foul magic permeating the air and giving the rough edges of the landscape a cruel finality.

Anika felt the blade of grass tingle, and she looked down knowing she should let it fall. When she did, it floated down perfectly still, no wind to dance with during its slow descent. The land itself seemed to *breathe* as the grass touched the unmade ground, and from that green shard, life cascaded across the world in green and brown waves. Anika felt the very power of Creation. It sent surges of an indescribable emotion through her: partly nostalgia and partly what she imagined a mother might feel like as she gave birth.

"The power of Creation courses through you, Child." The halfling's voice brought her back to the verdant lands of Ruke's stone. "You are able to project to the Nethering domains, a trick that took me a lifetime to learn and has earned me eternal bondage."

"What do you want from me?"

Ruke inclined her head in curiosity. "I am here for you, Child. You have come to the gateway between our world and the domain of Oakus, and our time is limited—the Shadow is breaking the chains that keep it from enveloping the world in its misery.

"What would you have of me, Child?"

Anika's mind was a blur—endless questions racing through it.

Why was she here?

Who was the monster from her visions?

Was her brother truly evil?

Where was her father?

"What is this?" Unknowingly, Anika lifted her knife that now held the blue stone that was her brother's gift to her.

"A magic weapon—a mighty one, forged by the Child of Light in time of need." Ruke touched her nose. "But, again, you knew that. You ask about the stone itself. It is a greater keyshard of Eyen, a very piece of Skythe. Each of our Keys were blessed by the old gods—those fools. After the Unthroning, the Keys were shattered, creating the greater keyshards. Unlike the lesser keyshards—which are remnants of the gods' crystallized power in other holy items—the pieces of the Keys themselves have near limitless power."

"And this?" Anika asked, raising the green shard.

"My prison," Ruke said with a smile, motioning to the lands around them, "and it is falling to Shadow. Each keyshard is imbued with three aspects—Light, Shadow, and the old gods' mastery of a single element of Creation. My prison is a lesser keyshard, one that I foolishly forged myself before the Unthroning—my mother always said, 'Make sure you always have a good place to hide.'" She laughed, her eyes distant.

"Halflings were hunted back in those days…"

"You forged your own prison?"

Ruke blinked her memories away, looking back to Anika. "It started as an experiment, based on the legend of the gnomes. I remember the stories of Wendal the Wanderer, a folk figure among halflings in the Acreage. He found his way to the unpronounceable Fey Domain, becoming the first gnome. I thought the other domains could be reached as well, so I vowed to find the way to Elysun." She looked around sadly. "But mortals are not meant for such journeys. Our minds cannot comprehend the enormity—the impossibility—of these places.

"But I ramble," Ruke said, her voice losing its melancholy. "We do not have time for my musings. The incarnate is coming for you at this very moment. You feel it, do you not?"

The word conjured up the image of the monster from her visions—wide, feathered wings and evil eyes full of malevolence. "Why?"

"Because you are the Child of Light!" Ruke said exasperatedly. "You have a piece of her!" She pointed to the blue keyshard. "She's a god in the flesh, but incomplete. She needs the other pieces of Skythe to fully possess Eyen's power. But she also knows that you are the only one that can stop her from building her malicious, tyrannical empire."

Corvanna's terible voice seemed to echo in the nothingness surrounding them as if in response.

"How do I stop her?"

"No one can stop him," Valix said, putting her hands behind her head as she stared up into the wooden rafters, watching a spider creep across a beam. "His Coming is as inevitable as death. It's just a matter of who ushers it in and who resists."

Layla lay back as well, her eyes closed. She was exhausted from their urgent passing of the Jathi Plains, and she was relieved to be out of Caraby. Most of the ship captains were similarly eager to be pulling anchor from Jath's shores now that the dragon had awoken. Finding passage was easy.

As assured as she was in Valix's company, Layla still held doubts about her new path in life. *Where else will you go?* she thought. She could never return to Andelor. Any royal seer would have the truth from her about what had happened in Jath, and even if she weren't held responsible for Desmond's death, she still didn't have the book that she had been sent to retrieve.

She had nothing to return to.

"What kind of god would Stane be, Valix?"

A brief silence.

"A just one," she said finally. "One with no further ambition, or any single faction to pit against another for his own gain. He would be the first true god, ruler over all. I find security in that—I do not want to be a pawn."

Layla turned to Valix. "Are we not pawns?"

Valix laughed. "For now, I suppose. Until the seals are broken."

"Are there no theories on what the seals are?"

"Plenty," Valix said, amused. "Perhaps too many. The most popular theory is that the seals have something to do with the Keys that the Purveyors foolishly used to trap their gods—as Stane had decreed. They say he split himself into seven aspects, one for each old god, as well as one to lurk in the Abyss until he could once more be whole."

"So would the theory be that the Keys somehow represent the seals—he would be restored if the Keys were restored?"

Valix shook her head. "Stane would require more than that—he would require sacrifice. Stane is complex, and the easiest solution is rarely the right one when it comes to him or his writings." She laughed lightly. "Just look at the mess the Purveyors made of the Unthroning."

Layla thought for a moment, analyzing the information. "So if he needs to unite his aspects to become whole, and they are trapped with the old gods in the shattered Keys…"

Valix rolled over on her side to look at Layla, staring at nothing in particular while she focused on the words.

"…it seems to me he would need to restore the Keys—in a fashion—so he could properly destroy them, freeing his aspects."

Valix gave the most genuine smile Layla had seen on her face. "I think Stane brought us together, sister. You speak of the scions."

"The scions?"

Valix waved the question away. "Rest for now, sister. We have plenty of time for prophecy."

Layla smiled, feeling at home with this stranger with whom she was now bound by blood. Closing her eyes, she felt herself falling into the comforting arms of deep purpose.

There was a time she might have feared sleep, unknowingly terrified of Desmond's dark words that waited in her dreams to deprive her of agency.

But that seemed like a lifetime ago already.

"You are the only one who can defeat her," Ruke said. "She is an incarnate of Eyen. Wick's flames might weaken her, but only the Light can defeat the Shadow that has consumed her almost entirely."

The Shadow, Anika thought, remembering the futility she felt in the Nethering before Ruke appeared and guided her here.

"My brother…"

Ruke shook her head. "You may have shared a home with him, but he is not your brother. He is the Child of Shadow, destined to kill you should you fail to slay him. He will come for you eventually—"

"He *is* my brother!"

The lands of Elysun darkened as Anika's voice rose with anger.

"Anika," Ruke said, "we do not have time. He is the Shadow—he may not know it yet, or even truly feel it yet, but he was born of malice and the Shadow will emerge however much he fights it."

Tears welled in Anika's eyes. "There must be some way to stop it."

"There is," Ruke said, without hesitation, but the surprised look on her face told Anika that she might not have meant to say that.

"Tell me."

Ruke swallowed. "It's dangerous, Anika…not just for you, but for the entire world."

"Just tell me."

"I am bound to tell you, though I fear the consequences," Ruke said, a tear streaming down one cheek. "The only way to break the cycle of Light versus Shadow is to kill the deceiver—Stane, the designer of the Purveyor's treachery. He is the foul presence that has always poisoned this world, and he seeks to come back." She placed her small hands on Anika's. "Child, I do not fear anything in this world or the beyond more than I fear Stane. He is the all-corrupting power that created the Light only to manipulate Shadow to his will."

The weight of the words felt like too much for Anika to bear, but she began to understand what would be required to save her brother.

Ruke swallowed. "The only way to defeat the Shadow that

consumes your brother is to defeat Stane, but doing so could also destroy the Light. And I don't know if you—if any of us—would survive that. They call him the inevitable.

"When you defeat the incarnate, you will have a choice, Anika. Stane's scion will emerge when its seal is broken. If you slay that scion, your only path is to destroy your brother before he inevitably accepts his own dark fate. If you allow the scion to live, and then you manage to break the remaining seals, Stane will be released from the Abyss.

"Only by defeating Stane himself can you hope to overcome your brother's destiny," Ruke said, the vision of her starting to fade away as the landscape darkened, "as well as your own."

"Wait," Anika said desperately, reaching out. Her hand found only mists, her surroundings fading in a swirl of greens and browns, replaced by blackness. All the talk of scions and seals and Stane seemed overwhelming, but something deep within her assured her this was knowledge she already knew.

She's right, Anika thought. *I know what she's talking about. How is this possible?*

Her final questions were left unanswered as the black void of the Nethering gave way to the scene in the baron's bedroom.

CHAPTER THIRTY-ONE

The Last Flight

"Anika!"

Ransil's voice pulled her from the vision, her eyes blankly watching the robed Xe'danni woman scramble to her feet, shoving Robin out of the way as the room shook. Something fell from the ceiling, crashing down onto the bed. Renay leapt up, crying out as the bed cracked under the weight of a falling masonry block nearly the size of her.

Naya cradled the bleeding remains of her wrist as she stumbled toward the secret door on the far side of the room. Grip had her blades drawn, ready to meet her, but as the distance between them closed, the priestess uttered a foul incantation and she disappeared into a shadowed crevice in the wall, leaving a cloud of wispy black smoke in her wake.

Anika ignored the fleeing woman as another stone fell. "We need to leave! Gage!"

Her brother got to his feet, grabbing his bloody dagger from the ground and taking Robin's hand. Renay rushed ahead of them toward Anika.

"Ransil!" Grip called out, motioning to the secret passage.

The halfling nodded, motioning for everyone to heed him. "Right, we should split up—easier to slip out of here in this mess. Robin, take Gage and his mother with Grip below—you know the way out?"

The half-elf nodded his head before jerking it low as something else came crashing from above. He looked up. "There's something up there!"

"I know the way," Avrim said, stepping forward. "I am Avrim Kaust, an errant priest of the Light. My companions and I can guide them."

"Your companions will come with us, if they don't mind," Ransil said, motioning to himself and Anika. "Matty, you're with us as well. We reconvene—discreetly—at the Breeze once we get clear. If any of us are caught on the way out, those that escape will come back for them. Agreed?"

They all nodded as three more chunks of the ceiling fell down, several of the companions nearly losing their balance as the ground rocked again. It was as if a giant was stomping around on the roof while something else shook the foundations.

There was a piercing cry from above like a giant bird of prey.

"It's here," Anika said with wide eyes. She turned to Gage, then her mother. She moved to embrace the latter. Renay wrapped her arms around her daughter, holding her fiercely, her body shaking with sobs.

"I'm sorry, Anika," she said through tears.

Anika shook her head, untangling herself and holding her mother's face in her hands. "I'm fine, Mother. I understand what you did." She looked at Gage sadly, her brother's head lowered in shame, but his eyes looking up at her as if desperate for her forgiveness. "Keep her safe. Brother."

Gage nodded and the room rocked more violently than before.

"Go!" Ransil shouted, diving out of the way of a falling chunk of the ceiling. The sky above could be seen, flashes of lightning revealing the poisoned clouds from Anika's vision.

"That's our cue," Grip said, motioning for them to follow her down into the Oakhold. Avrim stood in front of Anika, a look of reverence carved onto his face.

"I will protect them, Child," the priest said.

Anika nodded. "Thank you." The priest followed the rest of the figures as they descended into the world below.

"Where is the Child?!" a shrill voice echoed from the darkness above. "My forces wait outside your gates. Bring me the Child or the town will fall." Cawing laughter came in booming waves.

Anika set her eyes to the hole in the ceiling. "I'm going up there."

Ransil started. "What?! Come on, we have to leave now. We don't even know what *that* is up there!"

"I know what it is," Anika said.

"Aye. The incarnate," Deina said. "Destructor of Rathen."

Melaine had her bow drawn, aimed at the hole. "Master of the harpies—she has drawn an army of Shadowfiends to her."

"More reason for us to go," Ransil said, moving toward the door. "Matty, come on. We need to secure the way out."

Matty looked at Anika, her face firmly set on the storm above. He loosened his grip on his sword, checking its weight. "I'm going with her."

She shook her head. "No, I need to do this alone. I can't put any of you in danger."

"I'm coming," Melaine said, her hard eyes set firmly on Anika. "That thing killed my entire company—the only life I knew. I saw it destroy Rathen. I will not run from it anymore. Yet, I do not know how it can be defeated."

"Worry about that later," Deina said, turning toward the door, carrying her axe in both hands. "Let's go find some stairs." Defiant, Matty fell in line right behind the dwarf.

Defeated, Ransil looked to Anika. "I hope you know what you're doing, kid." He spun two knives as he joined the half-orc, swiftly following the dwarf down the shaking hall.

They heard the noisy retreat of guards and servants rushing for the main door, leaving Anika and her company a clear route to the stairs leading up to the battlements. The climb was perilous, with dust and stone falling from above, clouding their vision and bruising them with debris shaken loose by the incarnate's assault on the building—*And something else*, thought Anika, feeling a powerful force from below as well.

The stairs quaked under the group's steps. One of the narrow footholds gave out as Renay's foot brushed it, nearly causing her to spill down the stairs. Grip caught her just in time.

"Step lively," the dark elf said, her pale eyes glowing like lanterns in the gathering dark. "Follow my lead if needed." Her own steps were light and confident, avoiding any troublesome stairs.

Gage's body trembled with each step he took in Grip's wake.

"Are you all right?" Robin asked Gage, keeping his voice low so that the priest would not overhear them. Avrim led the party with the Light he held in his closed fist.

Gage gave his partner a nervous glance. "I don't know." He looked up at his mother with nervous, darting eyes. "That Xe'danni woman was a priestess of Shadow. I think she did something to me." He knew the lie before he uttered it, but he hoped speaking it aloud would make him believe it.

He had to believe it—the darkness within him had to be someone else's doing.

Robin gave his shoulder a firm squeeze. "You fought her off. You and Anika both. We just need to get out of here. My mother will know what to do."

Gage shot him a glance. "Your mother?"

Robin ducked his head to avoid falling debris as the very earth seemed to shudder. "I have secrets as well, Gage. We will share them when we get out of here. Together." He held up his hand.

Gage took it, and they continued down the treacherous path into the rumbling darkness below.

Deina threw open the port door that led up to the floor of a turret on the north side of the battlements. She scrambled out as the incarnate continued screeching out its threats, flapping its wings in the windless night sky. The storm overhead could be seen even in the dark as conjured lightning constantly tore through the rotting flesh of the sky.

Melaine came out of the port next, followed by Anika, Ransil, and then Matty.

"Light condemn," Ransil cursed, finally seeing the beast that haunted Anika's visions. His eyes went to the sky, his face becoming a mask of apocalyptic terror. "This is Eyen?"

"Nay," the dwarf woman grunted, stepping out the turret's door into the open air, "that…'tis not Eyen. She's an upstart deity that's stolen Eyen's power for her own."

"She was born from Skythe," Anika said, drawing her knife, wishing she had brought Farrah's bow as she saw the harpies wheeling in the stormy sky. She held up the blade, her hand steadier than her breathing. "But she needs to gather the rest of Eyen's greater keyshards to truly ascend to godhood." She spun the knife and stepped past her allies toward her sworn foe. "But she will not have this one."

"The Child has come to Corvanna!" The incarnate laughed wickedly as it lurched through the air to land atop the conical roof of the turret nearest the one Anika and her allies emerged from. "If you want to see your father again, you will give me the shard."

"You can have it," Anika shouted. In the blink of an eye, she pulled her arm back and launched her knife, summoning a gust of wind that blew from behind her allies. The air was so powerful that it lifted Ransil off the ground, but Melaine caught him and brought him back down.

The knife spun—*Stormender*, Anika thought, as she watched it split the storm's stagnant air in a whirl of death that flew toward the incarnate—making a vertical disc of blue energy.

Corvanna's eyes widened, frozen in place by the mesmerizing relic that she had long yearned for coming straight for her wicked heart.

"No!"

A nearby harpy dove in front of the blade, letting it bury itself in her chest. It was hurled back by the force of the knife, but carried Anika's weapon with her as she fell dead to the ground.

Corvanna moved toward the corpse in a show of impressive speed for a hulking creature. Anika panicked, reversing the summoned wind that she still hadn't mastered, urging Stormender to return to her. The blade flew free of the corpse, trailing dark blood that splattered across the walls as it spun toward Anika.

"Watch out!" Matty called, rushing toward Anika, who didn't see the other harpy diving for her.

Anika felt cruel talons dig into her flesh as she fell to her side, Stormender spinning past her to clatter against the wall of the turret. Ransil rolled over to retrieve the blade as Matty slashed at the harpy, severing a wing with a deft stroke of his sword.

Melaine unleashed arrow after arrow at Corvanna, the incarnate waving her wings to deflect the useless missiles, gathering her own wind behind her as lightning crashed from the restless sky. Deina charged, but was easily knocked aside by a long wing, smashing the dwarf against the crenellations that ran along the outer edge of the wall.

"Anika!" Ransil flung Stormender toward her, rolling out of the way as another harpy dove to attack, razor-like talons snapping the air where the halfling had been. There were dozens of harpies now falling from the sky, screeching their war cries. Several threw the limp bodies of the baron's guards as weapons, their armored corpses crashing hard against the stone like lodes from catapults.

Melaine cursed as one of the dead guards knocked her over.

Anika reached out and grasped Stormender, standing to face Corvanna, who was now towering over her, talons digging into the stone wall. A huge grasping hand swooped out from under the incarnate's wings and closed tightly around Anika, its razor claws pinning her arms to her sides. Stormender was useless.

Corvanna lifted Anika, bringing them face-to-horrible-face. The incarnate's black, Shadow-corrupted eyes narrowed angrily on her. "I have had enough of this. I came here to offer you a seat at the table in my empire. The Light and Shadow can coexist—I see that in you. Your father told me of you and your brother, the Child of Shadow. There is no need for war! All I require," she squeezed Anika tightly, "is worship."

Anika screamed in pain.

Matty rushed toward Corvanna, cleaving an attacking harpy in two, but was knocked to the ground by another attacker that dove in from the opposite direction. "Anika!" Quickly, he was pinned to the ground, his sword knocked away, and a harpy restrained him while another sang sweetly into his ear.

Ransil threw his last knife at the singing harpy, catching it in the throat and turning the serene music into a gurgling death cry. Matty knocked the other harpy away and rolled for his sword.

"Give me the stone and end this, Child," Corvanna said, struggling to maintain her control on the wind. Lightning crashed again, weaker this time. The incarnate looked to the sky angrily and saw patches of clouds receding.

"It's not yours," Anika growled, struggling for air. "The sky...is mine."

Anika's eyes glowed like two small suns, sparking with snaps of lightning. In response, the storm overhead gathered into a single mighty cloud that sat right over Corvanna. The harpies that had hidden in the clouds were exposed, and Melaine began to quickly nock and fire, bringing them down one by one with expert precision.

"This can't be," Corvanna said, looking at the sky, reaching up toward it with her free hand. "I am Eyen! I am the keeper of the wind!"

In response, the wind swirled around Anika and Corvanna, knocking everyone else away. They were alone in a cyclone of wind that embodied every ounce of fury Anika felt toward this wretched creature.

Bright lightning struck Corvanna from the storm cloud, descending like a white-hot crack splitting the icy night sky. It hit the incarnate in an explosion of blue energy, thousands of feathers taking flight in the surrounding cyclone. The force of the blast released Corvanna's grip on Anika.

But the Child of Light did not fall.

The cyclone fell away and the storm cloud above dissipated. Anika's allies slowly got to their feet to see the incarnate shaking violently, holy lighting coursing through its body. Its wings were held wide as its body continued to seize.

In front of the incarnate was Anika, floating in the clear night sky, her body glowing like she was hanging in front of the sun. Her clothes were torn and she bled from where the incarnate's claws had mauled her. She held Stormender in one hand, the blade fiercely glowing blue.

"You are not a god," Anika said, her voice a soft roll of thunder across the clear spring sky. "You are merely the Shadow of one. And I," she raised her knife, "I am the Light."

She dove toward Corvanna as the incarnate let out a terrible, desperate wail. As the blade pierced Corvanna's breast, the lightning left her body and she fell back onto the wall, her dead wings draped over the edge of the baron's keep.

Anika descended back down to the ground, staring at her foe's body. Tendrils of energy drifted from Corvanna's feathers, returning to the sky. As Anika watched those twisting streams of faintly blue magic lift skyward, she felt the wind breeze through her hair. She did not call the wind. It was Eyen, free from Skythe, and returned to the sky that he forged.

"It's over," Deina said, rubbing her neck as she approached the dead incarnate.

"No," Anika said, turning to her companions as the cool night breeze reminded her of Ruke's words. "The scion will come now; the first of six."

They all looked at her, in both confusion and reverence. Matty thrust his sword into his scabbard and nodded. As did Ransil, hooking his thumbs into the belt that rested under his portly stomach

"This is not over until I kill Stane," Anika continued, the soothing wind filling her with the knowledge of Eyen that in turn filled the gaps in what Ruke had told her. "The incarnates are coming. Each one is a seal on Stane's prison in the Abyss." She turned to Corvanna's body that still leaked its magic into the sky. "This is the first. Its death will bring the scion."

"Well," Deina said, spitting off the edge of the wall. "Where is he then?"

"Here."

The voice startled them all save Anika, who turned slowly to see the figure emerging from the turret.

It was a young, pale man, with ash covering his eyes, streaming down his cheeks as if he had been crying.

"Please," the scion said, reaching out to Anika with both hands in desperation. "Please kill me."

CHAPTER THIRTY-TWO

The Fading Light

"How much farther?"

Quinn shrugged, focusing on the spell that kept their passage lit. He held out his hand, holding an orb of light. "I've never led my own expedition into the Old Ways, Fallon. I told you, Master Audreese is the only one in the spire that has trekked farther than Nest."

Fallon gripped her staff tightly, praying silently to Oakus for guidance in his domain. She did not tell Quinn, but she felt something curious down here. It wasn't her first time in the Old Ways, but there was a presence here when she prayed to Oakus that she normally did not feel. Her prayers to the old god were usually answered with a crinkled leaf in the distance, or the sound of an old root cracking. But down here, she *heard* Oakus, like whispers on the edge of her hearing.

Each step she took, the whispers grew louder until she actually began to hear words in those whispers. *The Light*, it said. *Beware the Light.*

The words stopped her heart. It was a warning. The Luminaura had already killed her father, and it was hiding a secret for which it was worth spilling the blood of its own.

I hear you, Oakus, she thought, *guide me to the truth.*

The crack of a root made her gasp.

Quinn spun toward a path they had not seen, hidden by the shadow of heavy roots. "Who's there?" The boy's voice quivered, which unsettled Fallon; she had never heard such fear or concern in Quinn's voice.

"Quiet," a voice answered, a shadow stepping out into the light. It was a robed Xe'danni woman. "They'll hear you."

"Who?" Fallon asked, stepping in front of Quinn. *This must be a druid*, she thought, *alone in the Old Ways.*

The woman held up a bleeding stump. "The Light."

Fallon gasped with sudden realization as the green keyshard in her hand awoke in a blinding glow. Around the three figures, a cacophony of creaking roots told Fallon that the god was waiting for her below.

To fight the Light.

The rumbling below finally stopped, giving Avrim pause at the head of the group. He held up a hand for his companions to wait. Together, they listened for what the priest had heard.

"Something's happened," Avrim said, turning to his new companions. The young half-elf stared back, his face searching for an explanation that the priest could not provide, while the dark elf crept around to the far end of the vast study. Avrim could clearly see she was a thief, evaluating the collected books, tomes, and parchment to see if anything might be worth stealing.

The older woman stepped toward him. "Father—"

"Brother," Avrim corrected.

"I feel the Shadow here." She clutched her thin robe tightly against the chill in the sprawling study.

Avrim nodded, now focusing on the heavy dread that still remained after the excitement of their flight. She was right. They were in the Shadow's domain.

"This way," the dark elf nodded.

The half-elf followed toward the wide archway that led to a twisting hall. The boy lingered for a brief moment, his eyes staring at the ground, searching for something beyond anyone else's reckoning.

"Gage," the half-elf hissed.

As if that name carried a weight he did not quite grasp, Avrim looked toward the boy. When their eyes met, Avrim felt the truth in that cold stare. As sure as he had seen the Child of Light above in the baron's keep, he was now staring into the eyes of her counterpart.

In that brief moment, Avrim saw the scene of the mutilated children, felt the struggling breaths as he had asked the Light to mend their wounds. *The Shadow*, he thought, realizing now how he knew all these truths, *he inflicted it upon them*. When Avrim healed those children, he touched the vile power that delivered their anguish.

Gage turned away to join the others. The woman was about to follow, but Avrim reached out a hand and clasped her wrist. When she spun to face him, he held a single Light-blessed finger to his lips for her silence. When the two figures disappeared around the bend in the hallway beyond the archway, following the dark elf, Avrim motioned toward them.

"He is the one," Avrim said. "The Child of Shadow. He tried to kill the baron's children tonight while they slept in their beds."

The woman stared at him flatly and said, "I know. I am his mother."

Looking into her eyes, Avrim felt the gravity of it all sink in. As he held onto the woman, the Light in his hand began to intensify, pulsating with power that was beyond his own. He stared at her in wonder, realizing the Light was at work in this woman. She was flooded with divine purpose.

He released her, giving her a slight nod of understanding. "I think we know what needs to be done then."

She stared at him in perfect understanding before turning to follow her son.

"We cannot kill him," Anika said, sheathing Stormender and holding her arms out to keep her companions away from the stranger. "He is the scion."

Desmond's eyes were wide with panic as he took in his surroundings, but ignored Anika's companions as if they weren't there. He only had eyes for the Child of Light. He took a step closer, his tattered black robes exposing gruesome scars across his entire body, as if he had been pieced back together from a thousand parts.

"You must," the man pleaded, reaching desperately. "No one else can! He—he told me that I must serve him, await his coming—the end of the world." He pointed to Anika. "He said that you could free me! If you kill me, I won't have to go back! Please! Do not let me go back!"

"Move aside!" Deina growled, stepping forward threateningly with her axe. "I won't kill ye, but I can certainly make your livin' more uncomfortable!"

Anika looked behind them. Their only escape—short of leaping from the wall, a fall her companions would not survive—was blocked by the ruins Corvanna left in her death, the wall broken and impassable. She turned back to the scion that stood between them and the turret.

"What happens if we kill him?" Matty whispered to Anika.

"Then Gage is doomed," Anika said, giving him a pleading look. "This is the only way I can save him. The scions must live—it's the only way Light and Shadow can be united."

Ransil motioned forward. "Then we must go."

The scion took another step toward Anika, the dwarf woman blocking his way. When he felt Deina's axe, he finally looked down at her, as if seeing her for the first time. He raised one of his hands that trailed smoky black tendrils and Deina arched back in pain, dropping her weapon.

"Sorcery!" Melaine shouted as she rushed to catch the dwarf before she nearly staggered off the edge of the wall.

"Kill me!" the scion screamed. "I cannot kill you," he said, more in fear than anger, "but I can kill your friends and family until you set me free! Do not play his damned games! Please! He will destroy the entire world if the scions are not sacrificed by the chosen!"

"Go!" Ransil slipped past the scion, hugging the outer wall. Anika followed behind him while Melaine dragged Deina around the scion the other way.

The black-robed man turned as if he was learning how to use his limbs all over again, reaching for Anika.

"Back!" Matty cried, rushing to shoulder the scion away from Anika.

"Don't!" Anika cried, but it was too late. The scion twisted one hand to spin Matty around and then wrapped the impossibly long fingers of his other hand around Matty's neck. Those fingers seemed to grow as they tightened.

"Kill me, Anika!" The scion was weeping black tears.

Matty reached up to pull the ensorcelled fingers from his throat, gasping desperately for air. His wild eyes went to Anika, seeing her make a move toward the scion. Matty held his arms up to keep her back, waving her to go.

"No!" Anika shouted, a violent wind blowing behind her, lifting her slightly off the ground. She clenched her fists and a small storm began brewing above the scion.

The man in tattered black robes looked up, smiling as flashes of lightning began brewing in those clouds.

"Yes!" he exclaimed. "Do it!"

"No!" Matty said in a choking gasp, shaking his head.

Tears ran down Anika's eyes as she released her fists. The storm above died away and the scion let out a tormented wail. He squeezed his long skeletal fingers and a popping sound ended Matty's struggles. His body fell limp.

Ransil dove with two daggers thrust downward, both of them burying themselves into the scion's chest. Anika and the scion both let out a shriek and Matty's lifeless body fell to the ground.

The scion swung his enlarged hand and knocked Ransil hard against the wall, the halfling falling to the ground in a heap. Dropping to his knee, the scion's hand shrank back down to normal size as he grabbed the small hilts and pulled Ransil's blades from his chest. They clattered to the ground, splattering his dark blood.

"Not him," the scion said, scowling at Anika. "Only you can set me free. I won't let anyone else kill me—I can't. Stane will know. This game is ancient and he sets the rules. Only you can end it before it starts. I will find you again…alone. And you will do what needs to be done."

With that, he raised his tattered robes and dropped them in a flash, disappearing in a burst of black feathers as an unkindness of ravens took to the sky.

Falling to her knees, Anika turned Matty over, cradled his head, and began to weep. Melaine and Deina knelt down next to her, as Ransil pushed himself up from the ground, shaking the dizziness from his head.

Matty's lifeless eyes stared up into the clear night sky.

As they emerged from the darkness of Oakhold, Robin and Gage stepped into the crisp evening air. Taking a deep breath, Gage felt an enormous weight lifted from him. He looked up and saw the stars, thinking of home.

The baron's gardens looked abandoned, but beyond the keep's walls there were torches moving about. The townsfolk were probably investigating the disturbances they had felt, Gage thought.

Turning around, he saw his mother step out of the darkness, her frame lit by the priest's blessing, giving her an angelic quality. He felt tears coming to his eyes, but did not fight them.

"Mother," he said, the voice of a lost child finally finding his way home.

Renay's raw eyes also glistened with tears as she stepped forward with her arms held out. He ran and embraced her, feeling free of the Shadow that cursed their last reunion.

Holding onto her son, Renay took a deep breath, feeling overwhelmed and grateful. But when she opened her eyes, she saw Avrim looking intentionally into her eyes, the Light fading from his hand.

She caught her breath, but then nodded before closing her eyes and resting her head on her child's for one moment longer.

CHAPTER THIRTY-THREE

The Crystal Sky

The sun shone brightly that morning, despite the heavy grief Anika carried down the stairs. She had slept under the stars with Matty's body, telling him everything that she always wanted to tell him back in Blakehurst. She wept, and laughed a little, as she reflected on simple memories from home.

But her sleep was restless, haunted by the Karranese woman—her birth mother. Anika couldn't remember the dreams each time she awoke, but felt the familiar dread.

When the sun came up, Ransil was the first one to find her, followed quickly by Dolly and Brood. The halflings sat with her for a long moment of silence, heads bowed in respect for her lost friend.

"Me heart aches for ye," Brood said to Anika, giving her an awkward hug around her waist. Afterward, she sat down with her legs crossed to be closer to eye level with the halflings, glad for the company.

"Yer always welcome 'ere," Dolly said, motioning toward The Harvest Breeze before wrapping her arms around Anika's neck. "We'll leave ye be for now though. C'mon, Rosh."

"Shhh," Brood said. "Not so loud, sis. It's Brood when peoples can hear."

Anika smiled as the halflings went back down the turret port.

"I don't mean to sound wrong here, Ani," Ransil said, looking from Matty to the clear morning sky above, "but this is where he would always have ended up, regardless of what we could have done." He looked at her with deep sorrow. "He would have always died for you. It was almost like his destiny."

Anika sniffed back a sob. "I don't want anyone dying for me."

"I know," Ransil said, looking back up into the sky. "But I would anyway."

"Did ye get it?"

Brood spun the green stone in his fingers, quickly returning it to his pouch. "I can't say I'm proud of it, but it was an easy pinch given the situation up there."

"Poor child," Dolly said. "I don't know what the rock means to her, but we can get it back once we make sure me girls are safe."

"To Andelor?" Brood asked, as they took the steps back into the keep.

Dolly nodded her head. "As if I could ever escape that damned place."

Deina and Melaine carried Matty down the many stairs of the keep, then out into the courtyard where a wagon awaited. The baron and baroness waited near it, their two children standing before them with bandaged limbs. Despite their injuries, the children seemed cheerful that morning.

Must be the weather, Anika thought as she approached. She looked up into the sky, feeling the sun's warmth against the crisp morning chill. *It is a beautiful day.*

Avrim stood next to the lord and lady of the keep, bowing his head as Matty was carried by and placed gently on the wagon. His body was covered in a light linen shroud, his sword resting on top of it.

Anika looked at the gathering, but didn't see her brother or Robin. She stopped and pulled Ransil aside. "Where are the rest?"

"At the Breeze," Ransil whispered. "We'll pick them up on the way out of this place." He motioned toward the wagon.

"And the horses?" Avrim asked the baron.

Alburn Caffery gave the man a pointed look, bristling. His face still displayed the results of the savage beating the priest had given him.

Listening carefully, Anika heard Avrim as he pulled the baron aside by the arm. "Do not think I am done with you, my good lord. I've seen what's below the keep. I may overlook certain consorting, but only so much as you give my companions the proper treatment."

The baron's shoulders slumped at that. He raised a hand.

"Errol!" The baron's voice was full of restrained anger as he called for his stable man. "Bring me three steeds ready to ride."

"Thank you, my lord," Avrim said with a slight bow. He smiled as he moved toward Anika. "Perhaps I may accompany you, Anika. I am in your service and you have my undying loyalty in whatever is required of the Light."

Anika smiled, "Thank you, Avrim. You would be a welcome companion. However, we are just traveling to my home, Blakehurst. I don't imagine there will be much excitement now that this is all over."

"That is very good," Avrim said. "I have never been, and would welcome the opportunity to serve your temple there, with your leave."

"Certainly," she said. She turned to Deina and Melaine. "And you?"

Deina motioned to Avrim. "I'm still in his debt, so I go where he goes. With your leave, of course."

"Of course." Anika turned to Melaine.

"I have no real home anymore," the half-orc said. "My place in Wickham was with my order that Corvanna slaughtered. You avenged them, my lady, and I am now yours. If you'll have me, that is."

"I will," Anika said. She turned to Avrim. "You protected my brother, and I owe you my loyalty, as well as my trust, which extends to those in your trust."

Avrim bowed his head again. "It is not misplaced, Child. I do assure you."

The stable man brought their horses and they mounted up, making their way to The Harvest Breeze.

"Well, this is quite the entourage," Grip said as she sauntered out of the inn. "It's a shame I can't join. Shall we, Ruse?"

Sitting in the wagon, Anika turned to Ransil next to her.

He avoided her gaze as he leapt out of the wagon. He looked up when he stood next to Grip. "I have to go to the Guild in Andelor, Ani. There's nothing left for me in Blakehurst."

Mouth agape, Anika stared in disbelief. "I—I will miss you, Ransil. Home won't be the same without you."

He inclined his head. "It will still be yours though. And I will return. I promise you." He looked at Grip as he said, "I just have some matters to attend to."

Anika fought back tears, having had her fill of loss already. She looked around. "Where is Gage?"

Gage looked out the window at the town, feeling homesick and thinking about his father. *Where are you?* He hadn't given his father much thought with everything that had happened, but now it was all he thought about. *I will find you*, he thought. *Anika and I—together—we will find you.*

There was a slight tap at his door. Gage turned to see his mother, a concerned look on her face.

"Mother?"

She approached slowly, the sun piercing the thin veil of her robe. He averted his eyes slightly at her nakedness, remembering too well the baron's bedroom.

"What's wrong, Mother?"

"I'm sorry, Gage," she said in a voice that pierced his ears.

His eyes were averted so he did not see the blade, but he felt it bite into his stomach. He didn't scream; he just gritted his teeth and pushed her away. When he looked up at her, he saw the Light in his mother's eyes.

"I'm sorry, son," her voice still thundering in his head. "I have been called. And as the Light commands," she raised the bloodied blade again, "I must obey."

Gage fell to his knees, weak from the wound, but also heartbroken, knowing he was helpless against her. He looked up futilely as his mother approached, her blade—his blade—raised high to do what she had failed to do all those years ago.

"I'm sorry, I—"

Her words were lost on choking blood as she stiffened, dropping the blade. The Light faded from her eyes, and his mother looked down on him with the most love and compassion he had felt in his entire life.

She fell to the ground with her eyes locked onto Gage's, Robin standing behind her with his own bloodied dagger. His eyes were wide with fear and sorrow, going wider when he saw Gage's wound. He knelt down to put pressure on it.

Gage's vision started to fade as he stared at his dead mother. Her eyes were still locked onto Gage's as the Shadow took him, consuming the world in cold, fearful oblivion. Robin's worried voice faded away, and all Gage knew was hate, growing stronger with each shallow breath he tried to take.

When Anika walked into Gage's room shortly after, she found her mother dead on the floor with no sign of her brother. She fell to her knees, wanting to weep, but she seemed to have run out of tears.

A dry, unsated rage began to blossom inside of her. Outside, the sun continued to rise into a clear blue sky.

The Keyguard

Bennik awoke to the peaceful buzz of insects and the soft rustle of leaves in the breeze. His aches were gone and his body felt twenty years younger as he sat up in a soft bed. He was in a room that looked like the hollowed-out trunk of a tree, decorated with simple floral arrangements and architecture carved from the wood itself.

He threw his legs out over the edge of the bed, the silky sheets so cool and smooth to the touch that he almost didn't want to get up. But he felt restless, as if he had slept for years.

Corvanna, he thought, remembering his final moments in Rathen. The orc witch that rode astride him, and then the elf.

Elves, he thought. *Am I in Lefayra?*

As he tried to stand up, his arm brushed against a brass tray, knocking it to the ground. He gritted his teeth at the sound of the crash, but he did not hear any movement in response. Reassured that he had not startled his keepers, he looked down to see that he wore a simple tunic of emerald-green with swirling elven patterns on it, as well as loose brown pants. No boots.

He looked around, eager to have an escape route planned, but his heart stopped when he heard the voice.

"The Eldercrowns await you."

Bennik spun to see a beautiful elf standing in the room. *Where did he come from?* There was no door visible anywhere in the room.

"This way," the elf said, motioning to the wall. His hand reached *into* the wall and drew it aside. *A curtain*, Bennik thought. *A cunning illusion.* The curtain had the same wood pattern of the walls, flawlessly blending in.

He had no choice but to follow, walking into a breathtaking hall that rose up at least twenty stories, with wooden balconies crisscrossing the upper expanse. Lights danced in that majestic hallway, green flashes that could be bugs or motes of magical energy for all Bennik knew. He followed the elf across the hall, becoming dizzy as he tried to take in all the elegant, flowing architecture of the place.

"The Eldercrowns?" He had so many pressing questions, but the most obvious one seemed to be their destination. "I'm going to see them?"

"Not quite yet," the elf replied, flashing Bennik a perfect smile. "They await you. But I have questions of my own first." The elf guided him into a room with a similar curtain, but darkness lay beyond it. Unlike the hall they came from, this place was primal and dirty, but still had a magical quality.

"My name is Lexeth," the elf said, reaching for a bow that leaned against the earthen wall. He slipped a quiver over his shoulder. "My sister's name was Farrah, a guide that was killed in a village called Blakehurst. Do you know it?"

Bennik couldn't hide his shock, and found no reason to lie. "Yes, that's my home. I knew Farrah well. She passed through many times."

"Take me there." Lexeth nodded to a pair of boots and a cloak that sat along the wall as well. "Here," he said as he extended an elegant knife to Bennik. "Something has awoken in the Old Ways. Corvanna was not the first incarnate, and I suspect Oakus is stirring. Are you ready?"

No! Bennik thought, but he took the knife anyway as he slipped his feet into the boots and grabbed the cloak. If there was danger coming to Blakehurst, he would not wait idly for his children to face it alone.

"Hurry," Lexeth said. "The elders will not wait long until they come looking for us. But the Keyguard needs answers before the Eldercrowns ask more questions of you."

Together they descended into the darkening earth.

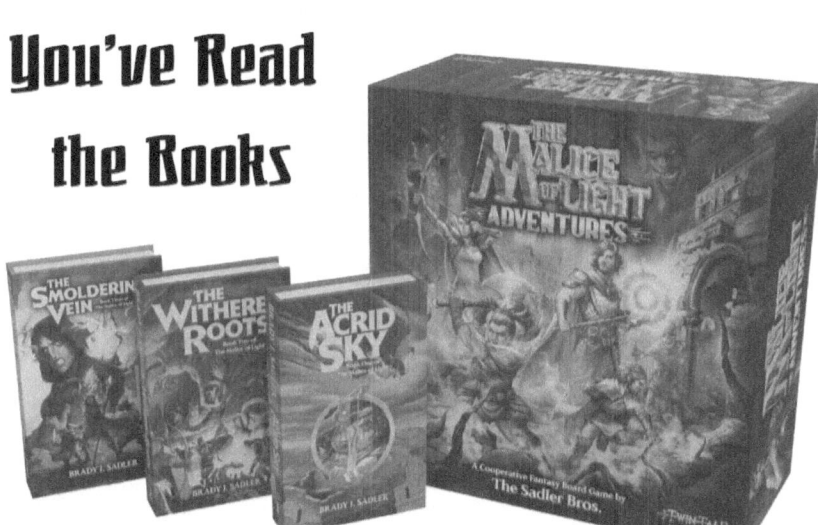

Please Review

THE ACRID SKY

About the Author

Brady J. Sadler is a drummer, game designer, and author. Along with his twin brother, Adam, he is the co-founder of the fantasy metal band Lorenguard and the publishing company Twin Tale Studios.

In addition to his novels, he has designed dozens of tabletop games and expansions and written for various TTRPG lines.

Brady lives in Indiana with his wife, two kids, and, unfortunately, a couple cats.

www.bradyjsadler.com
www.twintalestudios.com

www.ingramcontent.com/pod-product-compliance
Lightning Source LLC
Chambersburg PA
CBHW030643260626
47157CB00007B/2464